LACHLANN'S LEGACY

ASHLEY YORK

For my mother

PROLOGUE

The damp cold seeped into the chieftain's tired bones. He tugged the wolfskin mantle tighter around his length as he paced the uneven terrain. At two score and eight, he was getting too old for traipsing along the open glen, sleeping on the stone-riddled ground each night. He longed for the peace of his own bed, his wife's warmth beside him.

A young child being dragged toward him yanked Colbán, chieftain of Clan MacDonell, out of his woolgathering. He looked to be the right age, about four winters. Although the boy was filthy with smoke and ash from the burning huts, Colbán knew in his gut it was the right child. He recognized the dark hair of his father, just sprouting after a close shearing, and the bright green eyes of his lovely mother.

God rest her soul.

"Enough!" The soldier's firm tone was directed at the lad, but had little effect as he continued to struggle against him, yanking and jerking as the man tried to explain. "This is… a wild one, m'lord… Dragged him… out of the shelter just before… it collapsed on us both."

"Still yer tongue!" Colbán's son, Garnait, had come up silently behind the two and proclaimed the order like the

1

pompous arse that he was demanding obedience, his cross expression making no secret of his exasperation. "Ye're in the presence of the chieftain. Quiet yerself now."

His son's nasal tone— nay, his whole manner!— grated against Colbán's skin, and his face suffused with angry heat. The child remained unaffected, even spewed gibberish at the warrior with the unrelenting death grip towering over him.

The warrior visibly stiffened and his face lost all its color. In a hushed tone, he uttered the unthinkable, "A pagan."

Despite the chill that passed down Colbán's back he asked impatiently, "There is no one else?"

His eyes scanned the surrounding stillness where a village once thrived, but no more, thanks to his heartless son, who had come in with war cries and axes waving, rending the morning quiet and burning the round houses to the ground.

It took a moment for the warrior to tear his wide-eyed gaze from the child. A quick shake of his head was the only response.

Colbán stood tall, crossed his arms about his chest, and glared down at the small child. "Verily a gallows tree may be required."

The boy ceased his movements, his jaw slackening.

"So ye understand our words?" Colbán asked.

No answer.

This lad would never be cowed into submission, never go willingly with them. He was very much like his father in that way.

"Do ye yield?" Colbán finally asked.

"Nay!" The boy's face tightened into a mask of outrage. "'Twas not a fair fight."

His attention remaining on the boy, the older man halted Garnait's hand just short of striking the boy. "What say ye?"

"With no one to lead us, how could it be fair?"

The lad considered himself a warrior. "Who was yer leader?"

"My da is chieftain here."

"Yer da?" The sense of loss struck Colbán anew, but confusion made him wonder if mayhap this was not the child. Word of his father's untimely death had sent Colbán on this journey in search of the child he had sworn before God to protect with his very life. "Where is yer da?"

The lad fidgeted. A crack in his brave front. "He has gone... for help."

"Forsooth! Leaving behind women and children?" Garnait barked a laugh. "Nay, he left because he was outnumbered. A coward."

That got him a baleful glance from the lad.

Colbán ignored his son's bragging. "Give us his name."

His young lips quivered, and the boy pulled a fist to his chest in a sort of salute. "I am the son of Barra, the High King."

Barra was not the name of the boy's father, but his uncle. The enormity of the claim caught Colbán unprepared, until he realized the truth of the matter. "The sly fox has taken the boy as his own. No doubt to replace the one he'd lost."

This would require more delicate questioning if he wished to guard the lad's strength. Colbán signaled the others to leave. The lad kept a wary eye on the two of them before turning back to give him his full attention.

"Ye show the courage of a much older lad."

"Courage is measured by action not age."

The lad spoke as if he'd heard that many times before, the words far too old for his young age. Colbán smiled. "Wise words. Ye truly are yer *father's* son."

Tears, big and fat, slipped down the boy's round face, but he kept his hand tucked to his small chest, focusing his eyes past Colbán. He couldn't help but wonder if the lad had any memories of his actual father, Branan. Probably not. And by the looks of him, he was not being trained as his father would have wanted him to be.

Not a demonstrative man, Colbán surprised himself by hunkering down in front of the boy. He needed to speak the truth to him, and he preferred they be on the same level. The boy was proud. Mayhap too proud. But setting him straight about the lie he'd been fed would not go over well.

"Yer da was a brave man." Colbán spoke from the heart, surprised by the tears flooding his throat. "My most loyal friend."

The young face turned suspicious. "I do not know ye."

Scoffing, Colbán said, "And mayhap ye dinna know yer true father."

Colbán would never have admitted how uncomfortable the intensity of the boy's piercing green eyes made him, but he dared not look away. He was too young to remember his real father, and that made Colbán's heart heavy.

Colbán pulled out a large pendant from inside his mantle. It immediately caught the boy's interest. Made of silver, the oval medallion was masterfully engraved with a hog pierced by a well-placed arrow. The symbol of Branan's clan. Colbán ran a hand lightly over the top, the grooves of the imprint smooth against his fingertips, then raised his gaze to the boy's expectant expression.

"This belonged to yer father." He placed the cord around the boy's neck. The lad studied the drawing, holding the medal closer to his face.

"How can it be that I have not seen this before?"

"Mayhap ye've not seen yer true father, not since ye were learning to walk."

The boy's face puckered with confusion, his eyes dark with skepticism, but he remained silent.

"Son of *Branan*," Colbán spoke the name with great reverence. "By what name will ye be known?"

The tears coursed freely down his cheeks now, and he allowed the pendant to drop. It hung past his small chest to land at his belly.

With a strong voice, he answered, "I am called Lachlann."

CHAPTER 1

Twenty years later

"Amen," the dark-robed priest intoned.

In the windowless chapel of Clan MacDonell, the people were gathered for their long-awaited mass, prayerfully seated with their eyes closed as Father Michael spoke over them. Three nuns lined the side wall, hands steepled and heads lowered in petition. A single candle glowed brightly at the altar between a simple chalice of specially prepared wine and a small plate of unleavened bread, both covered by a linen cloth.

"Is that ye?"

Lachlann paused in crossing himself long enough to question if his ears deceived him. No. He rolled his eyes. That raspy whisper had indeed come from the man seated beside him on the hard bench.

Aldred.

Unlike other men, Lachlann wasn't the least bit intimidated by the dark, accusing Norseman's scowl, even if it did make the tiny scar above his brow throb. He recognized it for what it was. An act.

A stomach growled loud enough to wake the dead. It came from the direction of the priest. Aldred faced front, the blond hair clubbed at his neck swinging with the motion. His stoic mask broken only by the occasional twitching lips that threatened to erupt into an outright guffaw at any moment.

Lachlann shook his head. He would be the mature one who did not lower himself to such childish behavior. Besides, the priest could very well be fasting. A worthy sacrifice. Jesus himself fasted for forty days in the desert.

Bodily functions were not something that should even be mentioned. And in the chapel? During Mass? Not the place for that type of behavior. Unless, of course, you were named Aldred.

The only problem was that Lachlann had known Aldred since they were young. Aldred knew how to set him off or get him to act against his better judgement, and it worked every time. Even now Lachlann's breath caught as he struggled to keep from responding to his friend's outrageous behavior. He clamped his teeth tight, holding in his laughter, and laughter was so much worse knowing you were about to be reprimanded. It wasn't right that a man full grown should cower in fear of getting caught by the priest for bad behavior, but the dread worming its way through Lachlann's gut did not agree.

Father Michael was a devout priest in his own way... though unable to pronounce Latin to save his life. The small amount of leeway he'd given Lachlann as a child had left its mark. He kept his emotions tightly reined. But even after three years of disciplined study at the Abbey of Mar Moutier, Lachlann's discipline evaporated like smoke on a windy day once Aldred started in. And this in spite of knowing the priest would lay the blame for any disruption firmly at Lachlann's feet.

Lachlann studied the priest, his back permanently stooped from so many hours in supplication, but he showed no sign of having heard Aldred's comment. To the contrary, he continued to swing the incense-filled orb, chanting the Latin words few understood even though they listened intently. Lachlann was one of those few.

"*Gaudeamus onmes...*" the priest murmured.

Om-nes, Lachlann corrected in his head.

"*...in Domino diem festum celebrantes sub horone...*"

Sub ho-nore. Lachlann had loved learning the language of the church.

"*Sanctorum onimum...*"

Om-ni-um.

This was painful to listen to so Lachlann focused instead on the priest's precise movement as he took communion. The act, which was comfortingly accurate, would be followed by the post-communion prayer.

The priest began, "*Quod ore mumpsimus, Domine—*"

"*Sumpsimus!*" Lachlann slammed his lips together and cringed at his slip. Had he actually said that aloud? No one else would have caught the priest's mistake. Mayhap it would go unnoticed.

The sudden silence confirmed that was not the case.

The priest moved closer with slow, heavy steps scraping along the stone floor. Lachlann swallowed past his tightening throat, but refused to confirm the priest's location even though he was fairly certain Aldred was the only thing between him and Father Michael.

"Ah, Lachlann." The interminable silence that followed demanded Lachlann turn his gaze to the priest. "Is there ought ye would like to share?"

Just like that, and he was again a lad receiving reprimands from the itinerant priest whose flock covered much of the highlands, but somehow knew *him* by name. Hoping the man would just ignore the correction and continue with the service, Lachlann shook his head. A wasted gesture.

"Hmmm."

The sarcastic lilt of the sound sent a wave of heat across Lachlann's chest.

"Did ye not correct my Latin?"

When Lachlann opened his mouth to apologize, the priest's eyes flared. "Think ye a man of the cloth deserves such a rebuke? Verily do ye test my patience, lad."

Shame swamped Lachlann. This priest could cause him to feel guilty for breathing. "Forgiveness for my outburst, Father. No insult was intended."

Lachlann held himself taut. That was all the man would get from him. He was a warrior. He did not apologize like some youngling.

The slight quiver of the blond Norseman beside Lachlann made matters so much worse. But it was the near uncontrollable twitch of Lachlann's own lips that Father Michael's piercing eyes did not seem willing to ignore. "Do ye find humor in this interruption?"

"Nay—"

Aldred made a strangled sound.

An answering high squeak slipped out, and although Lachlann cleared his throat into his hand in an attempt to cover the noise, his face was in flames. "I do not, Father Michael."

After a hard, quelling glare, the priest turned about. Aldred bestowed a face-splitting grin on him. Lachlann's relief was short-lived.

"Enough!" The deep warning voice came from the man to Lachlann's left, Niall, who gave a sharp shake of his red head.

Lachlann poked his elbow into Aldred's side. He shouldn't be surprised by Aldred's blatant disrespect, but he was. He always hoped for a change, but the truth was the man had no shame.

The priest stopped before the altar. Lachlann's breath stilled in his chest. But Father Michael kept his back to them, his eyes heavenward as he chanted on in more far-from-perfect Latin.

The many churchgoers surrounding them showed no sign of having been disturbed by the encounter. It had been a long while since any priest had visited, and the masses were in desperate need of penance. When one could drop dead at any moment, acceptance into God's kingdom was an essential part of life. Their focus was on Father Michael. Unlike Aldred, who had no respect for anyone. Not even the Almighty.

Lachlann knew better than to sit next to Aldred even on a good day, but especially when he'd not slept for two days. And certainly *not* after he'd had enough to drink the night before and still felt the effects this morning. Though he had to admit, his endurance for the stuff was diminishing the older he became.

As one, the congregation kneeled to accept the priest's final blessing.

At the end of the service, both Lachlann and Aldred pressed back to allow Niall to lead the way, but Lachlann yanked Aldred's shoulder to pull him back from the coveted second position, forcing him instead to follow at the rear. He was being petty, but the small gesture made him feel better. Lachlann snorted at his own idiocy.

Outside the chapel, Niall stopped just to the side of the entrance. Lachlann cringed at his own behavior and tried to ignore Niall's overly firm tugs as he donned his leather riding gloves.

Those passing by as they exited the church said nothing, but the darting glances of the young lasses accompanying their parents were not lost on any of them. Niall, Lachlann, and Aldred were unmarried warriors, flesh-and-blood versions of the heroes haunting their maidenly dreams. They always returned the smiles even when a glowering mother or father intercepted the young lady's show of interest.

"Aldred, what ails ye? Yer lack of respect can be trying," Niall finally said.

Lachlann's sigh of relief was quickly replaced by a feeling of dismay. How childish it was to be happy someone else was being taken to task. He opened his mouth to accept responsibility, but Niall cut him off.

"And whose bed were ye in this morning when the chapel bell began ringing?" Niall's patient expression, his eyebrows raised in expectation, filled Lachlann with satisfaction. It was only right that Aldred be taken to task.

Aldred chuckled a quiet sound, then stretched his torso as if only now feeling the tiredness of that particular event. "Ah, not just the one bed, my friend."

Their eyes wide, Lachlann and Niall turned toward the shorter man. Lachlann recovered first. His irritation unchecked, he lowered his brow and quirked his lips into his most doubtful expression. "Ye always claim such grand experiences yet offer no proof."

Aldred shrugged then tapped at the multi-colored sash that lay across his chest. The braided hair of his many virgin conquests, or so he claimed. "Look closely, lads. These locks are given willingly with no shame involved."

"No shame until they're tossed out by their new husbands on their wedding night." Niall crossed the open green of the village with long strides.

"Men old enough to be their fathers," Aldred spouted his usual justification. "Why should a young lass be used so?"

They headed toward the narrow path that led into the woods and away from the villagers to where their prized horses were stabled.

Niall merely huffed, having heard the argument many times before, but Lachlann shoved the shorter man. "Ye're full of shite."

"Doubt it not." Aldred kept up the pace Niall had set

and spoke over his shoulder to Lachlann. "And what of ye and the twin lasses?"

Lachlann shrugged, not willing to share more than was necessary, though the twins' interest in pleasing him was something he'd not experienced for quite some time and certainly not from simple highland lasses. The more exotic, dark-skinned lasses had taught him quite a bit about lovemaking while he was away learning Latin.

"Oh, forsooth! I canna help that the two thought I could more easily choose between them if they each took a turn so I could better compare their...abilities."

"*Choose* between them? As in taking one to wife?" Aldred scoffed. "And ye with no plans to marry either." He spat out the words and added, "For pity's sake."

A twinge of guilt settled in, but Lachlann quickly dismissed it. He was not about to share that he'd made that exact point to both of them, repeatedly, but they refused to be convinced. Quite the opposite. They believed they could change his mind once he had experienced their prowess. For pity's sake indeed. If there was a woman intended for him, he'd know it not from the bedding, but from his own willingness to lay down his life for her. Like the great love stories the Bards sang of, his wife would be a gentle woman, passionate certainly, and caring. He didn't need to try her out like a horse. They would discover together the private intimacies of being married, teaching each other what pleasured them most.

Lachlann spent too much time with such thoughts. He'd found no such woman. He sighed. "Leastwise I am not on a mission to find every virgin in our midst."

"So 'tis fine then. . ." Niall halted to confront him where they stood in the middle of the open area, ". . . as long as they have been with another?"

Lachlann was surprised Niall was even listening, but before he could put words to his defense, Aldred responded. "He believes he is a better man than me by not taking a virgin. Even avoiding them like the plague! Never mind the service I provide by accommodating the married ones who have more desire than their aging husbands."

"And that is called adultery." Lachlann only said what they all knew and had no regrets at sounding so pious.

The shorter man smirked, his nose in the air, and swerved away.

Lachlann flattened his lips. "*I* am only about the pleasure. *I* give as well as receive, and *I* have no bone to pick or hidden reason to make a fool of some husband." He straightened to his full height, more than a head taller than Aldred. "And I *am* a better man than ye."

Aldred turned about to reveal his anger in a nasty grimace. Lachlann prepared for the shove: shoulders back, feet firmly planted, body tight. When it came, he barely budged. The fist he planted into Aldred's jaw had a satisfying thud despite the sting that shot up his arm. The man had a damn hard head.

"Enough!" Niall's declaration halted them in their tracks as they were about to go at it. He glanced about before lowering his voice, which brought them in closer. "Ye're both getting into trouble because ye're bored, as am I. Besides…" The tall redhead got between them, his blue eyes glowering at each in the dramatic way he had. "We all know...*I am* the better man."

He shoved them both. Lachlann and Aldred staggered back with quick steps to catch themselves before they fell. Niall continued down the path, his shoulders shaking with his loud laughter. Aldred winked at Lachlann before trotting to catch up. Exhaling a deep breath, Lachlann shook his head. This had been the way of it for as long as he could remember. Rivalry. Competition. Though the three of them were closer than brothers, they were easily riled to anger.

He rose to take the bait every time, much to his

irritation. And just like brothers, they were there for each other without question, having each other's backs when it mattered. Like the time Niall's father put his little sister, Thomasina, in harm's way. After being shunned from their clan, he'd become a drunkard. Both Aldred and Lachlann stepped up to protect her as if she were their own sister.

Though glad to see her happily married to Sean, the Irish warrior, Lachlann missed her still.

"Move yer arse now!" Aldred called to him from the direction of the stable.

Besides, who would the man have to argue with if Lachlann went and took a wife?

"Settle yer own arse. I'm coming." Lachlann started off at a slower pace to give himself some space to shake off these thoughts.

There'd been no one that had tugged at his heart, sparked a desire to protect her. Not since Thomasina, and she was like a sister. Tommy, as they called her, was a special lass. Beautiful. Kind. No one had ever come close to her in spirit.

The sight of the chieftain's treasured daughter, her brother at her side and coming his way, had Lachlann's jaw tightening. The direct opposite of Tommy. With long auburn hair and smoky gray eyes, she was named for the Virgin Mary herself, but she asked for trouble with all her carrying on.

"Murchadh." Lachlann acknowledged her lanky escort, guarding her, and trying to keep the lass out of any trouble she seemed more than ready to get into. Of Niall's two cousins, this man was the one Lachlann preferred with his easy demeanor and jovial expression.

He smiled now in his relaxed way. "How fare ye? Have ye heard the Campbell is returning?"

"I had not."

A thorn in their side, in any loyal Scot's side, since the

Campbells seemed bent on ingratiating themselves with the Normans, any Norman, who could give them the power and titles they craved so deeply. Rumor had it the clan had even gone so far as to organize a hunt for the pleasure of the visiting Norman king, Rufus. When his court had last ventured this far north, it was the Campbell who so openly embraced him. In truth, Rufus's very presence this far north hit a sore spot, indicating, as it did, that the man believed the entire island was under his domain.

Lachlann hardened his expression. "Might it be possible for ye and yer brother to be the ones sent off this time?"

"Not after my brother's latest exploits. My father may be requiring yer assistance again to improve his fighting abilities."

"No doubt I could teach him more with my bare fists."

Murchadh barked a laugh. "Ah, and I believe ye know my da's favorite form of punishment."

Banishment. "Aye. Yer father is not the most creative, my friend. He could use with some battle training himself."

"And I would enjoy being there when ye tell him as much."

Lachlann continued past, irritation worming its way through his innards. He didn't need reminding of the shunning. A hard time indeed. And now the Campbells? Their arrival was not a good omen. Timing for this visit, after having just returned from a battle with the Northumbrians, was suspicious at best.

"Lachlann!" a voice in the distance called out.

Lachlann paused when he recognized the voice of the priest and turned back the way they'd come. He squinted his eyes. Father Michael? He stood in the doorway of the chapel, motioning him closer.

Niall and Aldred had just reached the edge of the tree

line and were disappearing over the rise, too far ahead to catch without hollering. For the smallest second, Lachlann was torn in what to do, but then the memory of the priest's hard glare came back. Ah, the reprimand. This might be the opportunity to set things right with the man, explain to him that he was no longer a child and the correction hadn't been intentional. And wasn't that quite apparent? He'd barely said it loud enough for anyone else to even hear.

From within the chapel, one of the nuns came alongside the priest. She also watched Lachlann, but with an anxious expression. That was enough to convince him to do the "proper thing," leastwise as far as the good priest was concerned.

With quite a bit of reluctance, Lachlann retraced the path back to the chapel. Guilt made his steps heavier than they needed to be, and the priest's dark expression seemed to confirm his first impression.

"Good day to ye, Lachlann," the nun spoke first. "And how are ye this fine day?"

Surprised by her cheery tone, he accepted the small hand she extended, bowing slightly. "Hearty and healthy, and how are ye, sister?"

Her eyes widened with surprise. "Do ye not remember me?"

"This is Sister Elizabeth from the priory." Father Michael looked down his nose at the two of them. "She assures me ye've met. That ye've even been there and helped them out on occasion."

The priest's tone carried so much doubt that Lachlann almost laughed at the man's bad opinion of him, but quickly swallowed the urge.

"Of course. Sister Elizabeth."

A small woman, slightly younger than himself, and always a gracious hostess. They had enjoyed her company.

"Ye've only just missed Niall and Aldred," he said.

He, Niall, and Aldred had gone to the priory often over the years to help with upkeep—cropping and herding, filling in the gaps along the roof, digging a new well. Mayhap as a way of penance for some of their foolishness, but they hadn't been there recently.

Her lips transformed into a genuine smile. "Oh. Please do tell Aldred I said hello. As always, I've kept him in my prayers."

"I can bring ye to him," Lachlan said with more enthusiasm than he intended, even turning toward the general direction of the stables as he spoke. Idly chatting with the priest, who always found him lacking, was not how he wanted to spend his day.

"Many thanks, but 'tis ye I wish to speak with."

Her piercing gaze held his, and his stomach dropped at the uncharacteristic insistence. Was he to be reprimanded by her as well? No doubt she'd been one of the nuns lined against the wall, probably listening to the Father's admonishment, but politely pretending not to hear it.

"I am returning to Restenneth shortly, but I had hoped to enlist yer help before I do," she said. "The three of ye."

"As always, we would be happy to help in any way we can, though I admit Niall's uncle keeps us quite busy in battle as of late."

So much so that when they weren't living off the land, sleeping wet and cold on the ground, they weren't sure what to do with themselves.

"I was hoping ye'd say that."

She seemed ready to burst with excitement and his heart quickened.

"Do ye have such exciting labor?" He asked half-jokingly.

"Ah, no." Sister Elizabeth laughed. "But we did find something that will interest ye. Completely unexpected.

The sisters and I have a journey we need the three of ye to make on our behalf."

"A journey." The idea immediately intrigued Lachlann. This might be the very thing they needed to escape Garnait's grasping clutches and ceaseless wars. And as long as he could convince his friends to go… Lachlann smiled. He had no doubt that he could do just that. "Tell me more."

CHAPTER 2

*L*achlann followed them into the dimly lit interior of the chapel. Father Michael directed them to sit, but he remained standing. A small leather parcel had appeared from somewhere among the nun's many layers of material and now rested in her lap.

When she looked at Lachlann, her eyes danced with excitement. "This winter has been exceedingly hard on the priory. Rivers changing course to divide our fields. Trees being ripped out from the roots to fall on the buttery."

Lachlann's shoulders tightened with concern. "But all are well? No one was hurt?"

She flashed a frown then shook her head. "No. No. All are fine."

He rubbed his chin. This didn't sound like a journey at all. "Then I'm stumped. Are ye looking to have repairs done?"

She fidgeted. "Aye, too many for the three of ye, but nay."

He couldn't remember ever seeing her so fretted.

"Not now—'tis not what I'm asking of ye." She blew a breath in frustration and picked up the parcel. "This! This is what I'm asking of ye. We have the funds, but what we need is for ye to collect them for us."

With great care, she untied the leather strap surrounding the deerskin package to reveal a palm-sized book. "We found this buried in the dirt."

The vellum leaves had been sewn together with a fine stitch and encased in a cloth cover, stiff with age.

"It was tucked beneath the floor of the buttery where the old priory had been. We believe it was more than likely written by a monk. 'Tis written in Latin."

Lachlann's gaze immediately went to the priest who raised his brows as if in challenge.

"Latin?" Lachlann didn't try to hide his surprise at the priest's heretofore unknown ability.

Father Michael cleared his throat and glanced away. "Not entirely."

Lachlann pressed his lips tight to keep from smiling.

"Aye," Sister Elizabeth said, though she never looked up from the precious item. "The sisters and I have gone through it with great interest."

"May I?" Lachlann opened his palm, and she gently placed the book into his hands.

Their eyes met, and he offered a reassuring smile until she released it. Studying it closely, he was impressed by the elaborate drawings and colorful writing. It was the writing of a well-trained cleric.

"Are ye familiar with Saint Columba?" Sister Elizabeth asked.

Lachlann nodded, the vellum pages stiff in his fingers as he turned one leaf after another. "The man who brought Christianity to Scotland."

"The writer was one of his followers. He writes of the Picts. Long ago, they lived where the priory is now. Columba turned them into followers of Christ."

Lachlann stopped reading to watch her. Her eyes

remained bright and her voice low, bringing him in closer as the story caught his imagination.

"This man writes that he was once called Oengus, a hired killer. Pillaging and raping for whoever would pay him the most: Celt, Pict, Anglo-Saxon. And all the spoils were his to take or use as he chose. He recalls one particularly savage battle; his arm was all but severed from his body. He was left for dead, discarded like he never mattered, while his life's blood seeped into the hard, cold ground. The blowing leaves covered him as they fell, because he hadn't the strength to clear them away. Hours and days went by while he waited for his death. That is when Columba found him.

"Columba gave him cool, refreshing water and spoke reassuring words of God's love and mercy. Oengus's body raged with fever. In his brokenness, he called Columba a liar, crying out that God could never forgive him for the atrocities he'd inflicted on the innocent. But Columba continued to care for Oengus's many wounds, insisting God would forgive a repentant heart.

"When the fever finally broke, Oengus awoke in the priory surrounded by monks praying over him. It was several weeks before he fully recovered, but he finally felt well enough to ask for Columba. The man had shown him great love and care, and Oengus wished to be baptized by the man. The monks told him Columba had been dead for hundreds of years."

Lachlann let out a slow breath. The wind blew against the chapel's stone walls and the sound sent a chill through him. It was not unheard of. He knew of many stories where saints were seen visiting a battlefield or a dying man. They gave courage where there was none.

"This man—" Sister Elizabeth tapped on the tough hide "—changed his life because of that encounter. He took the vows of a monk, praying and caring for the sick in the surrounding area as far as he was able." She lifted her gaze to Lachlann. "When he found his true calling, he gave all that he had acquired as a mercenary to the church and lived a peaceful life...until the Norsemen came. That was when the life he'd come to know ended. The monks implored Oengus to again don the garb of a mercenary and take the silver to where it would be safe from the heathens. Oengus finally agreed, taking along their youngest ward to pose as his squire."

She turned to the next page and pointed out a section. "Here. He tells how he planned to travel to the caves along the north shores that he had visited in his youth. He would wait there for word that the priory had survived the heathen attacks and he could return, but they'd all heard about the savagery committed in these attacks."

Lachlann asked, "Could this man not have served them better by staying behind and fighting the attackers?"

Father Michael sighed, a woeful sound. "Sister neglected to mention that when the monks took him in and nursed him back to health, they were unable to save his arm."

Lachlann thought of the man, sitting in the quiet cave with the ocean his constant companion. The cold, wet nights. The fear he must have felt for the brothers he had left behind.

"But word never came." Sister Elizabeth shook her head. "The monks did not survive the attack."

"A traveler came at Michaelmas, the year I first was in residence at the priory." Father Michael took over the telling of the story. "I remember him well. Broad in the shoulders and quite tall, but he struck me as menacing. I shared this with the sisters to be sure they were never alone with him. One night, as we supped, he told us of the legend of silver that had been hidden in the caves along the northern shore. Quite a tale. Enough details to make the story seem...true."

"A *skald*. No more. The stories they tell have no root in

truth." Lachlann scoffed. "Surely ye dinna believe he spoke of the silver from this warrior."

The nun's eyes were piercing in their intensity. "It was money intended for the church, money that had been moved to protect it from raiders, just like ours."

Lachlann waited, but she had apparently run out of things to add so he turned to the priest. "What say ye?"

"Trust me when I tell ye I was not even slightly interested in the man's legends. He was full of himself and his own importance." Father Michael indicated the small journal with a tilt of his chin. "When Sister brought me this, I recognized the similarities to the man's story. Since it seems they just left the silver hidden in a cave somewhere, and there was never any large amounts added to the priory's coffers, the legends may be true."

Sister Elizabeth shifted her attention back to the small journal. "He writes about the safest location for the coin being in some cave and promises to bring it back to the church as soon as he gets word. I believe this is where the silver remains even now. We need only for ye to retrieve it for us."

Lachlann held her steady gaze. "Think ye I can just walk in and someone will point me to it?"

Her voice remained quiet. "The silver is there."

"Where?"

Her earnest expression never faltered. "In the caves."

"Which caves?"

"The ones along the northern coast in Moray."

"That area is overrun with lawlessness. They speak our language, but they're no longer ruled by our King. The Danes and the Islanders to the far north fight over control."

"'Tis a bit…wild up there." Sister visibly stiffened.

Lachlann waited, his lips pinched together to keep from begging her to open her eyes and see the truth. Someone else would certainly have found the silver by now. If no one had, then it must be so well hidden that it never would be found.

She cleared her throat. "I would not ask if it were not so important to us, Lachlann."

He held himself stiff, resisting the urge to fall into the trap these two were both in. Before he could speak, she placed her small hand on his arm. It was quite warm, and her expression revealed her fear of his refusal. His guilt increased.

"Please, Lachlann." She implored him. "We have no one else to send. The money is meant for the church, but we *can* pay ye for yer service…leastwise once the silver coins are retrieved."

He understood her desperation. He heaved a sigh, before flashing a smile. "*If* it is retrieved." He kept his voice low and quiet. "Ye have verra little to go by with this."

"But I believe we are meant to have it. God will surely watch over ye in yer travels, and ye will have much success." She spoke quickly, her words all running together in her enthusiasm.

"We all think well of ye, Sister." Lachlann didn't want to disappoint her. "I will see if Niall and Aldred can be persuaded to travel so far north at this time of year, but I make no promises."

She held his gaze and shook her head ever so slightly. "Ye need to convince them, Lachlann. *Ye* understand the way of it. This must be done."

Father Michael and Sister Elizabeth remained as still as stones and watched him. They couldn't understand the totality of what they were asking of him. A foolhardy quest at best. To convince anyone they should do this when he himself could think of a hundred reasons why they should not left him reluctant to agree. But agree to it he did.

"I will do what I can."

"Wonderful!" Sister Elizabeth beamed. To the priest, she added, "Ye were correct, Father Michael. A wonderful group of men."

A wonderful group of men? Had the man actually said that about them?

She turned back to Lachlann, her warm smile remaining. "Ye will not be disappointed. I promise ye. Can ye leave at once?"

They could go nowhere without their chieftain's leave. "The 'when' will be determined by another…"

Her face closed down in disappointment.

"But I will accept this mission as my own and act accordingly." He quirked a brow at Father Michael. "I just hope the worst is disappointment and not the loss of my soul."

CHAPTER 3

When Lachlann joined Niall and Aldred at the small stabling area, they were still discussing the Norseman's lack of respect. Their horses munched among the tall grasses, unbothered by the loud, angry voices beside them. Instead, they looked to be preparing for a brisk morning trot. Lachlann hoped for the same once he had his friends' agreement on what he'd promised Sister Elizabeth.

Niall towered over Aldred, who sat cross-legged on the ground, a piece of long grass between his lips and his back leaning against the post. Niall's stern manner matched his angry tone. "I believe if ye put as much effort into not offending others as ye do in seeing to yer baser pleasure, ye'd be sainted!"

A scowl was Aldred's only response.

Niall sighed in defeat before tending to his horse. "But I still think it's the boredom of our current situation that is the problem. Only three days back in the bosom of our loving clan, and we're at each other's throats"

The perfect opening.

"An adventure would be just the thing to put an end to that boredom," Lachlann said when he came within earshot.

"Did ye get lost?" Aldred turned his irritation on his favorite target.

"I was approached by Sister Elizabeth." Lachlann leveled his gaze at the man. "She sends her greetings and wants *ye* to know she continues to pray for ye."

Niall stroked the black warhorse's long nose. His favorite courser shifted uncomfortably as if sensing Niall's still simmering irritation. "I thought I noticed her among the nuns."

"With their faces barely visible," Aldred offered, "'tis difficult to tell them apart."

Before Lachlann could get the words of explanation out, Aldred halted him with a raised hand.

"I know. I know. 'Tis why they're covered. As a nun, they're not to be seen as women anymore." He rolled his eyes. "Between yer Bible teaching and being prayed over by the Brides of Christ, I'm sure to find myself in the fires of hell."

Lachlann took a breath, ready to explain that's not how it worked, but shook his head instead.

"Women or not— " he spoke pointedly toward Aldred before continuing— "they have a job for us. There's been much damage to their priory."

"We're not trained in such work, as I'm sure ye told her."

Aldred was pushing for an argument now, and Lachlann glared at him. "Costly repairs. They're needing some funds to pay for the work."

"We've none of that either." Aldred's scowl returned.

"Oh, they have the funds." He offered a crooked grin. "Or, leastwise, they *believe* they have the funds."

Aldred frowned. "Good. Then they have no need of us."

"And what do we have to do, but fight my uncle's petty fights?" Niall shouted and shook his head at the shorter man before facing Lachlann. "I would be happy for any distraction about now."

"Well, my friend, a distraction they have. They need us to retrieve their funds."

"Hmm, from where?"

"The northeast coast."

"Too bad." The redhead rubbed down the side of his horse. "What did she say when ye told her my uncle was bent on sending us out to start a fight with yet another clan and would never give us leave to take such a long journey now?" He turned to him mid-swipe. "I assume ye didn't tell her in quite that way."

"I told her we'd do it."

"What?" Aldred scrambled to his feet, ready for a fight.

Niall remained calm and came to stand beside Lachlann, the slightest tilt to his head as if searching for clarity. "Am I missing something? Why would ye agree to it without discussing it with us first?"

In the short walk from the chapel, Lachlann realized he'd become quite excited for this trip. It was the perfect solution to a bad situation.

"Niall, yer uncle is not just bent on starting another fight. His plans include sending ye to meet his wife's niece, Lily. That would be the same Lily who jumps in fear at the mere sound of a man's voice, and I'm sure I dinna need to remind ye of winter last.

"At St. Stephen's Day, she was telling everyone she'd be marrying ye. Apparently, all the maidens gather up the last of the crabapples and carve the initial of their favorite lads on them. She put an *N* into hers." He raised a single brow at Niall. "The *N* could be seen a month later, even as it rotted—a sure sign she and ye were meant to be together."

Aldred beamed. "Aye, she's mighty smitten with ye."

Niall spit on the ground. "And I'll not be used by my uncle in that way. Damn him! She is a child."

"He does seem bent on it." Aldred sounded more thoughtful than his usual blustery self.

"If he announces the betrothal," Lachlann said, "ye have only outright refusal to save ye. Are ye willing to take the chance of getting on his bad side now that ye're finally being acknowledged as his nephew?"

"Better I marry a woman who canna accept a man's touch?"

"And that is my point." Lachlann understood Niall's frustrations. It had not been so very long ago that his entire family had been banished for his father's failings as clan leader. "Yer uncle is now acknowledging ye, but he doesn't appreciate yer worth. He'd rather bow down to the southern tribes that cater to the landed lords in *England*, using *ye* as his prized warrior."

"No doubt he's hoping for a title of his own and riches to go with it." Aldred's tone hardened in his outrage at Niall's treatment.

Niall's face had turned a blotchy red. "I shouldn't have to prostrate myself for respect rightly earned."

Months of groveling to Garnait, of proving Niall was not like his father, yet being treated as little more than a slave to order about, had worn thin...for all of them. Both Lachlann and Aldred always saw Niall as their rightful leader and Garnait used that to his advantage time and again.

"That's why we need to take this journey for the nuns. Do ye not see? An act for the church? Even yer uncle wouldn't detain ye from such a noble trek."

Niall blew a gusty breath, his ire seeming to dissipate with the action.

Lachlann breathed a sigh of his own and pressed his advantage. "'Tis why I agreed to go retrieve their treasure."

"A treasure?" Niall's surprised tone brought a smile to Lachlann's lips. "What kind of treasure would that be?"

"Silver."

"And where is this hidden treasure? More exactly," Niall asked.

"More exactly is hard to say, but 'tis somewhere beyond the firth of Moray."

"Moray? A good sennight ride away! Well, then, let us go and get this treasure." Niall's face mottled again, his tone hardened. "Ye try my patience. Ye truly do."

Lachlann scoffed. "I didna say 'twould be easy."

No doubt they'd find great humor in the fact that Father Michael had joined in the convincing. That alone should have made Lachlann refuse but, damn it, it was the noble thing to do. "Where is yer sense of adventure, my friend? Sister Elizabeth trusts us. She knows what we are able to accomplish unlike yer uncle. This will be a small matter, finding the silver—"

Niall's snort interrupted him momentarily.

Lachlann refused to be discouraged. "A damsel in need who has no one else? The bards will sing of our adventure."

Aldred chuckled. "Even the bishop pays the priory little mind, preferring to visit the areas with a greater population and more influence with our king."

"She has no one else," Lachlann said, "and she is willing to pay us. Handsomely."

"Handsomely?" Niall's nostrils flared "Are we for hire now? And what exactly is our worth?"

Niall was serving no purpose with this belligerence. Lachlann clamped his teeth tight. He understood his friend's struggles. Even with his father in a drunken stupor, brokenhearted over the loss of his wife, he had been a far better leader than Garnait. That fact always made Lachlann question the events that caused him to be replaced and shunned. Now, Niall was at a disadvantage, always shoved to the side so his cousins and his uncle could shine.

Lachlann squared his shoulders. He needed to confront this stubbornness head-on.

"The clan yer uncle claims as his own was stolen from yer father, Niall. We all know that. Short of fighting him directly..." Lachlann forced himself to pause, his chest tightening with the effort, then forced out the words. "If ye've decided to confront him, then let us wait no longer. Say so now and I will be at yer side as I always have been."

The silence hung there between them so thick that even Aldred remained motionless. It wasn't that Lachlann minded confronting the chieftain. He didn't. Not at all. But Niall's own father had never done so. He never set things right and now, the rest of the clan knew only what had been told to them. Their allegiance would be questionable at best.

The small shake of Niall's head released the tension. Air whooshed from Lachlann. Aldred's shoulders rounded in relief. Speaking in a lighter tone, Lachlann said, "Then make yerself known. Make alliances. Mayhap even find a wife of yer *own* choosing. Does that not sound like a better option than waiting around for your uncle's blessing? For some acknowledgement of yer importance —our importance—to the clan?"

Niall's brows were furrowed in concentration, but at least the bright red had faded from his cheeks.

"How much will she pay?" His voice was quieter.

"A portion of what is found." Lachlann dared not look away. "A finder's fee of sorts."

Niall pressed his lips together, but there was now a definite curl to them. "Ye dinna know the value."

"Truth be told it may amount to nothing. Then we will have wasted our time, but *they* will know for certain 'tis gone, and we shall regale the multitudes with our stories."

"So, tell us of this great adventure ye would take us on."

"The nuns found a journal. It tells how to find the

silver hidden in some cave. It was hidden by a monk." He explained to them what Sister Elizabeth had said. "They have the proof. The coin was intended for the church. We have only to retrieve it for them."

"But yer uncle will have yer head for abandoning him." Aldred made no attempt to hide his irritation with the situation. "He makes his own plans. Daily."

Judging by the sudden tightening of Niall's face, Aldred's matter-of-fact tone was not lost on him.

"His plans. Not mine. He'll have a hard time catching that head once we're gone." Niall smiled, his eyes creasing. "But as ye say, Lachlann, 'twould be for the church. A work of great value."

"He could say, 'Not at this time.'" Lachlann added this fact with great reluctance as it had just occurred to him. "Going without his leave is burning bridges." He didn't like the idea of disappearing without a word to their leader, no matter how bad a leader he was. "Never good for a battle plan when ye might need to return the same way."

Lachlann had a thought. "Think ye he may give his blessing if he believes 'twill profit him?"

The three exchanged glances and burst into smiles. Garnait was the greediest man alive with no feelings of guilt. How he was able to take communion without choking on the host was beyond Lachlann.

"At least three clans along the way may be happy to receive gifts and salutations from our mighty chieftain."

Niall's expression darkened.

"Not a mighty chieftain then, but mayhap from his fearless warriors. We can convince yer uncle of how it could improve his standing and influence with the other clans. There's been talk, and the highland clans know yer uncle is currying favor with those lowlanders. Let him believe we're doing his work as well as helping out the nuns."

"What of his mighty plans?" Aldred asked.

"Let his precious son lead his battles for him." Niall's demeanor brightened considerably. "Lachlann, ye're a wise man indeed. 'Twill be *me* they see, *me* they'll be getting to know. These men could be future allies, known to me, and I to them. Verra wise indeed." Niall slapped him on the back. "Mayhap I can convince my uncle of the importance of this journey after all."

"Making alliances should always be the goal of a wise leader," Lachlann said. "Yer uncle doesn't seem to understand that. He prefers making enemies of those closest to him."

Aldred waggled his bushy blond brows. "I enjoy making alliances."

Lachlann shoved the man against the wooden post, but Aldred just laughed, even as he struggled to keep his footing.

Niall didn't return the Norseman's grin. "And not keeping yer hands to yerself can sometimes make enemies."

Aldred spit on the ground. "Are ye all expecting me to remain celibate?"

As in so many other instances when Aldred shot off his mouth without thinking, Niall and Lachlann merely glared back at the man.

"Well, do ye?" In supplication, he raised his upturned hands. "I hate it when ye act this way. I'd much prefer my lusty friends to join in on the conquests we could make."

"I'm wondering why it is that ye seem to be the only one of us who still acts like a spry young buck? After any white-tailed doe he sees?"

"I'm not that bad."

Lachlann stopped short of rolling his eyes. Instead, he met Aldred's whining with a stoic face.

Aldred kicked at a stone and said in a petulant tone, "I will if 'tis needed."

"It may be," Niall said. "Ye've offended enough fathers by yer pursuit—"

"Not only pursuit, but claiming as well."

"And yer proud of it?" Lachlann didn't hide his annoyance. "'Tis the deflowering that causes us problems."

Niall continued. "And conquering of their daughters. As a warrior, ye know just fine how to withstand temptation, no matter what ye may claim."

Aldred puckered his lips then shrugged. When Niall raised a brow, not satisfied with his half agreement, Aldred nodded. A slow reflective nod.

Lachlann asked, "So shall we approach yer uncle tonight?"

Niall placed a hand on Aldred's shoulder before facing Lachlann. "I think tonight will be fine. I'll do my best to convince him, but my decision is made. We'll leave by week's end with or without his blessing."

The large, open longhouse was set up for the evening meal with the room near to overflowing with men from the clan. All talking, drinking, and eating. The darkness just settling in, a few flaming torches were set up to offset the gloom. Garnait, his long gray hair flowing around his shoulders, sat on his raised dais centered on the far wall and looked out over his men. Lachlann's scalp prickled. He knew of no justification for the man's arrogance, but he basked in the title of chieftain as if he had somehow earned it. If Niall ever chose to confront the man for leadership, Lachlann would definitely receive great satisfaction in taking him off his throne. Even now, Garnait was the only one surrounded by women as was his custom whenever his wife was not nearby.

Lachlann and Niall weaved their way through the

mass of loud, smelly warriors to settle at a quiet table tucked along the eave of the low, thatched roof, nearly hidden in shadows, with their sopping trenchers. Aldred quickly joined them, plopping down opposite on his own long bench.

"How am I to stay strong and ready to fight if they give me no meat?" he grumbled.

Lachlann held his tongue, though he was at the end of his patience as well. Warriors should never be treated so. They needed sustenance. They should be revered, treated to the best accommodations and fed like kings. Without them, the safety of the clan was in question.

Aldred's downcast eyes lit up at the sight of an unexpected piece of meat in the watery broth. He speared it, then closed his eyes to savor the delicacy, groaning in satisfaction.

"Hey, Heathen!" Garnait's oldest son Douglas called from the next table. He was surrounded by his minions, which included his younger brother Murchadh. His amicable tone did nothing to mask the nasty scowl. "Are ye eating or pleasuring yerself?"

Lachlann tensed at the insult, the ribald comments loud enough for everyone to hear. Despite his repeated attempts, Douglas had yet to be successful at riling Aldred, who again remained imperturbable. Even now, he merely opened his eyes, paused, and took a sip of his mead.

After what seemed like an eternity—Lachlann was ready to take down the man if he said even one more word—Aldred turned to Douglas and said, "Ye tell me, Douglas. Has it been so long since ye've lain with a woman that any pleasure must involve yer prick?"

The large man threw down his wooden plate and stood, ready for a fight. Lachlann lurched forward. His arse kicking was long overdue.

"Enough!" Niall's tone left no room for discussion. He

grasped Aldred's shoulder before he could stand. Without another word, Aldred resumed eating and gave Douglas his back. This forced Lachlann to ease back as well, but his vexation remained.

"Hey, Douglas." Lachlann's lips turned up into a genuine smile. "Did ye not just come back from battle? Entertain us all with yer stories of conquests."

By the look of Douglas's reddening cheeks, his brother had been kind in his recounting of the battle. Any battle was better off without the man...unless the goal was to lose.

"No?" Satisfaction spread across Lachlann's chest. "Mayhap another time then."

Douglas scowled at them, before settling back and returning to his own talk.

After a few minutes, Niall said, "That man is a glutton of the worst kind."

Lachlann knew he referred to Garnait without being told and his and Aldred's gazes went to the dais. The man's hands roved the supple swells of the ladies flitting about him in the guise of being fed. That the man would chastise the three of them the harshest, while showing no restraint himself behind his wife's back and allowing the same from his sons, was as insulting as the tone he used every time he spoke to them. That he could gainsay any of their plans was galling.

"I've heard this is all show." Aldred washed down the last of his mead, tipping it back twice for good measure. "And the best show is for strangers since they do not know him as we do."

"And have ye any idea who those *coigrich* are?" Lachlann motioned to the warriors opposite Garnait's trestle.

Their pale skin and light hair marked them as Saxons: their fine clothing as earls. They lifted their mugs toward

Garnait. With a wolfish grin on his ugly face, he winked in return.

"My guess would be they're from the same southern clans making alliances with the Normans. My dear uncle's own fondest wish for our clan."

Lachlann wiped the back of his hand across his mouth. "The man flirts with danger, courting those leaders. They would as soon slit yer throat if they believed it would please the English."

"When the cat's away…" Aldred spoke in a lilting tone, his eyes on the entrance to the hall. "And the cat is about to return."

The rough-hewn door was thrown open. Garnait turned the flash of a fearful gaze toward the sound. His dark-haired spouse, flanked on either side by her ever-present hand*maidens*, entered. Lachlann knew from Aldred's boasting that at least two of them could no longer claim the title. The din hushed to silence in tense anticipation.

"Garnait." She strode forward, a slow but determined gait, her long walrus-skin *brat* hugging her regal length, her hair flowing down her back. "What are ye about?"

"Ma-Margaret," her husband stuttered, his eyes wide with guilt.

Margaret's eyes followed the young ladies as they were ushered away from her husband. "Up to no good, I see."

She paused to accept a kiss on the cheek from the Saxon earls who'd risen to greet her. Each held her hands, in turn, while quiet words were exchanged.

"Friends of yer aunt?" Lachlann's face tightened. Thoughts of her niece, Lily, came to mind.

Niall merely shrugged.

It was becoming even more imperative that they take their leave of this place and soon.

"Not at all." Garnait cleared his throat and motioned

to the vacated spot beside him. "Not at all, my dear. Come, come sit beside yer husband."

The sharp flick of a brow was the only further acknowledgement.

"Of course, my husband."

Margaret assumed her rightful place at Garnait's side. It seemed as if someone had opened both doors to let the air out of the hall.

"I am glad to see ye have taken yer repast in my absence. Some things take precedence and time is of the essence now."

Her gaze settled on Niall, and she smiled. His face blanched at the sudden interest. Lachlann's stomach dropped. The undue attention could only mean one thing. She was advancing her plans for her niece to wed Niall. Mayhap burning bridges had its advantages.

"It seems we may not have a chance to speak to Garnait." Lachlann turned his attention to Niall.

Niall's scowl turned from his aunt to Lachlann. "We will speak to my uncle about our journey this night. Come sunrise, we are taking our leave of this place."

Lachlann prayed those would be the only plans settled on this night.

CHAPTER 4

Knee-deep in the cold brook, Ethne forced herself to be still as the silver fish weaved about her ankles. The young child on the bank beside her squeezed his mouth shut even as he hunkered down, struggling to contain his excitement. It wasn't that her nephew had never seen her catch fish before, because he had. No, this was at the prospect of her using her bare hands to do so.

Ethne caught sight of her reflection peering back at her from the smooth surface of the water. Her long dark hair plastered to both sides of her face from her many unsuccessful attempts, her mouth tightened into a determined line, and her eyes narrowed in concentration. And why wouldn't she look so obstinate? Finn had laughed—laughed!— uncontrollably, even rolling on the ground, when she told him of how she had learned to catch fish. Her own childhood had been spent farther inland among the deep, lush forests where many creatures Finn had never seen lived.

Here, along the north shore of Scotia, there were no trees. The relentless wind had stripped the land clear except for the tall grasses that easily shifted along with the currents. The only creatures that could survive here were of a much tougher bend to withstand the harsh elements. And, certainly, they could never be caught with bare hands.

"Finn!" The sound of the angry voice startled them both, and Ethne jumped enough that the fish she'd been waiting so patiently for was gone in the flash of its silver back. "Finn!"

Her stomach clenched at the tone of Finn's mother shifting higher and louder as she searched for him.

"Ye'd best get to her." Ethne's pronouncement was not entirely necessary since the boy was moving in that direction even now. She trudged along the banks as quickly as she could, barely noticing the dark mire splattering her short *léine* once she had cleared the muddy strand, where she ran in earnest to catch up with the lad.

The scene she came upon made her breath catch. Finn was crying, his mother's arms clasping him to her bosom where she kneeled beside him. The woman seldom ever touched the boy. His own small arm was wrapped around the huge swell of his little brother or sister. Domelch glared at her, and the fury in those dark green eyes slowed Ethne in her steps.

"Ethne! What have ye done to scare the boy?"

Thoughts whirled in her head as Ethne tried to pinpoint when the boy had shown any fear, but before she could respond, the woman raised her hand up to stop her. "Bother me not with yer excuses. We know well how ye lie!"

Ethne's body went rigid, but she kept an even tone despite her outrage. "I never lie."

In three steps, the irate woman was in her face. The slap was hard, stinging Ethne's cheek. "Ye will not speak back to me."

Ethne tasted blood flooding her mouth. The cut in her

cheek from yesterday's slap had reopened. She turned dry eyes on her sister-in-law with her lips tightly closed. This was Domelch's latest tactic meant to belittle her, but Ethne refused to cower.

Domelch's nostrils flared with indignation. When she raised a hand a second time, Ethne easily caught the wrist mid swing. This infuriated her sister-in-law even more.

"How. Dare. Ye. Touch. Me." Domelch squeezed out the words from her clenched jaw, the bulge of her unborn child heaving between them in her upset.

Ethne's cheek throbbed. She released the wrist, her own hands falling to her sides.

"Yer brother will hear of this."

There would be hell to pay for Ethne's single act of defiance, and though her brother would listen to her explain, he would allow Domelch to deal with her as her sister-in-law saw fit. Ethne dropped her head so the woman would not see her intense anger. Anger that squeezed her throat tight, nearly cutting off her breath. There was no help for it. Or for her. She had been at Domelch's mercy since the day her brother had married the awful woman.

"I beg yer forgiveness, m'lady." Bile flooded her mouth, the result of the tart taste of her own blood or having to use such a respectful title for such a vile creature, she couldn't be certain which. She prayed Domelch would not take some offense at her tone, or the tilt of her head, or the rigidity of her stance, or a million other things the woman took pleasure objecting to.

"She looks scared, Mama." Finn tried to mimic his mother's stance, but his glaring scowl looked more humorous than mean.

Domelch's disdainful snort sharpened Ethne's hearing to what might happen next. She dare not even breathe. Not if she had any hope of avoiding further damage to her person.

"So, tell me why ye've dragged my son so far upstream?"

It hadn't been far at all. Ethne glanced at the boy, who just a few minutes earlier had been all but dancing in glee at the adventure. "I'd hoped to show—"

"She was showing me what she could do, Mama."

"Showing off again, Ethne?" Domelch's contemptuous tone matched her expression. That was one of Domelch's favorite insults.

"She made me stay quiet," Finn said, his small forehead furrowed like his mother's. "And still."

"She ordered ye not to speak?"

Ethne had told him that so that he wouldn't scare away the fish.

Finn was kind, loving even, but never when he was with his mother. Even now his mother's look of pride and the way the woman held him against her side when she refused to even kiss him goodnight was no doubt causing all kinds of confusing feelings for the boy.

Domelch's heavy brow lowered ever so slowly. Her eyes narrow, angry slits of cold emerald, prompted Ethne to speak just as Domelch knew it would.

"I am verra sorry for treating ye thus." The lies came easy now, much more easily than they used to when Ethne had struggled to understand what she did wrong. To explain. To defend herself. She knew better now. She would not be found blameless in any situation.

"On. Yer. Knees." Domelch's satisfaction complete, her nose held high and her long, red hair piled high atop her head, gave her an imperious look.

Once, Ethne and Malcolm had lived among people who were kind and loving. Her great-great-grandmother had been a woman of some importance.

Not anymore. Now, their mother and father were both dead, and Malcolm had married this miserable woman and returned to the "old" ways. Old ways Ethne had no experience with before she came here. Old ways that used words like "tribe" instead of "clan." Old ways the church considered heathen practices. They lived away from the protection of the village so their ceremonies would not be banned, and Ethne would continue to be their slave in all but title.

Knowing what Domelch wanted, she knelt before the two of them, head bowed, hoping she remained far enough away to avoid being kicked this time. "I ask for yer mercy in allowing me to remove this slight against ye. Pray tell me what I can do to make amends."

"What do ye think, my little man? What would ye like this night?"

"I would love lamprey cakes! Ethne makes the best, and it has been such a long time." His tone held the same enthusiasm as earlier when she'd believed the child might enjoy a simple walk in the woods.

"Then she will make lamprey cakes."

"For all of us?" he asked.

"For all of us," Domelch said, her tone pure gloating. "How generous ye are, my little man."

It was forbidden by the mormaer at the castle to catch lampreys and it mattered very little that these were disputed lands. *Anyone* caught breaking that law would need to pay just compensation. A silly law created as a way of honoring the Norman king's love of the slimy creature. A hard law to enforce, but it was there for anyone wishing to cause trouble. A fine could be exacted, even payment in kind when no coin was held. Payment in kind could be anything. *Anything.*

Ethne and Finn had been stopped just a fortnight ago after they'd been left behind when his parents went south to sell the skins they'd collected. Digging for crabs at low tide, the sounds of the surf surrounding them, she hadn't heard the mounted warriors coming at them until it was too late.

Four wealthy islanders by the look of them, but only one dismounted—the largest one. A gold medallion prominently displayed against his chest indicated his authority. She was at his mercy. No one would dare gainsay him. His fine leather gloves signified his great wealth. He swaggered toward her, peeling them off his enormous hands. The gold ring on his finger bore the seal of an island tribe. With no strong leadership of their own, the people in this area had no recourse against the outrageous treatment of being stopped and searched. Their tribe was afforded no protection, not from the mormaer, who considered this land the property of his king, or from these islanders who coveted the area. After all, they were outcasts by choice. Outcasts and unwanted.

Wearing a leering smile, he'd searched her with hot grasping fingers that lingered in places she should not be touched. His men laughed. She stood there, as still as she could, and took it because she had no choice.

In her mind, she'd stood up to him and demanded to know where, exactly, they believed she was hiding the slimy delicacy. But when he had finished his "inspection" and turned her about, he stood nose to nose with her. His breathing heavy and his eyes hooded. She was glad she'd held her tongue. With his lust sparked, he was even more dangerous. If he decided to rape her, the others who had enjoyed watching the humiliating examination, might even be allowed to take their turn. In that brief moment, she could read his indecision. She prayed to God for mercy.

"Ye stink!" He spat the words, then shoved at her chest, pushing her back so that she lost her footing and fell with a splash into the rising tide swirling around her. She had no recourse then, and she had no recourse now. And she didn't like feeling helpless.

The "loving" smile Domelch turned on her son never

reached her eyes. Ethne was convinced the woman had no feelings for anyone but herself. A heart of solid rock.

Ethne could not refuse and lowered her gaze, relieved they hadn't noticed her watching them as Domelch saw that as a sign of disrespect. "As ye wish. I thank ye."

"And tell him ye will not treat him so again!" Domelch demanded of her.

Ethne cringed, but stopped short of fisting her hands. Domelch watched her like a hawk high in the trees, ready to swoop down on her at any sign of insolence.

"Never again will I treat ye so." Ethne was beyond angry with this little boy whom she had raised as her own, but she doubted he understood the consequences of his actions.

"Ye may return when ye have collected enough lampreys for our evening meal." The words were thrown over Domelch's shoulder as she walked away, Finn's hand firmly in hers. Neither looked back.

~

Twilight had long passed, the rising moon the only light to guide Ethne across the boulder-strewn path. She paused to stretch her back, enjoying the quiet *whoosh* of the surf, and took a deep breath, trying to loosen the knot tightening her stomach. Domelch would no doubt object to the paltry number of fish she'd been able to catch. If her brother were not away, mayhap this time he'd come to her defense. She shook her head. Not likely, best to linger out here no longer. As if in answer to her troubled thoughts, music drifted toward her on the faint breeze. A whistle being played by someone far better than her brother.

Visitors. Her brother must be back. She closed the short distance to the cave's hidden entrance with quickened steps. Unnoticed, she paused just inside the cave to search him out. Malcolm sat with his back against the far wall as always, talking with their chieftain and three other tribe's men. They were back from their hunt, a success by the amount of drinking and loud talking. They had been gone since the new moon, and this celebration could last many days.

Malcom looked exhausted. His dark-hair matted against his head, along with filthy clothing, demonstrated how little his wife revered him. Ethne's heart squeezed. Domelch had not even provided him a bath. Instead, she flaunted about, distributing the dripping meat and seeing to the others. Another thing Ethne was helpless to change.

The smell of roasting boar made her stomach growl. Her smelly catch waited in her makeshift sack—her *léine* turned up at the hem with its ends tucked into the rope securing her waist—but she leaned back to appreciate the lovely music. Soon enough she'd be noticed and ordered about. The fire cast dancing shadows against the curved walls as nearly a dozen people moved around the tiny space, looking very much like the drawings that adorned the wall.

Five burly men were just joining Malcolm, their backs to her. She only recognized two of them for certain.

"Ethne!" Finn flung his hot, little body at her. He always got overly excited when people came to visit, refusing to leave the gathering for his much-needed sleep for fear he'd miss something.

After a moment's hesitation, she hugged him back. The boy was a victim as much as her. It was his mother who deserved Ethne's wrath.

He squeezed her tight, more tightly than normal. That gave her pause. He usually enjoyed the celebrations after hunt.

"I thought ye'd never return." He sounded winded.

"Lampreys can be difficult to catch."

His wide eyes and haunted expression surprised her. Could he feel guilty? When he glanced behind him, she followed his gaze toward his mother, who continued to entertain the others.

Ethne turned him about and placed a gentle hand on his head. "Do not fret, Finn."

"But—"

A deep male voice interrupted. "And do ye still stink?"

Ethne froze, struggling to convince herself it could not be the same man. Her hearing was playing tricks on her. She glanced down at the forbidden lampreys before turning around.

The sight of the arrogant islander standing there, his huge body casting her in shadow, made her flesh crawl. Her breath quickened. She glanced at the others and realized they hadn't noticed him singling her out, coming toward her.

When he stepped close enough to tower over her, he jutted out his chin and sniffed at her as if she were some dog who'd rolled in horse dung.

"Ye do." His voice was low, for her ears only. "And what do ye have here?"

He dropped his hand to the lampreys, his eyes glistening with that same excitement she'd seen at the shore, and moved so close that his body rubbed against her shoulder. Her face heated at the memory of the humiliating search.

"But I am not here to find...poachers," he said.

A black-haired man joined them, a clay whistle in his hand. He was one of the men who had remained mounted, watching as she'd been groped. He dropped the instrument into the sack at his waist. His eyes lit up with recognition, followed by the same leering grin. A squire, mayhap.

He glanced at the lampreys. "It appears ye were correct in yer suspicions."

The two exchanged glances. The bigger man wiped the back of his bare hand across his mouth while his eyes traveled the length of her, missing nothing, and she shuddered.

She recognized another of the men sitting beside Aidan, heads close together, intent on some story. Her mind reeled, trying to make sense of why these men were here, in their cave. Serving as entertainment for her brother's celebration? Listening to their aging chieftain's stories? These were powerful islanders.

Ethne gritted her teeth and forced herself to look at the men. Their appearance had changed. Their wealthy attire had been replaced by well-worn tunics and trews, and the medallion and gold ring were missing as well.

"I made an impression, I see, even without all my finery." The large man quirked a brow. He studied her, as if reading her thoughts. "Hmm, ye didna strike me as a stupid lass, but stupid ye are if ye think to expose me now."

"Ethne!" Domelch's voice boomed, echoing around them. She shoved her way forward, protruding belly first, sidestepping the islanders to grab at the lampreys nested in Ethne's upturned skirt.

Ethne shrieked. The eels poured onto the ground.

"Cover yer legs. Have ye no decency?"

Finn clung to Ethne's side, trembling, and she wrapped a protective arm about him.

Malcolm shuffled up behind the two men. His calm expression and the way he grasped the large man's shoulder had Ethne's heart pounding against her ribs. Her brother could have no idea of the man's power or he would not be touching him so.

"Ethne. Have ye met our travelers?"

Travelers? They were pretending to be travelers? Her

heart slammed into her throat, and she couldn't speak, barely managed to shake her head. She needed to let Aidan know of this deception.

"This is my sister," Malcolm said. "The one I mentioned."

The large man's face relaxed into a smile. "Ah, Ethne."

"That's it." Malcolm slapped him on the back before arching his brows at her expectantly. "This is Olaf. He is from the islands. Came here to get away from all their warmongering. A good hunter, too. Thinks he may like to join our tribe."

Her brother chuckled. He was drunk. Glancing around, she realized they were all drunk, though that wasn't unusual. They were celebrating. But it did not bode well for whatever these pretenders had in mind.

Ethne couldn't control the frown, but Malcolm paid her no mind, instead turning to drape his other arm around the shoulders of the squire, pulling him close against him. "And this is…"

Malcolm turned to the man, nearly nose to nose. "Damn, man, I canna remember how to say yer name."

The younger man sunk his teeth into his upper lip to check his grimace, then smiled. A tight-lipped smile. A grotesque expression.

"Keer-awn." He spoke the name deliberately, as if annoyed at having to again pronounce it. "My name is Ciaran."

"For his dark hair," Malcolm added, as if just remembering. "A good hunter as well."

Olaf's eyes never left her. When he reached out to hand her one of the lampreys from the ground, she jumped back without thinking. Her panic rose.

But when Olaf glanced around at the others and then turned back to her with a questioning smile, she realized he saw her dread and didn't care. Who could she tell that they had the enemy in their midst?

Malcolm dipped his head, an apologetic expression, and dropped to his knees. "Need to get these picked up."

The others went back to their drinking. All but Olaf, who remained close, keeping her in his sight.

"Ye look done in," Malcom whispered, his wife's loud laughter echoing around them.

Ethne glanced at the warrior before answering, "'Tis ye who looks done in. Shall I see to a bath?"

He smiled, weaving a little when he stood. "I am fine, and ye look to have yer hands full."

She glanced toward Olaf. The uneasy tension between the mormaer and the powerful islanders was unrelenting. Though not living on royal lands or covered by royal laws, the ongoing abuse of their power was well-known. Hiding their identity now didn't seem to fit in with their arrogance.

Malcolm brushed the sand off the last eel. Pausing before handing it to her, he squeezed the large fish's mouth as if it were speaking and said in a high voice, "Did ye get these yerself?"

Finn laughed beside her, his thumb dropping from his mouth, a concerning sight since he hadn't sucked his thumb since he started to walk.

It eased the tension enough for her to respond, "These were all I could find."

When he smiled at her again, Malcolm's kind, brown eyes creased at the corners. "Ye have done well then."

"Come away now, Malcolm." Domelch's orders were not to be disobeyed.

He and Ethne's eyes met, but he said no more, instead swaying slightly as he moved to rejoin the others.

His wife was quick to turn back to her guests and explain, "Malcolm is a kind brother. More kind than Ethne deserves."

"Ethne," Olaf said again and turned to Ciaran, always close at hand it seemed, who smirked in return.

Ethne's breath quickened. He quirked a brow, no doubt entertained by her distress.

"And what about Ethne, Malcolm?" It was Aidan, their chieftain, who spoke. "She is your sister, but surely ye see she is ripe for the taking."

Her face flamed and she dropped beside the fire.

The scraping of the iron pot on the stone hearth hid her quiet groan. Her heart racing, she needed to focus on seeing to the meal. Finn sat near, understandably afraid to leave her side.

Aidan was the only chieftain Ethne had known here, but his interest no longer seemed fatherly.

"We will decide when the time comes," Domelch said with a light tone, as if the man had asked a silly question.

Ethne's fingers were white where she gripped the iron pan. It was no secret they considered her their slave. Worth very little. As breeding stock, however, her price increased.

"Ripe, indeed." It was Olaf, but the others laughed quietly rather than upbraiding him. "I say her time has come this night."

The lampreys splashed into the pan with a loud, sizzling sound. A great billow of smoke surrounded her, hiding her from the man's perusal.

He was an outsider. Certainly, Aidan would protect her from him.

Domelch pinned her with a nasty scowl. "Finn asked for lamprey cakes."

Ethne opened her mouth to defend herself, but Finn was quicker.

"I am tired of cakes. This is better." Finn's animated expression made Ethne smile despite the rising tension.

Domelch grumbled under her breath before turning her attention back to the others.

"We will see, but for now, let us celebrate our

successful hunt." Aidan lifted his mug, and the others followed. All but the islanders who gathered together.

"I've heard such kind things about yer hospitality." Olaf crossed his arms about his chest, flanked by his two men. "But I'd prefer to settle this first."

The room became quiet. Insulting their hospitality was never a good thing. The longbows and shields might have been left at the door, but daggers large enough to do damage glimmered in the firelight.

"Am I not to be rewarded for helping ye take down the boar?" Olaf asked. "I want the girl."

Ethne froze, her breath stilled.

Aidan nodded, a slow, thoughtful movement. "Indeed. But Ethne has great value to us."

"Especially to *me*." Domelch put a fist to her hip. "She serves an important purpose for me."

"I have a better purpose for her," Olaf countered.

The wolfish grin on the face of the man at his side said plainly enough what that purpose was. They moved toward her. Olaf hunkered down beside her. When he moved to brush her hair away from her face, she drew back. He smiled, continuing to search her like he would some animal he considered buying. "How much would ye sell her to me for?"

"Sell her?" Aidan asked, his interest not well hidden. "More than *ye* could pay. As I said, she has great value to us."

Olaf's eyes held Aidan's gaze. "And I think ye wish to take her for yerself."

Aidan opened his hands as if acquiescing. Ethne struggled to take a breath and ease the burning in her chest.

"How much would ye give me?" Domelch might as soon sell Ethne for a pretty trinket.

Ethne kept her head down, her eyes fixed on the

lampreys, and her jaw tight. She *did* serve a purpose for Domelch, and Ethne prayed she'd not forget that.

"Is she untried?"

"Ha!" The derogatory tone gave Ethne pause. Domelch was not usually so obvious with people outside their own group. She'd prefer them believing she was all sweetness. After all, she considered Ethne her own property, but that also gave her the power to sell her. "Verily, she is a virgin. I know her value. But we also know her many faults. Arrogant. Prideful. Demanding. And look—" Domelch grabbed Ethne's arm, shaking it— "too skinny. She's good for nothing but cooking." Domelch let Ethne's arm drop from her grasp, her face a mask of disgust. "And look! She has one job, and even that she is not good at. Ye've got the lampreys burning in their own oil."

When Domelch reached to grab the hot iron handle, Ethne moved to intercept without a thought. The woman's hand would be burned with no protection. But Domelch elbowed her away, touching the edge of the pan just enough to flick it, burning oil and all, into Olaf's face. The man's howl vibrated back at his men, who closed in, their jaws dropping open. Olaf grabbed at his face, staggering back in pain.

With wide eyes, Ethne stared at Domelch. Why had she done such a thing?

Aidan and his men reacted quickly despite the unexpected assault, using the weapons piled harmlessly by the entrance against the three men who would be seeking their revenge.

Olaf groped forward with hands flailing and spewed threats of recourse. Malcolm grabbed him from behind, a blade to his throat. His lips moved, but the erupting chaos was too loud for her to distinguish her brother's threat.

When Ethne caught sight of Finn huddled against the far wall, her heart clenched at the wide-eyed fear on his young face. She gave her hand to him, and he took it without hesitation. His obvious relief stirred her deeply. She needed to get him to safety and away from the fighting surrounding them. She led the way to a tiny passage, no more than a wide crevice hidden in the shadows at the back of the cave, and they slipped away unseen.

55

The aftermath of the melee would take longer to clean up than the fight itself. Domelch called Ethne out from her hiding place once the visitors-turned-intruders had been chased away. Domelch was not about to set things to right herself.

Finn had fallen asleep nestled against Ethne so she was content to sit and listen while the most important men in the tribe discussed what should be done next. They were convened in a tight circle around the fire, fully sober now and their dour expression reflected in the light. They were discussing how best to prepare for the imminent retribution. Malcolm sat cross-legged at Aidan's right.

"Will they return?" asked the man with the missing finger. He rarely spoke, and Ethne couldn't remember his name.

Aidan glanced toward the shadows where the man sat. "Talorc has gone to follow them. There is little more we can do. If they go to the castle to complain, they may stir up more trouble for us. Let us hope they do not since I do not feel inclined to relocate at this time."

"It will be a choice of who the Scots at the castle hate less. Us or them?" Malcolm voiced what everyone knew.

"They could easily use this unprovoked attack as a reason to run us off for good."

Aidan smiled. "Ah, but they are only suspicious of us and why we live away from the safety of their clans. They may wonder why we keep to ourselves. Islanders like Olaf, have been openly aggressive toward them, taking what they want as if they have a right to it. The laird at that castle has no love for us, but I believe he thinks he can win us to his side if they are openly attacked, even if his man Brian prefers to see us gone."

"Mayhap we should set aside our solstice observance? Get word to the others that 'tis not a good time?" Malcolm's tone seemed surprisingly hopeful. His expression as well.

"We will not!" Aidan's booming voice nearly shook the very stones surrounding them. "I will not be setting aside our chance for greatness, our chance to ally with the others, our chance to once again be in control of our own destiny. By joining with the others on the most important evening of the year, we will follow the ancient customs *exactly*. And we will be rewarded!"

Content that Finn's sleep remained undisturbed with the talking around him, Ethne parted from his warm little body to tuck him safely on his pallet. There was no need to awaken the exhausted child.

She stopped to stretch her stiff back. The child was getting far too heavy for her to easily carry him, especially through the narrow passage. When she caught sight of Aidan watching her, she shivered in repulsion. His persistent gaze left no part of her untouched. She shrugged forward to hide herself from him.

"Ethne," Aidan called, and she was filled with dread. "Come to me, lass."

Easing in a breath, she closed her eyes and prayed for a reprieve. The continued silence said there would be none this time. She fought to hide her resentment as she crossed the distance to the man.

"Sit by me." He raised his brow in expectation, a slow smile on his face while the others made room for her.

As a child, she'd enjoyed the man's attention. Domelch had always been cruel to her, but sitting next to the chieftain had protected her. It had made her feel like she belonged. No longer.

With great care, she sat as far away as she dared without causing comment, but he placed his hand on her head as always. Her flesh crawled. He caressed her hair with long, slow strokes, signaling to the other men to continue.

"We found nothing wrong with these men. Yer wife's attack was unprovoked." Thomas, Malcolm's closest friend, held up a hand. "We had to defend against them or we'd have been slaughtered."

"I defended what is mine." Domelch stood and pointed an accusing finger at Ethne, her face twisted in an ugly scowl. "*He* wanted her."

"Ye insulted them…and us!" Thomas rebuked her in a stern tone.

Domelch's chin jutted out. "How so?"

Thomas rolled his eyes and turned away, his disgust obvious. Ethne had to agree, though she remained silent. Domelch always pushed the boundaries placed on her, no matter who it hurt.

"We welcomed them into the group. Into our home. We could have discussed it." Malcom sounded as if he spoke to a child, but the way he glared at his wife said something else. "They served us well, helping us catch and slaughter the boar. Their presence was a good omen. If they were given what they wanted, we could have made powerful allies."

Ethne sucked in her breath at the betrayal.

Someone running outside put the men on full alert.

Aidan stood, his body tense. Malcolm moved closer to the entrance. The sight of Talorc, disheveled and gasping for breath, put them at ease.

"Well?" Malcolm's patience was at an end.

"They have boats…" Talorc heaved, trying to catch his breath. "On…the shore. Hidden."

Ethne tensed. She knew of at least one other man as well as their horses. Were they hidden nearby?

Malcolm shrugged at Aidan's frown. "But we knew they were islanders. They said as much when they joined us. There was no reason to hold that against them."

Aidan snorted, shooting a flash of disdain toward Malcolm before addressing Talorc. "More than one boat?"

"Leastwise three, though 'twas difficult to see."

"So, men of wealth pretending to be poor." Aidan pulled at his bottom lip while he ruminated.

Talorc continued with his report. "They've camped there for the night, seeing to Olaf's burn when I left. They'll not be leaving anytime soon."

"They questioned us about the caves." Malcolm had settled back down, his back to the wall. "I thought it odd until they told me they were seeking a place to settle. They'd heard of the caves."

Aidan leaned forward. "What is it they had heard?" It sounded more like an accusation than a question.

Malcolm looked toward Thomas, no doubt hoping his friend had been paying closer attention. "Legends?"

"Aye, legends they'd heard growing up," Thomas added. "Some kind of wealth?"

"A wealthy man…?" Malcolm never had a good memory. "Living here? Mayhap he had died and left the wealth behind."

"And have ye ever found any such a thing?" Aidan asked, his gaze sweeping across all of them. They shook their heads. "A legend with no truth to it is no legend at all."

Talorc dropped down to eye level with the chieftain, almost in his face. "Their leader? Olaf? He seemed the most disappointed, walking away with no money. And no Ethne."

As one, they turned to her with mixed expressions of confusion and curiosity. She clasped her hands, trying to appear disinterested. They didn't know she'd come across him before or about his humiliating treatment of her.

"They said something about a treasure." Talorc gave a little laugh. "Mayhap Ethne is a treasure now?"

"Oh, ho." Thomas shifted closer. "He may have wanted our Ethne, but we dinna need to give her to him."

"Why ever not?" the fingerless man asked. His tone became teasing when he added, "He wanted her so much he was willing to fight us for her. Our little treasure, Ethne."

"Enough!"

Aidan's bellow silenced their belittling discussion, but not their scrutiny of her. She'd always thought Thomas was a good man, but even his eyes were searching her now. When the chieftain tunneled his thick fingers beneath her hair to cup her neck, she tried not to flinch.

"What say ye, Ethne?" His eyes were bright on her. "Did ye want the man to have at ye?"

Ethne's face heated with embarrassment. As if she'd want someone so disgusting to come anywhere near her. She shook her head—adamantly—and used the opportunity to pull away from Aidan's disgusting touch. Finally, out of his filthy reach, she faced him. "I didna want him to come near me."

"He wanted more than to come near ye!" Talorc guffawed at his own joke.

Others joined in much to her dismay, but Malcolm and Thomas, thankfully, did not.

Aidan merely studied her with that stoic expression, as if discerning what was in her mind.

"Nay." His voice was surprisingly quiet and the ribald comments stopped. "Ethne never wants to be touched by a man."

He was correct, but she merely held his gaze, wishing this discussion of her would cease. She knew how men touched women. Brutal. Like animals. What woman ever sought such treatment? Not ever her!

When Aidan reached a hand toward her again, she clamped her teeth tight. With no choice but to return to her earlier spot beside him, she prepared herself for his unwanted touching.

But Aidan pressed her. "Did ye not find the man handsome?"

Her body tight, she raised her shoulders in a stiff motion. What was it he was looking for?

Knowing the man was determined to keep touching her didn't halt the tremor that passed through her body when his hand landed on her shoulder and he urged her closer, to lean back against him.

"He desired ye greatly."

The low timbre of his voice sickened her. The others watched as if unable to stop, as if held by some morbid curiosity. Malcolm sat up straighter, too. She didn't dare take a breath.

"If we had decided to give ye to him, that he could take ye—" Malcolm moved closer, his eyes intent on her— "would ye not have been an obedient sister?"

His betrayal squeezed her throat tight and her mouth went dry. How little Malcolm held to the values they had been raised with. Women were not to be handed off to a group of men as a show of thanks. They were to be protected and valued.

Oh, Malcolm!

"The taking is easier if ye submit, Ethne," Aidan said.

She jerked her head toward the old man, her ears

ringing with the words that showed how little they valued her.

"She will do as she is told." Malcolm's firm tone was intended to reassure the man, his solemn gaze confirming that belief.

Not likely. She swallowed the lump in her throat. That was the way of this tribe. If a woman was a virgin, she could be taken to wife, but the consummation was performed in front of everyone. The few times she'd been a witness, her own face had heated in sympathy and embarrassment for the poor lass. The eyes of the onlookers glazed over with lust as the woman was bared for their inspection. Thankfully, after Finn was born, she was no longer required to attend and was left with the child so his parents could participate. That suited her fine.

"There is only one first time." Domelch huffed. "Why waste her on some travelers where we get nothing from it?"

Ethne thanked God she had not told them of her earlier encounter with their "travelers."

"They were offering to pay for her." Thomas's tone had turned combative. He ignored Ethne's deepening frown. She had considered him a loyal friend, but no longer.

"Better to trade her for something of value." Domelch gave Ethne a look of disdain before rolling her eyes and settling back on her precious gilded stool, her large bottom nearly hiding the intricate designs of leaves and flowers that ran along the edge. It was the only embellished stool to be found in any of the caves because she had insisted on having one. Aidan had several in his round house perched on the hill and surrounded by high grasses. He enjoyed his wealth and showing it off. And he enjoyed keeping separate from them.

"They had boats!" Thomas countered, unleashing his frustration on the woman.

"We didna know that!" Domelch said.

With a huff, she began brushing her hair with slow, deliberate strokes. The latest tool she and Malcolm had acquired from their travels south, smoothing out her otherwise tangled red tresses and acting like she'd done nothing wrong.

"Piss and wind." Malcolm's expression matched his tone. The others shifted around him. "Get yerself to bed, wife. Ye have made enough trouble this night. Ye, too, Ethne. The cleaning can wait until morning."

Aidan's gaze followed her, as did the others, when she spread out her pallet. Domelch did the same, but then pulled down the heavy cloth that closed off her small area toward the back of the cave, where the lower ceiling offered privacy. Ethne had no such protection from prying eyes, so she lay down just as she was, covered herself with the coarse wool blanket, and gave them her back.

The room remained quiet except for the occasional popping of the wood as it burned. Ethne began to drift off, memories of her parents flooding her mind, giving her peace. Her father's kind eyes and his gentle voice reminding her that one day she would become a wonderful wife just like her mother. And her mother's bright smile, so big her eyes nearly closed.

"Will ye abide by my decision, Malcolm?"

Aidan's voice came to her, rousing her from sleep, but he made little sense.

"I have waited for ye, hoping ye'd be more comfortable with my plans."

"I do not take the decision lightly." Malcolm's low voice was harder to hear, and she began to drift off again.

"I gave ye time to adjust. The decision will be mine alone."

"I will not interfere." Her brother's tone had sharpened, forcing her to listen. "I ask only that ye wait until the solstice observance."

The solstice observance at Goats' Cave. The only creature easily able to access the steep trail to the entrance except when the low tide exposed the path to it.

Ethne yawned; the crackling of the fire soothed her.

The cave could be used for more elaborate ceremonies during certain full moons, and the summer solstice when the tide was at its lowest. That gave them just enough time for their ritual before the ocean rushed back in and cut off their only path of escape. No one knew for certain how high the water reached in the cave since no one had survived a flooding. But she couldn't remember ever seeing a drowned goat. She yawned again.

The summer solstice was just a few weeks off. The men's voices dropped, and the quiet lulled her to the edge of sleep.

"Would ye have sold her to them?" Malcolm asked. "I mean, if ye knew of the boats and their wealth?"

Ethne's eyes jerked open. Fully awake for that question, she held her breath for their chieftain's answer.

Aidan laughed, and someone else coughed. Talorc or Thomas? She wasn't certain.

"I wished to witness her reaction," Aidan said, his voice calm. "My plans remain the same."

The sound of pouring liquid. "And what did ye see? How did she react?"

"Young Ethne is a child no more. She keeps her emotions well hidden, but I see more than she knows. I may need to take her in hand myself."

Her stomach tightened. Aidan's possessiveness tonight could have been him wanting to be her first, taking her in front of all the others as he had his third wife, Moira. That poor lass was as young as her. There had been pain because she'd had no desire for her husband, leastwise that was how Domelch had explained it when they'd brought her to Ethne after the bleeding did not abate.

If Aidan forced her, Ethne would be screaming out since she hated the man.

"She is of great help to us," Malcolm said.

"But after yer wife has delivered..."

"We will have an even greater need for her."

Another long pause. Ethne's chest tightened for lack of air. She was ready to scream.

Aidan finally spoke again. "She will remain here. For now. I will let ye know if that changes."

"I will abide by yer decision. Do not doubt it," Malcolm said.

Tears flooded her throat, but Ethne dared not make a sound. Despite her confusion about specifics, one thing was clear: it was not safe for her to remain here. When next she went to the village, she would look for a place to hide. Mayhap a church.

Her thoughts turned to Finn as they often did. A sweet child except when he mimicked his mother. She was training him to be hard-hearted and cruel. Ethne's plans needed to include him. Abandoning him was no more an option than ripping out her own heart.

Decided, she took a quiet breath and soon drifted off to the memories of happier times.

Garnait refused to speak to Niall about their possible travel to the priory, instead sending them into battle with a promise to grant them any request upon their return.

More than a sennight later, Lachlann stood with Niall before their chieftain. They were both exhausted and the scream of dying men still sounded in Lachlann's ears. While they had fought under the command of the bloodthirsty Campbell, Garnait had stayed behind ensconced on his raised dais as if overlooking his royal subjects.

"And I should allow ye to make such a trip to what purpose?" Garnait MacDonell settled himself in his favorite seat in the longhouse. He crooked a single brow before smiling. Definitely a smile intended to let them know groveling would be involved in order to get his permission.

His wife and daughter huddled beside the open fire in the center of the open space with their sewing, their heads close together as they spoke. His sons slouched about the only trestle table remaining after the evening meal had been cleared away, drinking and gambling over a game of dice. The rest of the warriors were within earshot of their chieftain, almost as if ready to assist at a moment's notice. It seemed their chieftain believed he needed protection.

Lachlann smiled to himself.

"The church has requested our assistance with some troubles there."

Garnait's expression twisted into a comical display of outrage. "But their priory is to the east."

"They have spiritual interests across the area," Lachlann added. "Certainly, God has no limit to where we may be of service to Him."

"What exactly is in it for me?" The aging warrior demanded before taking a deep swallow from his silver bejeweled chalice.

"Is it not obvious?" Too late, Lachlann realized his irritation came through in his tone. Rustling came from his left where the warriors feigned disinterest.

"Uncle." Niall's voice was tight. "We will offer yer well wishes to the chieftains whose lands we cross, both as a tribute and to avoid any useless fighting. Reaching out to these other clans could verra well put ye in a favorable light, as I'm sure ye realize."

Lachlann hoped Garnait wouldn't ask too many questions. Just as Niall's temper had settled enough that he obeyed his uncle to support the Campbell in battle, he could choose now to leave without another word.

At the narrowing of his uncle's eyes, Niall's face reddened. "*Or* I could not mention ye at all and do the work of the church faster and with God's blessing. Surely, helping the Brides of Christ will cover many of the sins laid at my feet."

His angry tone had not been missed by those around them. Garnait's men shifted in the suddenly quiet room.

Sensing danger, Lachlann closed the distance between Niall and him. He squared his shoulders and ignored the men moving ever closer. "Did ye not promise us a boon, Garnait?"

"My uncle's word holds little value." Niall spat out the insult, a hand on the hilt of the blade at his side.

The women were grabbing up their needlework to make a quick exit.

Garnait stroked his long beard. "I see ye have yer father's temper."

Niall snorted through flared nostrils. "They are called principles, Uncle."

Insulting murmurings became more distinguishable, but Garnait raised a hand to silence them.

"And what are these *principles*?" Garnait's disparaging tone was difficult to ignore. "Have I offended yer honor yet again, nephew?"

"I have never claimed such an offense," Niall said.

Lachlann began to count the many times that day alone the man had belittled the three of them, making light of the battles they'd been subjected to with the blood and dust still clinging to their mail.

"And yet I see it in the way ye look at me, the way ye speak to me when ye believe I am too deep in my cup to notice, and yer reluctance to follow the simplest of orders, orders I have every right to give to those who swear fealty to me."

Fealty to a fool. Garnait's choice of alliances was galling. It would take very little to spark the resentment stirring in the Danes, who still had claim to the area. With the Norsemen and islanders patiently waiting for an opening to take a stab at them, as well as the English King William—Rufus as he was called—traipsing about as if he owned the entire island, unity and trust were all the Scots had and the only way they could remain a force to be reckoned with. The ones Garnait so easily scorned were the very clans he would need to look to for support should any decide to pick a fight with them.

"Battling on the side of those fighting against our own? And with the southern aggressors?" Niall's voice was tight. "That does not bode well for us here."

Garnait guffawed. "And yet we won."

Lachlann clamped his jaw just short of barking out an outraged "We?"

"It does not sit well with me to fight alongside the enemy."

"What enemy? The Campbells are our neighbors."

Niall shook his head. "The Campbell himself would willingly watch as the English run us down with their horses for a chance at an earldom."

Garnait's expression turned to disgust. "Ah, and ye are as weakhearted as yer father was."

Lachlann's blood boiled.

Niall's face stiffened at the insult. "My father was many things, but weakhearted was not one of them."

"Ye need to gird yer loins, boy."

"We will be leaving at first light, Uncle, with or without yer permission. If ye have gifts ye would like to offer to the other chieftains, have them packed for us and ready to take. Otherwise..." Niall held the man's angry gaze, his expression surprisingly calm. "I will see ye come the harvest."

Niall choosing to stand up to his uncle was a balm. Mayhap his closest friend was coming to his senses and remembering who he actually was. The son of a chieftain. Lachlann's spirits lifted considerably and a strong sense of accomplishment brought a smile to his face. Things were finally looking up.

In a fortnight, they'd traveled across glens and over mountains, through fewer rainy days than they could have expected this time of year and arrived at the coast. The highlanders were as welcoming as Lachlann knew they would be sharing food, fodder for their animals, and a place to rest safely. As planned, Niall offered gifts of seal skin and silver from what his uncle had provided for them. The gifts had been well received and it put them in a favorable light.

Although Garnait's name was mentioned as their chieftain, it was Niall they wrapped their arms around and welcomed into their clan and whose face would come to mind when they thought of the Clan MacDonell to the west. Niall who they would speak of with friendly warmth. The man was a natural leader, setting them immediately at ease when he showed interest, listening to their stories with great respect.

When the ocean came into view, they slowed their horses at the crest of the forested hill. The clouds hung low, thick and dark. The water churned white. An angry sea, indeed. Lachlann shivered. The knee-length tunics made of coarse wool and thick hose that they now wore as their pilgrim attire kept them warm enough. It was the roiling ocean that was a bad omen. They stopped to cover up with their mantles.

Aldred said, "That rain will be near impossible to travel through."

"The castle shouldn't be far now." Niall tucked the heavy material of the *brat* around his legs as he spoke.

"Halt!" an unknown voice commanded.

They obeyed, raising their empty hands, but exchanged perplexed glances.

"Turn about now. Slowly." The voice, though forceful, cracked.

They maneuvered their horses toward the sound.

A tall, thin man, covered from crown to toe in dark green cloth, stood a stone's throw away, his bow and arrow poised on the three of them. He looked to be about six and ten. They again looked at each other.

"What do ye here?" the slim man demanded.

A loud crack of thunder sounded out over the ocean.

"We want no trouble." Niall opened his palms to show

again they carried no weapons. "May we lower our hands?"

The green man trembled before them, his eyes darting skyward as the lightning hit the water. As if catching himself, he fixed his gaze on them and lifted his bow higher still. "Aye, but slowly now."

Even though he stood farther away than his bow could hit a mark with any degree of accuracy, it was three of them to his one arrow, and they were mounted, they did as commanded.

"Are ye islanders?" he asked.

"No. We are travelers from the south. I am Niall." He gestured toward them. "This is Lachlann and Aldred."

Lachlann tipped his chin to the man, who kept glancing behind them as if more interested in the storm at sea. The next strike of lightning revealed his paling countenance.

Niall continued. "We're on a pilgrimage from Restenneth Priory. Do ye know of it?"

"I do not." As the slim man searched the sky, his arrow dipped again.

With the slightest shake of his head, Niall dismounted but indicated he did not want Lachlann or Aldred to follow him. Instead, he alone moved toward the young man and asked, "What is yer name?"

Startled by Niall's sudden closeness, the boy glanced toward Lachlann and Aldred, who hadn't moved. He seemed to collapse a bit in relief.

"I am called Cull." Unnocking the arrow, he tucked it back into his quiver and extended a hand to Niall. "Welcome, travelers."

"Many thanks." Niall gripped his wrist before remounting. "Is there a place about where we might find shelter?"

They had seen nothing to indicate any sort of refuge

nearby, but Cull nodded, his eyes again darting heavenward.

"Is it far from here?" Lachlann asked. "We are about to be doused with a heavy rain."

"Not far." Cull glanced at their horses, a grin on his lips. "Especially not if ye're mounted."

Niall smiled as well, offering a hand to the slim man to help him up. "Well, then, let us be about it."

They were off at a gallop in the direction Cull indicated. The sound of the rain against the water came ominously closer. At the bend in the road, he released what looked like a death grip from around Niall's waist just long enough to indicate the highest point across the clearing. The dark outline of a large building enclosed with a tall fence was just visible. The sturdy wooden gates closed tight against intruders.

"Hail!" Cull called out when they were close and forced to slow their pace or take the chance of being mistaken as assailants. He pulled back his hood, revealing a good head of dark, curly locks. "I have returned. 'Tis Cull!"

The first drops of the cold, heavy rain hit them just as the gates opened and a young lad darted out to reach for their horses. Cull dropped off Niall's horse and ran to embrace a dark-haired woman who came from the castle to meet him. The gates quickly closed behind them.

Niall, Lachlann, and Aldred dismounted more slowly.

"This way," Cull called over his shoulder, his arm about her slim shoulders. "See to their mounts." Cull had to speak loudly to be heard over the wind, but the stable lad nodded.

The five of them dodged the huge raindrops, running toward the open door where the light streamed out in welcome. They made it inside just as the deluge began. Surrounded by the warmth of a huge fire built right into the wall of the cooking area and the smell of baking bread, they wiped the dampness from their faces, removed their *brats* with a shake, and handed their mantles to a waiting servant. Cull smiled at the lass and kissed her soundly on the mouth.

"Ye've taken forever," she said, her warm smile belying her angry tone. "And ye've brought prisoners besides?"

Cull clearly appreciated her jest, winking at the men to confirm that it was just humor.

"These are pilgrims from Restenneth Priory."

Niall bowed and introduced each of them.

She held Cull's hand close to her side even when she curtsied. "Pleased to meet ye."

"This is Rhona, my wife." Cull offered a shy smile as if the use of the title was still new to him.

He might be a bit reluctant to tear his gaze away and back to them. The lass's blue eyes dwelt on him so fondly. Lachlann understood if that were the case.

Cull asked, "So, tell us what ye seek?"

Rhona swatted at her husband, pressing her lips in an irritated way. "Will ye not even offer them something to eat?" She rolled her eyes. "Ye have the manners of a wild boar. Without our mormaer here to greet them proper, *ye'll* have to make them welcome."

Cull laughed, kissed her cheek. "My lovely bride, as always, is correct. Come, let me take ye to the Great Hall."

The large room was filled with men, women, and children happily chatting as copious amounts of food and drink were passed around, but there was no head table where a chieftain or mormaer might be found.

"Sit." Cull sat at a table only partly occupied, Rhona close beside him, and accepted the platter of meat before passing it their way. The three of them settled on the benches beside Rhona.

Niall took a mug, brimming with sweet mead, from Rhona's hands. "My thanks. It has been awhile since we've been so fortuitously welcomed. The route through the mountains has little to offer wanderers."

Lachlann ripped off a hunk of the dark brown bread before handing it off to Aldred, who sat beside him.

"And well I know it. I was sent to guard the perimeter even though there's been nothing to guard against for quite a while." Cull took a large bite of a leg of lamb, chewing loudly.

"And where is yer mormaer?" Niall speared a piece of the dark meat with his dagger.

"They've gone to sea, him and his sons. There was some trouble with the islanders, and he hoped to settle it peacefully."

"Have ye no protection then?" Aldred asked.

The same question was in Lachlann's mind, but he knew better than to be so blunt. The immediate silence of the others at the table, including Cull and his wife, was chilling. The drinks were set down, the food pushed away. The men crossed their arms about their chests, while the women and children dropped their hands to their laps.

"And what do ye think we are?" A large red-headed man on the far side of Cull stood. His face was nearly hidden by a massively thick auburn beard.

Aldred should have reddened, but Lachlann could tell by the set of his shoulders that he was instead preparing for battle. Not a wise move.

Niall drank his mead, showing no sign of having noticed the change, but his gaze on the bearded man was intense. "No insult was intended from my loose-lipped friend."

"They're pilgrims," Cull offered more as an explanation than any defense. He wiped his mouth with his sleeve. "They'd have been lost out in the storm if I'd not offered assistance. They'll be gone once the storm passes."

"And what is it ye seek?" the bearded man asked, not backing down a bit.

For lack of a better title for the place, Lachlann said, "The Holy Man's cave."

"Holy Man? St. Gervadius?" The shift was nothing short of miraculous. The bearded man dropped to his bench, a big smile lightening his otherwise dark face. "They're to the caves!"

The others had similar reactions, enthusiastically bobbing their heads and with wide grins. Lachlann was a bit perplexed at the sudden change. When Aldred opened his mouth to speak, Lachlann jabbed him in the side with his elbow for silence.

"Have ye been there?" Lachlann asked, even while Aldred shot daggers at him with his look.

"Ah, no. We're not about to go stirring up trouble, but glad we are ye've come to see to them."

"Them?" Niall asked the question.

"Those loons that live there. They've taken over all the caves, living like animals. 'Tis disgraceful. Have ye not come to rid us of their vile presence?"

"Are they actual birds then?" Aldred asked, and for once, Lachlann was glad the man had asked the question that sounded far too asinine to be asked...except by Aldred.

The bearded man paused before slapping his hand on the trestle and breaking into hearty laughter. Others joined in and they soon had the attention of all the other tables, craning their necks to see what was happening.

"The church has sent us protection and entertainment." The man stood, raising his mug as he did so to include the onlookers. "My friends, we have three pilgrims here who've come to rid us of the pagan filth that occupy our shores. Huzzah!"

The entire assembly followed suit, lifting their drinks as well. "Huzzah!"

Lachlann swallowed hard. He'd expected empty caves not people living in them and surely, they'd have found any silver no matter how well it might have been hidden. He glanced at Aldred and Niall, who wore the same perplexed look, but they quickly covered it up, smiling and drinking with the rest of them.

In a small hut beyond the castle gardens, Lachlann stretched his back in the steaming water of a deep wooden tub. Niall and Aldred, in identical tubs, were on either side of him. After having been given the best spot in the Great Hall for the night and each offered a willing lass that only Aldred accepted, they were feeling quite appreciated. Apparently, their mission to visit Holy Man's cave and remove the unwanted inhabitants raised them to hero status. They'd found no opportunity to correct the assumption.

Lachlann had spent most of the night attempting to ignore the "attention" Aldred was giving to the pretty green-eyed lass, and tried to work out the best approach to searching inhabited caves. Even now she hovered near his friend, pouring in yet another pitcher of heated water. When she reached for the cloth to wash him, Aldred stopped her hand. Caressing her long, red tresses, he spoke in a quiet voice to her, "I will see to myself. Go. Rest yerself."

They were finally alone.

Lachlann glanced at Niall. "St. Gervadius. Well, now, we have the name of this Holy Man."

"And now we have to find a way to gain entrance before we can even search for the treasure." Niall's hard tone was not unexpected.

Lachlann blew a breath. "I readily admit 'twill make the search more difficult—"

"—Impossible ye mean."

Lachlann closed his eyes to fight his own irritation with the situation. When he sat forward, the water sloshed. "We had no reason to believe one way or another about the caves."

Niall tipped his head non-committedly. Lachlann refused to mention that the cave might not be the right one.

"I wonder what these pagans are actually like that these people want them run off. How bad can they be?" Aldred asked, steam rising around him. "I mean, they canna have two heads or three arms."

"Pagans," Lachlann said, "in the truest sense, would have little regard for people. There are even stories of human sacrifices."

"Ye're called Pagan all the time," Niall looked around Lachlann to see Aldred.

Aldred stared blankly. "They call me pagan to roil me."

"I am a bit perplexed about the loyalties here." Lachlann shrugged. "To whom do they swear fealty? Fight for? Pay taxes to?"

Niall shifted in his tub. "Our bearded friend—I believe he said his name was Brian the Red—is in charge here while the mormaer is away."

"We've nothing left from yer uncle," Aldred said.

"If needs be, I brought some items with me that ye can offer in tribute." Lachlann still had the items he'd gathered in case Garnait had offered nothing. The gem-encrusted goblet from a lass he'd saved in his youth had great value. She'd been put out by her husband, a man of some importance, for adultery she never committed. An armlet her brother had pressed upon him when they'd been reunited did as well. These things meant little to Lachlann, unlike his father's medallion that lay buried deep in his sack. He'd removed it when he took on his present guise.

"As pilgrims, I do not believe they expect anything of us." Niall climbed out the tub.

Lachlann did the same, yanking the scratchy tunic

over his head and securing it with the leather strap. He chose to go barelegged, which was not an unusual custom for highlanders, but it might be so near the sea.

It was decided they would find out what they could about the people living in the caves. They could always offer something from what Lachlann had brought if tensions arose, but it made more sense to offer their services for any work that needed doing since pilgrims usually had little of value.

CHAPTER 7

After Lachlann had convinced Niall to remain within the castle in the hopes of learning about the people living in the caves, he'd been disappointed by their lack of information. The castle folk did not trust the cave dwellers. They wanted them gone from the area and they expected the three pilgrims to do the removing.

Going to them with the intent of kicking them out wouldn't serve their purpose. Strategy was what they needed. And strategy required knowledge. Cull's invitation to join him and his wife on their trip to the market coming in a few days came at an auspicious time.

Lachlann, Niall, and Aldred said their goodbyes at the castle, tied their mounts to the back of a short, wooden cart, and put their faith in Cull's ability to direct them to the people who dwelt in the caves. The three of them squeezed into the back of a cart never intended for people or their comfort. Lachlann wedged himself into a corner, one leg bent, one out in front with Niall in the middle. With all its bouncing and tipping from side to side, the tall sides were a blessing.

"The pagans always come to our market days." Cull spoke calmly from his perch on the bench at the front of the cart, reins in hands, and his bride nestled close beside him as always. "And this is the first market day since Michaelmas. Sure to be a jovial event. Verra well attended, so they may not be easy to spot."

"What is it that makes ye believe they are pagans?" Niall asked.

"They are never seen in our chapel, and the priest has expressed a concern for their souls. They also have an unusual liking for nighttime ceremonies." Cull shuddered. "We've all come across one, but its best witnessed from the sea. A long procession of their torches moving along the ridges at all hours."

"So how is it ye spot them at a fair among so many?" Lachlann asked, unable to keep irritation from his voice.

Cull's shrugged. "It is more a sense of them rather than anything I can say to watch for."

Lachlann's challenging tone was thankfully ignored. He'd not anticipated having to retrieve the priory's silver coin from among cave dwellers. He assumed the caves would be empty. Surely by now, those people would have discovered it themselves.

Aldred snored quietly beside Niall, who elbowed him and received no response. Lachlann would not have been so patient with the man.

"Lachlann, tell me again how long we have been here?" Niall whispered, an exasperated tone.

Lachlann snorted. "A mere two days that we have been amongst these kind and generous people."

Niall's expression remained stoic. "And three very long nights."

Aldred had kept them awake each night with Sophie— they finally had a name for the green-eyed lass.

"Have ye found the hall not to yer liking?" Cull kept his eyes on the road ahead and turned only enough for his words to be heard from the back.

"Forgiveness, please. Yer hall suits us fine," Niall spoke louder, shoving the sleeping Aldred away when the cart bounced over the rutted road and his drooling mouth wiped against Niall's shoulder.

The colorful flags set up along the road leading down into a large valley, resplendent with even more color, signaled an end to the journey. Lachlann twisted at the waist to search the area as Cull led the cart from the well-traveled road to a field of sweet grass and rye and a roughly hewn lean-to. The smell of the ocean teased Lachlann's nose, but the water remained hidden.

Once on their feet, Niall stretched and untied their mounts while Lachlann retrieved the satchel from his courser to wear across his chest. Reaching inside, he worked his hand to the bottom and rubbed the medallion from his youth. They'd worked hard to appear as simple travelers, wearing rough leggings that had seen better days and simple, knee-length tunics. As a pilgrim, such ornamentation would seem out of place.

The smell of roasting meats set his stomach to growling. He grabbed the end of the rein from Niall's hand and snapped it at Aldred, who'd remained asleep. "Up with ye now."

The Norseman jerked awake and Lachlann barked a laugh. Cull and Rhona were busy taking great care with the horses Brian the Red had given them the use of.

"Niall, did ye not say Aldred would see to our horses? *All* the horses?" Lachlann asked.

Aldred's belly scratch halted abruptly, his jaw dropped open in protest.

"I believe I did."

Aldred barely caught the reins Niall tossed to him. Any protest he would have made was silenced by Niall's raised hands. "I've a good mind to leave ye here."

"A fine idea." Lachlann tipped his head in agreement. "And would he even notice? We'd no doubt find him sleeping under an elm."

Aldred quirked a blond brow, but remained

uncharacteristically quiet, even offering to take the reins from Cull, and headed toward a small lean-to with a single elm to shade it.

"There!" Cull had come alongside them and pointed to a youngster of mayhap five years. "And that woman there." He pointed toward a couple. The man was quite a bit older than the woman, ancient in fact. His hands were possessively wrapped around her middle. She was quite lovely.

Lachlann could see nothing that distinguished these people as cave dwellers. "Seems a bit of an intimate grasp."

The woman pulled back and grabbed the youngster's hand, leading him away, but the older man's eyes followed them.

Cull's face tightened. "As I said, they are not Christians. I think they have strange family groups. Use care when approaching them."

"So that is probably not the woman's father?" Niall crossed his arms.

"Could be her husband." Rhona snuggled closer to Cull's side, no doubt glad she did not suffer with an ancient man for a mate.

Lachlann's gaze remained on the old man, who wandered alone by a few booths, purchasing both food and drink. He eventually settled in an area set up for entertainment. A raised, center stage, surrounded by benches, served as the arena where jugglers, musicians, and exotic animals would no doubt be performing soon.

"He seems familiar, but I dinna remember his name. I can speak to them if ye like. The woman or the man." Cull's offer was a surprise.

A juggler with bright red clothing and a pointed hat had the man laughing, one of only a few in the audience since it was still early in the day.

"I appreciate yer kind offer, Cull, but no," Niall said. "I'll walk around a bit first."

"I dinna see anyone else." Cull continued to scan the area as he spoke, his gaze finally settling on Niall. "Sorry I am that I canna be of more help. Be wary around them. Think ye they'd mind themselves and stay out of trouble when they come to town, but there is some problem every time."

"We will," Niall said.

"Let us say our goodbyes now. There'll be little chance of finding ye again in this crowd." Rhona lowered her head and curtsied to Niall. "Pleased I've been to meet ye, fine pilgrim. May God go with ye."

Niall bowed over her hand, then Lachlann, and the couple went off in the direction of the music.

"We'll split up and meet back here at gloaming. Learn what ye can," Niall said and disappeared into the crowd.

Lachlann made his way toward the cooking fires where he could get himself some sustenance.

A table laden with dark, heavy breads, a variety of soft and hard cheeses, and flavorful meats soaking in their own juices sat just off the busy path. The area was crowded and he waited his turn.

"Have ye a leg to sell?" Lachlann asked, his head down as he searched through the few coins in his sack.

"If only I could breed an animal with more than four legs." A short man with a large belly came from the fire behind the trestle, a platter of roasted meat still sizzling in his arms. "I do have some tasty pieces for ye to choose from, warrior."

Lachlann paused at the term then placed a single coin on the table. Certainly his clothing had not given him away. Had his gaze been too direct? He helped himself to some hard cheese, still warm meat, and dark, heavy bread. It was a busy place, and a very good location from which to watch the goings on. With such a fine location, this man must get a look at nearly everyone here, if not all.

"Do ye know this area well?" Lachlann hoped not to sound overly curious, but the man's hawk-like attention told him he'd failed.

Damn. He'd never been good at deception!

"Some." A man of few words.

"Do ye know of the Holy Man?" Lachlann bit into the mutton.

The shake of the man's head was barely perceptible, but he offered Lachlann a mug of mead from his own supply.

"My thanks," Lachlann said, accepting his generosity.

The crowds around them were subsiding. Resting his hip against the table, the man took a sip of his own drink. "I was a warrior once, and I can spot a thief or a murderer while he's still a stone's throw away."

Ah. The man recognized his own. And if the man wasn't bragging, he had the best of a warrior's traits. The ability to see through a man's disguise. The mead was refreshing and cooled Lachlann's parched throat. "Impressive. And how did ye know I was a warrior...once?"

"A warrior still, I'd venture. The stance. Though I can see ye're trying to pass yerself off as a pilgrim." He indicated the satchel Lachlann had slung across his chest. "But ye've no wear on it and ye fumble with it when searching within. That tells me ye're new to such deception."

Lachlann laughed and brushed his hands clean before accepting the newly filled drink. "Ye have me, then."

"I've not seen ye afore. Ye're new to these parts." The round man extended an arm and said, "My name is Baker."

"Baker? Not Cook?" Lachlann grabbed his wrist with a smile. "Lachlann."

Lachlann could play the same guessing game. Narrowing his eyes, he perused the man's attire and the staples he had lined up behind him. "And ye dinna bake. Ye get yer bread from the man across the way, the one with the brightly woven cloth."

Baker's face lit up. "Buggar me! Ye're right! And ye're near as good at this as I am."

"Only near as good?"

"Well, I have my reputation to think of."

The dark-haired child Cull had pointed out earlier ran toward Lachlann, only to stop right beside him, breathing heavily.

Baker slouched slightly to meet the boy at his own level. "And what can I get ye?"

The lad didn't respond except to turn wide eyes on Lachlann. "Ye're as big as a whale."

"I am." Lachlann didn't mind the comparison...too much... and this was an opportunity to speak to a "pagan." "And ye're as small as a..."

"Sparling?" Baker offered, his heavy brow raised.

Lachlann smiled his thanks. Turning his attention back to the boy, he repeated, "A sparling."

"Dinna eat me!" The boy feigned his fear then laughed, his little body heaving with the action.

"I dinna find little boys satisfying enough."

He laughed even louder at that.

"Glad I am that ye find me so amusing."

"Finn!"

The boy gasped, ducked behind Lachlann, and whispered a little too loudly, "Hide me."

Lachlann and Baker exchanged glances, but then the other man shrugged and moved farther down the table to see to another customer.

"Finn!" the woman's voice called again.

"Ye wouldn't be named Finn, would ye?" Lachlann

spoke out of the side of his mouth, hoping to avoid drawing attention.

"I am." Finn's whisper was quite loud.

The woman calling the lad's name turned in their direction. She was even more lovely than Lachlann had first thought. Though tightened brows gave her a questioning look, she did not seem overly worried. Her long, dark hair hung down her back in a single plait. When she started toward them, the gentle sway of her hips entranced him, walking as she was with a slow gait. Then he remembered the ancient man who'd held her to his side. He blocked out the disappointment washing over him.

Lachlann asked, "Are ye playing a game with yer mum?"

Finn snorted, peaking his head out enough to glare up at Lachlann, his little arms gripping Lachlann's legs. "Ye dinna play games with yer mum."

So, she wasn't his mother.

"Oh, forgiveness, please." Lachlann sought the woman again, only to find her standing at the opposite end of the table. She stepped closer and stopped in front of him, a slight frown furrowing her brow.

Understanding dawned. Her brown eyes twinkled with mischief. "Do ye have Finn hiding behind ye?"

Lachlann found himself smiling back at her. "I may."

When the lad decided he deserved a slap on his bottom for the answer, Lachlann jumped. "Forsooth! Verily, I have not."

The lass's pretty pink cheeks rounded with a smile, and Lachlann's breath caught. She was a beauty. Doe eyes and a perfect little nose. Her head was well covered with a separate hood. The long *léine* went all the way down to her bare feet.

"Ye're lying." She struggled for a straight face.

"I never lie." He cleared his throat and pressed his lips tight.

"Findláech?" The woman's warning tone was met with a loud giggle. "Are ye hiding behind a tall man? With long black hair?"

A disgruntled sigh was followed by the lad stomping out from behind Lachlann. His head bent, he grumbled, "Ye always win."

The lass turned her surprised gaze to the boy and snorted through her nose. "Finn, ye know 'tis not true. *Ye* always win."

The dark head bobbed up, his face lit with glee. "I do!" He laughed loudly. "But ye won this time, Ethne. Ye truly did." Finn cast a sideways glance at Lachlann before his face dropped into a scowl of reprimand. "I think ye could have done a better job hiding me."

Lachlann raised his arms in surrender. "Think ye I knew I was even playing?"

Finn's wide smile was contagious. "Ye played well enough, man."

His response made Lachlann laugh. "Ah, well, thank ye for such a gracious appraisal."

A glance at the lovely lass, whose warm gaze remained on the boy, filled him with the urge to see if he could receive the same attention. "Shall I try again?"

When she looked up at him, he offered his most dazzling smile.

"How would ye do that?" Finn asked, awe in his voice. "Would *ye* hide?"

Lachlann laughed at the question. "I dinna think I'd find any place big enough…"

Ethne glanced beyond Lachlann now, her expression changing to distress. She reached for Finn's hand. "Come along now." Her lips were tight. "We should not be here."

"Is ought amiss?" When the boy glanced the same way and his eyes widened in fear, Lachlann's confusion increased. Finn latched onto the woman's outstretched hand.

"Finn?" Lachlann's concern deepened, but Finn turned back to him and vigorously shook his head.

Bewildered, Lachlann could do nothing but watch as the two moved away, swallowed up by the crowd around them. He kept his eye on them as they weaved in and out, the lass glancing over her shoulder several times, until he lost them.

"Ye mentioned the caves?" Baker asked in a gruff tone, breaking into Lachlann's disquietude.

He had only mentioned the Holy Man, but obviously Baker knew the story as well, so he nodded.

"Ye've just met two of the people who live there."

CHAPTER 8

After only the slightest hesitation, Lachlann shoved the food he'd purchased into his satchel and pursued the woman with Finn. According to Baker, the two lived in the caves and those were the people he and his friends were here to become acquainted with. The perfect opportunity. Just what Lachlann might have hoped for. It certainly was not because his stomach had clenched when he lost sight of them after they'd hurried away so unexpectedly.

It took but a few seconds to get them in his sights again. The two weaved among the crowds, but he remained to their right. They'd glanced back several times but try as he might, Lachlann could not locate who it was she avoided. When they made a wide arc around the entertainment area, now overflowing with a lively, loud audience, he surveyed the area for the old man who had been her escort. He sat there, squeezed tightly between two young and pretty women, laughing so hard at the brightly colored jugglers that his whole body shook. So he wasn't the one Ethne shunned.

At a clearing between two booths—one selling ornate silverwork and the other reading fortunes—the two ducked down the gentle green slope toward the trees lining the banks of a small burn. Lachlann paused at the table covered with combs, ribbons, and cloth, surreptitiously watching them duck behind a large, red-leafed tree and disappear. Lachlann glanced about, but no one showed them any interest.

"Anything ye like?" A dark-haired woman, a provocative grin on her lips, broke into his thoughts.

"Ah, no." Lachlann quirked a smile before descending the path to the brook. At the river's edge, he paused. His gaze searched up river and down, as well as both banks. They were nowhere to be found.

A tiny giggle from the tree above had him smiling. Hands on his hips, he eased out a breath before speaking. "Ye can come down now. No one follows ye."

"No one but ye!"

His face heated at her sharp rebuke, but he kept his gaze on the drumly water. He hadn't meant to anger her. He was simply concerned for her safety. That wasn't true. He hoped to get information from her since she lived in the caves.

He cleared the sudden tightness in his throat, not wishing to think too much further about the why. "I dinna believe we were done speaking."

"We weren't!" Finn's loud response was quickly followed by a louder *shushing*.

"Is there anything I can do for ye, lass?" Lachlann faced the busy market lane, blocked from view by the many booths lining the country path. One woman, a few stalls to his right, carried a bucket to the river's edge, but never glanced his way. "I'll leave ye be if 'tis what ye truly want."

"Nay!" Finn spoke at the same time as the lass, who said, "Aye."

"Well, as long as we have that worked out."

Lachlann's sarcastic comment was met with a solid laugh from the lass. A hopeful sign.

In a tight voice, she finally asked, "Are ye certain no one is about?"

"I see no one. This area is well protected from the road with the many stalls lining this side." He withdrew the satchel from his shoulder and dropped it to the ground. "I have food I'm willing to share if ye're hungry." At last, he looked straight up into the faces of the two looking down at him. "But I must insist ye come down since I've no desire to be climbing trees."

The two exchanged glances a moment more before Finn nodded and climbed down from the tree as if he'd been born to it. He went straight to Lachlann's satchel. The lass clambered down a bit more slowly, but Lachlann was there to lift her off and set her gently on her feet. His hands remained at her narrow waist a moment longer than was necessary. She stood only as tall as his chest.

"Ye've made it."

When she smiled, her eyes sparkled. "My thanks."

She walked away, and Lachlann felt the loss of her closeness. He mentally shook himself. He barely knew her. Untying the mantle from his shoulders, he spread it out for them to sit on. "Would ye join me?"

Finn went to his knees and quickly tipped the satchel upside down. Bread and cheese were quickly sorted through. He held up the dark loaf of bread, a look of expectation on his young face.

Lachlann encouraged the lad with a wave. "Eat what ye like."

"A generous man." The lass accepted the cheese Finn tossed at her before sitting down beside the boy.

She closed her eyes as she nibbled at the cheese, its tart smell wafting around them. "My favorite."

Lachlann rifled through the mantle's folds to retrieve some figs. His father's medallion flashed from amongst his belongings that created a hollow in the fabric. Indecision clawed at him. Pick it up or leave it? In the end, the decision was made for him. The lass lifted it, still cradled in the soft cloth he'd had it wrapped in, and gently brought it closer to inspect.

A sudden, overwhelming sense of being totally exposed made Lachlann catch his breath. With great care she unwrapped the only connection he had to the man who had sired him.

"This is lovely." Her fingertip lightly grazed the metal. "Such intricate carvings." She looked up at him with a reverent expression. "This belongs to ye?"

"It does." An immense sense of pride swelled in his chest. "'Tis from my father."

"An important man, truly." She emphasized the word *important*. "So, ye must be as his son."

He scoffed, uncomfortable with such an assessment. "Long ago times. Things were different then. My father was never known to me. Leastwise, not that I can remember."

Her lovely eyes rounded with sympathy, and he had the definite impression she knew exactly what he meant. A great warmth spread out from his belly and left him breathless. And surprisingly speechless.

"A treasured object." She quickly wrapped the medallion in the cloth with trembling hands. "Forgiveness, please. I dinna mean to intrude."

Lachlann placed his hand over hers. "Not an intrusion."

He accepted the small bundle she handed him, righted his satchel, and placed the medallion back in the bottom before returning the other scattered items on top of it.

The dark bread and most of the cheese gone, Finn sat back with his mouth flapping as he chewed loudly on the figs.

"Finn!" The lass might be trying for a stern tone, but the twinkle in her eye said something else.

Lachlann grinned. "A drink would be good about now."

Before the lad could respond, she stood abruptly and glanced about. "We've kept ye too long. Forgiveness, please." She seemed embarrassed. "Our thanks for yer kindness."

"My pleasure." Lachlann meant it and stood as well. "Is there somewhere I can bring ye?"

She was making her way to the road. The closer they got, the quicker her pace became.

"My thanks for the offer," she said, clearly distracted. "There is no need."

Her eyes landed somewhere behind him. When he scanned the same direction, he saw no one.

Lachlann replied, "It appears there may indeed be a need."

Her eyes stilled their darting about long enough to focus on him. He swore he felt the weight of that gaze all the way to the soles of his feet.

"I promise 'twill be my pleasure," he added.

Just as quickly, the spell was broken. She clutched Finn's hand in her own. "We've kept ye long enough."

She all but dragged the lad, his little legs struggling to keep up, as they headed toward the next stall and away from him.

Lachlann would have called her back, followed her at the very least, but decided against it. He didn't want to call any undue attention her way, not when he was at such a disadvantage. He didn't know who she was running from.

She had shown him open admiration, and his heart warmed at the memory. It was not admiration for his ability with the sword. That feeling he knew quite well. It was admiration for who he was, who his father had been. The awe and acceptance in her expression had stirred something deep inside. With all the priest's belittling of him, Lachlann was unfamiliar with such feelings. Although he'd preferred to have stayed with her, she had been too afeared to remain.

With a fierce and sudden urge to protect that he preferred not to examine too closely, he headed in the direction she'd been watching. He needed to learn who had prompted her to leave in such haste.

Ah! A noble cause indeed. Of course, finding whoever stalked her would require he approach her again. There was no help for it.

He beamed.

The need to reassure her, to let her know of his success in protecting her...it couldn't be avoided. Nor should it be. The lass's concern was obvious. When he did so, mayhap he'd find the opportunity to ask her more about the caves.

CHAPTER 9

*D*espite his failure at locating whoever seemed to be hunting the lovely lass, Lachlann spent the remainder of the day searching for her and Finn. He'd even gone so far as to look along the riverbanks, craning his neck back to view the treetops, which brought curious stares and one comment about the condition of his mind. The two were nowhere to be found.

He and Niall met by the horses as planned. No Aldred.

"I had great hope in the man," Lachlann lied. He wanted to keep Niall from letting loose his irritation at Aldred's behavior. "I thought he might search us out at some point today. Did ye see him?"

Niall huffed and shook his head, but said nothing.

Having cleared the shade trees, they stopped midway across the open field at the single elm and scanned the surrounding area for any sign of their friend. Instead of finding Aldred, they found a man trying to make off with Lachlann's horse. The other horses were safely tethered and appeared unmolested.

"By God's bones!" Lachlann said under his breath before running to intercept the large man in well-worn trews, who was trying to lead off his prized courser.

Amica was having none of it, jerking her head as if avoiding bees. "Ye'd best drop the reins."

When the man turned, Lachlann recoiled. The side of the man's face was covered with angry red sores. He had all the markings of a warrior: broad in the chest, thick muscles, and a swagger meant to intimidate. But his clothing didn't match. Not at all. No protective leather, not even deer hide, and a dagger was his only weapon. Baker would say the man was only pretending to be a traveler, and Lachlann would have to agree.

"Are ye sp-speaking to me?" His belligerent tone and unwavering posture, despite his slurred speech, confirmed that the man had money enough to get himself well soused.

A man with a thick crop of dark hair came out from behind the lean-to, still adjusting his trews after seeing to nature's call, and trotted toward the thief with an expression of concern.

"I am." Lachlann did not lighten his tone. He stopped within an arm's reach and placed a heavy hand on the agitated mare's back. The beast, recognizing its owner, stilled immediately. "Ye've got the wrong horse."

The drunkard's expression spoke of his disbelief. His mouth hung open, as he looked from Lachlann to the horse and back again.

"I dinna think so." The man barked out a loud laugh, then said to the man arriving at his side, "Can ye believe the bollocks of this one? Saying I stole his horse?"

The dark-haired man averted his eyes, and Lachlann had the sneaking suspicion he knew the man had the wrong horse.

Lachlann pointed toward the holding. "That other horse has similar markings. Do ye think ye may have made a mistake?"

The drunkard threw down the reins like a gauntlet,

grabbed the dagger from his belt, and got in Lachlann's face. "I know I dinna."

His companion laid a hand on the aggressor's shoulder without getting too close. He seemed a bit intimidated by the drunkard and worried about setting him off further. He pulled gently, but remained quiet.

Lachlann held his tongue as well. For the moment. Mayhap the dark-haired man knew of some way to settle his drunken friend. Although Lachlann would admit he would not mind if a fight ensued.

"Ye impudent dog! I've got the seal right here—" The man slapped his chest then ran his hand across his front. His tone switched to alarm. "Zounds!"

When the big man turned to search behind him, the other man just cleared the arm that swung his way.

"Ciaran!" the drunkard yelled before noticing the man right beside him. "Oh, there ye are."

"Aye, m'lord." The man appeared frightened, his eyes darting toward Lachlann.

"'Tis gone. I've lost it."

"No. Ye put *all things* aside. Do ye not remember?"

"No! Why would I take off my—" The man wavered a bit and gazed above their heads in a thoughtful manner. The puffiness from the injured side of his face left one eye a mere slit. "Ach, right. 'Twas that bitch I wanted a taste of."

Lachlann caught the dragging rein of the horse.

The younger man nodded toward him. "My thanks."

"What are ye thanking that man for?" The bigger man shoved away his friend, who surprisingly kept his footing. "I need something to drink…and that damn bitch."

The horse forgotten, the two of them headed back toward the table where more drink could be found.

"That was strange," Niall said.

"He was drunk," Lachlann said, though he agreed with the comment.

When the man stumbled, Ciaran helped him back up, wrapping his arm about his shoulder in an effort to support him.

Lachlann stroked the mare to soothe it. "Was that a burn on his face?"

"Something recent. Fiercely painful," Niall said. "It will leave a nasty scar. Probably the entire length of his face."

"And how have ye fared? Well enough I think." Lachlann ran his hand down the mare's side. "I think we arrived before any harm befell Amica."

They headed across the field in the hope of locating Aldred. "Surely he'd not just disobey my orders."

A loud voice could be heard from the direction the drunken man had taken. An affray, by the sounds of it.

"Is that—" Niall asked.

Lachlann nodded.

Niall smiled. "Shall we have a little entertainment?"

After safely tethering the horse with the others, he and Niall rushed toward the sound coming from just beyond the last booth near the musicians. The music continued, but the voices grew louder. The older man, whom Cull had identified as one of the cave dwellers, stood with arms crossed and two younger men on each side of him, confronting the drunken would-be thief.

"Ye asked for it!" The old man's voice was surprisingly forceful for someone of his age. "Now be on yer way, and we'll not make a fuss."

The drunkard seemed oblivious to the gathering crowds and sneered, reaching for him. The younger men blocked his advance.

"Those men with him may be from the cave." Lachlann kept his voice quiet. "They're willing to fight for him."

They guarded the older gentleman well. He hadn't needed to move a step. "I told ye to be off."

"Be off, Olaf." The taller of the two protectors took a

step forward. "Ye dinna want to be pushing him too far. Ye'll not like the results."

Ciaran interceded. "Ye called us friends, Malcolm. *We* did nothing to betray that title."

Olaf bellowed. "Where is the bitch? I'll have her now whether ye say aye or nay."

Malcolm didn't seem repelled by the grotesque sores even when he got up in Olaf's face. "Move. Along."

The older man kept the same firm tone. "Move on now, and we'll forget it. Dinna believe we won't alert the guards."

Malcolm and the other protector's darting gazes showed their concern. They'd prefer not to call attention to any of this. Cull had said they always started trouble, but this did not appear to be their doing.

Ciaran reacted to the threat as well, yanking at his friend's shoulder as he spoke quietly to him. If he was attempting to console Olaf, he failed miserably.

"Shall we offer aid?" Niall asked without taking his eyes from the men.

"If it gets violent, surely we have no choice." Olaf was huge and even soused, could easily do damage to these men. "It may be only a petty quarrel, blowing smoke."

A third man approached and assisted in leading Olaf away toward the ale.

Lachlann sighed, a bit disappointed. "It could well have been our introduction to the cave dwellers."

"Aye, and in their appreciation, they would welcome us into their caves." Niall looked away long enough to wink at Lachlann.

Olaf stopped abruptly to confront the two leading him away. "But I dinna want to let it go."

Tension gripped Lachlann's shoulders. Mayhap he'd be offering aid after all.

Olaf swung at the old man before anyone could react. He knocked him right on his arse.

"What th—" A man with thinning hair rushed at Olaf with a lowered shoulder and tight fists but was easily knocked aside.

Three cave dwellers came to assist him, but he pushed them away and got up on his own. "Leave me. Help Aidan."

The melee had begun. Fists flailed. Insults were exchanged.

Lachlann grinned widely. "They have a history that didna end well."

"And when a woman is involved..." Niall didn't finish his thought, his gaze intent on the scene playing out before him. When Olaf downed Aidan again, the younger men were more alert to his condition than defending their position.

"They need our help. What say ye?"

"The only thing to do." Lachlann shrugged. "Besides he tried to steal my damn horse."

Niall moved to intercept Olaf, who charged like a bull toward Aidan for a third time. Momentarily distracted, Lachlann didn't see Malcolm flying toward him until they were rolling on the ground together. He landed on top, catching Lachlann on the chin.

"Sorry," Malcolm said, before yanking Lachlann back to his feet with an arm adorned with a wide, silver band. The man turned back to the fighting.

Lachlann squared his shoulders. Neither having the wind knocked out of him nor the unexpected punch to his face sat well with him. These men might not be as defenseless as they first appeared.

Lachlann dodged a punch from Ciaran. The fist he planted in Ciaran's gut met solid muscle. The body of a trained warrior.

One of the sheriff's men broke up the fight. The drunkard, along with his two friends, were tossed out of the fair and ordered to sober up before they returned.

The crowds that had gathered to watch the fighting quickly dispersed.

"Many thanks." The older man took Lachlann's wrist. "I am called Aidan. I lead this rabble, though they've given a good show this day. Aye?"

The men joined in with a resounding "Aye."

Aidan wiped at the blood dripping from his lip, his gaze full of pride as he looked over the others. "Ye've earned yer keep, I tell ye that."

The men smiled at the comment. None seemed badly bruised.

Malcolm moved closer, a wide grin on his face. "I am Malcolm."

Niall shook the man's extended hand. "Though I didna believe ye could defend yerselves so well, ye proved me wrong. Niall."

"We fight only by necessity."

A third man with curly hair came to stand beside Malcolm. "Call me Thomas. Ye carried yerselves well."

Lachlann accepted his hand.

Malcolm chuckled. "And can ye not tell these are seasoned warriors?"

Niall said, "Warriors at one time. Pilgrims now."

Lachlann smiled. He didn't need the people in the cave to wonder about their presence here. It would be best if they didn't see them as a possible threat.

"Pilgrims?" Aidan spit the word out like it was an insult. "And ye've come here?"

Lachlann nodded. Mayhap this group didn't know the story of the Holy man.

Aidan grumbled something under his breath, but Malcolm quickly stepped in front of him and asked, "Have ye got a place to stay this night?"

"Not as of yet." Lachlann rubbed his jaw. This man had a fist like a rock.

"My apologies again," Malcolm said.

"Do ye know of a place?" Niall asked.

Aidan and Malcolm exchanged glances. With a curt nod, the older man's consent seemed grudgingly given.

Malcolm said, "Ye can stay with me and mine."

"My thanks. And where would that be?"

"In the caves," Malcolm said.

CHAPTER 10

If there was a moon over head, it was well hidden by a dark cloud high above the trees. Only the abundant number of stars cast light on the path that had been filled with travelers when she'd come to the fair just that morning and was now empty except for her and the rest of the tribe. They'd be staying on, mayhap as long as the entertaining event lasted. She trudged alongside Domelch and Malcolm who led the way, with the others trailing behind in twos and threes.

"It is as I told ye, Ethne."

Domelch's irritation was, as usual, directed at her. All she had done was ask why they could not stay near the fair tonight as they usually did.

"I am just concerned with Finn so exhausted." She wanted to bite her tongue for trying to explain herself to this woman. Always a wasted effort.

She and Finn exchanged glances. The truth was they'd spotted Olaf and his lackeys from a few nights ago, still not dressed with the authority they possessed, but as poor travelers. His face looked horrible where he'd been burned. Bright red with ugly blisters. She was afraid of what he might do if he saw her again, so they had climbed a sturdy tree, high above the festivities, and remained there until dusk.

Ethne assumed the tribe would be back on the morrow. She'd been looking forward to the music and the dancing that happened every night of the fair, though she was never allowed to participate. Watching was enough. To see the people smiling and laughing as they swung each other about, men and women alike. Not a concern in the world. Certainly not a concern about needing to escape from their home to avoid being violated. But that was not meant to be this time.

"I saw ye walking with a strange, fat man," Ethne said. "Who was that?"

Malcolm roared with laughter while Domelch frowned her disapproval, first at him and then at her.

"Shut yer mouth," Domelch said. "That was my brother, Uradech. He is coming to stay with us for awhile."

Malcolm snickered and Domelch huffed, pushing a few steps ahead of them.

He turned to Ethne and winked. "We have heard from some of the other tribes." His voice was full of pride. "Our observance will be well attended."

"The solstice observance?" She shuddered at the reminder. The solstice was her day to be gone. Either that or be handed over to Aidan. That wink meant so much more since she'd heard them discussing her.

Hoping to hide her trepidation from her brother who knew her so well, she dropped to her knees for Finn to get on her back.

"The verra same." Malcolm belched loudly.

Fear gurgled in her stomach. She'd only understood half of what was discussed. Malcolm had always been protective of her when they were children. With his strong profile and determined chin, he certainly didn't look like a man who was willing to give her up without a fight. How deceiving men could be.

He continued. "It will be a boon for us all, the time together with the many tribes coming forward."

Domelch grinned now, her teeth bright against her skin. She stroked her fine red hair from her face and sidled up to her husband. "It will be. The child will be borne by then."

"That is the hope." Malcolm's smile didn't reach his eyes.

Domelch paid no attention, rubbing her belly as she always did when she wanted to call attention to her pregnant state. But she never spoke of the upcoming birth. She never seemed excited about it. She'd been the same with Finn. It seemed odd that a woman wouldn't look forward to having a child.

When she was young, living safe with her parents who loved her, Ethne had looked forward to marrying. She dreamed of finding a handsome man—as handsome as her father—from some faraway village. He would sweep her off her feet and into his strong arms. She understood so little about the world her parents had protected her from. But hearing Domelch and Malcolm grunting from behind their curtain every night did not leave Ethne with any interest in marrying now. Or coupling.

Curious, she asked Finn, "Will *ye* be happy to have a little baby?"

"I do no—"

"Cease yer prattling." Domelch's eyes widened on Ethne. A forbidden topic?

Even where he hung on her back, she felt him tense. The little hand that had been gripping her shoulder was no doubt in his mouth again. The gentle sucking sound at her ear confirmed it.

She slowed a bit. Then a bit more. Just enough to avoid comment until the rest had passed the two of them.

Domelch babbled about some new carved bowl she'd taken a liking to, asking if Malcolm would get it for her. Aidan had ridden his horse off somewhere, although he had allowed his many wives to remain behind at the fair. She envied them until she remembered Moira.

Before long, she and Finn were far enough back that their talking could no longer be overheard.

"How fare ye, my little man?" she asked, bouncing him lightly with each word.

He made a sound in his voice that sounded like no answer at all.

"And did ye enjoy that elephant ride?"

"Oh, it was so high up. Where did it come from again?"

Ethne laughed. He'd asked her three times, and three times she had told him she did not know. The man who cared for it and allowed Finn to take the ride knew, but she couldn't remember. He had been a stout man with bushy black eyebrows, not handsome like the man who had played along with Finn.

She said, "Ye picked a fine man to hide behind. Tall as a tree."

Finn laughed. "I told him he was as big as a whale."

Gasping, Ethne stopped. "Ye did not. Tell me ye said no such thing."

"What is wrong with a whale? They are good. They stay together as a family and they love each other." Finn leaned his chin on her shoulder. "They are happy."

His moping tone squeezed her heart.

"Who knows, Finn, if they are truly happy?"

"They blow the water up into the air!" He picked up his head, sounding quite put out by having to explain this to her. "That is how they show they are happy."

"I am not convinced." She hoped to prod him into more conversation, but he remained quiet for so long she became lost in her own thoughts, thinking again about the stranger with the broad shoulders and kind smile. She wished she could have spent more time with him. In her mind, they would talk about things. Him and her. They'd talk about this and that. He would ask her if she was well taken care of. She would tell him how miserable her life was and how much she wished to be away from the caves. And he would offer his assistance—

"Ethne?"

She shook herself. How silly to be wasting her thoughts on something that could never happen.

"Up ahead, Ethne." Finn wiggled to get down, and she dropped to her knees so he could. When he grabbed at her leg, she flinched at how tight his hold was.

"What is amiss?" she asked.

Thumb shoved inside his mouth, he pointed with his other hand up the road.

Three men stood abreast, blocking the way.

"Ethne."

Olaf called, and she couldn't catch her breath. He said her name the way he had in the cave. Low and intimate.

Finn squeezed tighter.

"I've been waiting for ye."

A squeak escaped her throat. Olaf confirmed her suspicions, and she clamped her jaw tight.

When Ciaran came toward them and yanked the child away, Finn's nails ripped through her clothes into her skin and she gasped in pain. He struggled against Ciaran so fiercely that the third man came to grab his feet. When he slapped the little boy, his body went limp. Ethne screamed. In the blink of an eye, Olaf had her mouth covered and an arm about her waist. He picked her up off the ground as if she weighed nothing. She continued kicking and flailing, and digging at his fingers to gain her release. His powerful arm squeezed tight. She couldn't breathe.

His hands clawed at her, stopping only long enough to

drop her behind the bushes that grew thick along the side of the road. He threw her down so hard she hit the back of her head against the ground. She winced. The pain shot all the way to her teeth.

"Tease me, will ye?"

"No." She shook her head, scrambling back on her elbows to get away. He hauled her back by her ankles. Her *léine* balled around her hips, and he pulled her knees apart to settle on his knees between her legs.

The taking is easier if ye submit.

Aidan's advice echoed in her head.

Never! She would never submit! But she could not panic. Not now!

The speed with which he worked at his trews, yanking out his stiff rod, was almost faster than her body could react. She jerked her knees against him, pulling and pushing to get a leg around him while he shoved her back against the ground at any attempt to sit up. He laughed, an enjoyable laugh as if the brutal attack entertained him. "I'll show ye I dinna even need to pay for ye."

"Stop. Please. Do not." Her voice was hoarse. "I beg ye."

When he dropped onto her chest, he all but crushed her beneath his weight. His stiffened appendage persistently tapped against her thigh and his foul-smelling breath in her face made her gag. Fresh sores, bright red and oozing along the side of his face, nearly closed one eye completely shut, creating a permanent grimace.

"Ye beg me? Nay. 'Tis what I want." He squeezed her chin painfully tight with his meaty fingers, turning her face toward him. "I get what I want."

She needed to slow him down, get herself a chance to escape. He was extremely drunk, and that was the only thing keeping him from being successful now.

"I didna know they would hurt ye." Tears clogged her throat. "I wanted to lay with ye."

She closed her eyes and turned away, preparing herself for the inevitable, but he stilled. When she faced him, his one good eye was narrowed with suspicion.

"Did ye now?" His tone was still hard, but suspicion was better than his anger. "Or are ye lying to me so that I will be gentle with ye?"

Seeing Domelch again tossing the hot oil at him, Ethne took a steadying breath and gulped down her fear. "I tried to stop her from hurting ye, reaching for her when she grabbed the pan, but I was too late." She had to convince him she told the truth. She widened her eyes in innocent supplication. "Do ye not remember that?"

He growled, his anger still intact. She needed another tactic.

"They do not need to sell me, Olaf, not with all their silver—"

"Silver?"

"They have it hidden away. A lot of it. They do not need to sell me. They will keep me with them forever, but ye..." His grip had lessened so that she could place her hand on his arm. He listened intently now. "Ye could take me from them."

"Do ye know where they hide the silver?"

Excitement tightened her chest. He had taken the bait! "I have not found it yet, but every time they leave me alone, I search for it."

Olaf squeezed her chin again, his gaze darting to her lips. "But can ye? Can ye find where it is hidden?"

"I am a smart woman." *Smarter than ye know.* "I think I am close to finding it, and they do not even suspect me."

He released her chin and thrust his hand between her legs. She gasped at the sudden pain.

"Are ye playing me for a fool?" His tone sharpened again. "Ye do not feel ready to lay with me. Ye have no interest at all."

She didn't understand what he meant, but his fingers were hurting her.

"Ye frightened me." She spoke as sternly as she dared and shook her head, fighting to steady her breath. "And I'm afeared for Finn. Is he well?"

Without hesitation, he called behind him, but kept his gaze locked on her face. "Ciaran!"

"My turn?" Ciaran's voice came from the road.

She gasped, and Olaf smiled at her. "And if I wish to share ye, Ethne? Will ye be willing?"

Bile rose in her throat. "I do not know about such things."

"I will teach ye."

"Whatever ye want. I ask only that ye take me away from them."

His nasty grin widened, and he jumped to his feet. He hiked up his trews as he turned toward the road and hollered, "Does the child live?"

There was a pause, and Ethne's imagination sparked: Finn had been murdered outright by the man. Or he'd stumbled and cracked his head open when he tried to escape. He'd been gutted like an animal as he struggled to save her. The world darkened around her.

"Of course, he lives." Ciaran's tone left no doubt about his irritation with the question.

"The boy lives." Olaf's voice was intimately quiet, and he glanced down the length of her, pausing at her bare legs. His anger was shifting back to desire. He dropped to his knees beside her this time, sliding his hands along her thighs. Gritting her teeth, she did not resist when he put his hand between her legs again, more gently this time. "I will admit I prefer my women willing."

Ethne was not prepared for him to drop his mouth to hers, crushing her lips. She dug her fingers into the earth to stop from hitting him. The sensation of his beard burning her skin where it scraped against her face sent her already racing heart into a full gallop, but she dared not turn away.

Instead, she opened her mouth to his forceful tongue and fought against the urge to clamp down on it. He made a pleased sound, but his cruel fingers were relentless, sliding and stroking, as if looking for something. She knew one thing for certain. If he saw through her lies, drunk or not, he would not hesitate to rape her.

She searched her thoughts for anything that would calm her fear, slow her beating heart, allow her to seem to submit so he would let down his guard. Surely with how drunk he was, it would only take one unexpected heave to get him off her.

The memory of the tall man with the long black hair came to her. With his kind eyes and welcoming smile, he would have a gentle touch. Careful of her. Careful not to give her any pain. Protecting her. In her mind, she was with the tall stranger, and he was the one kissing her. She kissed him back, lifting her head in urgency.

Olaf pulled back, withdrawing his hand. His expression full of smugness, he sucked at one finger and then the next. "So, ye speak the truth."

He stood to refasten his trews, leaving her struggling to get up on her own. Ciaran came through the bushes with a crash.

"What is amiss? Why is she covering herself?" He took a step closer, his eyes hooded with lust, but Olaf yanked him away from her.

"Not now. We have a more profitable alliance with this one."

"No!" Ciaran's disappointment was great, and he moved closer, yanking his slim shoulder from the bigger man's grip.

Olaf shoved him to the ground where he landed face

first. "I said, we have an alliance. Ye will not touch her"—he leered at her and winked—"yet."

The squire pulled himself together enough to stand and brush off the dirt from his threadbare knees and elbows. With a thoughtful expression, he said, "And what is this alliance?"

"Do ye question me? Ye insolent little pup." Olaf's anger was even more fierce directed at the other warrior.

Ethne shrank back in fear.

"I ask because I fear she has tricked ye."

Olaf guffawed. "And how could this girl trick *me*?"

"By convincing ye of something that is not true."

The larger man turned a gimlet eye on her, but quickly smiled instead. Broadly. "I had the proof. She does not lie." Olaf moved to hold her flush against him while his large hand grasped her bottom. "Besides...I will have her one way or another, but I am willing to wait for now. I believe she will care for a more gentle taking, mayhap even a soft pallet beneath her. Is that not right, Ethne?"

"Ethne!" Malcolm was calling her. She took a breath to respond, but Ciaran's smug smile was like a slap. If she called to Malcolm, Ciaran would be proven correct. Besides, what could Malcolm do to protect her from these men? He could end up hurt or even dead.

She clamped her jaw and turned wide, innocent eyes on Olaf. She asked, "Should I respond? Or do ye wish me to remain quiet?"

He beamed at her, sliding his hand up her back to the nape of her neck. A gentle caress. His eyes staring deeply into hers, he said, "Ye need to find the silver. Ye have a fortnight before I return for it...and ye." The unexpected yanking of her hair made her cry out. "If ye do not, I have many men who will have a taste of ye when I am through, and ye will not need to worry about escaping. Ye will probably be dead."

Olaf called to the other man, and the three of them left

her standing there. The distant sound of their laughter carried to her, and then horses pounding the hard earth as they rode deeper into the darkened woods back toward the fair. She took a deep breath, her knees trembling, straining to support her.

"Finn?" she called.

"Ethne?" The little boy stumbled as he ran toward her, tears staining his dirty face.

She took him in her arms. "Did they hurt ye?"

Finn shook his head against her bosom.

"Ethne!" Malcolm called again from much closer.

"I am here, Malcolm. We've had an accident." She looked into Finn's eyes and continued calling to her brother. "Finn has fallen."

She nodded to him, an expectant expression. When he returned her nod, she clasped him to her breast again, his hot tears dampening her clothes.

"All will be well, Finn. Do not speak of any of this. It must be our secret. I will take care of ye."

His tears continued in a torrent, his sobs breaking her heart. When Malcolm got to them, his obvious anger immediately cleared up Finn's tears.

"Why must ye two always dawdle?" Malcolm's voice slurred slightly. "Get on my back, boy. We need to catch up to the others."

She helped him to get on his father's back. They hurried down the road until they caught up to the others. Domelch's complaints could be heard before they were seen.

Malcolm said something under his breath that sounded a lot like "miserable woman," but Ethne couldn't be certain. She had too many other things to worry about. First and foremost was how to get back to the fair and find a way to escape. She didn't need to worry about finding where the silver was in a fortnight. She was the only one who knew.

CHAPTER 11

Come morning, Malcolm's offer to take Finn to gather wild berries was an unusual treat for the boy. It left her and Domelch alone in the cave. Ethne wouldn't be surprised if it were Domelch's incessant chatter that prompted the exit, but hoped Finn would remember not to say anything about the men who had accosted them.

She had kept Finn talking on the way back from the fair so that he wouldn't be preoccupied with the earlier encounter. She needed to talk to him about it and had hoped for an opportunity when they'd arrived at their home, but by then it was too late and had to wait.

"We have much to celebrate this day," Domelch said yet again.

Again, Ethne refused to rise to the bait; her curiosity would not be sparked. Instead, she concentrated on which herbs to add to the boiling water.

But Domelch's reaction to being ignored was to be more demanding, which made it so much worse for Ethne. It almost made her want to ask the question Domelch was dying for her to ask. When she became suddenly quiet, Ethne's entire body tensed. She prayed Malcolm and Finn would return this very moment.

"Is that what ye will wear?" Domelch finally asked, scowling when she perused Ethne's one and only *léine*.

Ethne could not have been more surprised by the question. She frowned. "I do not understand."

Domelch rolled her eyes and went to the chest that was kept beside their private sleeping area at the back of the cave. She grumbled as she went through her many items, finally pulling out a dark brown gown Ethne could not remember ever seeing before.

"Ye will wear this." Domelch's smile was nothing short of radiant when she tossed it to Ethne.

Ethne's breath caught in her throat. She swallowed hard. "And why would I wear this?"

"Why not?"

Because Domelch never paid attention to anything about her, only that she kept Finn quiet.

"Why does it matter what I'm wearing? I cook the meal, clean up, and get Finn out of yer hair. No one will even notice me."

"Today ye will be noticed."

Ethne's stomach clenched. "I do not wish to be noticed."

Her sister-in-law had no idea how true that was. Aidan had always kept his eyes on her, but it wasn't until she'd started her menses that it had become a more intimate attention. As leader, it was his duty to see her married, if that was what they had planned for her. But there had never been any mention of it so, she had always assumed it wouldn't happen. She had nothing of value to be offered as an enticement for any type of advantageous marriage, advantageous to Aidan that was. Well, that was until the islanders had come.

She ripped the last remaining berries from the stems, dropping them with a loud plop into the steaming pot that sat snug against the fire. What was taking Malcolm so long since the berries were less than a stone's throw away?

"Why are ye so irritable this morning?" Domelch asked.

Domelch? Inquiring about her feelings? This did not look good at all.

"I am overtired and didna sleep well."

The pregnant woman's quirked brow shot fear right through the center of Ethne's heart, but she struggled to remain calm. "And why are ye suddenly so interested in me?"

"I am always interested in ye."

Domelch lied and her honey-sweet smile did nothing to lessen Ethne's trepidation. "Ye are only interested that I do as ye bid me to do."

"When the men follow ye with their eyes instead of me?" Domelch shrugged. "Do not think I do not notice—"

"But I do nothing to attract their attention."

"And when Aidan replaces my seat at his left with *ye*?" Domelch scoffed, continuing as if she'd not heard Ethne. "I see yer tricks."

Ethne was beside herself. She wasn't sure how to respond. Especially since she was more than willing to be replaced by Domelch at Aidan's side. "I do not wish the attention, Domelch. Surely, ye see that?"

But Domelch wasn't listening. "Does Aidan not remember my long line of royalty?"

Everyone remembered Domelch's lineage. A direct line to a powerful Pictish queen. She never let them forget it. But this was the first Ethne had heard about Aidan.

"Ye should be at his side." Her desperation made her voice tight. "As ye said, ye are royalty. I am…nothing."

Domelch rolled her eyes. "Ye are a stupid lass who does not appreciate Aidan's power." She closed her eyes and took a slow, deep breath. After a moment, she turned her bright green eyes on Ethne. "My brother comes to take ye to wife. Today."

The fat little man who had been with Domelch at the fair?

"No!" Ethne squeezed the single word out of her tight chest. When she stood, the rest of the branches that had rested on her lap dropped to the floor.

She would never allow that man to touch her, and she refused to be cowered by the woman's scathing look. "I will not be his wife."

"Ye will do as ye are told." Domelch's tone was the same one she used with Finn, but Ethne was not a child to be ordered about, and this woman was definitely not her mother.

"I will not."

The sounds in the room seemed to get louder. The constant drip at the back of the cave sounded like it was dripping right onto her head. The distant roar of the ocean and the birds above it could have been right here in the cave with them. Panic was taking over.

"I will obey when it has to do with Finn. Or with the food. Or how ye want me to wash yer back. But I will not obey when it has to do with me. I do not wish to be with a man in that way." Ethne's voice cracked, tears welling in her eyes. She had to stop speaking.

"Are those tears, Ethne?" Domelch pursed her lips. "They will not work on me."

She took a quivering breath, but held her head high. "They are not meant to work on ye. I will not be ordered to take yer brother as my husband. Or to lay with him. If ye force me in this way, I will not remain here. Doubt me not."

Her voice had remained strong. Ethne squared her shoulders.

Domelch measured her resistance before she finally

replied, "If ye run away, we will find ye. And then we will keep ye tied up."

Ethne's mouth fell open. She did not doubt it, which left her with no choice except to leave and not get caught.

"Ethne! We found more red berries." Finn burst through the door ahead of his father. His excitement quickly diminished as he sensed the tension in the room. He faced his mother. "What is amiss?"

Malcolm came in more quietly, dropping his sack beside the fire before glancing between the two of them. His expression revealed nothing. Ethne held Domelch's gaze, her jaw tight. The sound of Malcolm helping himself to the ale filled the tense silence. He said nothing. Instead, he smacked loudly, enjoying the taste, then settled in his spot against the wall. Finn remained standing. Watching.

"Ethne?" Malcolm began, and Ethne's stomach dropped. She knew that tone.

No. He could not be insisting as well. Did he not care at all for her? She refused to turn to him. She refused to acknowledge she had no one in this whole world who cared about her or what she wanted.

"Look at me."

She shook her head, her gaze remaining steady on the bull painted on the wall in front of her. An outline really, in a bright blue that had lasted many years in the cave.

"Now." His voice remained calm.

When Domelch's ugly red lips curled up at the corner, a sob slipped from Ethne.

"Poppa, what is wrong with Ethne?" Finn moved to stand in front of his father. His concerned question broke the dam, and tears rolled down her cheeks. "Why is she crying?"

"Because she doesn't listen." Domelch's clipped words hung in the air.

Ethne's quiet sobs blended with the sound of the

crackling fire. Finn came to stand beside her, his little hand taking hers.

"Do not cry. All will be well," the boy repeated her earlier words.

They were a lie then, and they were a lie now. She looked into his imploring face, fat tears rolling down her cheeks, unable to correct him. She knew in her heart.

It will not, Finn.

~

Malcolm blew into his wooden flute yet again, filling the air with that terrible sound. Domelch stretched herself before the fire, the swell of her baby keeping her from falling forward. They were both drunk.

Uradech, Domelch's brother, was not drunk. He'd arrived just after the morning meal, his hair still damp and smelling of pine, with presents for each of them. A dark green ribbon for his sister. A jug of ale for Malcolm. A sack with a game inside for Finn. And for Ethne, a spray of forget-me-nots. He must have bathed in the burn, hoping to make a good impression. He failed.

At present, he sat cross-legged and tossed the painted pebbles once more onto the ground between him and Finn. The boy, full of excitement to have someone new to play with him, studied the way the stones landed, even dropping to the ground with his bottom in the air to decide whose had landed closest to the center circle.

"Ha! I win," Finn said.

But Uradech's bright eyes remained on Ethne, watching everything she did. When she stirred the iron pot. When she dished the food. When she moved around the little circle, their family, to fill the empty cups. His gaze remained steady as he assessed her dressed in Domelch's dark *léine*, the low top so loose on her that she had to be careful not to reveal too much as she went about her duties.

The man had come, but there had been no talk of a marriage contract. No talk of marriage at all. Instead, he had been welcomed in by his sister like a long-lost sheep coming home. And no one spoke directly to Ethne.

It was just as well since she was coiled tight enough to let loose her outrage at any moment if *anyone* were to speak directly to her. Not at all acceptable. She'd have to make a run for it or she would be quickly caught...and tied up if Domelch had any say in it. Which she, unfortunately for Ethne, certainly did.

It was well past mid-day when the sun finally broke through the clouds enough to warm the air in the cave.

"What was that?" Finn turned toward the opening.

"I dinna hear anything." Ethne gave it little thought, keeping her attention on her stitching. Domelch had strained the seam of her gown far enough that it had shredded. It was a difficult repair.

A footfall outside brought Ethne's head up. Malcolm was again playing so she moved closer to the door. Uradech's eyes followed her.

"Greetings!"

She recognized Aidan's tone, but it was a tall redheaded man standing there, and she jumped. Aidan stood just behind him.

"I am sorry to startle ye." The man reached a hand toward her, stopping just short of touching her. "My friends and I are travelers and yer chieftain was kind enough to offer to put us up."

Ethne was joined by Finn and Uradech, who stood close enough that his breath stirred the hairs on her neck, which sent a shiver of revulsion down her back.

"Who is this?" Uradech sounded far too proprietary.

She rolled her eyes and sighed. "I do not know."

The redhead's eyes lit up with humor as if he'd caught

her irritated tone. She glanced at the two men with him: a blond, stocky man and the man with long black hair from the fair. Heat spread across her chest at the familiarity in his eyes.

Aidan pushed himself to the front. His face lit up when he spotted Uradech. "Ah! So ye've arrived."

Uradech mumbled something inaudible, his eyes downcast. Aidan grimaced at the large man's lack of response before shaking his head in dismissal and continuing.

"These men are visitors here. Malcolm invited them to stay with ye." Aidan gazed around, picking up the condition of everyone with a single scan, before settling on her. "Please show them a warm welcome." His gray eyes sparkled as if he laughed at some private joke. "And I will see ye all within a sennight for the celebration announcement."

Ethne *humphed.* When his eyes narrowed, she clenched her jaw tight. There'd be no such announcement if he referred to her wedding Uradech.

The men nodded, exchanged hand clasps, and Aidan was gone. The awkward silence that followed made her shift uncomfortably, that and the mention of the announcement and some impending celebration she'd not heard of before. She ground her teeth in irritation. Her brother should be seeing to this. When she turned back to call to him, she had to shove the massive weight that was Uradech aside to do so.

"Malcolm? We have visitors," she said.

Visitors would make it impossible for any marriage talk. A spark of hope was lit, and she beamed at her rescuers. She pulled at the redheaded stranger's arm, his friends following. She led them into the cave where Malcolm was just staggering his way to a stand. Domelch snored loudly but didn't move.

The redheaded man approached Malcolm, not

seeming to notice his drunken state, and extended his arm. "I thank ye for the offer to take us into yer home." He had to catch Malcolm's arm when it wavered past his hand, to grab his wrist in greeting, then turned to Ethne. "I am called Niall and these are my companions, Aldred and Lachlann."

Lachlann. The man's name was Lachlann. They each moved forward, but only nodded their greeting, apparently not willing to chase after her brother's drunken limbs.

"Aye, I remember ye now. How's the jaw?" Malcolm's question was directed at Lachlann.

He wiggled his jaw. "None the worse."

"Welcome. Stay as long as ye like," Malcolm said, right before dropping again to the ground, and Ethne came forward in his place.

"Ye have met my brother, Malcolm. And this is his wife..." As one, they turned toward the sleeping woman. "Domelch."

"I am called Finn." The lad had come with Ethne, standing in front of her now. He stretched his neck to look up at them. "Welcome. Come join us by the fire."

The lad's words startled Ethne until she realized he was only repeating what Malcolm always said, what he would be saying if he had not over-imbibed. It was still endearing and brought a smile to her face. She wasn't certain if he recognized Lachlann.

"Please." Directing them to sit, she climbed over Domelch to grab what was left of their ale. "Would ye care for some?"

Niall said, "We do not mean to put ye out...?"

"Ethne." She was quick to answer the unasked question, scanned the three of them, pausing at Lachlann, and said, "I am called Ethne."

CHAPTER 12

*L*achlann lay on his back, his eyes fixed on the brightening sky through the cave opening. The cave was surprisingly warm, easily holding the heat from the fire that had long since burned out. Domelch, who never did wake up, snored loudly, then mumbled something incoherent. She lay right where she had apparently passed out. Her husband, Malcolm, had moved to their pallet where the ceiling sloped lower. The large man, whom Ethne had introduced as Uradech, lay in the space between them both.

Leaning on an elbow, Lachlann turned toward the small pallet hidden in the shadows. The boy was curled up in the arms of his aunt. Ethne. Now, Lachlann had a name to go with the lovely face of the woman he'd encountered. For the slightest of moments, he thought she had not recognized him, but then she smiled. A smile of recognition from a beautiful woman, and his heart had quickened.

Finn had recognized him for certain, speaking about the size of the whales they could see, but not claiming to remember him outright. That was just as well. It made their shared meeting more intimate.

Intimate? Lachlann shook his head and lay his head back down.

Aldred snored behind him like the dead. Served him right after the way he'd been carrying on with Sophie. Yet he'd had no qualms about setting her aside when they learned where Holy Man's cave was. But she'd had none either.

"Are ye awake?" Niall asked, his voice barely a whisper.

Lachlann turned to him and nodded. Niall motioned to the door, and they went out into the light.

"Have we found the place? Or is there another cave?" Niall spoke quietly.

Lachlann kept his eyes on the horizon, watching for the sun. "This is the cave that opens up to the sea. It must be the one."

"And with these people living here, would they not have found anything once hidden? How long did the girl say they'd lived here?"

"*Ethne* told us they've been here five summers." She had become very animated once her brother had passed out, sharing with the young Finn the entertainment expected from hosts. They were quite close, their love for each other more like that of a mother and son. But Malcolm? Even drunk, he'd been overbearing. The question was where did Uradech fit in. He mostly sat brooding like an old hen, darting angry glances at the three of them as if they'd ruined his fun.

"But *Ethne* also said they grew up in the highlands, so how is that possible?" Niall stressed her name just as Lachlann had, but making no comment about it.

"I took it to mean there have always been people living here. Their people."

Niall snorted. "And what people are those?"

"Is it not obvious?" Lachlann asked. "The drawings on the wall? The game the boy was playing? These are the

Picts. Or rather this is where the Picts lived, and these are the drawings they left behind. A *verra* long time ago. These people appear to have chosen to follow in the same path for some reason."

"And somehow they know the games the Picts would have played?"

Lachlann scoffed. "*I* know the games as well."

"But pagans?"

"I suppose the Picts *were* pagans, but were we not all pagans until we accepted Christ as our Lord and Savior? The Scots? The Celts? The Saxons? The Danes? These are people playing at being Picts. They are not truly so. I dinna believe there are any of them around anymore. They've intermarried, just as the Normans do with the Saxons. Our grandchildren may one day wonder where all the powerful Saxons went."

Niall's shrug indicated his lack of interest in the subject. Lachlann was the only one who had been schooled in a monastery that included the Christianization carried on by Columba and other saints. Sometimes that teaching reared its head. Like now. And his friend's lack of knowledge reminded him that, although they might be like brothers, they had not that much in common.

Someone stirred inside the cave.

"Shall we?" Niall asked, directing Lachlann to enter.

Lachlann led the way, his gaze immediately going to Ethne, but she was no longer alone. Uradech knelt beside her pallet, blocking whatever was happening from Lachlann.

"No." Ethne's quiet voice carried and Lachlann's whole body tensed.

Enraged, he strode across the cave to where the heavy man hunched over her. The child had been set aside, still asleep. Lachlann yanked back on Uradech's shoulder, pulling him away from her so hard that he fell back on his arse, sliding along the sand a few feet away.

"Hey!" Uradech said.

The brown gown Ethne had slept in was up around her hips, and her eyes were wide in fear. Lachlann hunkered down beside her curled up figure to cover her bare legs with the wool blanket. When she focused on him, he was surprised to see her redden and turn away.

"What is amiss?" Malcolm called from behind him, still sounding half asleep.

Uradech opened his mouth to respond, but Lachlann raised a finger at the man along with a warning glare. "Do not. I heard her. She told ye no."

Ethne shrank back and yanked the rough wool up to her neck, her small shoulders heaving. Lachlann held her gaze, watching as she took a deep breath before responding to her brother. "There is naught."

The fat man sneered at Lachlann before standing, brushing off his backside and returning to the others just beginning to stir.

Lachlann turned his attention to Ethne and spoke in a quiet voice, unsure what to say to her. "Is there ought I can do for ye?"

She lowered her gaze and shook her head no.

"Ethne!" A demanding voice Lachlann didn't recognize barked from behind. The woman Ethne had called Domelch? "The fire!"

When Ethne moved to get off the pallet, Lachlann extended his hand as he stood. She hesitated, her eyes darting between his hand and his face with suspicion. Was she so seldom offered a kindness that his simple offer must be met with mistrust? When her gaze remained on his face, he swore her doubt changed right before his eyes. Then her small hand was in his, still warm from sleep, and he lightly caressed her fingers with his thumb while assisting her up. His heart swelled as if a great battle had been won.

She offered him a shy smile then said in a louder voice intended for the others, "Are ye ready to break yer fast?"

Ethne left him behind as she moved toward the fire.

He went to stand alongside Niall, who stood at the hearth near to where Ethne blew the fire aflame. His arms crossed, Niall quirked a brow. Lachlann nodded. This was indeed a strange place.

Aldred came in from outside to pause in the doorway, scratching his stomach while all eyes turned to him. "Good morn!" he offered, a slight shrug to his shoulders. "How did ye all sleep?"

Lachlann and Niall exchanged glances right before Niall turned away, shaking his head.

"And who are ye three?" Domelch stood, her hair matted to the side of her face and spittle whitening the corners of her mouth. She didn't seem a bit embarrassed to have three men she didn't know seeing her disheveled from sleep. Just the opposite, in fact. She smiled, adjusting the gold bangles at her ears that had become entangled in her hair. It might have been a flirty smile, but Lachlann couldn't be certain. He only knew that when her gaze had traveled the length of them in a slow perusal, there had been a definite spark in those green eyes.

"These are visitors from…" Malcolm threw water on his face from a bowl Ethne was just filling from a clay pitcher that had been set near the hot coals overnight. "Where did ye say?"

Niall answered. "We are Pilgrims from Restenneth Priory."

Domelch grunted her dislike. She accepted the brush Ethne handed her with a jingle from the arm bands at her wrist and deposited herself on a small stool that her sister-in-law had set beside her. "Well, we won't hold that against ye. Ye are welcome here no matter where ye hail from."

"I'm hungry." Finn looked exhausted, big red eyes, a smudge of ashes on the bridge of his nose. When he noticed Lachlann, he perked up.

Lachlann returned the smile. "And what about the whales? Do ye have many whales about?"

The lad cupped his hands for the berries Ethne offered to him. He beamed at her, and she patted him lightly on the head before returning to the fire. An iron pot tucked neatly against the coals was filled with steaming porridge.

Ethne smiled. "Finn knows quite a bit about them, dinna ye, Finn?"

"Ethne!" Domelch turned a mean expression on the lass. "I need my mead. Now!" Once Ethne was scrambling to do the woman's bidding, Domelch turned a bright smile toward the men. "And what can I get ye three?"

Niall shrugged. "Mead will do fine if 'tis not too much trouble."

"Ach, no trouble at all. Ethne is just lazy." The woman paused, offering them a sweet smile, then hollered, "Ethne!"

The lass was the only one moving about, seeing to the things that needed to get done, doing as she was told.

Niall and Aldred settled not far from the fire, but Lachlann remained closer to Ethne. It seemed a safer place to remain for her sake. He didn't miss the way Uradech glared at her from across the room.

Malcolm interrupted the companionable silence . "And what are ye three doing around here? 'Tis a bit out of the way."

"We heard of the caves along the coast. Holy Man's cave in particular." Niall turned to include Aldred and Lachlann. "As pilgrims, it seemed a worthy journey to come to such a holy place."

"Pilgrims? Ye're claiming to be pilgrims?" Uradech's

sarcastic comment made Domelch sit up at attention. Malcolm, too, if at a little slower pace.

Something was making the man bolder. He'd had little to say the night before.

"Holy Man? We have our own holy man," Malcolm said.

"Oh?" Niall asked.

Unexpected tension tightened Lachlann's limbs, peaking his alertness.

"Aidan. He is our leader. A holy man."

Lachlann relaxed. That didn't sound quite the same as a monk. Or a clerk.

Niall wasn't sure either. "Yer chieftain?"

"He was marked as our leader when still a child. When he was grown, he was anointed as such. If ye choose to stay with us awhile, I'm sure ye'll meet him."

Malcolm seemed to have no memory of how they'd met the day before or, at the very least, that Aidan had been there.

Niall frowned. "He was the one who brought us here."

Malcolm scrunched his face, no doubt searching his foggy memory. Apparently finding nothing, he shrugged.

"And have ye always been 'pilgrims'?" Uradech asked in the same sarcastic tone as his earlier comment.

Aldred sat forward. He was primed for an argument now. It was there in his eyes, which never wavered from the large man. "Pilgrim is what a man is called when he is on a journey to a sacred place. A religious place. A *holy* place."

Lachlann hoped his friend would keep to their plan and not start any trouble for them. Uradech was irritating in the extreme, even if Aldred hadn't witnessed the man bothering Ethne.

"No, we have not always been traveling," Aldred said, then turned away. Leastwise he was trying to avoid an argument.

"And ye, Uradech?" Lachlann tried to sound more amicable than he felt. When Ethne paused in stirring the pot, he had doubts about his success but kept his attention on Uradech. "What is it ye do here?"

"He is my brother." Domelch sounded defensive but, as if realizing that, she offered a wide smile that didn't reach her eyes and continued. "He has been away for many years, but now, he is here among us and we have much to celebrate."

Ah! Now that Uradech's sister was awake, he could be more outspoken. Lachlann followed her gaze to Ethne, who kept her head averted. She did not look interested in any celebration.

"The porridge is done, m'lady," Ethne said.

Strange use of the title. Niall and Aldred seemed to notice it as well.

Uradech swaggered over to her side, but with such a large stomach, could he honestly walk any other way? Not a handsome man. Not with that large nose and those beady little eyes. The red hair that might be becoming on his sister made him look sickly and pale. He had a smug look on his face when he passed Lachlann and placed an arm about Ethne's small shoulders, who immediately tried to shake it off. "I can assist ye."

Domelch all but gushed at the exchange, even smacking Malcolm's arm so he would see it, too. Lachlann had a sick feeling in the pit of his stomach.

"I am fine," Ethne said in a low voice. She did not seem fine.

A glance toward Malcolm refilling his own mead, after offering no more than a shrug at the awkward exchange, made Lachlann's ire rise. Quite a bit.

"Ethne?" Domelch's eyes narrowed on her.

The lass immediately stopped her struggle to get out from the large man's grasp, her gaze steadfastly landing on Domelch's stern expression. Uradech caressed her arm, a smile on his ugly face. Ethne stiffened at the intimate gesture.

"Do as ye should." The irritated command came from Malcolm, but he barely glanced their way. No doubt he had spoken at the urging of Domelch, who had turned her frown on the man. An effective gesture.

Lachlann stood before he'd even considered what he would do.

"Come." Lachlann extended a hand to assist Domelch, who gasped with pleasure at the gallant gesture, smiling and fawning as he took her hand just as he knew she would. "Surely, ye are famished."

After Lachlann saw her settled closer to the fire—more of a plopping down with her round belly—the woman immediately started chatting with Niall and Aldred and forgot all about Ethne. Lachlann came alongside Ethne and, giving no warning, shoved Uradech from her side. With his sister's back to them, the man had no recourse but to trot off to a spot at the feet of "m'lady," like any good dog.

"Allow me to assist," Lachlann said in a quiet voice, standing beside Ethne.

The corners of her lips turned up ever so slightly, revealing her appreciation. When her gaze turned back to the others, she shied toward him. She was sore afraid.

He hated to see a lady in distress.

~

Outside the cave, a cool breeze blew in off the sea where Ethne crouched low and rubbed the sand into the pot, adding more water to get a good paste. Finn played nearby as she cleaned while the rest had gone off to the shore. She kept an eye on them. Uradech hung on every word from his sister. *Ugh.* The man was intolerable, and when she'd been awakened by his hand sliding up her leg, she had taken in a breath, ready to scream until he shushed her.

"This is what they want, and ye know it," he'd said.

That realization alone gave her the strength to clamp her knees together as tight as she could and voice her objection. Then Lachlann was there. His determined expression once he'd yanked Uradech away had made her heart soar.

In her imagination, she'd been brave, cupping his cheek and telling him how much his protection meant to her. But when he asked if there was anything he could do for her, she managed to keep from begging him to take her some place safe. Deep down, she knew there was nothing he could do to help her. Besides, he'd be gone soon.

"Look what I found." Finn held a shiny object between his fingers.

She rinsed the last of the mud out of the pot, left the item upside down to dry, and came closer. "Another coin."

He beamed.

"And see? The same tiny hole…right…there!"

"Right near the man's head?" he asked, even though he knew the answer.

She smiled, an expression she hoped spoke of her pride in him.

He made a face, the silver close to his face to study it. "He is a funny looking man."

"He was a king."

"And that is why they made the coin in his image." Finn recited the information he'd heard from her many times before.

Ethne tapped his nose. "And someday ye will wear this hanging from around yer neck. Ye will be verra wealthy."

"I will."

"But ye must not tell anyone," she whispered, her wide eyes keeping his attention. "It shall be our secret."

His eyes widened as well. "A secret. Our secret." He inspected the coin. "Can we tell Lachlann?"

Her breath caught at the boy's perception. "Why would we do that?"

"He can be trusted."

She again saw the man grinning at the boy as they played along the surf earlier, kicking at the waves when they looked for clams.

"He is a good man," she said, sounding more wistful than she intended.

"He is."

She sighed. It was best not to get the boy too attached to a man who'd soon be leaving. "For now, we will keep it to ourselves."

"Shall we put it with the others?"

Ethne searched the horizon, finding all six of their group busy with other things. It would be awhile before they returned. "We must be quick."

Giving Finn the lead, she followed the boy into the cave. The narrow opening in the back was hidden completely. When they'd first come to live there, Domelch and Malcolm had been small enough to fit through the passage when Ethne had located it. The strong smell of rotted eggs sent them back out, but it didn't bother her and Finn. Now only he and she fit, and they slipped through the crack.

This had become their refuge, especially when they were alone and unexpected visitors might plague them. Including Aidan.

Ethne went to the large rock, just the right size for sitting on, and rolled it up against the back wall. The flat side set perfectly alongside the engraving in the wall, an outline of a bearded man carrying an axe, carved by someone from long ago. She motioned to Finn, and he climbed onto the rock to reach his small hand into a crevice that was barely discernible among the natural striations of color throughout the stone. He withdrew a small deerskin pouch and jumped off the rock, the dusty sand rising around him.

He opened the pouch wide, revealing the other coins inside.

"Shall we count them?" He loved to practice his counting, but it wasn't safe to do so now.

Ethne's mother had taught both her and Malcolm to count and to read, but he never practiced like she did. Instead, he always asked her to do his reading and counting. Their mother would be greatly disappointed with him.

"We should wait. It will not be so verra long before the pilgrims leave. We'll have more time then."

"Even Lachlann?"

She paused. "He has places to go as well." Finn's expression turned sad, but she pushed on. "We will count them all then."

Finn shoved the coin down into the middle of the sack then closed it. With careful precision, he replaced it in the same spot before rolling the stone, all by himself, back to the center of the small chamber. "My silver is safe now."

Ethne nodded with the same enthusiasm, even while her heart tightened with sadness. Finn was growing quickly. Too quickly. She wasn't prepared when Finn crumbled into tears and threw himself into her arms, squeezing her in his tight little grasp.

"What is amiss, my little man?"

"I do not like Uradech."

She patted his back, forcing a light tone. "Whyever not?"

"He pulled me aside earlier and pinched me."

Ethne's mouth dropped open. "To what purpose?"

"He told me to sleep alone tonight, or he would pinch me even harder."

Finn sobbed against her chest. He was exhausted, and things were changing so fast now. For Ethne, too.

"Do not be afraid." Brave words. She was only able to use them because she ignored the increased pounding of her own heart.

Finn pulled back, his tears halting. "Will Lachlann protect us from Uradech and those mean men on horses?"

The islanders. Dare she offer him false hope? She had no choice. "I believe he will."

Finn's relief was immediate, and she was glad she'd chosen to lie to the boy. He didn't need to know how precarious their situation was. Better he had hope in someone he could see and trust. Even if that man would probably be gone when they would need him most.

CHAPTER 13

They'd been there only a few days, but catering to Domelch's need for constant attention was trying Lachlann's patience—as was the way she ordered Ethne about. They decided to try flattery that third night since it proved to be the most effective way to get her to talk. Ethne, with Uradech following close behind, had taken Finn down to the shore to wash before bed.

It didn't take long to learn that Domelch and Uradech had been raised in the caves with Aidan as their leader. An idyllic childhood according to them. It appeared her many complaints only started once she'd married Malcom.

"If ye know me at all," Domelch explained with rounded eyes, her expression imploring, "ye know I am a loving woman."

Surely if that were true, her husband, who now lay asleep beside the fire snoring loudly from overindulgence, would choose to spend more time with her. Instead, they barely spoke to each other.

"Verra kind ...even to Ethne."

Lachlann locked his jaw. Tight.

She grasped at her fleshy chest. "I refused to leave the

child behind when her parents passed. I asked 'who would care for her?' and I said, 'I will care for her.'"

He wanted to applaud the performance.

"Of course, ye did," Niall was the first to reply. He even had a straight face, which Lachlann had to admire.

"Verra kind. I see that ye are. A truly loving," Aldred said, after clearing his throat, "caring woman."

Lachlann would not lie and refused to be pinned down by those doe eyes she batted at him. He looked away. Ethne must have been no more than a child herself since she'd come here before Finn was born. No doubt she'd always been ordered to do Domelch's bidding.

When Ethne finally returned from the shore with the boy, no one offered her help with the child who had apparently fallen into the waves. Lachlann quickly stood.

"Go. I am fine." She elbowed Uradech away, but he refused to leave.

Lachlann came closer, returning the child's smile. "Shall I get ye a blanket?"

"There was a big whale." His eyes lit up with excitement. "I wanted him to see me."

Ethne rolled her eyes before responding. "Please, Lachlann, that would be helpful."

Uradech's expression turned into an ugly scowl. "I'll see to it."

The large man rambled off, giving Lachlann a place to stand beside Ethne so he could assist her in taking off Finn's soaked clothing.

"Ye canna go chasing after the whales." Lachlann stood him up so she could see to him.

"But I wanted to!" Finn yawned. "I like the whales. They can be trusted."

Odd sentiment, but Lachlann merely smiled. When Uradech returned with the cloth and made to wipe at Finn's skin, the child drew back, his eyes widening.

Lachlann didn't hesitate to rip it from the man's chubby fingers.

"Canna ye find something to keep yerself busy?" He let his annoyance come through in his tone.

Uradech snorted, but slithered over to the fire to sit beside his sister, who didn't even notice him because she was so engrossed in her storytelling. Ethne looked over at her then shot a quick glance at Lachlann.

"Is she telling ye all about how Malcolm didn't want to take me in after our parent's died?" she asked, her voice low.

Lachlann held up the sleeve of the dry *leine* so Finn could slip his arm through. "Something like that."

Her jaw tightened. "'Tis a lie. He had to convince *her* I would not be a problem."

There was great pain in her eyes and he wished he could soothe the hurt. "I believe ye."

Her expression immediately closed down, almost as if she felt she had said too much. He attempted a reassuring smile and put his hand on her delicate shoulder. She carried a heavy weight.

"Ethne." Domelch barked her name. By the smug expression on Uradech's face, it must have been at his behest. Lachlann shook his head. That man needed a good beating. His gaze met Niall's whose brow furrowed. Disapproval? With *him*?

Ethne took Finn into her arms. "I need to get him to bed."

There was no response from Domelch because Aldred had her attention again. He was quite good at that. Hmm. Something the man was good at. Lachlann smiled only momentarily, his eyes drawn to the little pallet where Ethne and Finn lay huddled together. So, who else would the lass have to confide in if not him?

~

At day break the next morning, Domelch and Malcolm prepared to take their small boat out fishing. Despite the man's constant overindulgence, he worked hard. Having Uradech join them seemed to be at Domelch's insistence and not of Malcolm's choosing or liking. Lachlann found the vision of the huge man struggling to sit within the *currach*, which quickly ran aground, extremely funny.

Malcolm did not. He scowled. When he tried to shoulder the vessel into the waves with little success, Lachlann came forward to help, but paused, motioning Niall and Aldred closer and called out, "Niall and Aldred are true fishermen."

The two exchanged puzzled glances. They were not fishermen.

"Mayhap ye can stay here," Lachlann moved closer to Malcolm, "and allow Niall and Aldred to go in yer stead."

Domelch's eyes lit up. "A verra good suggestion indeed."

She preened as Lachlann knew she would. Having Aldred and Niall all to herself and without a husband to gainsay her? A dream come true.

"I noticed ye have some skins drying." Lachlann tipped his chin toward the large, low table set up and ready to use just beyond the sand. "Mayhap ye and I can remain here and I can assist ye with the scraping. I have never prepared seal skin."

One on one with Malcolm, he hoped to ingratiate himself with the man, mayhap gain his trust so his questions about possible hiding places or even silver would not seem suspicious.

"Indeed." Malcolm nodded, scratching at his chin. "That would be a great help."

Niall and Aldred made quick work of getting the boat afloat, jumping in when they were thigh deep in the water. Malcolm and Lachlann stood watching the vessel as it broke through the incoming waves.

Lachlann knew the way to loosen Malcolm's mouth and opened his satchel. Before lifting out the dark clay jar, he skimmed his fingertips against the medallion safely tucked within. Withdrawing the jug, he swished its contents. "A drink before we start?"

As expected, he had Malcolm's full attention. He nodded and reached for the jug.

"'Tis a fine silver arm band ye wear."

"Indeed." Malcolm sat up straighter, admiring it. "A wedding gift from my wife's leader, Aidan."

"And all the baubles yer wife adorns herself with?"

Malcolm's hawk-like glance made Lachlann want to kick himself. He moved too fast. Unsure exactly how to appear innocent, he curled his lips and kept quiet.

"They are gifts from me." The man shrugged. "And Aidan has sent word that our tribe's celebration will be anon and that you and your friends are expected. The others in our tribe will be there as well."

Lachlann remembered Aidan's invitation. "How many are in yer clan?"

"Tribe."

Malcolm's correction surprised Lachlann, but he didn't interrupt.

"Twenty warriors," Malcolm continued. "Ye've met Thomas. Some of the others were at the fair as well."

"I thought ye had trouble remembering the event."

Malcolm laughed, a genuine chuckle that brought out a dimple on both cheeks. "Domelch had been nagging me that night. I did not want her to think I remembered any of it, but I did. I will soon be giving her the gift she requested."

"Such generosity." Lachlann smiled, drinking directly from the jug. "A true Scot. A drink before we start?"

Malcolm nodded, took a drink, then scowled slightly before answering. "My father was a Scot. *I* am a Pict. That is how Aidan refers to us."

That seemed odd. Aidan seemed fairly intelligent so he must know that Picts disappeared hundreds of years ago.

"Truly?"

"We all have Pictish blood in us from long ago. It's what unites this odd group of men. That and Aidan's leadership."

Long ago would have to be even further back than the stories the bards told, but Lachlann remained quiet.

"Aidan seems to think 'tis important to keep that fact foremost in our tribe."

"And is that why ye refer to yerselves as a tribe?"

Malcolm chuckled, and his cheeks reddened. "My mistake. Aidan does not believe we should be speaking openly about that fact."

He pulled up the long sleeve of his tunic to reveal the dark coloring of an odd symbol tattooed on his lower arm. "And yet, I was given this after Domelch and I had been wed and came to live here among her people."

"Does it mean ye are married?"

"No." Malcolm laughed. "It means I have been accepted into this tribe—" He flashed a smile. "I mean clan. Come." He handed the jug back to Lachlann. "Let us see to these skins."

"I know little about the Picts." Lachlann pushed the jug into the sandy ground to secure it and followed Malcolm to the skins.

"I never had much interest in them. Not until I came here to live. Aidan is a great storyteller, although I'm not sure where he gets his stories from."

"Our clan tells stories as well. Stories of our great warriors. Or great battles. That is how we keep our past from being forgotten," Lachlann said.

"Ah, that is how we remember the power the Picts once had and remind ourselves that we will be powerful again."

A dark cloud drifted by the sun, casting them in shadows. Lachlann steeled himself against the involuntary shiver that began at the back of his neck.

"Powerful again?" he asked.

Malcolm nodded. "Aidan believes we can work toward being as powerful as the Picts were so that we will be able to take care of our own." He shook out the seal skin, stiff from drying, and spread it across the trestle. "We will again have land, riches, and power, and we will do so by coming together with the rituals of our past. Like for our solstice observance."

"Observance? Is it similar to a church observance?"

Pagan cultures performed rituals about nature—the creation—as if God himself was unimportant as the Creator of it all. But in the monastery where he'd studied, he was taught the creation was nothing without knowledge of the Creator.

Malcolm shook his head thoughtfully. "A bit like that, but first we must return to the old ways."

Lachlann accepted the flat stone from Malcolm. It fit perfectly in the palm of his hand.

"There will be much happening at this year's solstice observance, but 'tis awhile off yet."

Lachlann didn't want to seem overly curious so he dragged the flat side of the sharpened rock against the tough skin, the rasping sound surrounding them as they worked. The repetitious movement was oddly soothing.

After awhile, Lachlann asked, "Domelch mentioned she was raised here, but ye were not so how did ye meet?"

"She was brought to our clan as an offering." Malcolm bent over the skin, smoothing it flat and blowing off the loosened, dried flesh. "We lived along the Spey, among the woods and water, far from this barren grassland of this coast."

There was bitterness in his tone.

"We were a powerful clan. My grandfather was a

bannerman for King Malcolm. When the King married the English princess, we lost favor with him. My uncle ended up leaving the clan entirely and moving here."

"The first time I remember meeting him was when he came to visit and brought Aidan. They dangled Domelch in front of me like a mouse in front of a hungry falcon." Malcolm stilled his hand, half stood, and gazed into the distance as if seeing the woman again. "Ripe for the taking. She was introduced as a Pictish princess, from a long line of royalty. I knew little about the Picts, but I knew I wanted her. I was young."

The man blew out a breath, looking sheepishly at Lachlann, as if he'd said more than he intended.

Lachlann nodded. "A good match. And a fine dowry? Silver? Gold?"

"The finest dowry and the ripest breasts." Malcolm winked and went back to his scraping.

Lachlann cleared his throat. He bent his back into his work, finding the manual labor relaxing. Finally, he stopped, placing his stone on the bare skin, and stretched his back. "'Tis a lovely day. Mayhap they will catch many fish."

"Not with Domelch and her need to talk."

Lachlann grinned then looked around. "Is this not the area breached by the Norsemen?"

"Aye. The islanders. The Norsemen. They all come. They all go. But the Picts remain. That is what Aidan says."

Apparently Malcolm thought a lot of what Aidan said.

"But why do they keep coming?" Lachlann smoothed his bare hand over the skin, assessing the cleanliness of the scraping. "Is it land they seek?"

"They fight for control over all things. Long ago, it was raiding the abbeys for the gold, then the land for farming, and sometimes people for slaves."

"And when ye came here, ye didna mind leaving yer clan?"

"We stayed with my clan at first. When my parents died unexpectedly, I had no reason to stay, so we came here. Besides, Domelch never liked my clan. She cried herself to sleep every night."

"And Ethne came as well?"

"Domelch said she could find something for the lass to do, so we brought her with us."

"Something for her to do like cooking and seeing to Finn?"

"Aye and now Domelch has decided she will be wife to Uradech."

When they returned with the boat, Malcolm went to help unload the fish, but Lachlann held back under the pretense of cleaning their tools. Aldred jumped out first into the shallow waves to beach the small vessel high on the shore, while Niall offered a hand to assist Domelch ashore.

Uradech was directed by Malcolm to grab the other side of the large basket now loaded with silver fish flapping for air, which he almost dropped. The man was inept at everything. Domelch followed, giving orders before they even made it all the way into the cave. Niall came, red-faced, soaked tunic, and hair messily clubbed back, to stand alongside Lachlann where he waited for the others to continue into the cave.

Lachlann couldn't contain his grin. "And how was the ocean this morning? Wet?"

Niall glowered at him before untying his hair and shaking loose the water and sand. In a quiet voice, he finally asked. "Was my discomfort worth it? Did ye learn anything?"

"Malcolm told me how he wed Domelch, and came here with her after the death of his parents," Lachlann said. "Except for his arm band, everything else was acquired by him."

"And did he say how he'd acquired them?"

Damn!

"He didn't specify." Lachlann cringed. Niall's question was a good one and he should have pressed Malcolm.

The redhead nodded thoughtfully.

"There is to be some big meeting later in the summer." Lachlann's voice was louder than it needed to be, but he felt some relief at this added information. "Aidan will attend. If anyone knows of any hidden silver, it's him. I dinna believe he will just tell us of it, not even if it's been found by them and used."

Aldred chose that moment to join them. He flashed a grin. "It seems ye may have been breaking up the consummation this morning. Sticking yer nose where it does not belong. Ethne and Uradech are to be married."

"Ye told him about that?" Lachlann turned on Niall, his accusation louder than he'd intended.

One single, red brow raised high, along with Aldred's perplexed frown, flooded Lachlann's face with heat. He continued defensively, "I heard her tell him no."

"As did I." Niall's brow remained raised.

"Ye've upset the apple cart. Explains why Uradech is always shooting arrows at ye from his beady little eyes."

"If there is to be a consummation, should she not be saying 'aye'?" Lachlann's heart was racing. Their damned expressions, accusing him, but he couldn't say for certain why he felt so disappointed.

"Overly chivalrous, even for ye," Aldred said.

Lachlann scowled. "There is no such thing as *overly* chivalrous. There is only chivalrous."

"And the way ye yanked him away from her side? He

fell right on his arse?" Aldred barked a laugh. "What a sight that must have been."

Lachlann shot another accusing glance at Niall before he explained. "He was taking advantage of her. The lass may be treated no better than a slave, but she still deserves protection. She probably has to wipe their arses when they take a shite."

Niall tipped his head in agreement, but offered nothing more, keeping his eyes on Lachlann.

Lachlann kicked at the ground. Dust rose about his tightly laced leggings. "I think she needs my—*our*—protection." When he raised his gaze to Niall, there was no doubt the man measured his motives.

"If she is a slave..." Niall spoke slowly as if choosing his words carefully, "there is little we can do to protect her."

"But if she is not a slave..." Lachlann glanced between both of them with a furrowed brow. Surely they could explain how he should have reacted.

Niall and Aldred exchanged a look that could have been concern, but Lachlann wasn't sure he'd convinced them, so he continued defensively, "I am just saying that a sister is to be protected by her brother when her father is not there to do so." Lachlann blew a breath. "Until she is wed. 'Tis the law."

Niall's expression tightened. "But what laws do these people follow?"

A good question. "Pictish law according to Malcolm. But I feel certain that means whatever Aidan tells them to do."

"And getting involved with marriages and consummations would be a mistake. Do ye not see that?" Niall's level tone sounded so reasonable.

Lachlann sighed. "I do not believe I acted in error, only out of concern for someone who is being taken advantage of."

"The silver is our goal. We need to find it for the church. And well we know it, but we dinna know their past or the reason they behave as they do, or the laws they follow. We do not need to get involved with any struggles here. We need only to find the treasure."

And if they didn't, Lachlann had taken his friends on a futile adventure. Best they find it.

CHAPTER 14

When the six of them returned from fishing, Ethne was there to accept their soaked clothing, their fine catch, and provide the requisite libations. Her brother and Lachlann had seen to their own cleaning up which lightened her load.

Malcolm sat stretched out in his usual spot against the far wall with Niall and Aldred sitting close by. Domelch, naturally, perched herself front and center. Why did the woman never tire of flirting? Why did Malcolm never try to stop her? Ethne had no answer for either question.

Uradech lolled in the shadows with a dark scowl, his beady eyes never wavering from her. She shivered and turned away from him to see to the bread she'd just been ordered to make. Finn had seemed so unhappy since their return that she tasked him with the job of sorting the remaining fish.

"And how are the fish coming?" Ethne spoke for Finn's ears only.

He looked at her with a sullen expression and shrugged. He'd been busy wiggling one about in the basket as if it were still in the water.

"Do some of them still live?"

"Only the whale," Finn replied.

She nodded and winked, but received no response.

Lachlann paced about the cave, pausing to glance outside or at one of the many drawings adorning the walls left by the cave's long-ago inhabitants. He seemed agitated.

Mayhap he paced because he had much on his mind that kept him alert. After all, he was a man of great importance. That medallion had said as much. Dressed in a dark knee-length tunic, there wasn't much of Lachlann's well-honed build that was left to the imagination. Even the tight fitted leggings, cinched to his footwear with a tight crisscross pattern about his solid calves, spoke of the mighty power in his body.

"Ethne!" Domelch called.

Ethne started and dropped her gaze, her face heating from guilt at having been caught thinking about the handsome pilgrim. Was the woman incapable of saying her name without barking it like a dog? Taking a deep breath, Ethne settled herself before looking up from her work. "Aye?"

"Something to slake our thirst."

She glanced at the work in front of her and the fish cooking on the fire. Could Domelch see to nothing on her own? Ethne sighed and brushed off her floured hands.

Domelch made an exasperated sound. "Can ye do nothing on yer own?"

Ethne bit her lip to keep from laughing out loud. That would not go over well with *m'lady*. She stepped outside to get the mead, but paused to take a deep breath, raising her shoulders with the motion, but her restlessness refused to settle. After retrieving the mead, she nearly collided with Lachlann.

"Forgiveness, please." He flashed her a smile and stepped aside with a flourish of his arm to allow her passage.

Feeling an odd fluttering in her belly, she dipped her head.

She moved about the group, offering food and drink to those settled about the fire. A much more enjoyable job with appreciative smiles and words of thanks from their visitors. Lachlann stopped in front of her and accepted the mead. The fingertips that grazed her hand were warm.

His voice quiet, he said, "My thanks."

"Ye're verra welcome," Domelch answered in a loud voice over her shoulder.

Lachlann tipped his head before raising his eyes to Ethne. They sparkled with humor, and her breath caught.

"Is there anything *I* can help ye with?" he asked in a deep rumbling voice.

Her wide grin made her feel ridiculous, but she couldn't seem to stop herself. She shuffled her feet. "Nay. Um...but thank ye."

"Ethne!" Domelch's impatient tone startled them both. "See to the fish. Then a bath."

She flashed Lachlann a shy smile before returning to her work.

"And how did ye find our rough seas this morning?" Malcolm's loud voice filled the small space as he spoke to no one in particular.

Niall chuckled. "I am not certain we were much help to yer wife. Highland Scots are not known for their open sea fishing skills."

"Now, if ye've a loch nearby..." Aldred added without finishing the sentence.

"'Tis true enough." Niall took a sip of the mead. "And the fowl. What are those dark-winged creatures?"

Malcolm seemed content to answer the pilgrim's many questions about the area. Ethne saw to the fish and the heating of the water for the bath. As long as she remained beside the fire and worked, she was not included in the conversation, but whenever she glanced up, she found Lachlann's eyes on her.

Finn kept to himself, saying nothing to the others. If anyone else noticed his sulking, they showed no sign of it. The boy needed some cheering up. When she was going for more water, she dropped down to his level and spoke quietly, "Finn, come with me."

Finn raised sad eyes to her, shaking his head. That broke her heart.

"But I need yer help, little man," she implored.

"I will help ye." Uradech stood, shoulders back, big belly hanging over the belted waist.

She rose slowly, her body aching and tired. She gave him a tight smile. "I dinna want yer help."

"But ye asked the boy—"

"The boy has a name. 'Tis Finn."

The room went quiet. Her sharp words hung in the air. The weight of every eye on her needed no confirmation.

With her last speck of patience, she said, "Finn can help me."

"Then I will help Finn."

Memories of the man's earlier threat to the child had her seeing red. "Finn does not need *yer* assistance. Not now. Not ever."

"Ethne!" Domelch stood, her face pale. "Ye overstep yerself when ye speak so to my brother."

Lachlann shifted beside the door where he had been standing. Ethne's face heated. She had had enough. Enough of the backbreaking work of lugging water, while Domelch sat on her gilded stool. Enough of the relentless heat from the open flame heating the water, while Domelch dazzled their visitors with her beauty and wit. Enough of the leering gazes of Domelch's brother every time Ethne bent over to lift the iron bucket or check the temperature of the water, while Domelch waited impatiently for her to finish filling her tub so she could take a pampered, luxurious soak.

With dripping sweat covering every bit of her stinking body, Ethne turned on Domelch. "If ye dinna keep yer beloved brother away from me—"

The woman gasped, then her mouth slackened and just as quickly slammed shut.

"Tell me," Domelch demanded, "what will ye do, *little* Ethne?"

"Do not call me that." She closed her eyes, regretting the outburst that gave her sister-in-law the upper hand. The woman knew well enough how to make her cower.

"But it is what ye are. Little. Of no consequence." Each word brought the woman closer.

Malcolm, a disgusted expression, kept his gaze leveled on Ethne. He'd be taking his wife's side. As always. The three seasoned warriors would surely have witnessed far worse than a woman screaming in her upset, but they exchanged surprised glances. Or was that only her imagination?

The heat of embarrassment at her own shrew-like behavior lingered despite the little voice in her head telling her she'd every right to be upset. "I will gut him in his sleep."

"Ye will not!"

Domelch flew at her, her hand poised for a hard slap, but Ethne was done with this belittling treatment. She grabbed the larger woman's wrist and shook her hard. Ethne was no longer a weak child but a strong woman, and she was more than willing to show Domelch that.

"Do. Not. Touch. Me. Again," Ethne said. Tears thickened her voice, but she gritted her teeth. Damn emotions! She'd be breaking down at any moment. Then Domelch would laugh at her as she always did. Uradech would take that as encouragement to do whatever he wanted. And her brother, Malcolm, would just sit there and expect his sister to submit.

Her gaze bore into Domelch's face, her hand squeezing the woman's wrist. When her arm began to shake, Ethne knew she was about to break. Something moved beyond Domelch. Ethne caught a glimpse of Lachlann.

He stood near the entryway behind everyone else, watching the scene unfold. He crossed his arms about his broad chest, his gaze intent on her. He winked.

Her breath caught in her throat.

He smiled, followed by a slightest dip of his head.

He was encouraging her?

She turned her focus back to Domelch and threw the woman's hand down so hard that the she stepped back in fear.

"Now, sit back down so that I can finish my work."

Uradech's mouth hung open.

Seeing that, Ethne added, "And keep yer puppy at yer side."

She reached toward Finn, and he took her hand, his mouth agape as well. Together, they went out of the cave. No one spoke behind them. Not even Malcolm.

CHAPTER 15

*L*achlann remained at the cave entrance. Guarding the lass. Ethne needed some time to herself and he would insist if needs be. Niall and Aldred proved to be most entertaining, taking Domelch's attention off her sister-in-law's rebellion.

When Ethne finally returned, there were no tears in sight. She resumed her duties, and no one said a word. Not a word of reprimand, warning, or concern. In fact, no one said a thing.

Lachlann gathered from Uradech's downtrodden expression that he expected any marriage plans might be forestalled because of the woman's obvious dislike of him, or until they were able to coerce her. Even though Lachlann had only the slightest knowledge of Ethne, he was fairly certain coercion would not be a simple task.

Seeing her standing up to that bully had been amazing to watch. Her proud demeanor, a vision to behold. It set Lachlann's heart afire. She was like a captured animal breaking free of its binding, racing across the open glen. Or some hawk's prey that managed to work its way out of the deadly talons to live another day.

Breathtaking.

Now, he had a hard time taking his eyes off her at all.

When she removed the loaves from the iron pans, he was right there to offer her a cloth to protect her hand. And when she lifted the fifth bucket of boiling water into the tub, he helped her to lift it that last little bit to empty it just as her arm gave out. She looked exhausted. They worked her hard.

He didn't notice Niall taking the few steps closer to him until his friend spoke.

"Ye best not be following in Aldred's footsteps." Niall's low voice was intended for his ears only. Niall's eyes looked about as if he wasn't speaking to him.

Lachlann merely glanced his way. "What are ye on about?"

Ethne beat the cream in the deep clay jar, her entire body moving with the motion. Lachlann licked his lower lip.

"That." Niall was staring at him now, piercing him with widened eyes and raised brows.

"Ye are speaking gibberish." Lachlann glanced back at Ethne, who wiped her hair from her face.

Niall gripped his arm. Hard. "Look at me."

Obligingly, he faced Niall, but Lachlann deeply resented the man bothering him right now, and he didn't bother to hide his irritation. "Why?"

"Ye've not let the lass out of yer sight."

"Not true," Lachlann said, but when he turned to search her out again, Niall moved to block his view so they were again eye to eye.

"Aldred is taken to task every time he behaves like a lovesick little puppy, and *ye* are the one most strongly admonishing him." Niall's face was tight.

"Aldred is out for a quick tumble with no care for the lass, and *that* is what I object to."

Niall shook his head. "Ye're enamored with her."

Lachlann opened his mouth to defend himself, but no words came to him. His shoulders dropped, and he slammed his lips together, snorting like a bull. His face heated. Either from embarrassment because it was true, or irritation at the suggestion. He wasn't certain which.

"She's beautiful." Niall's matter-of-fact tone, though still quiet, had lost its edge. "I can see why ye'd be attracted to her."

"Ye're seeing something that's not there." Lachlann sounded far too defensive so he took another breath and started again. "She's spirited despite the way she's treated. She's stronger than she realizes."

"She's a virgin."

The word hung in the air between them, but Lachlann refused to address it. It mattered little since she would be another man's wife. Although he doubted it would be Uradech. That man had no abilities at all that Lachlann had seen. But then again, it didn't matter what he thought since no one sought his council.

"I've no interest in the lass. Ye are wrong." Lachlann hadn't meant to sound quite so emphatic. "Where is Aldred?"

When his search of the cave stopped on Ethne smiling at Finn, who growled like some fierce animal beside her, Lachlann couldn't help but smile despite the gnawing worry about Niall being correct.

"Lachlann, I—" Niall said.

And Lachlann didn't care.

"Is that a bear, I hear?" he asked, feigning fear and totally dismissing Niall.

"It is!" Ethne beamed up at him as he approached.

Lachlann settled beside the boy. "I canna tell what type of bear ye are."

"I've never seen a bear." Finn's face scrunched up in his confusion. "What types are there?"

"Well..." Lachlan lowered his voice. He glanced around before leaning in closer. Ethne's scent drifted to him, and he stilled. She was lovely, her eyes bright with excitement, delicate lips slightly parted, her breath gentle on his cheek.

Niall was wrong.

Lachlann turned his gaze to Finn. "I have heard of bears as white as the snow."

"No!" Finn's exclamation came on a sigh of disbelief.

"Tell us," Ethne prompted.

Lachlann's gulp was painful. "They're to the north. Far, far north."

"By the lights," Finn said. "Have ye ever been there? Have ye ever seen the lights?"

"Oh, no. Not me." Lachlann shook his head as if afeared to even consider the trek. "I am not a wild man."

He moved in close and tickled the boy. Finn laughed and rolled onto his back.

Ethne laughed at their antics. "Ye are verra entertaining, Lachlann."

When he turned to her, she mouthed the words, "Thank ye."

His chest tightened, and despite his dismissal of Niall's wild accusations, Lachlann knew he was in trouble.

Ethne kept to her work within the cave and waited for a chance to make her way back to the fair unnoticed. It would be there another sennight, but the rains were coming. The clouds were even now heavy on the horizon and the ocean full of foaming swells. Many merchants might choose to move farther south to their next stop where the weather would be dryer, rather than tolerate these coastal storms. If that happened, the castle would be the only place she could seek help, and they did not like the "pagans" coming too close. She doubted she'd even be able to make it through their gates.

"Ethne, I canna find my brush." Domelch whined in a

loud voice, showing her true colors since it was only her and Ethne in the cave.

"'Tis where ye left it." She brought it to Domelch.

The woman was having a harder time sitting down and getting up now that the babe had dropped, although Ethne doubted she had noticed. Even her favorite stool could only accommodate by Domelch spreading her legs so the bulge that was her child could hang unobstructed between her thighs.

"Do ye need me to see to yer hair?"

"Aye." Domelch gave her back to Ethne, who settled to her knees to work through the tangled tresses. The puffiness of the woman's face was only getting worse, as were the dark circles under her eyes, and Ethne was concerned about the babe.

"I've seen to yer dress if ye'd care to wear the green one today."

Domelch mumbled something incoherent.

"Did the babe keep ye awake again?"

Domelch had not mentioned the child's movements lately. She did love to complain about every little ailment. Mayhap the constant attention from their guests kept her mind too busy to complain, although Lachlann preferred to play with Finn. They were inseparable. The lad would miss him when he was gone.

"'Twas the pains here." Domelch rubbed her lower back, stretching slightly.

With a firm hand, Ethne rubbed the tight area. "Does that help?"

"Aye," Domelch said. "I hope I am able to make the celebration."

Ethne stiffened. This was the first time the woman had mentioned the event that was to mark her own marriage to Uradech. Since the outburst, no one had spoken of the marriage. Or the celebration.

"If the green dress is ready, that would be the perfect time to wear it." Domelch turned to add, "Wash it well."

The *léine* had been washed, but Ethne said, "I've nothing to add to the water. We were to get that at the fair."

The large woman sighed in disgust. "Nothing?"

Keeping her voice unconcerned, Ethne assured her, "It will be fine. I will use the fresh water."

"It will not. It will stink," Domelch barked her unhappiness.

Ethne kept at the tangles even when she noticed Domelch glancing toward the opening where Malcolm sat out of ear shot. He was working at repairing the tears in their fishing net.

"Ethne?"

The whisper was unexpected, and she moved in closer. "Aye?"

"Ye could go yerself. Get the flour and the lye. And anything else ye need."

Excitement tingled all the way to the tips of her toes, but she forced her breath to remain steady. She didn't want to reveal her excitement. "I dinna believe Aidan will be pleased with that. Did he not say we were not to return?"

Domelch batted at the air. "Yet he leaves his wives there." She snorted, glancing again toward the opening. The men moved about, helping Malcolm to spread out the material as they searched for more holes that needed mending. "No one needs to know."

Their eyes met. Ethne dared not breathe. It was exactly what she had been hoping for, a chance to get to town and find someone to help her get away from these people. What would she do? Where would she go? She squared her shoulders. "If ye wish me to go for ye, Domelch, I will go."

The woman's green eyes rounded and she tsked. "But

ye'd need protection. Aidan would beat me if anything were to happen to *ye*."

An odd statement, and Domelch seemed to have changed her mind. The quieter she got the more Ethne wanted to scream at her. She hadn't anticipated this, and disappointment tightened her gut.

"I do not need protection." Ethne tried not to sound desperate. "I will take care and not call attention to myself."

Domelch's disgusted gaze traveled over her. "I think not."

Ethne had planned to walk hidden among the bushes and trees, off the traveling paths. Olaf was the only one she was afraid of running into, but he'd said he was going away. Her breath quickened. Her chance for escape was at hand. She had to believe in herself. Believe she'd be able to look out for herself once she was away from these people. Believe she could find someone willing to help her, mayhap allow her to do work for them.

"I can take Finn." She blurted out the words without thinking them through. Truth was, bringing him would make it easier for her. She would not need to come back for him. "I think that will be enough."

"He is a child, Ethne. Besides, Malcolm wants to keep Finn with him this day."

Ethne was devastated, her heart squeezed tight. She shouldn't be surprised. Nothing about this would be easy. "I didna know of that plan."

"He's promised to take him to Aidan's so he can see Niall's horse."

The silence dragged on as each of them tried to work out the dilemma. When Ethne was about to suggest again that she would cover herself and avoid attention, Domelch's eyes lit up in excitement.

"Uradech can take ye."

Ethne's stomach dropped.

CHAPTER 16

Repairing the nets went quickly and Lachlann enjoyed the work. Malcolm left them alone on the rise to go down to secure his *currach*. A storm was brewing. Lachlann looked out over the ocean and imagined the islands that lay far off the coast. Too far away to see.

"The waves look mean." Aldred's gaze searched the horizon as well. "Did someone not tell us the islanders come here often."

"To what purpose?" Niall's contemplative tone required no answer but Aldred shrugged.

"There's a power struggle for the area," Lachlann said. "Malcolm explained as much to me. The keep we stayed at has been captured by the Danes, the Norse, and the Scots. The area is under no one's control at present."

"Verily, the islanders wish to stake their claim as well," Niall said.

That made sense. The Norse Kingdom might have stretched as far south as the River Spey and beyond, but that was a distant memory, only kept alive by the bards and storytellers.

Niall continued. "Some islanders may come on their

own and for their own purposes. Like our wounded man in black. Our would-be horse thief."

"Olaf. He and his men were verra well trained for simple travelers," Aldred said. "Do ye not think they were here to stir up trouble?"

"And just disguising themselves. Verra good!" Niall acknowledged his pleasure at the answer with a dip of his chin and a widening grin. "Mayhap their warriors are deserting the islands, looking for a new home. Or mayhap they were sent ahead by their leader to bring back information."

"Aye, like scouts before an attack."

Lachlann scoffed. "I think not. Leastwise not that man. He'd been speaking about some woman so we have no reason to believe it was any more than what it appeared. The man was drunk."

"Mayhap he'd been ordered out of the group." Niall laughed. A wry sound. "I hear that happens for many different reasons."

He referred to his own father's unspeakable offense, and his somber tone confirmed it. His entire family had been cast out of the clan, even his little sister. For them, it had been anything but a humorous situation.

"Well, ye enjoy yer trip to Aidan's." Uradech's voice interrupted them. The mere sound of it grated on Lachlann's nerves. He had come up behind them unheard, which was surprising for such a large man.

"Are ye not joining us?" Niall asked.

"Ah, no, I have my own duties this day."

Something about the way he said *duties* set Lachlann on full alert. He turned to study the man. Uradech's shoulders were back, his expression pure gloating.

"I dinna hear about yer duty." Niall smiled. An amicable smile. One ye would give a friend or ally. But Lachlann assumed he was only giving Uradech the opportunity to elaborate on this duty, an opportunity he was so obviously looking for.

Uradech beamed as he spoke. "Aye, well, I need to see Ethne to the fair."

Lachlann's entire body tightened.

"Today?" Aldred voiced their surprise. Malcolm had just mentioned they would not be returning to the fair. When they pressed him, he would not say why.

"Aye, today. I'll be there to see to her, be her protection." He nodded. With his puffed-out chest and smug expression, his extreme sense of importance was easy to read.

Lachlann would like nothing better than to wipe that smug expression right off his face.

Instead he crossed his arms about his chest and said, "Well then, she'll have no protection at all."

Niall tensed beside him, but Aldred cracked a huge grin.

Uradech's mouth dropped open before he slammed it shut, his nostrils flaring. "Why, ye arrogant little sod. She's to be my wife."

Lachlann stroked his bearded chin, the course stubble rough against his skin, and puckered his lips in a mock display of searching his memory. Then a shake of his head, a slow shake, not intended to be convincing. "As ye say. Yet I've heard no such thing,"

"Lachlann—" Niall took a firm grip of Lachlann's arm.

Lachlann ignored Niall's warning tone and yanked his arm free. He stepped closer to Uradech. Though Uradech was a large man, Lachlann towered over him, his own broad torso nearly touching Uradech's flabby chest.

"And if the words are not from the lady's mouth"— Lachlann's smile was tight—"ye're blowing hot air."

Resisting the urge to shove the man on his arse again, Lachlann faced him down, but this time Uradech showed no resistance. He just shrugged and sauntered back toward the cave. A very unrewarding encounter. Lachlann would have preferred to beat the man.

"Was that needed?" Niall finally asked, his lips in a flat line.

"I believe so." Lachlann frowned at his friend. "Since when are we men that allow a woman to be mistreated?"

"Slav—" Niall interrupted, but Lachlann pressed on.

"She. Is. Malcolm's. Sister. Not a slave."

"Then as Malcolm's sister, he has the right—a duty even—to see her wed," Niall said.

Aldred came closer. "And they're going against Malcolm's wishes by going to the fair."

"This doesn't sit right with me." A strong sense of foreboding filled Lachlann's chest, but the set of Niall's jaw told him there'd be no help from either of them. "We should not be remiss. She has no one else who will look out for her."

"Ethne has her brother. She does not need us." Done with talking, Niall turned to follow the path Uradech had taken.

Lachlann preferred not to go against Niall, but he could not let Ethne be put in harm's way like this. Why could they not see she was in need of saving? When he and his friends reached the cave, Uradech was seated on the ground outside and puffed up like a peacock, sharpening a short dagger against a stone.

Lachlann snickered. "Do ye even know which side to use?"

"I'm quite good." Uradech peered closely at the blade, lightly swiping the edge with the pad of his thumb. "I've an effective thrust as well."

When he lifted his gaze to Lachlann, the man's arrogant smirk left no doubt of his meaning.

"It'd be a shame if ye lost a hand…or anything else."

Uradech paused, holding Lachlann's steady gaze, then

said, "Aye, *my wife* would surely be saddened by such a loss."

Aldred's hand gripped Lachlann's shoulder, holding him back when he wanted to charge the man. "We should go inside."

"We can break our fast." Niall led the way with Aldred right behind him, but they paused at the entrance when Lachlann didn't follow.

Lachlann didn't move. "I pray someday ye find a *willing* woman to take to wife. Mayhap she'll accept yer *great* ability."

Uradech merely shook his head and chuckled.

Lachlann's blood began to boil. "Do ye find humor in that?"

"Yer jealousy? Aye." Uradech stood, his shoulders back and his double chin jutting out. "Ye show yer weakness, *pilgrim.*"

"I have no weakness." Lachlann struggled for composure at the slight, his rage simmering just below the surface. "Nor do I force myself on women who have no interest in me."

"Ho, ho, is that it then? Can ye not find yer own women?"

That challenge released the dam holding back Lachlann's anger. He got in Uradech's angry face, but the man kept his belligerent stance so he punched the fat man squarely in his arrogant jaw. "Ye'd better guard her well."

As he growled the warning, Aldred yanked Lachlann's arms behind him. He strained so hard against the restraint a sharp pain stabbed his side. "Damn ye!"

Niall shoved Uradech out of harm's way. The newly sharpened blade dropped to the ground between them.

"Let me test yer mettle, Uradech," Lachlann yelled over Niall and ignored the annoying hand he started waving in his face. "If ye're found wanting, ye'll have me to answer to."

"Lachlann!" Niall yelled. "Aldred, let him go."

Before Aldred could respond, Lachlann jerked his arm loose to wipe at the sweat dripping against his tunic. Instead of water, blood smeared his hand. His knees buckled slightly. "What the hell?"

"He's injured ye," Niall said.

"I dinna mean to. It was an accident." Uradech's whining protest was as muffled as Niall's voice.

"Ye stay put!" Niall shoved the fat man, who dropped to the ground.

Aldred yanked at Lachlann's tunic. "He didn't lie. He does know how to sharpen a blade."

Niall assessed the wound. His hand came away bloody.

"It's nothing." Lachlann's voice came from far away.

"Ye need to staunch the flow." Uradech ripped off his own tunic and shoved it at Niall. "Here."

Niall pressed the material firmly against Lachlann's side. "'Tis not that bad."

"What is amiss?" Domelch came from within the cave, Finn just behind her, and hurried to her brother. "Are ye hurt?"

The blood dripped down Lachlann's leg to puddle on the ground. His world darkened around him as he slumped to the ground. "Not as hurt as he soon will be."

Ethne's concerned expression as she ran toward him was the last thing he saw.

*L*achlann was burning up. Try as he might, he couldn't seem to remove himself from the fire. Loud voices carried to him, knocking against his brain, and someone groaned.

"Whisht." A woman's voice.

He knew without opening his eyes that she was lovely, and the sound of her voice soothed his aching head.

"Drink this," she said.

When he moved to raise his head, pain shot up his side.

"I'll do the work." She supported his head with a cool hand under his neck. The bitter taste against his lips and the foul smell had him coughing uncontrollably.

"Easy now. Just a bit. 'Tis all ye need."

When he gagged at the taste, her chuckle had him questioning her role. Was she seeing to him or was she the source of his discomfort?

"Ye laugh at my pain?" he asked.

"Ah, so ye are among the living?" It was Ethne. She was worth opening his eyes for. Her tone had been light, but her deep frown spoke of her concern. "I was afeared our Uradech was a greater warrior than we knew."

Lachlann turned to search out the man in the room, but sharp pain stabbed at his temple, stilling the motion.

"Oh, none of that now. Keep yer head still." She put the foul-tasting broth to his lips again. "Get a little more of this into ye, and the pain will ease."

With that promise, Lachlann forced down as much as she gave him.

"Verra good." She smiled, moving a refreshingly cool cloth about his face.

"I heard voices. Where are the others?" Lachlann asked.

"They've left ye to my tender care. Ye'll sleep now, but I'll be here by yer side."

He grabbed her wrist, the damp cloth still in her grasp. "Promise me?"

She stilled and searched his face. "I promise ye."

A large blaze heated the cave, but still Lachlann shivered. A heavy skin covered him, the fur soft against his bare torso.

"How is yer head?" Ethne swished a cloth in a pan of water.

He turned slightly. "Better. As ye had said it would be."

"If ye can eat, ye'll feel even better."

She squeezed the soaking material and leaned over him again to follow the curve of his face with the warm cloth. His eyes closed in pleasure, and he moaned.

"Now that sounds like a man over the worst of it." Her breath was warm against his face, and her voice was pleasant to his ears. Comforting.

He wanted to keep her talking. "Where is everyone?"

"My brother has taken yer friends to Aidan's as ye'd planned. Finn is sleeping."

His eyes flew open. "'Tis night time?"

"'Tis night time *again*. Nearly daybreak."

"I have slept so many days?"

She shrugged, focusing instead on the cloth that soothed him.

"My friends care so little for me that they left me here?" He made light of the situation. "But ye stayed by my side." He held her gaze until she lowered her eyes. The coverings suddenly seemed a bit too warm, and he pushed them down around his hips. His side still burned. "Did they, at the verra least, make sure I would live before they abandoned me?"

Ethne chuckled, gliding the refreshed cloth across his bare chest and the designs prominently displayed there. "Well, Finn was so concerned about ye that he missed the chance to see yer horses."

Lachlann watched her, her eyes on her work, not noticing him looking at her.

"But aye, the bleeding had stopped, and I was able to secure the poultice. That is the pain ye feel in yer side."

Wetting her mouth with a swipe of her tongue, she rubbed her lips together. When she let out a long, slow breath, his discomfort was quickly forgotten.

He studied her, the quickened breath and mesmerizing motion. "And how long will I have this pain?"

When their eyes met, her hand stopped. "Ye should be careful not to rip it open."

He glanced beyond her where Finn slept beside the fire, no doubt having fallen asleep waiting for her to be done caring for his wound. "Did Domelch go as well?"

"She decided to join them at the last minute." Ethne dropped the cloth into the bowl. With a single finger, she traced the roundness of the impressions on his skin, the straight lines crossed like feathers on the shaft of an arrow. "Where did ye get these markings?"

"I do not know. I have always had them." He looked around him. "Is my satchel about?"

"Aye." She picked it up from the side of his pallet and handed it to him. "Niall left it for ye. I placed it safely beside ye."

He opened the sack and rummaged within. The cold medallion was easily located on the bottom, and he pulled it out, holding it by the thick chain.

"Ah, the standard of yer father's clan." She flashed a grin.

He turned his gaze from its twisting length and smiled back at her. "Of sorts."

The shifting light revealed she again had that expression of awe.

"I'd not thought of it as such, but I'll admit I find great comfort in the thought."

"As ye should."

His chest tightened with the truth of her words. Slowly, he nodded but words refused to come.

"He was yer sire, yer family, yer clan." With her hand on top of his hands, she fisted his fingers around the precious metal. "Best to keep it safely tucked away."

"Ye're right." He put the medallion back where it belonged. "My thanks for keeping it safe."

The perfect opening to ask of her own knowledge of valuable items but he shoved the thought aside. Instead he gently fingered her hair behind an ear. "Ethne?"

She looked at him with complete trust in her eyes.

"I want to kiss ye." Lachlann could barely catch a breath, for how strong this "want" was.

Her eyes clouded for the barest second as if distracted by some troubling thought. But then she took a slow intake of breath. Acquiescence?

"Come to me," he said.

After the slightest hesitation, she lowered her soft lips to his, then lightly kissed him. She lingered there above him, smelling like a warm summer day. When he slid his hand up her bare arm, goose bumps spread across her smooth skin.

She sat back up and smiled.

"It was as I feared," he said, shaking his head.

Her eyes rounded in distress. "I did it wrong?"

"Oh, no. Ye were fine." He slipped his hand beneath her heavy hair, drawing her toward him again. "But it didn't satisfy my desire. It only made me want more."

The flash of a smile, and then she kissed him again. And again. Each one longer than the previous one. Each one gentler. Each one more frustrating for him.

He couldn't read her emotions this time but she didn't move away. Instead she sat back, remaining close enough for him to still touch her.

"Forgive me. I have wanted to taste ye since the first time I met ye calling for Finn at the fair."

Her eyes widened in her innocence. Innocence. Virginity. He gasped in frustration, confronting himself with where he was going with this...this...seduction.

Her concern was immediate, and she leaned close, checking his pallor. "Is it yer side?"

Why did she have to look so lovely with the firelight behind her? Her gentle touch on his skin was driving him mad.

"I am fine. I will rest as ye said." He indicated her pallet. "Ye should sleep as well."

Unable to turn his body away because of the wound, he closed his eyes and crossed his hands over his racing heart. There was no way he'd be able to sleep, but he didn't move until he heard her quiet retreat.

What was Niall thinking to leave him alone with her like this? The man knew how he felt toward her. Niall should have realized what might happen. Did he believe Lachlann had the control of a monk?

He growled deep in his throat.

"Do ye need something, Lachlann?" Her sweet voice carried to him from her pallet where she lay.

He clamped his teeth, then blew a breath, puffing out his cheeks. He decided not to answer her at all. Best if she believed he was asleep. Never had his hands, his entire body ached so, urging him to set aside his chivalry and test the desire smoldering in her eyes. A need she probably couldn't name. No, it was better to find an experienced wench to see to him. Soon. As soon as they were done here. As soon as they found the silver, returned it to the priory, and were done with this. As soon as he could get Ethne out of his thoughts.

It would be another full day before any of the others returned to the cave. A day of pure hell for Lachlann. Finn came to sit beside him in bed, shoulder to shoulder, because Ethne insisted he stay there. His wound barely throbbed and his pent-up frustration was near unbearable. He needed to be up and about. And away from the temptation that she was. If she cared at all about his need to get out of bed, it was well hidden. Every time he broached the subject with her, she would not even consider allowing him to get up. When she started to feed him, he had had enough and pushed her hand away none too gently.

"I am able to feed myself, Ethne." His forehead was tight, partly a result of the ongoing throbbing behind his eyes, but much more from the irritation at the situation. That included her sitting beside him, her thigh warm against his. Close enough to touch, but out of reach. "Ye said yerself 'twas a small scratch."

"I never said scratch." She stood, the food left forgotten on the ground between them, and crossed her arms. Stubborn.

Finn turned to him. "She never said scratch."

She gave Lachlann her back after a flash of an I-told-ye-so look and returned to the fire. He whispered to Finn, "A lot of good *ye* are."

The lad shrugged. "Then I won't tell anyone about the kiss. How would that be?"

Lachlann stilled. The boy's expression showed no surprise, no judgement, no feelings one way or another from this unexpected witness of Lachlann's gut-wrenching debacle.

"If ye were awake, why did ye not say anything?" Lachlann asked.

"I dinna mind ye kissing Ethne." Finn shrugged again. "I would like it if ye took her to wife. She would take good care of ye. She takes good care of me."

Lachlann couldn't help but smile at the way his young mind worked. Finn was correct, of course, but he and his friends were not there to see him married off. They were there to find hidden silver and bring it back to Restenneth Priory. He would probably never see Ethne or Finn again.

His chest tightened at the thought. He put an arm about the boy's small shoulders, hugging him against him, and whispered, "That would be fine if ye kept the kiss to yerself."

Watching Ethne work about the cave, seeing to the cooking and the cleaning, maintaining the food stuff and returning with what she had gathered from the forest, making this cold, damp place a welcoming home, Lachlann swallowed past the lump in his throat. Finn was correct. She would be the perfect lass to see to him. He required little: food, care of his few belongings, a willing woman to warm his bed at night, or whenever he sought her out.

She stomped over to retrieve his untouched porridge.

She scoffed, adding over her shoulder as she left, "So glad I am that ye can feed yerself."

Unrepentant, he bent close to Finn's ear. "Can ye collect the painted pebbles for us to play with? And some of those berries Ethne likes so much?"

The lad's face lit up, and he nodded with great enthusiasm, wiggling to the edge of the pallet then running toward the door.

Ethne frowned. "Where are ye off to?"

"Surprise!" Finn called from beyond the cave entrance.

She snorted again, but barely glanced Lachlann's way. She was piqued at him in the extreme.

"Ethne." He waited, but she showed no sign of answering him. "Forgiveness, please. I am not a good patient. Ask Niall. Even ask Aldred."

A disparaging glance his way, and she was back to her endless mending. "That's obvious to anyone with eyes in their head."

"And ye've been so kind to me. Verra patient. I do appreciate all ye've done."

She stopped her busy hands and lifted her gaze toward the ceiling as if considering what to do. He hoped he'd chosen the right words that would make her forget her angst.

"Come sit by me," he said.

She blew a breath, but his patience was quickly fading.

"Sit with me or I will get up on my own."

She glared at him. "Do not!"

"Then come." He patted the spot Finn had left. "Sit by me. I grow tired of my own thoughts."

With a grump, she came toward him. "I have much to do, Lachlann. Domelch will not be happy with me if—"

"She does not hold ye in high regard."

Ethne laughed. "Ye've noticed."

"I notice everything."

She ignored that last comment and settled against the

wall, keeping their arms from touching, but he could feel her relaxing. He turned to her. "I am verra grateful for yer care."

"I know ye are. Ye are a good man, Lachlann."

When his gaze dropped to her lips, she shook her head. "That was a mistake. We were both exhausted."

He looked into her eyes, searching for that desire he'd caught a glimpse of earlier. It was gone. "I will not kiss ye if ye say nay, but it was no mistake. I waited a long time. I watched and I waited. A verra long time."

"Then what stopped ye?" Ethne's wise expression told him she knew the answer. "Mistake or not, 'tis in the past. Let us leave it there."

"Ethne, come quick. 'Tis Momma." Finn stopped in the entry, his face covered with dirt and tears and his tunic stained with berry juice. "I think she's dying."

Ethne's thoughts scattered, but she took Finn's little hand and followed where he pulled her. Hard as she tried to make sense of what he was saying, she could not understand how Domelch could have fallen into any harm. She had left only a few moments behind Malcolm and the others to meet Aidan. They would not have gotten any farther than the rocky ledge just before the upper glen. When Finn led her across the grassy hill instead of toward Aidan's round house, her heart sped up. This was the path to the fair.

"Dear God, no!"

Lachlann was little more than a breath away. "Did she speak to ye, Finn?"

Finn shook his head, his speed never lessening. When his first try at answering came out garbled, he struggled with his voice. "She didna know me."

The scene they came upon was of Domelch, sitting in

a pool of sticky fluid speckled with blood, perched up against a rowan tree. Unconscious. Finn held back to take Ethne's hand, and Lachlann went to her, obstructing their view.

"She has breath," Lachlann said, his tone steady. A good sign.

As if in answer, she moaned.

He added, "I'm not certain about the babe."

Ethne lurched forward and dropped to her knees beside him. With the lightest touch, she pressed against the swell. Domelch groaned something incoherent.

"I am here, Domelch. I will help ye." Ethne moved her hands in search of the baby's head. What she found instead was a small shoulder lodged awkwardly where it should not be. God alone knew how long the woman had been sitting like this, trying to deliver a babe that was stuck. With practiced hands, she pressed against Domelch's side.

"What is she saying?" Finn cried. "I canna understand her."

Lachlann turned to the boy, who kneeled on the other side of Ethne. "Being born is not easy, Finn. Ye have done well to find her."

Try as she might, Ethne could not remember the last time the babe had moved, and she feared for the worst. A small lump dragged against Domelch's side and Ethne winced at the moaning woman but continued to encourage the shifting babe.

"I need to see to her," Ethne said, meeting Lachlann's concerned gaze with a meaningful glance of her own.

He stood and offered his hand to Finn. "Let us give them some room."

"I dinna want Momma to die." Finn wailed, clasping himself to Lachlann's leg.

"I will do my best," Ethne promised and hoped she would not be sorry to have said it.

Lowering her to the ground, she bent the woman's knees and lifted her skirt. The head was now visible. She sighed in relief.

"Yer child wishes to be born."

The tight grasp of the woman's hand on her wrist startled Ethne. Nearly as much as Domelch's next words. "Do not let the baby die."

"I will not! Glad I am that ye can hear me." With the lightest touch, Ethne searched the curves along the baby's face for anything gone awry. All was as it should be. "I need yer help. Can ye push?"

"I've *been* pushing. All for naught."

She rubbed Domelch's leg in a comforting way. "But I am here now. I will help ye."

The contraction was powerful enough that she feared for the babe. If the cord had wrapped around the little neck, it would never survive. Domelch stopped responding, but there was definitely a sudden bearing down from her.

With a firm hand, Ethne turned the tiny shoulders and gave the slightest encouragement to clear the tight grasp of Domelch's body. The child slithered into her hands. A girl. She quickly wiped its face, holding its body against her and near to her mouth. There was no breath. Silent tears slid down Ethne's cheeks.

"Come now, little one. Let me hear ye sing." She tapped a cheek. Then her back. And finally, her chest. "Sing yer beautiful song for me, lass."

Nothing. Ethne repeated the process, each time with a firmer hand. The little face puckered so slightly she couldn't be certain she hadn't imagined it, but kept her eyes on the delicate features. Then the child's expression crumbled, and she let forth a loud, strong wail.

"Thank, God!" Ethne held the tiny body against her own for added warmth.

Lachlann was there beside her, followed by Finn. The

boy's wide grin when he looked at his little sister made Ethne's tears drop even faster.

Finn wrinkled his nose. "She's loud."

"A good thing," Lachlann said, accepting the little bundle without hesitation so that Ethne could see to Domelch.

The rest of the ordeal went without any problem, and Domelch soon stirred, accepting the water Finn had run to get for her.

"Does the child live?" Domelch clutched at Ethne, her eyes wide with sudden concern. Ethne might have been wrong about Domelch's desire for this child. But when the little girl let loose a wail, the woman rolled her eyes and Ethne knew she had not.

"The babe is hungry." Lachlann placed the babe in Ethne's arms, a gentle smile on his face.

The flash of what this moment could mean if it were *their* child—Ethne's and Lachlann's—flooded her mind. Her heart clenched with a deep need, but quickly shifted to pain. She was overwhelmed with sadness. Such a thing could never be. But if it could, he would be the man she'd want it with.

She cleared her throat and simply smiled her thanks, too overwhelmed for words.

He returned to Finn, who had lost any interest in the goings-on. Now that he was a hero and had done well finding his mother and she would be fine, he wanted to get back to the game Lachlann had promised him.

Once Domelch was settled back in the cave, the child fed and resting in her arms, Lachlann refused to get back in his bed, but allowed Ethne to check that the wound did not bleed. He then proceeded to see to her instead, getting her some warmed mead and a blanket. The air in the cave had turned chilly as soon as the fire went out in their absence.

"I wonder where she was going along that path." Lachlann settled across from her, sipping his own mead.

Ethne considered whether she should share what she knew. The urge to do so was strong. With a start, she realized how much she trusted Lachlann and his judgement. Not a good thing to feel toward someone who would be leaving soon. She refused to consider how his rejection would feel if she asked him to help her escape. Besides, Niall and Aldred did not seem as forthcoming as Lachlann. They always kept their distance from her.

"That's the road to the fair," Finn said from Ethne's pallet where he had gone to lay down. "I wonder why she dinna take me."

Lachlann's gaze questioned her. Did she agree? She gulped, assessing whether trusting him actually required her sharing this with him. She decided it did.

"She had wanted me to return to the fair. There was something she wanted me to get."

"Ah, and that was when Uradech would have 'protected' ye." Lachlann's tone had turned bitter. Very bitter. His lips were tight while he shook his head. "That man could have done nothing to protect ye."

His anger seemed...unusually strong.

"But he harmed *ye*. The pain so great, ye could not stand." She had no idea why she had the sudden need to protect Uradech. She had no liking for the man.

"He is not a good protector. He is slow on his feet. He seeks his own pleasure."

This odd conversation was causing all sorts of emotions to chase around her head like squirrels in spring. All that was missing was their inane chatter.

Suddenly all the thoughts stopped save one: Lachlann was jealous.

That was the only explanation for this talk. He wanted her to look to him for protection. Sudden heat flushed her face.

He stopped. "What is amiss?"

She shook her head, afraid to speak. Afraid to move. Afraid to believe such a ridiculous thought. The great warrior turned man of God, seeking to protect the never-quite-good-enough slave girl? Ridiculous.

His nostrils flared. "Do ye doubt me?"

She shook her head and said in a quiet voice, "Never would I doubt ye."

Something was there in his eyes, something she couldn't name.

"'Twas not the pain that made me drop." He averted his gaze before facing her again. "I do not tolerate the sight of blood well."

Finn giggled. Lachlann and she both turned their eyes to him. He shrugged, still giggling. "But ye are a great warrior!"

The man's embarrassment at the condition was obvious, but she found it endearing. Too much so. She found the idea absurd as well.

"It must make for difficult battles," she teased, barely holding her smile in check.

"Ye may laugh, but it makes me an even better fighter. A more determined fighter."

"More determined? That ye not make them bleed?" She openly laughed at that, but quickly covered her mouth.

Lachlann's scowl shifted to a grin. "That they drop dead without delay and I can continue with my attack. I seldom miss my mark."

I seldom miss my mark.

He was correct in that. He had not missed with her. If love were only about trusting, sharing, and desiring... then there would be no doubt she was in love with this man.

CHAPTER 18

"*D*oes yer side still pain ye?"

Standing beside the cave's entrance, Lachlann ignored Niall's question. He crossed his arms about his chest and studied the wispy clouds making their way across the bright blue sky. Although his friends had returned to check on him, they had left him behind and that decision gnawed at him. As did his lack of progress in learning anything about the silver. As did his inability to deny his attraction to Ethne.

Niall poured himself some mead and came alongside him. They had returned the night before to check on Lachlann's condition. "I said, does yer side still pain ye?"

"Ye didna need to leave me here." He slammed his mouth shut and glanced toward the fire where Aldred distracted Domelch with his chatter, but no one looked their way.

She had recovered quickly from the birthing and was enjoying her slightly thinner frame, dancing about the fire after a long, luxurious bath. Malcom snored beside Aldred, oblivious.

"A few hours and I would have been strong enough to travel."

Niall laughed, but no one paid them any attention. "Ye think much of yerself."

Lachlann struggled to control his gut-wrenching frustration. He grumbled, "The wound was nothing I could not have ignored and well ye know it, but my thanks for coming back to see if I still lived."

"Aldred and I had to convince Malcolm 'twould be best to find out what was taking ye so long. He was quite content to remain at Aidan's."

Domelch twirled about in her green *léine*. The gold trim at the neck and wrists and her silver earrings twinkled in the firelight.

"A fine garment and a fine figure of a woman." Aldred said, smiling brightly and sounding as if he meant every word.

"My thanks, kind sir." Domelch smiled at him, dropping into a quick curtsy, then accepted the crying babe from Ethne and settled beside her husband.

"Do ye not agree?" Aldred asked, elbowing the sleeping man none too gently.

Malcolm awoke with a start. "Ah, aye. Aye! Of course. My Domelch is a beautiful woman. Ripe breasts that beg…"

The words drifted off as he did the same. His cheek pressed against Aldred's shoulder made Malcolm look near dead instead of asleep. Aldred raised his shoulder with another sharp jab at the man. Malcolm jerked awake again. "And how well she is adorned by her generous husband."

Leaning against the cold stone wall, right above the picture of the bull pierced with a feather tipped arrow, Lachlann laughed to himself. He didn't expect any information to be gained with these questions. Malcolm seemed to be drinking even more since they'd returned from Aidan's to find his daughter had been born in his absence. Surely it should be a source for celebration.

"How goes it?" Niall's whispered words came as he was about to take a drink.

"Think ye I was up and searching about? I was bedridden! Ethne's orders." Lachlann's face heated at Niall's disgruntled look. "Where is the great warrior that laid me so low?"

"He was sent off to ask Aidan for a postponement to their announcement."

Lachlann swallowed hard against the disappointment. He'd hoped this celebration was not intended as some type of marriage announcement. A ridiculous hope after all. He squared his shoulders. They needed to find the silver and be gone.

He spoke in the same hushed tone. "The walls along the pictures have a few crevices, but nothing large enough to store a treasure."

"Since we don't know the size of the treasure, how large would it have to be?"

He shrugged, forgetting his irritation for the moment. "Not even big enough for a small stash of coins. I've not searched further."

"Returning to Aidan's will gain us more time here if one of us can remain behind to search." Niall stepped away. After refilling his mug, he sat down beside Aldred.

"And yer own lovely child at her...bosom." Aldred never grew tired of laying it on quite thick. "Does that not make her more beautiful in yer eyes?"

Malcolm's pained expression was so fleeting that Lachlann questioned his own sight. That would be an odd reaction even from a drunken man. Then again, both he and his wife had shown little interest in the babe. Just the opposite of Ethne.

His gaze sought her out. As expected, her bright eyes were on the child. But Lachlann was alert to Ethne's every move ever since their kiss. That sweet kiss left him wanting so much more. He cleared his throat.

"Mongfind." Domelch whispered the name in the child's face before resting her against a shoulder for a jostling burp, which came quickly.

"Will there be a naming ceremony?" Niall had been showing a keen interest in everything about this group since their return from Aidan's.

"Aye! She is named for a princess and will be offered at the solstice observance."

Offered? Odd way to refer to a naming ceremony.

Uradech chose that moment to return and announced that Aidan would wait no longer for the celebration to begin.

Domelch turned a wistful gaze on her child, gently stroking her tiny head, then handed the babe back to Ethne and sat up straighter. She pushed against Malcolm. His narrowed gaze spoke of his disgruntlement.

"Are ye certain ye should be going to Aidan's?" Discontent laced his tone as well. "Mayhap ye need rest."

Domelch groaned before answering. "I can rest no more. I have little pain and do not want to miss the celebration. Think ye Aidan is a patient man? The babe will be fine for a short while without me. Is that not right, Ethne?"

Lifting her eyes from the babe, Ethne frowned. Lachlann would swear she'd not been listening. She'd had all of her attention on Mongfind. Ethne had been quiet since the others returned, but it could be simply because the babe required so much of her time.

Only Finn had been able to rouse much of a response from her whenever the child was in her arms.

"Ethne seems capable," Lachlann offered, receiving a quick smile from her.

"Are ye ready?" Malcolm staggered slightly before finding his footing.

"We best not be late." Domelch rolled her eyes. "I have but a few hours to myself."

"Ethne, will ye not be joining us?" Uradech asked, darting a glance toward Ethne, his hand thumbing the ends of the rope tied about his waist. He avoided looking directly at her or Lachlann.

"Not yet. She'll be seeing to the sleeping child." Domelch placed two milk-soaked cloths beside Ethne. "Let us hope she does not awaken before daybreak."

"Dinna forget to empty the tub." Domelch threw the comment over her shoulder as she went into the cool night.

~

Ethne had laid the sleeping baby a short distance from her and was seeing to the latest catch of fish. Her slow movements revealed her exhaustion. Finn snuggled against her, his head on her lap, not minding that she was constantly moving.

"Can I help ye with some of that?" Lachlann asked.

She jumped.

"I didna mean to startle ye."

She gave a little laugh. "My mind is tired. Picking these tiny bones is making my eyes close."

He settled beside her, their knees almost touching where they sat cross-legged on the ground. He picked up the last fish, its mean bones still poking out from it. "We dinna have this type of fish where I live."

"No?"

"They have smaller eyes and a longer fin, the same white insides."

She nodded, stifling a yawn as she worked.

"Are ye sorry to be missing the celebration tonight?"

Ethne stiffened. "I prefer to stay here with Finn."

"And me and my friends have given ye an added burden."

Their tribe had been very welcoming, giving no date

that they would expect Niall, Lachlann, and Aldred gone by. Even including them in this celebration, though they didn't mention their inclusion in the solstice observance.

She simply smiled at that.

"Ye are often here? Just the two of ye?"

"And now it will be three," Ethne said.

"Ach," Finn said, picking up his head to look at Lachlann. "And that is when the big white bear comes to us."

He spoke in the same low tone that Lachlann had used earlier when they were playing.

"A big white bear is it now?" Lachlann asked, his gaze on the child. "And what do ye do when the bear comes by, scratching and growling outside?"

"What should we do, Ethne?" Finn's voice had grown serious. "The bear is out there."

Ethne's hands stilled, and there were tears in her eyes. "I dinna know what to do, Finn, but we canna let the bear have at us."

Lachlann's chest tightened at her pain. He had no idea what they spoke of.

The boy seemed to understand her sudden sadness and wrapped his little arms around her neck. No doubt it had nothing to do with hidden silver, but for the life of him, Lachlann could not turn away.

A light hand to her shoulder, he asked, "Tell me what I can do."

She shook her head, the movement sending her unshed tears rushing down her cheeks. Finn pulled back to look at her. "Ye must tell him."

She held a finger to his lips and shook her head.

The lad's expression turned angry. "Ye told me he would protect us."

She reddened and looked away.

Something Lachlann couldn't name bloomed in his chest. "Ye tell me, Finn."

"Do not!" Ethne was as near to yelling at the boy as Lachlann had ever heard.

He asked, "How can he not, when I am to protect ye?"

Ethne turned a warning eye on the boy and said, "Finn, I should not have sa—"

"Do not lie to the boy." Lachlann shook his head.

She opened her mouth, but no words came out.

He turned back to Finn. "Tell me. What is this thing that frightens ye?"

"Ethne?" Someone called from outside the cave.

Finn cringed, his expression crumbling into fear.

"That's Uradech," Ethne said, regret apparent at her unchecked outburst.

"They dinna say he would come back for ye."

Lachlann went to the entrance, ready to face the man coming through the opening. Uradech's expectant expression darkened as soon as he saw Lachlann standing there.

The man hesitated, then moved past Lachlann to approach Ethne, remaining a few feet away from her as if she were a goose about to squawk at him.

"Aidan is asking for ye," Uradech said, breathing heavily.

Ethne stood, laughing, a hollow sound. "Did ye run the entire way?"

His face red from exertion, Uradech nodded. "I came to escort ye to him."

Lachlann squared his shoulders and moved between the two of them, narrowing his gaze at the man. "Ye can return to them. I will bring her if she chooses to go."

Uradech leveled his gaze at him, assessing him. "How is the pain?"

The man seemed to speak with a new confidence, a new sense of purpose.

"A scratch. No more."

"Good." Uradech seemed to expand his chest. "I was concerned with ye ending up bedridden."

Lachlann locked his jaw. He'd prefer the man not have known quite so many details about his injury and wasn't about to set him straight. He merely said, "Not truly necessary."

One questioning brow rose, and his gut tightened, but he added, "Ethne is verra thorough in her care of a wounded man."

The cheeks that had barely lost their ruddiness from exertion flushed to an even deeper red. It was a moment before Uradech responded, "So, I've decided to bring Ethne to Aidan myself. I dinna believe we should ask any more of ye." His expression hardened. "Ye are only a visitor here, after all. Ye'll not be staying."

Finn's reaction to Uradech's arrival seemed to confirm Lachlann's suspicions , and although there was more happening here than he was privy to, he had cause to intervene.

"And I am happy to do what I can for people who have been so kind and generous to me." He indicated Ethne, who once again sat beside the fire surrounded by fish that still needed salting, a babe moving a short distance away, and Finn's wide-eyed expression. "She is not ready as of yet."

"Please return to Aidan's. I dinna want ye to miss anything on account of me." Ethne sounded breathier than usual.

Uradech was about to object, but seemed to think better of it. Turning about, he stopped at the door without facing them. "I am not certain I appreciate ye being here alone with her."

"Finn is here," Ethne said, her tone outraged.

Uradech left, but his comment had the desired effect. She looked uncomfortable now.

Finn still cowered, so Lachlann bent close and said, "Show me yer fiercest scowl, bear."

"Grrrrr." Finn scowled and raised his hands, making his fingers like claws. "I'll rip yer stomach out."

Lachlann beamed. "A fine bear ye'd make."

"And I'm a rich bear! So, I will rip out yer entrails and throw them into the water for the gulls."

Lachlann fell back. Odd detail. Ethne's shoulders had rounded again and that irked him. He would not have her so downtrodden. "Did ye wish to go to the gathering so soon?"

"I have no choice if Aidan is asking for me."

Following orders was her life. She deserved much more. He said, "Tell me what ye would have me do. Shall I go to Aidan and make yer excuses?"

She laughed. "Ye sound as if I am a woman of great importance, declining an invitation. I am just their slave. I must follow what I'm told."

"Ye should not be a slave. Malcolm is yer brother." Lachlann's ire rose at the wrongness of her situation, but he squeezed his jaw closed before he said too much.

"And ye see how much that matters to any of them." She sighed, a defeated sound.

Finn came to sit in his lap, breaking the awkward silence. "We want to stay here."

She turned a genuine smile on the boy, then on Lachlann. "I must go, but I need to see to the tub first."

The large wooden barrel sat a few feet from the fire, several large wooden panels acting as a screen to block the bather from view and ward off any drafts. Domelch and Malcolm had made use of the tub, then offered it to Lachlann, Niall, and Aldred. No one had been as considerate to Ethne.

Lachlann said, "They have been remiss."

"How so?"

"By not offering ye the use of the tub."

Ethne sneered.

"Shall I watch Finn so ye may do so now?" he asked. "The babe is still asleep."

Her face lit up with excitement, but just as quickly it faded. "I best not."

Lachlann added the last bucket of hot water beside the fire to the tub. "I disagree." He bowed low to her. "Yer tub awaits ye."

Finn quickly accepted the hand he offered, and they went outside together, leaving her to her ablutions.

The gloaming was nearly upon them. The air was heavily scented from the large, yellow lily blossoms just opening. There was a chill in the air. Finn led him to the clearing farther down the path, and turned to him with a fierce scowl. He growled and crouched down, low and menacing.

"Are ye a bear attacking me?" Lachlann asked, appearing shocked right before ducking into a defensive posture himself.

Finn growled louder, his hands curled into claws. They paced each other in a small circle, the boy's short *léine* making it easy for him to move about, darting and retreating.

"I am a wealthy bear, and I'm here to rip yer throat apart," the lad said.

A fair offense, Lachlann nodded. "And I'll stop ye so ye canna hurt me or anyone I love."

He raised his arm to ward off Finn, ignoring the minor tug at his wound. It was well on its way to healing. The boy understood and jumped at him, then rolled onto the ground, rebounding.

Trying not to smile, Lachlann surged ahead, a pretend dagger in his grip, but Finn was too fast, rolling away to land on his feet. Hunching forward, he advanced again. This time, Lachlann spun out of harm's way. Turning about, he ducked low. Finn did the same, forgetting the growl as they acted out their attack and defense. The boy never tired, his gaze intent on his prey. When Lachlann shifted to one side then the other, Finn repeated the gesture, very quick on his feet. He lunged at Lachlann, who held the lad while they dropped to the ground. They rolled until Finn was on top, Lachlann allowing his attacker a fleeting moment of success.

The silver coin flashed from beneath the heavy material of Finn's *léine*. When Lachlann stilled, Finn "slashed" his curved fingers toward Lachlann's face before jumping off and landing on his feet.

"Ha! I marked ye, and I'll do so again," Finn announced just before jumping on top of Lachlann again.

Wind whooshed out of Lachlann's lungs, but he caught the boy by his waist. "Ye are a wealthy bear."

Finn gasped and scrambled away, grabbing at the item hanging from a leather strap around his throat. He backed away, still working to shove it back inside and unseen.

Lachlann stayed on the ground, but leaned on an elbow, watching him, trying to assess the fear reddening his young face. He must have been told the coin should remain hidden. Was it by Malcolm? Or Domelch?

No.

There was only one person who gave any guidance to this child.

"Dinna worry, bear, I will not steal yer wealth from ye." Finn looked ready to bolt and Lachlann hoped to calm him down. "I want only to take yer hide."

Jumping to a standing stance, he crouched low and grabbed Finn by the middle to lift him high in the air. The boy laughed in enjoyment, his fear subsiding. Lachlann laughed as well, depositing him on his feet and breathing hard.

"Mayhap yer aunt has finished with her bath?"

Finn shrugged, the incident forgotten. "I have never known her to use the tub. How long should it take?"

Every woman loved a bath. Her treatment was even worse than he imagined. The weight on his shoulders doubled, and the dread in his heart grew even thicker. "I think we have given her enough time, my little friend. Let us return and see."

CHAPTER 19

*E*thne lounged in the tub, her under gown plastered against her skin, and leaned back her head. The panel perched alongside the fire kept in the heat surrounding the tub and the sleeping babe in her basket tucked against the low cave walls. Her long, damp hair swirled about her while she idly rubbed the cloth along her arms. It felt wonderful to be clean, and the warm water was a luxury she'd not enjoyed since childhood.

If Domelch ever learned of this, Ethne would probably be beaten. The shame of having to bare her bottom to receive such treatment was not something she wished to relive. That was no doubt the point of the humiliating treatment. She'd only been beaten twice. Etched on her brain, she remembered each event in great detail.

Domelch had been ordering Ethne around and gotten fed up with her lack of respect, or so Domelch said. This was early on, and Ethne had yet to realize how useless defending herself would be. And the threat of a beating? That did not make Ethne more submissive; it made her more defensive. Malcolm had spoken up once he realized his wife planned to actually beat her. He tried to help

Domelch see reason, but strode off when she refused to back down, leaving Ethne to the woman's mercy. And she'd had none. The reed burned Ethne's bottom so bad she was unable to sit for two days. Finn had been a baby then, easily roused to crying, so her constant need to pace had settled him down.

She was much older when Domelch had again taken a reed to her. She never understood what she had done wrong; she only remembered that her menses had started. Her clothes were too tight from her burgeoning curves. The changes disgusted her and when Domelch yelled at her, she started to cry. Aidan had sat her close to him and stroked her hair, speaking to her in a quiet voice. He'd never done that before. But that hadn't stopped Domelch. She took great pleasure in striking her with slow, deliberate whacks that left no place unbruised. The hard beating left her bedridden for a week. Slipping between sleep and wakefulness, Ethne had heard strange voices discussing her condition. Her brother's voice had been one of them, raised in anger at Domelch. He'd forbidden her to ever beat Ethne again.

Startled awake, Ethne leaned forward. Had she heard something, or were her drifting thoughts affecting her? The babe hadn't moved. Mayhap Finn and Lachlann were returning. She had no idea how long they'd been gone, but she climbed out of the tub. Wrapping the cloth about her, she paused, dripping water on the ground, to listen for another footfall.

"Lachlann?" Ethne called.

There was no answer.

She briskly rubbed herself before wrapping herself up again. Her *léine*, well-worn and still stained with mud from the river and the encounter with Olaf, did not look appealing.

A footfall carried to her. She jerked her head toward

the noise. There was definitely someone outside. Her heart started racing. She had to hurry.

"One moment." Hidden behind the panel, she doffed the clean, soaking shift. Better to let it dry so she could wear the clean undergarment later tonight.

A quiet sound, but much closer. With her filthy *léine* in her grasp, she stilled. Too close. She forced out her breath and refused to turn around to see if someone truly stood right behind her.

"Finn?" Her voice trembled.

"Well!" A throaty sigh. "I see I have been given a beauty indeed."

Her body tightened at that voice, but she refused to cower. Pulling the *léine* against her like a shield, she turned with a scowl on her face. "Uradech. Ye should not be—"

"Should not be what?" His eyes bulged in his outrage. "Taking what is mine?"

He'd never spoken so forcefully to her. She swallowed down her sudden fear.

"I will not be taken to wife by ye." She spoke with more confidence than she felt and spread her fingers along the edge of the material to hug it about her breasts. "I have said as much."

His eyes narrowed, assessing her, right before his face split into a huge grin. He moved steadily closer. She backed away, matching his movements. That confident smile petrified her, making her even more desperate to keep him at bay.

"Yer brother says otherwise." Uradech stopped. His gaze traveled along her body, an expression of appreciation settling on his face. "We discussed it just this night...with Aidan."

She gasped, the material slipping from her fingers, but she grabbed it back. "I dinna believe ye."

He darted forward and laughed when she retreated just as forcefully, hitting her head against the low ceiling. He was a cat playing with a mouse.

"Why do ye think I ran the entire way?" His gaze fell to her bare legs where the material did not cover her entirely. "I could barely wait to have at ye."

Using her most commanding tone, she said, "Leave me. I will be out anon, and we can discuss—"

"No!" He shook his head, a slow, deliberate movement, his eyes bright with excitement. "There will be no discussion. Ye are mine."

His hand traipsed along her bare shoulder while her back scraped painfully along the cave wall. She could move no farther.

"The pilgrim's interruption is the only thing that stopped me from making ye mine." His tone was quiet and firm.

She trembled inside, but scoffed, "And he'll stop ye again."

"He is busy with the boy." Uradech fingered the material covering her, his eyes darting from it to her, before following along her shielded curves.

Cringing, she glanced beyond the huge man. There would be no one to rescue her this time.

His gaze settled on her face, piercing her with his eyes. "I think I prefer the consummation this way. I want to see my wife. All of her."

He yanked at the only thing protecting her from him, but her fists squeezed the thin material as she fought against his strength. "I am not now and will not ever be yer wife. I promise ye that."

It became a tug of war, and she struggled to remain hidden, but he yanked hard enough to pull her from the wall. Still, she resisted, shifting about the cavernous space. There were no weapons here, none to move toward in a last-ditch effort to protect herself. She shoved the panel toward him, but he sidestepped it. Panic grew in her chest, increasing with the steady rise of her breathing. Clenching her teeth, she fought with all that she had. She was the stronger of the two. He was nothing but a fat man who sat on his arse all day.

He stalked her. When she faltered in her step, he was right there to claw up the material. Within reach, he raised a hand to grab her, but she regained her footing and shoved him, all of her weight behind the movement. The material ripped from her hold. When it slackened, he lost his balance.

Stumbling back, he crashed onto Domelch's prized stool. A terrible crack sounded as it buckled beneath his great weight. The babe started crying.

Ethne wasted no time. Retrieving her gown, she jerked it over her head, covered herself, and wrapped her arms around the child. Certain the man would lunge at her at any moment, she backed away until the cold, rough wall was once again behind her. The only thing that supported her. She took a deep, shaky breath.

Uradech did not get up.

Her steady rocking continued even when the babe drifted off again. She held her trembling hand to her mouth.

The fire crackled. She jumped. The child slept on, unaware

The sound of people talking outside came closer, and she recognized Finn's voice. He and Lachlann paused in the entry way. Taking in the scene before him, Lachlann's face tightened. "What is amiss?"

"Uradech came back?" Lachlann asked the question, but the answer was right before him.

The cave was disheveled. Items strewn around the

place, the privacy panel broken on the floor, and the flames leaping toward the ceiling. Ethne cowered against the back wall with the babe clutched to her chest, her eyes wide with fear. The huge body of Uradech lay on the ground between them. Unmoving.

Lachlann realized why. "He came back for *ye*."

"He said Aidan sent him to me. I was to be his bride, and he was to tak—" She turned her face away, as if in denial of what lay before her.

Aidan had given the man permission to rape her. Outrage at Ethne's treatment tightened Lachlann's gut. He gave a solemn shake of his head, unable to hide his disgust. With an insistent tug and great care, he took the babe from her arms to settle her back in the little basket before facing Ethne.

"Did he hurt ye, Ethne?" She didn't seem to hear him. "Ethne, look at me. Did he hurt ye?"

She covered her mouth and finally faced him. "I was sore afeared he would force me and…"

Lachlann opened his arms to her and she came to him without hesitation. Tight against him, she trembled. He held her close and rubbed her back, watching the man for any sign of life. "I dinna know. I took Finn to the water to play. I dinna mean to leave ye unprotected."

The attack must have just happened, and that was galling. A moment sooner, and he'd have been able to protect her. And he had no doubt it had been an attack. One with their chieftain's blessing.

She stiffened against him and pulled away. "Is he dead?"

Lachlann went to the body and squatted beside the man. He searched the body, ignoring the puddle of blood growing steadily beneath it. No breath. Uradech's eyes stared out. Lifeless. He eased them closed and offered a prayer for the soul of the miserable man, asking forgiveness even as he thought the unkind words, though he knew in his heart they were true.

The injury, and the source of the blood, were easily located. His side, sticky even now, had been pierced through with a shard of wood as big as a man's arm. Lachlann noticed the stool for the first time, poking out from beneath the large man. It was surprisingly easy to piece together what had happened, but his experience with the group told him how the man's sister would react. That it had involved Ethne would make it so much worse.

She had no color. Her fear was undeniable, just like the fear of the quaking little boy who came to stand beside him as soon as Lachlann stood. The rhythmic sucking of his thumb was the only sound. This was too much.

Lachlann hefted the lad up into his arms and crossed to Ethne. She held Lachlann's gaze, her eyes a depth of confusion and terror. Panic. When the boy reached out to her, she finally saw him, and her expression softened. She accepted the bundle without hesitation.

"Finn," she said, her face crumbling into tears.

The boy ducked his face into the crook of her neck, crying as well.

Lachlann had an unexpected tightening in his throat. He wrapped one arm around Ethne, who trembled against him, and rubbed Finn's back with large strokes intended to comfort.

"Do not be afraid." He said the words in a gentle voice, but her eyes had glazed over. "I will see to this."

Guiding her to the entrance, he blocked her view of Uradech. Getting her safely outside and away from this scene took priority right now.

Smelling of horses and covered with dust, Aldred filled the entrance. Lachlann's relief at the unexpected arrival of his friend was quickly overshadowed by the events. His jaw tightened. It looked bad. It *was* bad. When

Aldred took in the scene, his expression quickly changed from confusion to anger.

"What...?" Aldred asked, including all of them, but when his piercing gaze settled on Lachlann, no words were required. He shook his head in answer to the unspoken accusation. It was not his doing. Aldred's deep sigh filled the small space, his shoulders rounding in relief.

"I realized the sly fox had sauntered off." Hands on his hips, Aldred indicated Uradech with a tip of his chin. "When I asked Aidan about it, he only smiled, and then I knew where he'd gone. If I'd been able to catch up with him, this—whatever this is—might have been avoided."

That didn't surprise Lachlann and his hands fisted. Aidan might be considered their holy man, but it never occurred to him to protect Ethne.

"It couldn't have been avoided." Lachlann spat out the words in his fury. "He was bent on this."

Finn trembled and Lachlann immediately regretted his outburst. He blew out a hefty breath, but it was useless. His greatest desire was to find Aidan and take a fist to the man.

"Can ye see to them? Mayhap get them some water from the spring?"

The blond gave a stiff nod of his head. His reluctance to abandon Lachlann to handle all this on his own was there in his taut mouth and the way he glanced over his shoulder more than once as he led Finn and Ethne into the night air.

Alone in the cave, Lachlann questioned what he needed to do next. The man was dead. The church believed seeing the man buried in hallowed ground was of the utmost importance, but Lachlann was having a hard time sorting out the purpose for such insistence, especially when he was fairly certain Uradech did not agree with those teachings. Nothing could be done for the dead, but the living he could still help. Ethne deserved to be seen to first.

He grabbed the woolen blanket then joined the others. They sat in the clearing amid the high grass and under an open sky. A crisp night with only a few clouds and a smattering of stars just starting to twinkle.

With a gentle touch, he wrapped the material around Ethne's shoulders, being sure to include Finn, who had nestled close to her, nose to nose with the resting babe. Her appreciative glance lightened the heavy weight on Lachlann's shoulders, and he smiled back. He cleared his throat and went to stand beside Aldred, who squatted quite a distance from them, his expression one of intense concentration.

"Did she say anything to ye?" Lachlann kept his voice too low to carry to her.

"Finn *said* the two of ye went off to play and came back to the dead man." Aldred didn't hide his disgust. "Is that what happened?"

"Uradech came while we were gone. Aidan had sent him back to do his husbandly duty." Lachlann ground his teeth in disgust, his nostrils flaring before he continued. "Willing or not."

Aldred scowled before turning his face away again.

"I need ye to go to the others," Lachlann said. "Tell them there has been an accident. Daylight will be soon enough for them to return safely."

Aldred showed no sign of having heard him, no indication he would do as asked. He just…squatted there.

It was difficult to think clearly. All Lachlann knew was that Ethne needed someone to look out for her, someone she could trust. "I will remain here with the three of them. See to them."

With an unexpected amount of impetus, Aldred stood. His shoulders back, his face a mask of fury, he said, "And what will ye do then, Lachlann?"

Lachlann drew back at the outburst and frowned. "As I said, I will see to them." He kept his voice steady despite his friend's accusatory tone.

"How far is it ye will go to 'see to them'? Shall we be honest? Ye will see to *her*."

Lachlann struggled to hide his irritation. "They've both suffered."

"Had a shock?" Aldred laughed, his face turning heavenward before glaring back at Lachlann. "Finn had a shock. He saw a dead man. A man he knew. A man he may or may not have cared for." He scrunched his face in disgust. "*She* had no shock. *She* committed murder."

"Murder?" Lachlann glanced toward them, but neither showed any sign of having heard Aldred's angry outburst. "'Twas an accident. The stool leg pierced his body when he fell on it. Ye saw how he treated her. He was waiting for a chance to get to her. I left her unprotected, and he found his chance. I dinna know how far he was able to get."

"Stop!"

If his friend had suddenly punched him in the face, Lachlann would have been able to make more sense of the man than he could right now.

Aldred tipped his head. "She is not Thomasina. Ye know that, do ye not?"

"I dinna underst—"

"Ye do! I'm afeared for ye. Ye've fallen hard for a lass we know little about, yet ye're willing to defend her, to make excuses for everything she does. As if she is a lass deserving yer protection."

"She *does* deserve my protection. Not only mine. Ours! She deserves *our* protection." It had been a night of revelations, and this side of Aldred was pushing Lachlann further than he wanted to go. "Ye've seen the way she's treated just as I have."

"We've come to locate the silver, not to come charging in to save anyone."

"How can I not?" Lachlann took a slow breath, steadying his desire to feel the fat of Aldred's cheek against his hard fist. "Ye and I are not alike. Ye dinna feel about things as I do. I try to respect that. I ask that ye do the same for me. Will ye do as I ask?"

Aldred's lips tightened into a flat line before he answered. "Do I tell Domelch that her beloved brother is dead at Ethne's hand?"

Clenching his teeth, Lachlann was glad for the darkness so his friend would not see the intense anger in his expression, churning up from the more intense anger deep in his chest. "Tell them there has been an accident and ye're not sure what happened, but they need to come back as soon as possible. I dinna want ye to lie."

"That is a lie."

Lachlann squared his shoulders. Counted to five. Nothing worked. He yanked at Aldred's tunic, pulling him up close to his face. He spoke through clenched teeth. "Ye are being an arse. Now, do as I told ye and dinna stray from what I've said."

The whites of Aldred's eyes gleamed in the darkness. He was livid and didn't speak until Lachlann allowed his feet to again flatten on the ground. Even then he pulled at his chest, readjusting his crumbled tunic before he finally spoke. "I'm afeared ye'll take the blame, Lachlann."

Lachlann said nothing. He hadn't considered that. He hadn't thought that far ahead. He hadn't thought of how to proceed at all, he'd only been reacting.

"There'll be no help for ye if ye do." Aldred all but bristled. "We've nothing of value to give them for the man's life. If they take ye as a hostage, we'll have to travel back and beg Niall's uncle for mercy and his help. And that man is a selfish whoreson who'll probably reject us outright."

Aldred was jumping ahead, and that wasn't helping. Lachlann needed to focus on the battle at hand and said nothing. He noticed Ethne standing behind them, the babe asleep in her arms and Finn beside her.

"I hope she is worth it." Aldred stomped off, avoiding Ethne's questioning glance.

"Lachlann?" Her eyes rounded in confusion. Even she could see the man's anger. "Where is Aldred going?"

"Let us sit." Lachlann waited until she was settled to answer her.

"He's gone to tell yer brother and Aidan. They will want to know what happened." Lachlann let go of his breath and asked, "Can ye tell *me* what happened?"

She turned a surprised look at him. "But I told ye."

"Specifics, Ethne. I need to know exactly."

There was the flash of a frown right before she started. "I was getting out of the tub, changing into my filthy *léine* so my underdress could dry." She faced him, her eyes glazed as if she were no longer seeing him but reliving the events. "Uradech came toward me, tried to pull the gown out of my hands, but I fought him. He stumbled back and…fell."

"And his purpose was to force himself on ye?" Lachlann studied her hand where it clenched his knee, her nails ripped and broken. "Ye didna want him to touch ye?

It seemed obvious to Lachlann, and even considering the possibility that Uradech had some right to her was ripping his heart right out of his chest. "Ye never agreed to it with the others? With Aidan?"

She frowned at him.

"He was nothing to me." Her voice angry. "I didna wish to be married to him. I didna want him to touch me." When Finn shifted at her loud voice, she smoothed his hair.

"But yer brother? And yer chieftain made the match

for ye?" Lachlann's throat was dry. "Are ye not to obey them?"

"My brother? My chieftain? They dinna care for me. A fortnight ago, they'd have given me to some islanders! I must get away from them. All of them." She glanced at the child. "I fear I am not long for this life."

I'll have her now whether ye say aye or nay.

The drunk from the fair. Olaf was an islander.

Ethne was right. They would put her to death for the murder of Domelch's brother. Even Malcolm could not save her, even if that was what he'd want.

"Listen to me." Lachlann waited until he could look her in the eye. "Ye must not contradict what I tell them. Ye. Must. Not."

Her brows lowered, a deep ridge between her eyes, but he held a finger to her lips so she couldn't interrupt him.

"He returned for ye and we argued. Him and I. Do ye understand? I ordered him to go back to the others, but he refused. We struggled. He fell against the stool."

Her eyes pleading with him, Ethne shook her head.

"'Tis the only way. I will not see ye put to death for this. That man dinna deserve such a sacrifice as ye."

"And what of ye? 'Twill be the same." Her expression tight, she turned away. "Ye should never have come here. Ye should never have gotten involved with all this."

He took a deep breath, stretching his shoulders with the action, then blew it out. A sudden and unexpected peace filled him. Peace? In all this mess? Aye. There was no other word for it.

"Not true." He knew he was doing the right thing, even if she couldn't see it. Even if Aldred couldn't see it. All she had to do was agree with him. Surely, she could do that.

Lachlann turned her back toward him. With a single finger under her chin he lifted her face to his.

"If this is my purpose in life, so be it. I swear to ye that if I had known he was in there, that he was trying to force himself on ye, I would have killed him myself and not by accident."

When he kissed her, her eyes drifted shut. A gentle kiss. A kiss meant to convey her worth to him. He pulled back and her lids fluttered open.

"Defending ye would be my honor. Do not doubt it."

CHAPTER 20

"That man never liked my brother." Domelch stabbed a finger toward Lachlann, paying no attention to the sleeping child precariously balanced in the crook of her arm.

Lachlann agreed about that, but it wasn't without reason. He swallowed down his ire and schooled his features.

The tribe had gathered in Malcolm's cave, moved Uradech's remains from inside, and been going back and forth about his murder for hours now. They refused to even consider it might have been an accident. He recognized the group assembled around him, hanging on to Domelch's every word. The same men they had fought alongside of at the fair against Olaf. That seemed a long time ago now.

"Uradech told me Lachlann was sniffing after his Ethne and more than once he'd interrupted their consummation."

Sniffing? Hardly. *His* Ethne? Never. Lachlann shifted uncomfortably on the hard floor of the cave where he'd been directed to sit ever since they returned in force from Aidan's. His emotions in check, the inner turmoil not so much.

He had told his story of what transpired while Niall and Aldred sat a short distance away, their bodies taut as they listened intently, though they appeared stone-faced.

Neither offered anything.

Not in his defense. Not in his guilt.

No doubt they kept to the themselves so they wouldn't reveal what they might have planned in case things went further awry. Lachlann prayed they had a plan.

"He came upon them just the other night!" Domelch's high-pitched voice startled the sleeping child, and crying ensued, but that didn't stop her rant. "He said Ethne had been kissing him when she was here alone with him."

Lachlann stilled, holding his breath, and willed his face not to get any warmer. The man had to have been guessing. Either that or he'd stood in the dark and watched rather than confront him. Coward. Lachlann turned toward Ethne. Their eyes met, but he couldn't tell what she was thinking. Finn, once again tucked against her side, winked, and Lachlann struggled not to smile at the show of support. At least someone was still on his side.

Aidan asked, "Did Uradech not injure the man? Was that not the reason his betrothed came to be here alone with Lachlann?"

Finally, Aidan rolled his eyes as the wailing baby got louder. "See to that child, woman. Ethne! Assist her."

"Aidan"—Malcolm advanced closer to the man —"there was bad blood between the two. He had been insulted by Uradech just that morning."

"How so?"

"Uradech didna believe they were pilgrims. He questioned everything about them being here."

It was getting harder and harder to sit quietly. Damn! He wanted to speak up.

"I have spent time with these men on the way here. I

found no deceit in them." The chieftain's sweeping hand indicated all three of them.

Lachlann's eyes locked with Niall's, who showed no indication of what he was thinking. If the tribe discovered who they truly were, there'd be no chance to save Lachlann.

"Too many outsiders puts us at risk!" Talorc scowled. He seemed far too young a man for his thinning hair. "We need to tread lightly here, Aidan."

By Talorc's tone Lachlann guessed that was some sort of warning. Apparently, everyone else understood that because they all nodded.

"*Nothing* about this will disrupt our plans," Aidan assured, his face a mask of fury at such insolence.

"There is always disruption," Domelch grumped, handing the fed baby to Ethne like a pile of wet clothes. "And now, my dear brother is dead!" She turned to Niall. "What say ye about yer man? Was he not lusting after Uradech's betrothed?"

"Domelch." Malcolm's warning tone was unmistakable. "Have ye not interfered enough?"

The dramatic shake of her head was followed by a shifting away from her husband. His warning ceased her contributions. Thankfully. The woman was far too observant.

Aidan turned the question to Niall. "What say ye to her claims?"

"We've given ye no reason to doubt our word, not any of us."

Aldred nodded as well, and Niall continued.

"I believe it happened the way Lachlann described it. He is not a man prone to prevarication. If he says it was an accident, I believe him."

With a solid intake of air, he sighed his relief. He was glad to hear some defense of him.

Malcolm said, "Mayhap we should finish the

preparations for the body and come back to this on our return?"

"I am in agreement." Aidan stood, indicating one of his men to come forward. "Tie the man up."

Lachlann squared his shoulders, a fine sheen of sweat immediately covered his face.

"What?" Niall straightened as if ready to jump to his feet, but seemed to check himself, his shoulders rounding instead. "Why must ye tie him up? He has done nothing wrong."

"One of our own is dead." Aidan seemed confused, glancing to the others for confirmation. "Yer man has confessed to the killing."

Niall's head shaking quite vehemently gave Lachlann a good bit of comfort.

"An accident. No malice intended," Niall said, his voice louder.

"They were fighting over a woman. How far the fighting went, and how aggressive yer man got, is what I will decide on. Until then, we will keep him secured so that our laws are followed."

"If I take responsibility for my man, can ye trust me with that?" Niall asked.

"No." Aidan shook his head. "I would not expect ye to stand by and watch him be sentenced to death."

Lachlann cleared his throat with some difficulty.

"Death?" Niall's eyes flared with indignation, his chest heaving. He jumped to his feet. "What law is this that would condemn a man in a fair fight, or an accident as Lachlann has said, to death?"

"'Tis our code. Ye have been here among us. Why would we follow a different law? We will not."

Niall was flustered. "We appreciate all ye've done for us, accepting us in and sharing with us what ye have."

Aidan nodded.

"But we are not part of yer tribe. Visitors only. And *we* have verra few laws that would put a man to death."

"As do we," Aidan said. "Murdering a man from the line of kings is such a law."

Lachlann's chest tightened with pain.

Silence fell over the group. Ethne's face had lost all color.

Niall tapped his fingers against his thigh. A sure sign of his mounting irritation. "Allow us to take Lachlann to the castle. Let us speak to the sheriff there."

"The castle is not *our* law and well ye know it." Aidan had spoken in a calm voice, and when he turned away, Lachlann didn't miss the tip of Niall's head.

Stand ready.

Aidan continued. "If we find Lachlann intended to kill Uradech, my sentence will be final. If I find him innocent, he will be allowed to leave. I would not want to put ye in a position that could lead to even more deaths. It is better if we hold him. He will be kept comfortable. Ye needn't worry about him."

A clear threat. Aldred shifted back toward the man closest to him, readying for an attack.

"Please!" Lachlann spoke to Niall and Aldred, although his eyes remained on Aidan. "I accept yer decision, and I believe my friends will as well."

Aldred's nostrils flared, his face tight as he shot daggers directly at Lachlann. They were not happy with this show of chivalry, but he continued.

"I regret Uradech's death, and I believe the truth will bear me out."

Thomas came beside him, a heavy, iron chain draped over his large hands and hanging to the ground. Lachlann held his breath, but didn't resist when the man secured his wrists behind him before shoving him toward the entry.

"Is that really necessary?" Niall's voice was tight with

unleashed fury. "The man has just given his word that he'll abide by yer laws, Aidan. Can ye not show him compassion?"

When Thomas yanked the chain, Lachlann pulled up short. Aldred made a sound of outrage behind them.

"This is the way of our tribe." Aidan indicated Thomas should continue. "And do not try to follow. We will keep him separate until after Uradech's burial ceremony."

The sun seemed brighter than usual as Lachlann was directed by way of shoving to a narrow clearing on the hill above the caves. Apparently, being a prisoner meant he could no longer be spoken to like a man; they would treat him instead like an animal.

Once they traveled up the brae, Thomas jerked him around to remove the restraints. Lachlann struggled to ease his mounting fear and gazed out at the beautiful sea, white with foam and breaking waves. The salty scent was fresh, stirring a memory from his childhood that he couldn't quite pin down. He rarely thought about his life before he'd been brought into Garnait's clan, before he'd been accepted into a family of eight children. He remembered so little of that time.

"Inside." Thomas barked the order and pointed to a hole in the ground.

Peering inside, Lachlann could make out little. He turned a questioning glance to the man.

Thomas indicated the opening with an angry gesture. The hole was barely large enough for a small man to go through. "Down ye go."

"Down?"

The man heaved an angry sigh. "Inside. 'Tis a pit, man."

The word alone sent waves of revulsion over Lachlann. Dark. Damp. Dank. Overrun with spiders and other creepy things. But he squared his shoulders. Raised his chin. "How do I get inside?"

Thomas kicked his legs out from under him and Lachlann landed on his arse. Hard. "Ye drop down."

Lachlann held back his angry retort. Left with no other choice, he turned onto his belly ready to drop down into the unseen abyss. How far before he'd stop, he had no clue. Something jabbed against his wound, sending shooting pain through his side.

"Hold!"

The man offered the end of the chain, and Lachlann grabbed it, a scowl on his face.

Thomas wrapped it around himself, digging in his feet before giving the signal to proceed. Not the most secure Lachlann had ever been, but he did as he was ordered. He hit the hard ground and stumbled, his shoulder smashing into a stone wall. He fell to his knees and looked up to the little bit of sky overhead, the opening too far to reach without an aid. The clamminess immediately swallowed him. The sound of the ocean was far off and muffled.

"What do ye think?" Thomas laughed. "Rest easy for now. If all goes yer way, ye'll be out in a few days' time."

"A few days?" Lachlann hadn't expected that answer or the man's biting laughter.

"And if I remember, I'll bring ye food and water. Ye might want to sleep to save yer strength in case I forget." Thomas's laughter faded as he walked away.

Lachlann rubbed his side, surprised to find blood on his hand. He inspected his skin. Something had pierced his wound and it was bleeding again. He glanced up at the thick roots and twigs sticking out of the earth.

He got a fire going. After he wiped the wound clean with his *léine*, it no longer pained him and he was able to get some sleep.

Despite Thomas's taunt, Lachlann was not forgotten. The tiny size of the cave made it difficult for him to stand upright except in the center where his food and water was lowered down to him by a rope. The ground remained damp, the cold adding to the miserable cramping that had started seizing him. A nasty aroma surrounded him, reminding him of the time Niall's sister, Thomasina, had thrown chicken eggs at the two of them. They'd been relentless in their teasing of her, but she gave back as good as she got.

By the second night, he was burning with fever and remembering far too much from when they were in their youth. His wound throbbed again and his body shook hard enough to rattle his teeth. He swore he heard a woman calling him, asking him if he was warm enough. In his delirium, he wasn't sure if it was Thomasina's voice or Ethne's. The past and the present collided in his mind.

"No!" Lachlann startled himself awake. The small fire had long since gone out. It seemed that had been quite awhile ago. He sat up to dig through the embers, not that he had anything more than a few twigs left to feed it, but he managed to keep it going.

Desperate now, he dragged his fingers along the floor in the darkness. He searched where he couldn't see and found a small stash of timber, ridiculously wet, and prayed for a miracle.

When the wind howled from his left, the stink increased. That must have been the sound his tired mind had turned into the voice of Thomasina. It would have been just like her to see if he needed anything, even going against any orders to do so. Wait! But that would have been Ethne who would have been ordered to keep away, and he did have some memory of her doing just that.

He pulled the small wool blanket—the only concession they'd made to the fact that he was not actually an animal—tight around as much of him as he could encircle and dropped to the ground. He'd convinced himself that the small rock protruding from the otherwise sandy ground was as soft as a pillow. He laid his head there now, having covered the stone with a portion of his *plaide*. His eyes drifted closed. He could see Ethne completing her duties, her hair disheveled about her shoulders. Her slim body moved as she worked the small needle, mending Domelch's gown, while sitting beside the fire.

What did she think about? Escape, no doubt. To a better life. His body convulsed, and he reached for the jug of water. It was empty. Mayhap she could now have that life. Mayhap even children of her own that she would care for just as she did Finn and Mongfind.

He didn't know how long he'd lain there like that, his head propped against a solid rock and his body shuddering, but he became aware just as the sun lightened the sky. It was a beautiful pink.

"Beautiful."

The wind whistled, and he heard the woman's voice again.

"As beautiful as Ethne's sweet smile."

CHAPTER 21

*E*thne was mortified. The funeral line went on forever and her brother and Domelch, who sobbed uncontrollably on his shoulder, were at the front. It wasn't bad enough that both had insisted Ethne stand behind them, in the place of honor as Uradech's betrothed, but they kept referring to her as such. And the funeral would last several days.

"Do ye need a hand?" Malcolm asked her over his shoulder as they ascended the steep hill to the funeral pyre.

"I am fine." She regretted her quiet tone as soon as he turned his searching gaze on her. "Really." She even offered the flash of a smile so that he would return to tending to his wife who was beside herself with grief.

It turned out Uradech was her younger brother, the one she'd always looked out for right up until the time she met Malcolm. The stories Ethne had heard over the past two days just shoved the stake further into her chest. She couldn't count the number of times she had to physically stop herself with a hand over her mouth so she wouldn't scream her confession at them. She was the one to end the man's life!

That they all suddenly treated her like...like...a

widow, acting as if she must be mourning the loss of the man, was too much. After everything she'd said and done to get him to leave her alone? She cringed. It was unconscionable.

She had not wanted to marry him. Not ever. Her life would have been a miserable existence had she been forced to do so. That did not change because the man was dead.

This guilt was the worst. Hearing Domelch in her bed and Malcolm's quiet words of comfort. It was all too much.

"Ethne?" Finn was gazing up at her, holding her hand. She hadn't even noticed him there. "Are ye sad?"

She smiled and nodded.

"I'm not." He whispered the words. No guilt in him. No shame. "Uradech was mean."

That was true. She hefted Finn into her arms and hugged him. He helped by holding her around the neck and wrapping his legs tight around her.

"Dear child, yet another thing ye need to keep to yerself." She said the words at his ear, glancing around to be sure no one had overheard.

They continued their trek across the glen, the wooden poles in the distance. The men would take Uradech's body and lay him across the logs on the top before starting a fire underneath. She'd been to a few of these ceremonies over the years, offering her own prayers to the one true God. It was out of consideration for Finn that she was usually able to stay behind, and she was fine with that. Not this time. This time they'd decided the lad needed to be a part of it. All of it. It was his uncle, after all.

When Finn got down, Ethne wrapped the blanket close against her, the wind blowing over their morose procession. A storm was coming. A strong one. It might rain for days. And poor Lachlann—poor *innocent* Lachlann—awaiting a trial for a crime *she* committed.

Every time she'd tried to find him, offering to bring him water or food, they refused to give her any information. Aidan had given each of them strict orders to keep her from seeing Lachlann. She was so desperate the second night when she found the food intended for him still beside their hearth. When she told Malcolm, she was reprimanded for trying to interfere and ordered to keep to her own work.

And now, here she was in the place of honor as Uradech's betrothed.

After several tries, the flames caught beneath the corpse and the men stepped away. A circle formed around the pyre and around the five of them: Malcolm, Domelch, Ethne, Finn and Mongfind. The baby slept peacefully in her father's arms despite the murmuring chant as those around them began their mournful prayer song.

The conflagration finally took, and when the flames licked high enough to singe the corpse, Ethne had to look away. The tightness in her chest threatened to do her in. The disgusting smell of burning flesh covered them just as the clouds moved in from the ocean, low and ominous, to fill the meadow. The smoke had nowhere to go, and still the ceremony droned on. She stopped paying attention. To Aidan when he stood beside the flames and spoke of Uradech's lineage. To Malcolm, whose gaze kept falling on her as if she had lost someone she cared for. To Domelch, who would probably never be the same.

When they'd all stopped their speeches, extolling the man's virtues, and turned to her, Ethne gasped. All their expectant gazes weighed on her!

They wanted *her* to speak?

Oh no. Mindlessly, she backed away from them. One step after another, knocking into two men forming the circle behind her. Malcolm lifted a hand toward her, his eyes rounded with concern, but she could not let him touch her. If he touched her, he'd unleash the scream trapped inside. The scream telling them all how much she disliked the man. The scream telling them all how *she* had killed him, not Lachlann. The scream that, once unleashed, would never be silenced again.

All she could do was shake her head and back away. She had to get away from these people, away from their sick ceremony. Away from the truth of what she'd done. All while Lachlann was kept apart, awaiting a possible death sentence, for being a good man. A better man than she'd ever known.

"Let her be, Malcolm." Aidan's voice carried to her. "I will deal with her when we return."

She turned and ran. That threat and what Aidan might mean spurred her back toward the hill. She ran harder, stumbling several times for her effort. When the trail split and the path to the cave came in sight, she resisted the urge to continue down the road to the castle, to seek out assistance for Lachlann, and escape once and for all. She would not leave Lachlann, not after he had lied to protect her. She didn't deserve such gallantry.

She groaned, a desperate sound. Lachlann had seemed so convinced it would work out. She had known better. As did his friends, or so it seemed since they'd completely abandoned him.

Gasping for breath and with every limb threatening to collapse, she stopped. She needed to rest. To make a plan. Mayhap after some time away from the others, a plan would come to her. Mayhap she'd figure out what to do. She prayed it would be so because, as of yet, she could barely think.

In the midst of the open heath, she slowly twirled to scan the area around her. Her heart clenched with hope. If only she could locate Lachlann, she could help him escape. She had a general idea of where the pit was located. Everyone did. It was along the ridge where the many shrubs, heather, and stiff tufts of grass seemed to mock her feeble attempt to discern the well-hidden entrance.

"Lachlann!" She bellowed his name, half-expecting to see Niall and Aldred poke their heads up, but there was nothing. No response except that every creature became silent. She called again. And again. Until she was hoarse and could scream no more.

Once within the cave, the strong draft blew about the small pile of kindling and cooking items that lay discarded. Left behind like they mattered little, like the people who lived here had just up and left, never to return. Ethne clutched her arms to her chest and let the desolation roll over her.

It was only the people that used the items that gave them their importance, to warm the small area and bring light into the darkness, to prepare a meal and sustain themselves for another day. It would take time to collect more dry leaves and twigs to build another fire once they returned and that would prolong their hunger. Domelch's treasured brush lay half-buried in the sand, no longer having a place on the gilded stool to keep it from harm. In her mind Ethne saw Domelch sitting there, Uradech beside her.

Some items could be easily replaced. Others not so much. Ethne closed her eyes and took a deep breath of the stale air. She could either curl into a ball and cry herself to sleep, or she could stiffen her back and work out a plan to move forward. With a firm shake of her head, she opened her eyes and began to gather fresh kindling.

After seeing to the fire, she sat and nibbled at her thumb nail. Her gaze went toward the narrow passage to the hidden area. It certainly didn't look like a passage, more like a shadow cast against the wall. It had often been a place of refuge for her and Finn, to be protected from visitors and those who would harm a young woman alone with a small child. Now, it was a place of hidden treasure. That silver could be the very thing she needed to get help. If she offered it to Aidan, could she arrange Lachlann's release? No. Their chieftain had little interest in material wealth.

Slipping through the narrow crevice, she thought of how to approach someone she didn't know. A woman traveling alone. And desperate. No one was more vulnerable. If she asked the wrong man, he'd realize she had no protector and take whatever he wanted from her. The right man might offer to be that protection.

She'd hoped for an opportunity to speak with Niall or Aldred alone to find out if they were planning to break Lachlann out of his hellhole, but they'd not been seen since Lachlann was imprisoned. And what could she say that would make them trust her enough to tell them of their plans anyway? Aldred's obvious irritation with Lachlann could only come from realizing that Lachlann was taking the blame for Uradech's death to protect her. Niall might also be privy to the information. They'd assume the worst since she was willing to allow an innocent man to suffer at the mercy of people who were not his own. They'd be right.

The cold was worse in this deepest part of the cave. She'd always avoided having a fire that might reveal the hiding place's very existence. The nasty smell surrounded her. A funeral for someone from the line of kings would take many days. Alone here and expecting no one back for days, she gathered the dried leaves that blew in from the darkened crevices to start a fire, piling on the twigs scattered about. The wood so dry, it was easy to blow the fire aflame. She held out her hands and rubbed her fingers.

With a heavy heart, she crossed to the crevice overhead where the coins were hidden and climbed the boulder to reach inside. She had no choice but to go out on her own to get help for Lachlann. The sound of someone coughing startled her. She jumped off the rock. It came again, and she instinctively glanced toward the darkness in the corner where the sound had come from. The distance was only a bit farther than her stretched arms, but the darkness had always kept her away from that end. That and the sound of small, scurrying creatures.

Everyone was gone now, so no one should be here. Only Lachlann had been left behind in some pit. When someone sneezed, she drifted toward the sound, her body casting an ominous shadow along the wall from the light of the fire. She slid her hands, scraping her palms along the crevices that remained, some deep and wide, others barely small veins. Another sneeze. Her breath stilled in her chest.

"Lachlann?" She whispered the name, closing her eyes to better use her other senses. She spoke louder. "Lachlann? Is that ye?"

She flattened her hand against the cold, hard stone wall and pushed herself forward into the darkness. There was no answer, and her heart squeezed tight with the pain. She fell to her knees.

Another sneeze. She jerked up her head.

That had been louder. He sounded as if he were just on the other side of the wall. She searched again. When her fingers slipped off the edge into nothingness, she yanked them back. Just as quickly, she put her hand back in and shifted her face closer. "Lachlann? Can ye hear me?"

A groan of pain wrenched her from complacency. With a louder voice, she called, "Lachlann, answer me."

Unlike the other crevices that were shallow, her arm easily slipped through this narrow opening. She put her head close, peering through with one eye, but saw only darkness.

"Ethne."

Lachlann!

He moaned as if in pain, but no one should have hurt him. He was to be held only, treated with respect. Verily, his friends would not allow him to be mistreated in any way. Would they?

"Lachlann?"

"Dear Father in Heaven, do not torture me so," he said, his voice raw with emotion.

She slid her hand down the length of the crevice to the ground. It widened and she gasped.

"Ethne?" Lachlann sounded as if he'd moved to a sitting position.

"I am here, Lachlann." She pressed herself into the opening, the walls squeezing against her on either side. Her face against the stone, she shifted her head up and down in desperation, but saw only darkness. "Can ye hear me?"

"I can hear ye." His voice was louder. "Are ye a dream?"

Something scraped along the sand. Suddenly there was a light, and she saw him.

"Lachlann!" She pressed her hand through the tiny opening toward him. "See my hand?"

When he turned toward her, a burning piece of timber in his grasp, she was shocked at his red-rimmed eyes and gray pallor.

He caught sight of her hand and moved toward her. "Ethne."

His hand was hot, his grasp weak. Her breath quickened.

She was just able to reach his shoulder, so she grabbed it and lodged herself tight between the walls until she could touch his face. "Lachlann, ye're burning up."

His expression slackened into a lazy smile, and he dropped to his knees, stopping just short of falling. He stuck the burning log into the ground a short distance from her and leaned his head against the wall that separated them.

He closed his eyes. "I thought I was imagining ye. Am I? Dinna tell me if I am. 'Tis a wonderful dream."

He settled onto his bottom to be closer and kissed her hand before cupping it to his cheek, rough from his growth of beard. "I have had many strange dreams. This one gives me great comfort. Please. Stay with me."

He sounded so weak. Her throat clogged with unshed tears. She needed to get some help for him. Aidan had wanted no outside witnesses to their private ritual and had said as much, but she couldn't believe Lachlann's friends would abandon him.

"Where are Niall and Aldred?"

He shrugged, his flattened lips dipping down at the corners. "I have seen no one."

"No one?" Ethne shook her head. That couldn't be true. "No one but the guard who brought ye water? And food, right?"

"Only at first. I've seen no one since."

And Ethne had seen no one when she'd searched the brae. Her chest tight, she realized she shouldn't have been looking for Thomas but the opening to the pit! Could she have been so near to finding him? In her mind, she saw the ridge and imagined the short distance to any opening that could connect to this area.

Her jaw slackened before she slammed it tight. That was no way to treat a prisoner. "I'll be right back."

When she tried to pull her hand back, Lachlann's grip tightened. "Ye said ye would not leave me."

"I'll fetch ye some water."

"Ye've said that before."

Great tears slid down her cheeks despite her struggle to remain strong and calm. "I have only just arrived, Lachlann. They've kept me from ye, but I promise to return. I will see to ye just as I did before."

"What a sight ye are, Ethne. With yer proud stance and yer fiery eyes." Lachlann sighed and continued his rambling. "In better times, who knows—?"

"Ye need to release my hand so I can go and get the water."

"So soon ye would leave me?" With slow, deliberate movements, he opened her hand and kissed her palm. "The sweetest hands, working too hard for others." He nuzzled her. "Ye smell like flowers."

"Please, Lachlann," she said, struggling to keep her fear in check. "Let me bring ye some fresh water and a bit of bread."

"Mmm, and a kiss. Would ye give me a kiss as well, dear lady?"

A strangled sound came from somewhere deep inside her. She cleared her throat. "Of course, ye know I will. Just a moment now." She pulled against his hold. "I promise ye."

With his eyes still closed, he heaved his shoulders in a great sigh of resignation.

"I promise ye, Lachlann. I'll see to ye."

He glanced at her then, his eyes bright with fever, and offered a sad smile. "If I thought killing Uradech would have made ye mine, I'd have done it at the first."

When he slumped down the rest of the way, she scraped her shoulder trying to grab him.

"Lachlann. Lachlann. Wake up. Ye're too close to the flame." It took three tries before she freed herself from the narrow crevice and ran toward the ridge that hid the entrance. She didn't see Niall until she bumped into him and he steadied her. She couldn't get his hands off her fast enough.

"Where is he?" she demanded.

"Who?"

"Lachlann. Help him."

But he wasn't reacting. He just stood there.

"He's going to catch fire!" She screamed the words at him. "Help him."

Niall glanced beyond her shoulder, as if trying to make sense of what she was saying. She clenched her jaw and yanked away, continuing toward where she now believed the entrance to the pit to be. Unable to contain herself and knowing full well he couldn't hear her, she screamed, "Lachlann!"

Pausing only long enough to assess the distance between the two caves, she dropped to her knees and frantically searched the ground. Niall grabbed the back of her gown and yanked her away.

"Stop. Ye'll hurt yerself."

She struggled against him, but he tossed her aside as if she weighed nothing, yanked a small ladder from beneath a nearby shrub, and dropped it into the opening that was an arm's length from her side.

"How did ye find that?"

"Aldred and I have been searching. That Thomas is a suspicious man." The ladder groaned under Niall's weight, and he jumped off halfway down. "That whoreson didn't even see to him before leaving for the burial ceremony."

"Then why weren't ye here with him now?"

"We couldn't find the damned ladder." Niall looked up at her just as she was putting a foot to the top rung. "Do not! Get water! Go!"

Ethne nodded, her mind frantically racing with what to do next. She heard Niall speaking to Lachlann and prayed he'd been quick enough as she raced to the rain barrel. She grabbed the bucket to fill it and started back all in one motion, but turned back into the cave to grab some hard bread.

"Lachlann." She gasped for air. Somewhere in her mind she believed if she kept calling him, he would be okay. "I'm coming. Here! I have water."

Searching down the dark pit, she could just make out Niall, sitting on the floor with Lachlann's head in his lap.

"I have water," she called down to him, her heart racing.

"Easy now. The ladder is broken."

It cracked beneath her weight, but she made it to the bottom, the heavy bucket hanging from her shoulder. "He's had no water at all."

She knelt next to Niall, using her hand to scoop the water into Lachlann's mouth. His lips were parched and dry. Glancing toward the torch, she saw it remained on its side. The little bit of light came from overhead

"I need to get him something to lower his fever."

Niall pointed out the blood at Lachlann's side. "His wound must have reopened."

Ethne gasped. Niall helped her to ease up the stained tunic. The sight of the angry red wound made her breath catch. "Water. It needs to be cleaned."

Niall held the bucket while she sluiced the wound clean, then he offered her the small sack from his waist. She frowned before accepting it.

"An assortment of herbs." Niall shrugged. "Take what ye need."

He cradled Lachlann's head against him to continue urging water between his lips, while Ethne squeezed the healing juices of the succulent plant around the tear.

"It had nearly healed." Her heart continued to race, her irritation and shame mounting. "It must have been his treatment at Thomas's hands that opened this back up. Damn him."

She glanced at Niall and her face heated. It was her fault Lachlann was here, but she wasn't certain how much Niall knew. It was best if they didn't speak.

It didn't take long for Lachlann's skin to cool. Once he seemed to be out of danger, Niall turned his stern expression on Ethne. "Why *are* ye here?"

An angry rebuke. Her exhausted body slumped, her shoulders rounding with defeat. He knew! Lachlann had told Aldred what Uradech had tried to do, so of course, he would tell Niall.

"I heard him groaning," Ethne said, unable to stop her voice from shaking.

"How?"

"There's a hidden passage." She scrubbed at her scalp and glanced in the direction it must be. "They all must connect."

"So ye've been there for him? Ye've known his condition?"

She winced at Niall's angry tone. "I just found it. I dinna know they were so close to each other…"

"Why are ye not with the others seeing to Uradech?"

Aldred called from overhead. "Niall?"

"Here!" Niall turned toward the opening then back at her. "I won't allow ye to stop us."

Ethne's jaw dropped, the wind knocked out of her.

Niall's sarcastic smile said it all. "Come now. A smart lass like ye? Are ye not here to stop us?"

Her thoughts scrambled in her head and she had a hard time answering. "I dinna know what ye're—"

"Enough!"

Aldred's head peered down at them. "What is *she* doing there?"

"Lachlann's too weak to get up the rungs." Niall glared at her as he called to the other man.

The blond turned to come down the ladder. "What have they done to him? Why is he so weak?"

Niall's face stiffened and he arched a single brow at her.

"I have no idea." She sounded as defensive as she felt.

These two thought the worst of her, and mayhap they should. She'd allowed their friend to take the blame for something she did.

"I thought they were caring for him," she said. "Each time I tried to bring him food or a blanket, they refused to allow me to see him."

Aldred snorted.

When he started to heft the unconscious man over his shoulder, Niall halted him. "We can't get him up the ladder like this."

"Damn!" Aldred repositioned Lachlann on the ground. "Then how will we get him out of here?"

Ethne glanced toward the darkness, the charred remains of the log tipped into the sand. With a steady hand, she followed along the curves of the wall. And prayed.

"What are ye doing?" Aldred demanded before turning his angry tone on Niall. "And why is she here?"

Lachlann stirred. "Ethne?"

"I'm here, Lachlann." When she moved closer to his face, the other two glared at her. "And I brought ye food and water."

Lachlann groaned as if in appreciation, but his voice was definitely stronger. She poured more water into his mouth. He drank his fill.

"My thanks." His voice still a bit hoarse, he sat up some and chewed the bread.

"Eat it slowly now." Ethne offered a small smile.

He nodded, his gaze steady on hers. "Ah, ye're a sight for these tired eyes."

When he cupped her cheek, she turned toward it, placing a kiss on his palm.

"Did I get to tell ye how beautiful ye are?"

"Oh, Lachlann, I am so sorry for all this." Tears dripped down her cheeks, even as she tried to stay strong.

"None of that. Uradech died the way he lived. They'll see that. Dinna worry so."

Niall held up his hand to Aldred when he would have commented.

"I do." Ethne shoved her hair back from her face. "They're treating ye as if ye've done something and ye haven't. I need to tell them."

"Do not." He sounded incredibly determined. "I will take yer punishment, Ethne. Do not speak of it again." He held a single, surprisingly cooler finger to her lips. "But kiss me as ye did before."

He must mean when they were in the cave. Her face heated.

Ethne couldn't keep herself from glancing to where Niall and Aldred stood in angry stances a few feet away. She moved close to Lachlann and whispered, "Ye'll get yer strength back."

He moved closer, pressing his lips to hers for the briefest moment.

A little breathless, she said, "I'll see to ye."

Wrapping a hand around the back of her head, he drew her close again. His lips were urgent against hers so that a slow heat grew in response from her head all the way down to her toes. Her lips parted eagerly for his tongue to gain entrance, moving against hers in a strange sort of dance. The knuckles of his hand swept across her cheek, the roughness of his fingers sending a shiver along her skin, and she moved closer still. His arms went about her to pull her flush against his upper body. It was a wonderful kiss, sparking all sorts of tiny fires along her skin wherever he touched her. She wanted it to go on forever.

A cough pulled her out of her enjoyment. She jerked away, but Lachlann's arm remained around her waist, his dark eyes steady on her, his passion clearly ignited. She refused to wipe the moisture from her lips or to look at his friends, but kept her eyes on him.

"Ye seem to be feeling better," Niall said. "Lachlann, do ye wish us to leave?"

"If Ethne will stay with me, I would like to be alone

with her. Will ye?"

The question was there in his eyes. Her breath caught. He was asking her to finish what they had started. He wanted to make love to her. She had never had this feeling before, low down in her belly. Even lower. And all he'd done was kiss her. The intensity of the kiss had set her aflame, and his steady gaze promised much. She wanted more.

"I will."

He heaved a great breath and beamed. Her face heated under his scrutiny.

"Ethne," Niall said. With great reluctance, she turned to him. "When will the others be back?"

With great reluctance, she raised her eyes to Niall. "Not until nightfall on the morrow."

He and Aldred exchanged glances she couldn't read, but she didn't care. She wanted to be alone with Lachlann. When she turned her attention back to him, his eyes were traveling the length of her and his hand lightly caressed her back.

"Lachlann," Niall said, "we will leave the ladder where it is so that ye can come out whenever ye are…ready to join us. Call us if ye need help."

"I have what I need right here," Lachlann said, his dark eyes hooded.

Sighing, Niall added, "We have information…"

Lachlann nodded, but his gaze remained on her face.

Niall paused beside them. "I suppose it can wait for now."

Without warning, Lachlann stretched out and pulled her beneath him before the other two were even gone, and the weight of him covering her was the sweetest thing Ethne had ever known. The sound of the creaking ladder signaled they were alone, and she turned all her attention to him. He appeared much stronger.

His lips became more persistent, as if he hadn't just

kissed her, as if he was indeed hungry and she was his food.

She relaxed against his broad chest. "Ye hold me so fiercely. Are ye feeling stronger then?"

"Ye give me strength."

When his lips traveled across her cheek and down to her neck, she shivered and rubbed her cheek against him. If she were a cat, she'd be purring.

His intensity was a bit frightening. She was afraid for him, but a warmth was steadily growing. "Ye do seem…better."

Between little nibbles, he said, "Oh, I'm not."

She stopped. "What are ye saying? Should we stop?"

He didn't stop his assault on her neck, one hand at the small of her back and the other sliding along her body with purpose.

"Oh no. I have a great need."

When he skimmed his lips toward her bosom, she stilled, but this time with nervousness.

His eyes were bright on her, the same intense gaze. "Shh, dinna be afraid,"

She took a steadying breath and said, "I am never afraid with ye."

~

Lachlann cupped her cheeks to peer down at her. "Oh, my sweet Ethne. Ye are so brave, lass." And then he kissed her soundly on the lips. "Would ye never halt me, even when I overwhelm ye with my need?"

"I want to be overwhelmed." Her words sounded breathless.

Searching her face, he saw the tender feelings he'd longed for reflected there. He swore he could feel her need. "I was sore afeared to never have this chance with ye again."

She ran her hand along his back, urging him closer.

"I was a fool to turn ye away." Lachlann admitted his mistake.

Her eyes wide, they seemed to be taking in every aspect of him, as if to commit it to memory. "Be a fool no longer and accept what I offer ye."

He dipped his head into the curve at her neck, afraid she'd see the tears. Tears of pure joy. *This* woman was what he wanted, what he'd been searching for without even knowing it. She moved against him, her legs widening to accommodate him.

"Easy now," he whispered into her ear, her breath gentle on his cheek. "I dinna want ye to have any pain."

When she stiffened beneath him, he nibbled her lips. "Trust me."

Brave words when he'd no experience with an untried lass. Could he breach her without pain? He wasn't certain. Her willingness, however, would go a long way. One thing he could count on from his own experience was that he could make her even more willing. And he set about doing just that, using everything he'd ever learned about lovemaking to increase her desire for him.

With long, sweeping strokes he caressed her side. Shifting and tugging at her gown, but being thwarted at her waist.

"I need to see all of ye, Ethne," he said, surprised at how needy he sounded.

She smiled and sat up. He took the opportunity to spread the wool out for her to lay upon. When he turned about, he was stilled at the sight of her, the way she doffed her *léine*. His breath caught at her exquisite form, her skin pale and soft, her breasts calling for his touch.

"Ah, Ethne, ye are lovely."

He dropped his head, not willing to disappoint such perfection, and suckled her. A timid hand around the back of his head held him there, encouraging him. A boon for certain, and he realized how much that meant to him.

Despite his many encounters with other females, this moment, with her, was taking on a whole new meaning. She was a virgin. The importance of her first time had every nerve taut as a bow string. He listened to every breath, some that sounded suspiciously like quiet sighs. A hand at the side of her neck and he knew the speed of her racing heart. When she finally stretched out alongside him, she pressed closer to him. Surely, he had died and gone to heaven. An angel in his arms. It felt like he'd spent his entire life waiting for this. Seeing to her pleasure felt like a matter of life and death.

With the utmost care, his fingertips glided down her bare side. Definitely a sigh. Grasping her, a hand on either side of her waist, he slid lower, dropping kisses along her belly and hips. So attuned to her, he knew the moment she tensed. He looked up at her as he moved lower, holding her gaze that widened but a moment, then quickly closed when he found his mark, wet and ready for him.

She groaned, shifting against him. He moved his fingers to where his mouth had been, exploring her further. He covered her—bare chest to bare chest—and was filled with a sudden sense of inadequacy. It gripped him, making him momentarily unable to move. When she opened her eyes, he saw such a look of…love, he set aside his fear.

Sliding his hand up along her generous curves to cup the back of her neck, he held her there with his mouth close to her ear. In his last offer for her to end this, he whispered, "Tell me now if ye want me to stop."

She groaned, "Do not stop, Lachlann."

Relief flooded him right before he obeyed, entering her in one swift movement. Her maidenhead was breached. Sheathed in her tightness, he held himself back despite a near overwhelming urge to move inside her. Her pleasure was his only priority.

"Are ye…fine?"

When she didn't answer immediately, regret flooded him, and he wanted to kick himself for taking her in such a manner and in such a place. She deserved much better, and now, there would be no other first time—

"Fine, indeed." She said the words on a sigh.

Searching her face, he couldn't hold back his smile. There was no fear, no regret, no shame. Without further delay, he dropped his mouth to hers and moved into her, setting the speed to match her racing heart, until his thrusts were met with her needy response. When she pulsed around his length, her sigh of pleasure set off his own. This was where he belonged. He'd never been so sure of anything in all his life.

Lachlann had been dreaming about Ethne, about making love to her, about taking her virginity for days it seemed. Ever since he'd been forgotten in this dark, wet cave, fearing he would die here. When he'd opened his eyes and saw her there, he wanted nothing more than to sate himself with her.

Now, she'd fallen asleep in his arms, her head on his chest. Well sated. She was an absolute delight, and he'd been fooling himself when he denied what Niall had said. Lachlann was most certainly enamored of her. Even more than enamored. Her quiet breathing and the weight of her in his arms gave him great peace. She felt right, as if she belonged there, and he was convinced that was true. He couldn't just let this end, not when he'd found the one woman he wanted. He dropped a kiss on her head.

"Rest now, sweet Ethne. We've plans to make come morning."

CHAPTER 22

*L*achlann stood in the pit they'd imprisoned him and stretched his arms high overhead. With Ethne here, it seemed much less imposing. The ladder was right there for him to climb, but he wasn't convinced he wanted to give up this time with her. He wanted to make love to her again. Now. Before they left this place. Even though he should feel well sated since she'd not held herself back from him all night, even initiating the last time just as dawn was lighting the sky.

"Is ought amiss?" Ethne glowed, or was that his imagination? No, she definitely glowed.

"I…no, all 'tis fine." He sat down beside her, an arm around her shoulders. "Is there pain?"

"A tiny bit sore. Nothing more."

She grinned, and he couldn't stop himself from kissing her again, full on the mouth. Her immediate response was difficult to ignore. He wasn't prepared for her to wrap her arms around his middle, or to pull herself close enough to crawl onto his lap. So willing. But he'd heed her words and give her body time to rest. He broke the kiss.

He considered the declaration he'd prepared all night, but to suddenly blurt it out seemed awkward, and the right words remained elusive. What if she didn't feel the same? What if his loving words weren't something she wanted from him? He didn't know what he would do if she turned him down.

She asked, "Are ye not worried about the news yer friends have? Ye've left them waiting."

"No. I need to say something..." Lachlann hesitated and started again. "I wanted ye...to tell ye—God, ye are beautiful."

She reddened, making her eyes seem even brighter while she struggled to right her clothes.

"How will I ever get enough of ye?" he asked.

Her answer was to kiss him again, her tongue sparring with his.

He was getting lost in his desire for her. "Ethne. Please. I will be gentle."

When he would have pulled her closer, Niall calling from overhead broke them apart.

"Lachlann!"

She smiled, a knowing expression. "I told ye they wanted to talk."

Niall's obvious fear of interrupting them made him sound ridiculously loud. Lachlann said, "We're here, Niall, not deaf."

Ethne was at the ladder before he could get to his feet.

"Wait! I wanted us to talk."

She grinned. "I will take my turn. They can have their say first."

"They can damn well wait!"

But she ignored his outburst and started up the ladder. Steadying her with his hand on her bottom made him want to yank her back down for another bout of lovemaking. But Niall offering her his hand doused that idea.

Lachlann squinted at the bright light. Easier to close his eyes. The outside air was so fresh and clean, it demanded his attention. Heaven could not feel as wonderful as this. He opened his eyes and, opening his arms, tipped his face toward the warmth of the sun. It felt so wonderful, he laughed out loud. His life, at this moment, seemed perfect.

"We've some food prepared in the cave. We'll talk there." Niall's stern tone jolted him out of his revelry.

Ethne striding across the glen ahead of them, rather than at his side, brought a sinking feeling to his stomach. He'd not settled things with her, and he didn't want to make it awkward for her. He was not about to deny his love for her. Not now. Trotting up, he was a step behind her as they entered the cave.

Aldred, who'd been waiting for them within, jerked forward and looked like he'd dozed off unexpectedly. Come to think of it, he looked as if he hadn't slept a wink when the three of them entered, but Lachlann had a hard time feeling sorry for the man.

"What are ye…? Is ought amiss?" Aldred asked.

"No." Ethne smiled, a tight smile, and averted her gaze. "Ye needed to talk to him. Here he is."

Niall and Lachlann exchanged glances. There was something more there than disappointment in Aldred's falling asleep. When Niall glanced toward Ethne, Lachlann's chest tightened. It seemed his disappointment was for the lack of interest Ethne was showing in Lachlann. Niall knew what he and Ethne were about when he and Aldred had left them alone.

Lachlann paused in the entrance to watch Ethne's movements as she went about her chores. Seeing to the fire that needed no attention. Seeing to the water that had, no doubt, just been filled. Seeing to the mending in preparation for the wash.

Finally glancing toward their silent faces, she raised her brows. "If ye wish to leave, I am fine here. Alone."

Leave? Lachlann took a step closer then stopped.

"I dinna think we need leave anon," Aldred said, his gaze moving between Niall and Lachlann.

That man must be very familiar with the awkwardness of having taken a virgin and then leaving her behind. The comparison sliced like a knife to Lachlann's heart. There was no comparison. He had no intention of leaving her behind.

"We do need to talk," Niall said. "Should we take a walk? Or can we remain here?"

Ethne's attempt at dismissing them did not sit well with Lachlann. Was she intending to show she had no need of him? No expectation? A moot point since he knew he had every need for her. He should have spoken to her, told her how he felt, instead of worrying about finding just the right words. Damn! Any words would have eased the angst her sudden coldness was unleashing in him.

Could she possibly believe he'd taken what he'd wanted and would now just leave her behind? That he could forget about her? He'd wanted to tell her about their mission for the priory, to tell her she had no idea of what she sparked in him with her spirited ways. He'd not told her. He wished to be alone with her again, and this time he'd keep his hands to himself.

Not likely.

The frown Niall was turning on Lachlann made him realize he'd not answered yet. He nodded his head, not really sure what it was he'd been asked.

"Well, to start, it appears there is nothing for us to find here," Niall said. "We've wasted our time."

When Ethne jerked her head up, Lachlann's stomach dropped. He turned his glare on Niall to shut the man up.

"We need to step outside." Hit with the realization that it might be too late to fix this, Lachlann's voice sounded unnaturally high.

"What? Ye just said 'twas fine," Aldred blurted out.

"'Twas not what I meant."

Ethne's eyes never wavered from Lachlann, a deep crease between her brows, and her mending forgotten.

He met her gaze. "I believe we have come to the right place."

The right place regardless of what they sought, he'd found her. His shy smile was not returned.

Niall and Aldred were waiting to hear the reasons for such information, the tension pouring out of them. Not unlike a hungry heron on the edge of a loch, desperate to catch a fish. Damn! He just needed to get them outside.

"I need a moment to speak to Ethne."

"Ye've not spoken a word to her?" Niall glanced toward her, but then quickly looked away. His expression was tight, no doubt catching her sense of outrage as well.

She confronted him. "What is it ye've come for?" She stood. The material forgotten, it dropped to the ground. "Are ye not simply pilgrims, coming to visit a holy sight?" She looked heavenward and sighed. A defeated sound. She crossed her arms and confronted them with her stern tone. "Was Uradech correct?"

When her gaze finally landed on Lachlann again, it was no longer trust that he saw. The trust she'd put in him had dissipated like smoke right before his eyes. And he could think of no way to contain it.

"We've come from Restenneth Priory...on a mission," Niall said.

Ethne faced him again. Her entire body stiffened and she gave Lachlann her back. Surely it was nothing less than what it appeared. She was turning her back on him. He had a hard time swallowing.

"Not penance then. Why should I be surprised?" She shook her head with an I-should-have-known-better expression. "Ye are warriors. Ye've come as warriors and only pretended to be something else."

When Lachlann came alongside her, she bent at the

waist with the strength of her indignation. "Do. Not."

He opened his mouth to speak, but she halted him with a raised palm and widening eyes.

Niall, who looked most concerned, said in a quiet voice, "We *are* warriors, but we have come here for the priory. They asked us to return something to them that was left behind many, many years ago."

"We've not come to deceive ye." Aldred frowned before continuing. "Not really."

Lachlann shook his head. This was getting worse and worse, but Ethne's glaring expression kept his words at bay.

"Oh?" Betrayal. It was there on her face and in her tone and her damned raise palm. She wanted answers, just not from Lachlann. "Have ye come to condemn us then? Domelch and Malcolm? Me?"

"What? No!" Aldred answered, but then seemed to think better of it.

Niall glanced toward Lachlann. No doubt his friend realized how much this was burying any chance he'd have with her. "Well, we are on a mission for the church, but 'tis not our way to condemn another. 'He who is without sin—"

"'—can cast the first stone.'" She finished the Bible quote for him. She shook her head, an expression of absolute disgust.

Lachlann reached for her upheld hand, but she yanked it away.

"Ye've been here." Her jaw was tight with fury and her gaze included all of them. "They took ye in. Trusted yer word. Gave ye a place to stay out of the wind and rain, but all along ye were using them? Searching for something?"

Speaking in a level tone unmarred by emotion, Niall said, "We've been sent here to retrieve silver intended for the church."

No one could have missed the heightening of her color, the way she reddened despite her settling back down on the ground and picking up her mending as if to feign indifference.

Ignoring Niall's questioning glance, Lachlann moved to sit beside her. She stiffened, but he placed a hand on the material she'd retrieved from the ground, the material she gripped as if it would save her. Finally, she looked up at him.

"Finn showed me a fine silver coin." Well, he didn't actually show it to him. It had slipped out from its hiding place, but Lachlann felt only slightly guilty for the lie. "Do ye know where he got it?"

Aldred and Niall circled them, moving closer.

Ethne shrugged as if it mattered little. She fell far short of convincing them. "What did it look like?"

She was lying. Lachlann was taken aback at how well he could read her lie, but he knew he was right. Had he always been able to do so with her? Niall and Aldred showed no sign of discerning it. Instead, their gazes shifted from her to Lachlann then back again.

"A man's likeness on the coin. With a hole in the center. Finn wears it around his neck." Sitting there beside her, Lachlann felt her entire body tighten as if ready to bolt, but at the same time, he recognized her inner struggle. Turning toward Niall, he asked, "Would ye two give us a moment?"

"I thought ye—" Aldred started, but Niall grabbed him by the front of his tunic to drag him outside.

"No!" Her voice boomed in the small space. Aldred and Niall stopped mid-step.

"Hear me, Ethne," Lachlann said, but her scathing glance stopped him from saying more.

"I would hear from all three of ye, so I can be sure and explain it to my brother when he returns and finds ye gone." Her jaw tightened. "And ye *will* be gone. Doubt it not."

Lachlann felt like he'd run a hundred miles, like all the wind in the world would never again fill his lungs. He couldn't leave her. Not now. Not even if she ordered him to leave.

"Tell us where the silver is," Niall asked in a calm, controlled voice. "Return it to us, and we will leave."

"No!"

They all ignored Lachlann's outburst.

"I have never seen this coin Lachlann described," Ethne answered. "Finn must have found it somewhere. He's never shown it to me."

Niall searched her with narrowed eyes, obviously trying to read her thoughts and if she told the truth.

"Lachlann?" Niall put his hands on his hips and shrugged. "Clearly, she knows nothing about the silver."

Lachlann pressed his lips flat, torn between knowing deep in his heart that she lied and calling her out, or simply agreeing with his friend. If he did the latter, they'd pack up their few belongings and be gone before the others returned, and that would not do. He had no plans to leave this place without her.

An idea came to him, and he turned to Ethne, wanting desperately to reach out a hand to her, but keeping himself rigid instead. "Is the silver what ye would use to make yer escape after we're gone?"

When she looked past him, the sadness in her eyes turned into wide-eyed fear. She stood and stiffened. The sound of men, a lot of them, had all of them turning toward the entrance. Lachlann jumped up ready to confront the threat.

Dressed in leather and stopping just within the entrance with a wide grin was the drunk man from the fair. His scar was hard to miss. As was the fact that he was no longer drunk.

"Ethne." The man said the single word like an intimate embrace. "Have ye been waiting for me?"

"Olaf." She sounded breathless.

The ground shifted beneath Lachlann. She knew this man?

Armed men pressed in from behind to flank him on both sides. Six or eight, Lachlann couldn't be certain, crowding along the walls. Damn! He couldn't think. Only about Ethne. Niall, Lachlann, and Aldred were unarmed. They had no choice but to back up to stand beside her.

Olaf strode in near enough to tower over Ethne. A smile of pleasure on his face, he stroked her cheek. Lachlann's heart slammed against his ribs and he shifted forward, but Niall jerked him back. Olaf didn't seem to notice. The galling man had eyes only for her.

"I have been waiting too long for ye," Olaf said.

When he lowered his head to kiss her, Lachlann's attempt to intercept was blocked by no less than three large warriors. One shoved him to the ground, a dark-bladed long sword poised at his neck.

"Mmm, ye taste even better than I remember." Olaf tenderly pushed her hair from her face, his eyes taking in all of her. "And what of yer other charms? I am anxious to taste them as well."

Watching the intimate scene right before his eyes had every fiber of Lachlann's body taut and ready. But she wasn't protesting. Or moving out of Olaf's reach. Or voicing any objection. If anything, she was submitting to his touch, much as she had Lachlann's. It became difficult to breathe.

Olaf glanced toward them, his scarred face healed well enough that both of his eyes were open now. "Ye have friends, I see."

"Pilgrims." She kept her eyes trained on Olaf. "They were just leaving."

He raised his brow, a skeptical look. "Are ye certain

they wouldna care to remain? One of them seems eager to defend ye."

The man had not missed Lachlann's ridiculous show of chivalry after all. He took a deep breath to calm his racing thoughts. Ethne obviously had expected Olaf, mayhap even wanted him here. Remaining rigid, it took every ounce of Lachlann's control and training to give no indication of his inner turmoil while the man held his gaze. Olaf was assessing him. Lachlann had done the same thing many times. Studying a possible opponent, weighing if they were worth the effort, if they required immediate confrontation, or if they were harmless and could be let free as she was suggesting.

When Olaf's glance moved to Niall, Lachlann saw the spark of recognition, and his gut clenched. A slow smile lit up Olaf's scarred face, but he called to his friend. "Ciaran!"

His squire, now properly dressed as one, came to stand beside him. "We have met this man before, have we not?"

Ciaran nodded. "We have."

"I'm having trouble placing him."

Ciaran crossed his arms about his chest and shook his head. "A minor misunderstanding. Ye handled it well as I recall."

In a flash of anger, Olaf confronted the young man. "I dinna seek yer council. I want only to remember the incident."

Clearing his throat, Ciaran kept his ready stance and his eyes on Olaf. "It involved a horse, m'lord. At the fair."

"Ah, I'm remembering now. He called me a thief?"

"He did not, m'lord. If he had"—Ciaran turned back to Niall and Lachlann—"verily he would be dead now."

Olaf laughed. A hearty laugh. The laugh of a man without a concern in the world. "Ye have the right of it. Well, no grudge then." He turned back to Ethne. "I think

I'll have my desserts first. Is there a soft pallet nearby for yer tender arse?"

When he grabbed her bottom and crushed her lower body against him, his men laughed, enjoying the performance. Lachlann did not feel so inclined, his hands fisting so tightly his fingers ached.

"Ye've not dallied with another now, have ye?" Olaf tipped his head toward Lachlann. "The pilgrim there? He'd have enjoyed taking ye. Did he try?"

"They canna offer me what ye can." Ethne shook her head, her nostrils flaring. "Ye have promised to take me away."

Lachlann's chest tightened with actual pain as sharp as the piercing of a warrior's blade.

"Good!" Olaf turned toward his men. "Keep yer weapons on these men. Tie them up if ye've a mind to, but take them outside. I'll decide how to proceed as soon as I'm finished here. The rest of ye can stay or leave. It matters not at all to me." He turned back to Ethne. "But she may mind. What say ye?"

"I thought... I—"

"Ach, ye thought a gentle taking would be unobserved?" He kissed her soundly on the mouth before continuing. "But that would be up to ye. Give them the silver, and they'll be too busy counting it."

When she turned her eyes to Lachlann, he was certain it had not been intended, but he read her as clear as the dark clouds before a storm. Regret. She was sorry for lying about the silver. But Olaf saw it, too, and Lachlann wished she'd not revealed herself.

"What is this?" He shoved her away, and she fell to the ground. "Are ye no longer chaste, ye little whore?"

"I...I am," she said, brushing off her hands as she stood. "They are men of God. I dinna wish to corrupt them." She threw herself at Olaf. "Do as ye like with me."

Olaf's eyes widened in delight. "Have ye found the silver as ye promised?"

"I have. I have found it."

"Take them outside." Olaf tossed the order over his shoulder as Ethne led the way toward the back of the cave.

~

Ethne moved like she was confronting her death. But death was the least of her problems. The pain in Lachlann's eyes when she had not fought against Olaf's advances had cut her to the depth of her soul. It had cost her every bit of strength to not lash out, shove him away, take his own knife and jab it into his black heart. Olaf was ruthless; he'd shown her that. Lachlann and his friends were outnumbered, and she needed to protect them.

A large hand around her waist lifted her into the air, making her cry out as Olaf swung her around.

"Easy now." Olaf settled her back against his broad chest to nuzzle the crook of her neck. His voice was low.

She cringed.

"The sway of yer fine arse has me thinking the silver can wait." When he caressed down the front of her, leaving no part of her untouched, she stiffened, but he growled in her ear. "Ye know what will happen if I find ye've given yerself to another? Tell me I've nothing to worry about."

He slipped his hand between her legs, pressing against the material that chafed her tender skin despite her attempt to keep her thighs together.

His touch was painful, and she gritted her teeth to keep from crying out. After a slow exhale, she answered, "Ye've nothing to worry about."

Jerking her around to face him, he ran a fingertip

along her lashes. "Ethne, why are there tears? Did ye want the pilgrim so badly?"

Her mouth dropped open with her gasp. "No."

Olaf narrowed his eyes to mere slits. His brows slashed down, his face an angry grimace. Her breath stilled in her chest. She'd given herself away somehow. He stunk of sweat and shite. She struggled not to cough and shove the man away. Without warning, he hefted her over his shoulder like the carcass of some animal he'd captured. "I should not have made ye wait. I'll not do so again."

Ciaran moved ahead of them, getting to Malcolm and Domelch's secluded pallet in time to lift the material that would give them privacy, *tsking* at her as if somehow, she deserved to be thrown up onto Olaf's shoulder. He dropped her onto the pallet with little care. A sharp jab into her hip made her cry out in pain.

"A soft landing and ye cry out? I thought ye were made of stronger stuff." He turned to Ciaran. "I dinna want anyone disturbing us. No matter what ye hear."

"But what of—" Ciaran asked.

"I need this first." Olaf glanced toward her. "If she is no longer a virgin, we'll know whose prick to cut off."

Ominous words that made it difficult for Ethne to control her heaving breath. When the curtain dropped, they were enclosed in near total darkness. Her heart throbbed in her ear. Olaf didn't hesitate to cover her with his hard body, his hands again making free with her. He moaned in appreciation right before propping up on his elbows to peer into her face. "Tell me about those men."

Ethne eased out a breath, struggling to seem unconcerned, and swallowed her fear. "They were warriors and now, they are pilgrims. 'Tis all I know. They wanted to pay homage to the Holy Man."

"Then why are they still here? Have they been with ye since the fair?"

Unable to decide what answer he wanted, she apparently took too long, and he growled before dropping his mouth to hers for a rough kiss. That was much worse. She'd prefer he stick to conversation.

The moment his lips left her mouth, she answered. "I think Malcolm likes them. He invited them to stay with us."

"Yer brother is fickle. He liked us as well." Olaf spoke between kisses that followed the line of her jaw, down her neck, ending at her bosom where he yanked at the material. Her breasts spilled over the top.

The sound of his warriors outside drifted to her. Olaf lifted his head from his relentless sucking on her to look over his shoulder. She reached to cover her bruised nipple.

"Those pilgrims are persistent." He turned back and jerked her hand away. "Why is that?" His gaze was fixed on her heaving bosom, his hands gripping and squeezing. She could barely catch her breath with his unrelenting assault.

"I dinna know." She searched underneath her hip to grab at the offending lump jabbing into her. "They are friendly with Aidan. He likes them as well."

Unexpectedly, Olaf cupped her face between his large hands, holding her head so tight she couldn't turn away. "Why do ye think I will not know if ye are telling me the truth or a lie?"

Her throat too dry to swallow, her mind searched frantically for an answer. "They want the silver."

"Ah! Finally, she speaks the truth." His face shifted to an ugly grimace. "So, who has left their mark on yer skin, lovely Ethne?"

She gasped, and he slapped her face hard. The tangy taste of blood flooded her mouth.

"Did ye think I wouldna smell him on ye?"

She could not stop her body from trembling. Surely,

he'd kill her now.

He clenched her jaw, his tight fingers jabbing into her skin. He was livid. "Do ye wish to die at my hand? Mayhap 'tis *him* I should kill for using what is mine."

"Do not." Her words were nothing short of a plea. The thought of Lachlann taking more punishment because of her…their tender moments of lovemaking raced through her mind.

"And ye've feelings for the man? Then convince him ye wish to stay with me, convince him he needs to leave without the silver, and I will not kill him. Mayhap I can overlook yer unfaithfulness."

She nodded frantically, and when she pushed away the lump in her hand, it jingled. They both looked at it. The leather purse that should be hidden. Finn was the only one who knew it was there. He was the only one who could have placed it here.

"What is this?" Olaf grabbed the sack and leaned on his elbows to pour the contents onto her bared chest. "Silver?" His eyes were wide, his surprise unchecked. "And how did ye know this is where I'd bed ye first?"

"First?"

His anger dissipating, Olaf smiled. A tolerant smile. A smile that said she had much to learn. "Ah, Ethne, there will be many beddings. Ye fill my dreams. Even when I've a willing wench to poke with my prick, 'tis yer face I see." He kissed her hard. "Ye may never be able to walk again."

Rest now, sweet Ethne. We've plans to make come morning.

Lachlann's gentle words echoed in her mind.

Her throat clogged with unshed tears over what might have been. Her trepidation blossomed into full-blown terror. Again, she had put Lachlann at risk. If she could get away from Olaf, mayhap she could save Lachlann. If she could not escape, Olaf would be relentless, forcing himself on her when she had no desire for him, and she would end up being ripped apart just like Moira.

CHAPTER 23

*P*er Olaf the Islander's orders, Lachlann, Niall, and Aldred were shoved out of the cave. When Lachlann tried to look over his shoulder for Ethne, one of the ugliest men he'd ever laid eyes on thrust him head first to the hard ground.

The whoreson laughed. "I think ye can give up that idea."

Lachlann heard again everything Ethne had said. She was putting on a brave front, but…He ran her answer about the silver over in his head. And again. She'd hesitated. Was he wrong? No! He was certain she'd paused, and that look of regret.

"Get some rope," a fat little man said, while he swished the jug of mead he'd found outside the cave. A third man pushed Niall and Aldred to their knees beside him.

When Ethne saw Olaf, her body had tensed. Lachlann was certain she'd also tensed when that man touched her. Damn! Was he right or was he just imagining it? Certainly, she'd been holding her breath.

There was no clear indication of what Niall wanted done and Lachlann didn't care! He couldn't wait. His focus remained on Ethne, whom he'd just left in the cruel hands of Olaf the Islander. Hands Lachlann had to believe she did not want on her.

He felt nothing as his arms were yanked back and tied by strong hands. Even his side seemed numb. His mind, instead, raced to the interior of the cave and what might be happening.

Olaf's little band quickly stepped away to share the mead.

If Lachlann was right, then Ethne had been afraid despite her act. He had to be right. But mayhap, he saw only what he wanted to see. The man's familiarity with her could not be denied, even his inference that they'd been together before, but Lachlann knew she had been with no other. Panic was setting in. He needed to halt these racing thoughts.

"So, are we to assume ye know that Ethne has the silver?"

Niall's voice felt like a sharp slap of awareness and it annoyed Lachlann deeply.

"What?" He spat out the question.

His angry retort was too loud and now, they had eyes on them. Niall waited until the closest islander turned away before saying it again, his voice barely audible and his lips not even moving.

With a tight expression, Lachlann gave a quick nod. The silver was the least of his problems right now. He worked on the knots at his wrist, his fingernails ripping to the quick. If he could have yanked free, he would have because he could do nothing to help her from here.

"Glad we figured that out."

"She didna seem surprised to see them," Aldred whispered as he settled on the ground, facing the men who'd left them here.

Niall nodded. "It sounded like they had a plan, the two of them. If we can get back inside bef—"

"No talking!" The same islander who had tied them up

barked the order, then accepted one of the horns of mead being distributed among the others. Only a few men had remained inside, so their numbers were less than they would have been, mayhap five large warriors.

The three of them had fought more men than this. And won.

After waiting a few minutes more for the men to lose interest in them again, Niall asked, "Did ye see the medal on the man's chest? He's from the islands. A jarl of some sort."

"Dinna ye meet the man before?" Aldred asked.

"Not dressed in such finery."

The mead was flowing among Olaf's men, and they were a thirsty lot. Despite the occasional glance coming their way, they'd moved farther away, obviously not seeing them as a threat.

Lachlann remained rigid except for his fingers nimbly attacking the knots. His chest was tight and he couldn't swear he'd taken a single breath since he'd seen Ethne's expression of regret and been unable to get to her. He had to get back inside. Fast. He needed to protect her from that savage.

"He was here before," Niall droned on. "Malcolm and Aidan brought them in for the night, but an argument ensued. That's Domelch's handiwork, the burn on his face."

Aldred made a sound of surprise. "She's a tough one."

Lachlann was painfully unsuccessful at blocking out them and their speculation.

"From a royal line of the Picts, or so she claims," Niall said. "She's the one who told me the story. Their rope is not well made. I almost have it untied."

"Me, too," Aldred said.

Olaf's men had shifted to their right, nearer the trail's edge to watch the sea as they enjoyed the mead Malcolm had probably left outside for when they returned from the funeral. One group of three was closer to Lachlann. All were well armed. Good. That would give him and his friends weapons to save Ethne.

"Ready?" Niall asked.

But Lachlann was already up, shoving back the largest man in the nearest group. He planted his fist firmly into the man's face, his other hand grabbing the hilt of the sword as the man fell. With a sweeping arch of the weapon, Lachlann sliced through the belly of the closest man. Intense satisfaction raced through Lachlann's veins. The entrance to the cave and Ethne, a few feet away.

Ducking and swaying, he avoided the downward swipe of the third man's sword and was able to turn the man's dagger, still gripped in his own hand, up into his heart.

The nearby struggle with the other islanders held no interest for Lachlann. His eyes remained on the cave. Let Niall and Aldred take down the rest. He needed to be inside.

With the sticky blood of his victims still on his hands, he squeezed the narrow hilt of the long sword in his right hand and the leather-strapped handle of the dagger in his left. He paused in the entrance only long enough to get his bearing and allow his eyes to adjust to the sudden darkness. This gave the men seated against the wall time to stand ready. It couldn't be helped. No sign of Ethne or Olaf.

Rushing forward, Lachlann threw the dagger with practiced precision into the chest of the closest target coming at him, and the man dropped to the ground. Two men remained aside from Ciaran. Lachlann readied his sword as he scoured the darkened pallet for any sign of Ethne. A slice to his forearm had him wincing. He needed to focus. He ducked low, sidestepping Ciaran's frontal assault, to elbow the gut of the islander who'd drawn blood.

"Olaf!" Ciaran's words echoed in the small chamber even while Lachlann's dagger penetrated his gut. He slumped to his knees. Dead or unconscious, it meant only that Lachlann could save Ethne now.

When his gaze landed on Olaf, who was just rising from Domelch and Malcolm's sleeping area, the sound of Aldred and Niall joining Lachlann from outside faded from his mind. The material dropped back down to hide the area behind him where Ethne must be. The man tied up his trews as he walked toward Lachlann. The sick realization that he had not been in time tightened his gut.

"Ah, ye've come to join us!" The man spoke as if he had all the time in the world, even as his men dropped around him, three dead or unconscious on the floor already. When his gaze stopped on Lachlann, he added, "She's a tasty morsel and not to be missed, but then ye know that as I've just found out."

A war cry erupted from Lachlann's lips as he charged. He drove his shoulder into the Olaf's stomach to ram him into the hard, stone wall, and he dropped to the ground, but Lachlann didn't relent. Landing a fist solidly in his face, Lachlann barely reacted to pain shooting up his arm while the man's skin puckered and tore with the motion. Olaf howled in pain.

"I'd stop if ye value her at all!" someone called from the area behind him. A voice Lachlann didn't recognize at first. "Back away, or I'll run her threw."

When he turned and saw the tall man with thinning hair, it took him a moment to place him as one of Aidan's men.

"Talorc?" Lachlann was surprised he even remembered the man's name. He'd swear the man had not been there when they'd first come in.

He held a nasty-looking blade to Ethne's throat while he worked her up to a standing position, using her as a shield. Her clothes were disheveled and gaping open at the top. Her eyes were wide with fear. Lachlann dropped his weapons and raised his open palms to the man.

Talorc snorted. "I'd have bet my last drink that ye never even noticed me. I'm beside myself with such flattery, ye arrogant sod."

The man who'd barely spoken at all had become livid at Niall, Lachlann, and Aldred's prolonged presence. He'd certainly upset Aidan with his not-so-wild accusations.

"Why do ye hold a knife to the throat of one of yer own?"

Lachlann's gaze never wavered from Ethne's face, even when the man dragged her with him to help Olaf, who was struggling to get up. Olaf yanked his clothes back into place and strode right up to Lachlann. The single punch to his gut doubled him over, knocking the air out of him. Olaf gripped Lachlann's shoulders while he kneed him in the groin with a loud *umph*. Lachlann dropped to the ground, his hands tight between his legs. Burning pain radiated through his genitals, burning all the way down both thighs and up to his teeth.

The sound of laughter barely registered through his fog of pain along with the presence of Aldred and Niall. A hand to his shoulder. Niall helped him up. Lachlann still couldn't see straight.

"Ethne is not one of us." It was Talorc speaking. "She is only here because she is Malcolm's sister. Domelch insisted we endure her presence after doing away with their parents."

Ethne's choked gasp jerked up Lachlann's head. Her eyes were tearing up. But Talorc held the blade fast and added, "Besides, it matters more to me that I can rescue Moira from our *chieftain's* lecherous grasp."

"And I will help him with that," Olaf said, coming to stand beside Ethne, the pain from his face having apparently subsided. "I found him rutting with the woman I knew to be Aidan's wife." He shrugged. "We easily came to an understanding."

He ran his gaze over Ethne, wiping the blood that trickled down her neck with a wetted thumb before continuing. "That lecher Aidan wanted Ethne as well, so I understood the man's pain. Talorc has sworn allegiance to me." He lifted a small sack from around the man's neck and said to him, "I see ye have found our silver." He turned back to Lachlann. "And now we have the silver as well."

Lachlann forced himself to breathe naturally. He wanted nothing more than to rip off the man's face.

"And are we to just leave now and allow ye to do whatever ye like here?" Lachlann's irritation was barely checked.

Olaf smiled. "Either that or we can kill ye. It matters not at all."

"Or we kill ye." Lachlann hunched slightly forward and fisted his hands. "Just say the word."

"Ye think much of yer abilities." Olaf rolled his eyes then turned to stroke Ethne's cheek. "Tell yer friends to drop their weapons. I prefer her to no longer be held at knife point. Either that, or I'll allow Talorc to slit her throat." At the slightest tip of Olaf's head, Talorc readied the blade. Lachlann gasped before slamming his jaw tight. Olaf glowered at him. "Do help me to decide."

It took every speck of control for Lachlann to continue to stand their while his friends' weapons clattered to the ground.

Talorc released Ethne and advanced with his dagger toward them, pressing them back toward the entrance. Olaf took Ethne into a one-armed embrace, holding her close against his side and talking quietly to her. It sounded like an apology. Lachlann's tongue wedged painfully against his teeth.

"Now, back against the wall." Talorc was joined by two other armed men who had only minor injuries.

Ethne nodded to Olaf, a small smile, almost as if in reassurance. Lachlann's chest tightened.

"What is it ye are doing back in here?" She squared her shoulders, her tone more demanding than questioning.

"Protecting ye," Lachlann said. The lack of air in his lungs made him lightheaded.

"From what?" She jutted out her chin, shook her head as if he were some loon, then placed a hand flat on Olaf's chest. "I have my own plans that dinna include ye. I've no need of yer protection now. Go. Be on yer way."

Olaf beamed. A gentle tug back, and he wrapped his large arms around her, holding her close.

Lachlann's body was rigid with anger. He searched her face for any sign that this was against her will. "We want the silver."

"Ah, the silver is it now?" Olaf shook his head. "Ye best make up yer mind, *Lachlann*. Is it the lass ye've come for or the silver?"

He took a step forward, pushing as much as he dare against Talorc, who stood between them. "Both. We've come for both."

"So ye'll take her against her will now?"

"I dinna bel—"

"Believe it!" Ethne's fierce scowl was convincing. "I dinna wish to go with ye. And ye'll not have the silver, so just leave us." She jerked her finger toward the entrance. "Now, before the others get back and ye take the punishment for something *I* did."

Confused now, Olaf frowned. "What is this? What are ye saying?"

She turned to him. "I've stolen their silver, but they'll believe these three did it. They trust *me*, so they'll never think I did it. If ye take me away like ye promised, they'll believe I went off with them. All the better."

Olaf had promised to protect her, take her away from all this. Lachlann's panic was rising. Could she actually want him to just leave her here with them? Surely, she knew him better than that.

"The plan works for me, little one." Olaf kissed her, a passionate kiss that ripped Lachlan's heart right out of his chest.

"Ye lie!" Talorc moved in closer to confront her. "Domelch believes Lachlann murdered Uradech."

She shrugged, wiping the back of her hand over her lips. Wiping off Olaf's kiss? Lachlann narrowed his eyes at her.

"And when they find the silver gone," she said, "that will be on his head as well."

Olaf punched the unsuspecting man in the face. Talorc staggered back, his hand desperately trying to staunch the flow of blood from his nose. "What was that for?"

"Ye dinna call my lass a liar." Olaf turned his attention back to Ethne. "Domelch will not be happy with that, will she?"

He said the question more like a statement. Ethne nodded.

With a grin as big as his raw skin allowed, he said, "Then that is what we shall do."

Lachlann turned to Niall. "If they're giving us an out, we should take it."

Niall held his gaze, no doubt trying to discern Lachlann's motives. When Niall turned to Olaf, he raised his hands in supplication. "Do ye give us yer leave?"

Olaf had his bright eyes on Ethne. Her eyes lacked their natural brightness. He asked, "Is that what ye would have me do?"

She glanced at Lachlann. For the smallest moment, he saw...something, but then her expression closed down. "If it suits ye, so be it. They are more trouble than they are worth."

~

Under Olaf's direct order, his men were to "run the vermin off," which meant Lachlann, Niall, and Aldred were escorted at the urging of an extremely sharp, spiked polearm away from the cave and toward the main road. Once they left Olaf's close scrutiny, his men visibly relaxed, choosing the path that led away from the shore and their boats and straight to the castle.

Olaf's men might have been following orders or they might have been more concerned about covering their own escape in case there was a need for fast action. Either way, Lachlann was quite certain they had no idea where they were going and he planned to use that to his advantage when given the opportunity. After all, these men were good at following orders and not reasoning things out for themselves.

When they stumbled upon three coursers, fully loaded with weapons, grazing in the meadow, Olaf's men simply stared. Speechless. Lachlann recognized his own horse, his satchel hanging like a pannier from the saddle. He turned a scowl toward Niall, which was met with a wide grin. He'd have worried a lot less if he'd been told their horses had been collected from Aidan's and were just ahead of them, ready and waiting.

At Niall's signal, the three ran the short distance and got ahead of Olaf's men, who, wobbling from too much mead, were far too slow to react. When Lachlann's blade cleared the scabbard secured to his horse, he did not hesitate to run the first man through, even wiping his blade on the dead man's tunic.

With an evil grimace, Lachlann asked, "Who's next?"

He meant to put fear in them. The group, wavering slightly with no leader telling them what to do, was dumbfounded. The point of Lachlann's blade helped them to work it out quickly enough. His menacing offer of "No takers?" had the men's hands up in the air.

Aldred moved in to relieve Olaf's men of their weapons. Holding up a few good lengths of rope he'd collected, he asked, "Shall I tie them up?"

"And do better than they tied us up, please." Niall smiled, his relief obvious.

Lachlann quickly turned away. He was in no mood to celebrate. Not when Ethne was still in that whoreson's hands.

"A bit ruthless, aren't ye?" Niall asked.

"Knowing ye'd retrieved our mounts would have settled my angst," Lachlann answered.

He didn't want to believe Ethne's act in the cave. Verily, she must be afeared of what Olaf would do to her. So, why had she forced Lachlann's hand and ordered him to leave? This type of behavior was not what he'd come to expect from her. She was a kind woman. A passionate woman. A protective woman—

Realization struck, and he groaned at his own stupidity. The man had threatened Lachlann's life! That was the only answer that made any sense.

Niall was readying his horse, but finally responded, "I was busy. I not only retrieved them, but I went to the castle on yer behalf."

Another surprise, but a step Lachlann had considered they might take. At least before the delirium took over. Then his only thoughts had been about Ethne and his inevitable demise. "And?"

"*And* they'll not allow ye to be tried by Aidan when he has no authority here. Brian the Red is madder than hell and only awaits his mormaer's return. Ye do remember his feelings toward these people?"

"I do." Lachlann allowed himself the slightest relief and sighed. "So, now we go back for Ethne."

He was grabbing his horse's reins, about to step into

his stirrup, when he noticed Niall and Aldred's expressions. "What is amiss?

Niall finally spoke. "Lachlann, did ye not hear what she said to ye?"

"'Twas a lie!"

"She has feelings for the man. She trusts him, and he is offering her what she wants."

Lachlann had never had the chance to make the offer. No. That wasn't true. He'd hesitated. Far worse. "I know it was an act, to get us to leave. I'll not be put off by her attempt to protect me."

Niall dropped his gaze, no doubt picking up on Lachlann's growing rage, but it was Aldred who had the nerve to get up in Lachlann's face. "And if we return, we put ourselves at risk yet again with no one to back us up."

"We go knowing what to expect this time. We will be prepared."

"Think ye she will not *again* order ye to leave her? The truth is, ye mean little to her."

Lachlann crossed his arms over his chest. "So, ye attempt to protect me as well?" He snorted in disgust. "Truly, I must be a simpleton to be in such need of protection, first from a lass and now from the both of ye."

"I dinna want ye to be hurt by a lass who would take yer love and crush it beneath her feet." Niall's tone was loud for all its sternness.

"And I tell ye, 'tis not the way of it."

They held his gaze. Measuring his stubbornness? Mayhap. They'd find he had no intention of backing down.

"I am returning to get her safely away from that man. And then, I'm going to run Olaf through." Lachlann mounted his horse. "We need to kill the man if she's to feel safe. If she refuses me again, I'll know I've hurt her more than I believe, and my betrayal has turned her away from me."

He lamented that he'd seen to his own carnal desires instead of setting things right with her first. Her rejection had stung more than either Aldred or Niall could guess, not with the number of brokenhearted lasses they'd left behind them.

Shield and weapons in hand, Lachlann led them across the open heath. With the red sun setting before them, they pushed their horses as if Ethne's life depended on it. And he was afraid it did.

Held in the grip of shock and despair, Ethne trembled on the hard-packed floor beside the pallet, her knees tucked under her chin.

Domelch murdered my parents?

Ethne couldn't move. She couldn't stop reliving those last few hours when her mother still lived. She couldn't get past the heartbreak it still caused her.

Their mother had risen late that last morning. She'd been disoriented, complaining of painful cramps. It was so unlike her to share such things that Ethne, though still young, had been concerned. When Mother started vomiting blood, they'd gone to the healer for help. There was nothing that could be done. Their mother had died that same day, their father a few days later.

Ethne's chest tightened so much she couldn't take a breath.

Domelch must have poisoned them both. But why would she do such a thing? They had been nothing but kind and loving to their new daughter-in-law, accepting her into their family despite how bossy, demanding, and critical she always behaved.

She had never been happy staying with them, constantly voicing her desire to go back to her home along the sea. They'd all hoped Domelch would adjust to her new life. Many new brides did. That must have been why she killed them. Malcolm's desire to be there for his parents, to help them, was the problem as Domelch saw it, so she murdered them. Because he was a good son.

The realization hit hard, like running into a stone wall with her face.

Covering her eyes, Ethne gave in to her wretchedness. If her parents had lived, how different her life would be now. She'd be wed to a kind man, mayhap even have children of her own. Safe. Loved. Cared for.

Instead, she was a slave for Domelch and a prize for the men who vied to take her maidenhead. Olaf. Aidan. Lachlann…not Lachlann. Never Lachlann. He'd offered her only his loving. His tenderness filled her mind, the way he saw to her after that first time, washing away her virgin's blood, the way he held her close and awoken her with his warm kisses and caresses. In his arms, she'd been loved and protected. She would never regret giving herself to him.

The problem was he was far too chivalrous, always doing for others and not thinking of himself. She needed to protect him from himself. It was better that she be taken as Olaf's whore; she would know then what to expect. At least Olaf was honest with what he wanted from her.

Her head snapped up. She should not be simply waiting here for Olaf. She stood.

So lost in her misery and the memories of her loving parents, she was acting like a deer stricken with fear at the sight of a hungry wolf. Fear squeezed her gut.

"I've Ethne to see to now." Olaf's voice carried from beyond the entrance to the cave.

Too late. He was coming to take her as he'd promised.

The taking is easier if ye submit.

She clamped her hands tight. No matter how hard she squeezed her fingers, the tremors refused to stop.

His low chuckle made her wince. "I've neglected her long enough."

Her gasp traveled from her mouth to her toes and back. She all but flew out of the enclosed area, along the wall, to the narrow crevice that led to the small cave. Flat against the cold wall within, she was awash with sweat and quaked with fear. She thanked God for the darkness of the cave. The change in light had given her the extra time she needed to escape unnoticed.

The sounds of someone moving on the other side of the wall were muffled, but she closed her eyes and imagined it. Olaf tearing back the curtain. His angry face when he realized she was gone. He would be livid.

"Ethne?"

"Oh, God," she whispered, her heart thumping against her ribs.

His cry of outrage sent her toward the dark recesses where she'd found the crack opening to the pit holding Lachlann.

"Where could she have gone? Were ye not guarding her as I'd ordered?"

Mumbled answers.

"Enough!"

She patted her open palm along the wall, high and low, desperately searching for an escape. It was too dark to see anything, but she heard water dripping and remembered how wet Lachlann's pit had been. Drifting closer to the sound, the stench increased. The smell had been much stronger in the pit as well.

She knew in her heart there didn't have to be a passage between the two spaces other than the gap she'd found, but she prayed there was. Locating the crevice again, she dropped to her knees to follow it along the floor. It did open a bit more at the base, and a slight breeze blew across her hand.

When she ducked closer, the rotten smell blew in her face. A break in the wall. She followed the contour of the opening, but the bottom was sand. An arch. Something traipsed over her hand and she yelped, yanking back her hand.

"Did ye hear that?" Olaf's voice was quieter, but close. Just beyond the solid rock wall beside her.

She moved away as if somehow that could keep him from knowing where she was.

With her head to the ground, she could just make out the light shining into the pit from outside. The space was not big enough even for Finn.

"Another room?"

Olaf's voice kept her hands shaking even while she dug at the sand like a dog.

"Ethne?"

When he called to her, she gasped. His voice was no longer muffled. He'd found the passage entry.

Paralyzed with fear, her back to the wall, she struggled to settle her brain. He was far too large to get through. She was safe.

Turning her attention back to the sand, she raked her hands at the dampened floor. She needed to widen the size of the arch and make it big enough for her to pass through.

"Ethne, I know ye are in there."

She froze, but pressed on, continuing to dig through the dryer sand she'd uncovered.

"I can smell yer fear."

Desperate now, she pushed her head through the opening. Her shoulders still could not make the squeeze.

"Ye dinna need to fear me." He used the same seductive tone that sent waves of repulsion over her. "I will be gentle with ye. Ye have my word."

Grabbing up handfuls of pebbles and sand, she shoved them behind her, her mind threatening to freeze in panic.

"Come to me now, and I'll not punish ye." His voice was losing its composure. It must be killing him to sound calm when he'd prefer to rail at her.

"Get Talorc. He can get through."

Ethne squeaked. Her fingers scraped along something smooth. Smooth and cold. She wiped away the last of the sand. Her digging had uncovered a large rock, lodged in tight, running from one side of the tiny arch to the other. Her exit was blocked.

"No. No. NO!" she sobbed, frustration threatening to undo her.

"Ethne?" Olaf's tone was more coaxing now. He'd heard her.

She leaned a shoulder against the cave wall and held her bloodied hand over her face. Her eyes burned from the sand, but it didn't matter. This had all been for naught, and now Olaf would beat her or worse. Despite using every ounce of courage to escape this lecherous man, she had failed and might pay the ultimate price. He'd kill her.

"Do not make me have another get ye. Ye will not like what I do if I must have ye dragged out for me."

Mayhap she should just let him take her, and then she could kill him while he slept.

"Come to me willingly, Ethne."

She had no weapon, not even one to end her miserable existence. That would be better than submitting.

"Do. So. Now!" Olaf's patience was gone.

Dropping her face to the ground, she sobbed her frustration, pounding her fists into the sand. The hand touching her from the other side made her scream and jump out of its reach.

"Shh, Ethne, I am here." Lachlann's sweet voice.

She moved in closer. "What are ye doing here?"

He didn't respond. Instead, he dug around the flat rock lodged at the bottom of the crawl through.

"Talorc! Come! Quick now," boomed Olaf's loud voice.

Lachlann tried wiggling the stone out from its tight fit. When it fell back into place, he swore. On the second try, his arms reached through to allow him to wrap his fingers around the open edge and force it toward him. It left a huge indent in the ground and Ethne did not hesitate to drop down to the ground, turning her shoulders to force herself through the opening. He helped her from the other side. When both sides squeezed in at her hips, she froze.

"I'm stuck!"

"No, ye're not. Relax. Try to breathe easy. I will pull ye through." Lachlann's voice calmed her, and she did as he said.

"Try the other way, ye fool," Olaf barked in irritation.

Lachlann turned her gently. One way and then the other. "Deep breath now. Blow it out, nice and slow."

With a final tug, she cleared the passage. Her trembling sobs didn't stop her from going on her knees to hug him close to her, her head on his solid chest. "Thank ye, Lachlann."

"We've not a moment." He lifted her into his arms and ran to the ladder, handing her up to Niall, who stood a few rungs down from the top. The steps groaned under the weight. He hefted her up to Aldred, and the cracking of the step was as loud as a thunderclap. The broken pieces of wood dropped to the ground.

Niall quickly climbed off the ladder and reached back to Lachlann. "Give me yer hand."

The ladder cracked again, breaking apart beneath Lachlann's feet as he clasped Niall's hand.

"I could use some help." Niall strained against the weight of the man who hung by the strength of his arm alone.

It seemed like an eternity until Aldred grabbed the back of his tunic and together, they yanked Lachlann onto the ground on his belly.

"Damn, man, ye're a heavy one!" Aldred stood upright as he heaved a breath.

Ethne was beside Lachlann, "Are ye hurt?"

"Not me." He sat up, his surprised expression reassuring. "Are *ye* hurt?"

"We dinna have time if we're to get her away," Niall said.

"I'm fine now." When they stood, she hugged Lachlann to her again. "Thank ye for coming back for me."

"There's no lie that will keep me from ye, Ethne." He tipped up her chin to look her in the eyes. "No lie I won't tear down to see ye safe."

He kissed her then, a gentle kiss full of meaning.

"We canna tarry here." Niall handed down the reins. "Take her on yer horse and head back toward the castle, but go by way of Aidan's. I expect Olaf and his men will have the other way watched. We will meet at the castle."

CHAPTER 25

*E*thne wrapped her hands tightly around Lachlann, her cheek warm against his back. He urged his horse into a steady gallop across the glen. The rise and fall as they moved as one with the horse soothed his inner turmoil. He wanted to speak to her, but there'd been no time. Her eyes wide with fear had tugged at his heart. His need to protect her so fierce it nearly overwhelmed him.

It was late by the time they arrived at the copse of trees tucked into the valley, far enough away from Aidan's that they'd not be getting any unexpected visitors. With great care he slipped off the horse, careful not to awaken Ethne, who leaned forward onto the saddle. He couldn't say he was surprised she'd fallen asleep. She'd been through a lot.

"Wha—where are we?" She sat up and stretched her back. "Where's the castle?"

Lifting his arms to take her by the waist, he helped her down, but wasn't willing to immediately release her. He liked the sight of her tucked neatly up against him, the horse at her back.

"I've taken us another way, a quicker route," he said in a quiet voice.

The horse snorted as if recognizing the lie for what it was—a chance for them to be alone.

"But Niall said the castle was safest," she said, her fear still apparent in the tightness of her voice.

"I will not let anyone harm ye, Ethne." Lachlann held her sparkling gaze on him before lowering his lips to hers. She reached up on the tips of her toes, her head close, and accepted his kiss. A tender moment, mayhap a touch of passion, but a steadfast seal was more his intent. He hoped he could replace her fears with the strength of his protection.

Breaking the kiss before it ignited into more than reassurances, he remained close. "Ye said ye'd no use for me."

"What I said was ye are more trouble than ye are worth." She flashed him a small smile. "I lied."

"I know."

She nibbled her lower lip before speaking. "He threatened to kill ye unless I could convince ye to leave me."

Lachlann closed his eyes and heaved a heavy sigh before looking at her again. He shook his head and cupped her cheek. "I was sore afeared that somehow ye dinna realize…"

The words were escaping him. All that practice to say it just so, and his thoughts just scattered.

She touched her lips to his. "What do ye think I dinna realize?"

"That I'm in love with ye." The simplicity of those words worked just fine. A huge weight lifted from his shoulders, and his chest expanded with a deep, relaxing sigh. It suddenly became far less important that she say she felt the same. It didn't change how he felt because he would not be leaving her side. Not again.

Her eyes welled, her gaze dropping to his lips where she lightly traced her finger along them. The bottom and then the top. "I am not sure if this is what love is but please"—she looked into his eyes again—"do not leave me behind again. No matter what I say."

His chest tightened, his heart seeming to explode with joy. Despite such strong emotions, he was gentle when he took her into his arms. Even taking time to marvel that the length of her fit so perfectly against him. Her head against his chest. His hardness against her softness.

He rubbed his cheek against the side of her head, her hair still smelling of the stinky cave, but it didn't matter. "I want to take ye now and love ye again."

She hugged him tighter. Her consent. The horse was quickly seen to and hidden from the sight of anyone coming across the glen.

"Come." Taking her hand in his, he was again amazed at how small it was and, as he'd done that first time, he ran his thumb along it before kissing her palm.

"Do I still smell like flowers?" she teased.

"Ye smell like heaven." He tucked her hand through the crook of his arm and led her deep into the woods.

It was a warm night, thick with moisture and the promise of rain come the morn. The nighttime birds went about their hunting, unbothered by their presence. The sliver of moon cast the slightest bit of light through the trees. Stopping there, he pushed her long plaited hair back over her shoulders and kissed her again.

"Ye were verra brave," Lachlann said.

"I didna feel brave. I felt petrified."

He dipped his head to nibble at her lower lip. "Ye were brave, my love. Do not doubt it."

His hands gently caressed up her sides, squeezing and rubbing, to finally rest at her breasts, which he cupped with the same reverence. "More than brave."

Finding the ties at the neck of her garment, he kept his voice quiet as he loosened them. "Ye have always been brave."

The gown's neck widened and slid easily down her length. Pulling back, he left no part of her untouched with his gaze, and when his hands followed along the thin material of her undergarment, she closed her eyes.

With a single sweep of his hands, he doffed the only thing keeping him from seeing all of her. "Ethne, ye are more beautiful than a sunrise on a warm summer's day."

She met his kiss with urgency, but he was not going to rush through this. He wanted to leave her sated and well loved, secure in his love. She would know whose she was. Even going back to deal with her brother would not shake her belief in that.

A palm flat against her rounded bottom, he kneaded her, pulling her against his hardness. "I plan to spend the rest of my life showing ye the depth of my love."

Dropping his head, he swept his tongue against the firm peak of her nipple and rested the weight of its fullness in his hand. "My children will suckle at these breasts."

Her quiet moans might have been her agreeing. He lifted her chin, raising her eyes to meet his gaze. "Taking ye to wife would give me great pleasure."

She held his gaze, still searching to discern the truth. Best he show her what his words could not.

A soft patch of grass covered by his *plaide* served as their pallet. With her eyes on him, he made quick work of his own clothing.

"Oh!" She sat up, a hand reaching toward him. "Yer side? Does it cause ye pain?"

His lips twitched. "I canna say it has bothered me at all." He wiped a hand over it. No blood. "Mayhap the rest of me hurts even more."

"Oh, Lachlann." Ethne's tone sounded far too serious and concerned.

"Whisht." He winked and dropped to his knees before her. "We've far more pressing matters."

He covered her, supporting his body with an arm on either side of her, and kissed her passionately. Without hesitation, she wrapped her arms around his back to pull him flush against her. Such unleashed passion sent him past any thought of holding off. When he entered her, he was reminded of how well she fit him in every way.

He rode her slowly, every movement a special gift to her of his undying promise of love. She cried out in her pleasure, and he tightened his control to not do the same. When her breathing eased, her expression was questioning.

He explained, "I would have ye cry out yer pleasure again."

Ethne watched him this time. And he kept his eyes on her to know when the moment neared.

When she cried out his name, he let lose his release and was overwhelmed by the explosion of pleasure flooding his entire body as he filled her. He'd never experienced such a feeling. A feeling of being where he belonged.

Spent, he collapsed onto her, but was quick to turn and tuck her against his side, her head on his chest and her leg over his. He sighed. All was right with the world once again. "How is it I have such peace with ye here beside me? I have never felt so before."

Her only response was a gentle snoring, and he chuckled. That would do for now.

Awakened by the sound of a single horse galloping at a great speed toward where Ethne lay asleep in his arms, Lachlann jerked the *plaide* from beneath him to cover her. He sprang to his feet and quickly yanked on his trews and tunic. Aidan's men surrounded him. His skin grew itchy, and he rolled to the balls of his feet, readying himself for whatever came next. How long had they watched them here in the dark, the sun not even having cleared the horizon?

Aidan jumped down from his horse, his men filling in behind him like a force to be reckoned with as he approached Lachlann. With angry strides and his red face tight with fury, saying he was enraged was no exaggeration.

"Oh, no." Ethne's quiet voice carried only as far as Lachlann. "I thought we were safe here."

"As did I." He spoke in the same quiet voice. He reached behind him, and she took his hand, coming up alongside him wrapped only in his *plaide*. "Get yerself dressed. Quick now."

"Are ye certain?" Her rounded eyes showed her fear. "I'm afeared for ye."

"I am certain. Go."

She collected her clothes that had been left forgotten in a pile on the ground. When she would have trotted to a more secluded spot out of the sight of prying eyes, Thomas moved to intercept her. He shifted course whenever she tried to go around him, a wide grin on his face.

"What is this? A game?" Lachlann exploded at the ridiculous action. "Allow her to pass, damn it!"

Aidan responded. "She bared herself for *ye*. There's no reason for modesty now."

Lachlann took a step closer to Thomas, the hilt of his dagger gripped tight in his hand. "There is. And well ye know it."

The old man shrugged. "Whores have no reason to hide themselves."

"Whore? What sort of chieftain treats the lasses in his care this way?"

"She's yers now. Ours only *if* we take her back." Aidan's anger had cooled or mayhap it just simmered below the surface. For the first time, he turned his gaze to Ethne. "Although we may not want her now that ye've soiled her."

Her pained expression sent Lachlann over the edge. If only they weren't outnumbered. Regret tightened his gut. He wished he'd gone the way Niall had said so there would at least be some hope of reinforcements against this angry mob that seemed bent on ripping what was left of her pride asunder.

"She doesn't need to go back," Lachlann said. "I am taking her to wife. She will be going with me."

The tiniest smile on Aidan's face sparked Lachlann's need to survive. He feared the worst.

"And where is it ye think ye are going, Lachlann?" Aidan asked. "Or should I call ye *murderer?*"

"I murdered no one." Lachlann let loose his irritation, ignoring a growing sense of doom. "'Twas an accident. No more."

"And that may be what we decide, but *we* are the ones to decide."

He scoffed. "Yer belittling her does not make it true. Just as calling me a murderer does not make it so."

"It does to us," Thomas piped up, his gaze traveling Ethne's body, waiting anxiously to see her bared for all.

Lachlann had wondered about this man's interest in her, and he appeared to have not been far from the mark. Mayhap they'd all been hoping to take her at some point.

"Allow her to withdraw so that she may cover herself." Lachlann would have gutted the man if the others didn't look so eager to take his place.

Thomas merely laughed, a cruel sound. "She can try."

Ethne took it upon herself to do just that, playing swerve and catch with the much larger, and surprisingly faster man. It was a risky game, and Lachlann wished she'd given him a moment more to reason with them before consenting to it.

Thomas yanked the *plaide* away just as she escaped into the bushes. And Lachlann had taken the two steps closer so that he was right there to punch him solidly in the face. The telltale sound of bones crushing was satisfying.

Thomas merely wiped at the blood from his nose and turned to the others. "A ripe piece indeed."

And that was all it took for Lachlann to give free rein to his anger with a punch to the man's stomach. A punch so hard that Thomas doubled over. A stupid move, but Lachlann was no longer thinking clearly. It didn't matter that he was outnumbered.

When Lachlann would have followed up with a downward pummel to Thomas's back, Malcolm grabbed his arm and jerked him away. He ripped the blade from Lachlann's grip. "Ye should have used this when ye had the chance."

Another man yanked Lachlann's arms tight behind him, holding him in place, but he ignored the man and instead, turned his fiercest scowl on Malcolm.

"Ye were her protector!" Lachlann shouted. "And yer friends speak of yer sister like that?"

Malcolm's face reddened right before he punched Lachlann in the stomach with a fist that felt like solid wood. He lifted his head only to be backhanded by the man, splitting his lip. With no consideration for his helplessness, Malcolm repeated the action to his jaw and then his side until Lachlann dropped to his knees. The man holding him finally released him to fall the rest of the way to the ground with a loud moan.

"I am a good brother," Malcolm said from where he stood over him, his breath heaving. "I'll beat the shite out of anyone who deflowers my little sister."

Bile rose in Lachlann's throat, and he rolled over, struggling to get up. His entire body burned; the pain was intense. His mouth full of his own blood, he lifted his head only enough to spit it onto the ground where it mingled with the blood from his many wounds.

Lachlann must have passed out because the next thing he became aware of was an excruciating kick to his side, followed by near drowning when water was poured over his head.

"Get up, ye miserable cur," Malcolm said. His steady breathing indicated Lachlann must have been out for a while.

The sight of Ethne fully clothed, her face awash with tears, but restrained by Thomas, sparked Lachlann's defenses. When he tried to stand, the quick movements sent sharp pain to his head, and he crashed to the ground a second time.

"Again."

Aidan's words made no sense until Lachlann was doused with water. He struggled to get up on all fours, unable to catch his breath, as if he were indeed drowning.

"Get. Him. Up." Aidan's orders were followed by a man on either side of Lachlann, pulling him to standing, supporting him when his legs crumpled beneath the weight of his own body.

Thomas spit on him and returned to Ethne's side, Malcolm close behind him.

"I hope she was worth it," Aidan said in a speculative tone before moving closer to Ethne, lifting her head, and wiping her tears. "Ah, but I'm sure ye are."

The way the man searched her... If there was ever a time in his life that Lachlann needed to force himself to stand against anything, it was now. No woman was in more need of his protection than she was. And at this very moment. He jerked himself away from the men to stand on his own feet, a wide stance making it slightly easier to hold himself upright, but only slightly.

"So ye belittle her still?" Lachlann asked, but expected no answer. "She deserves a champion, not yer insults."

"And ye are in no position to judge us," Malcolm shouted back, but Aidan merely raised a finger to silence him.

Aidan turned his steady gaze back to Lachlann. "So have ye taken what ye came for?"

"I've found more than what I came for," Lachlann said, turning his gaze on Ethne in the hope she would understand his words of love.

"Ethne said it was silver they came for," Malcolm said to Aidan.

Her expression revealed her regret at revealing the truth, but Lachlann didn't need to witness it to know her confession had come under duress. Mayhap even in *his* defense.

"We've come from the priory." His jaw clamped tight, but then he thought better of keeping silent. "'Twas the silver they wanted us to retrieve for them."

"So deflowering virgins was an added benefit?" Aidan questioned him as if he'd come into their tribe with the sole purpose of doing just that. "Ah, but ye've promised to take her to wife. Is that not what ye promised her?"

It had not been that way at all. The man was making Lachlann sound lecherous, but he refused to bare his soul to Aidan. Instead, Lachlann asked, "Think ye she would choose to stay with ye? And yer belittling?"

"Unless ye can pay us for the life of the one ye murdered, ye can go nowhere until we deal with the loss. Just compensation must be made."

Lachlann's gut squeezed. He had no such funds, and he was fairly certain Aidan knew that.

"I am the one who killed him." Ethne's declaration made Lachlann cringe. The others in the group began murmuring, and Aidan had new eyes for the lass beside him.

"Is that so?" he asked, amazingly unperturbed by the revelation.

Lachlann spoke up, gasping with pain as he did. "She lies. She's trying to protect me."

Aidan did not even glance his way, but held his hand up to silence the others. "Well, ye wish to claim the murder was at yer hand?"

"Not murder. An accident," she said.

With a slow sweep of his tongue, Aidan wetted his lips as if he were about to eat his favorite meal. "Go on, little Ethne. Tell me what ye did."

"Uradech came to the cave and found me undressed."

"Were ye with Lachlann?" Aidan's question was an accusation.

"Nay!" Lachlann and Ethne answered at the same time.

"But did Lachlann not stay behind with ye? Did he not try to get betwixt yer legs?" Aidan's guttural laugh brought a smile to those around him. "How long have ye been laying with him?"

"'Twas not like that!" She sounded defensive. "He was outside with Finn. I was taking a bath"

"A bath?" Thomas barked a laugh. "After he took yer maidenhead?"

"We had not yet—nay!" She wiped at her face, but Lachlann could think of nothing to stop this terrible confession. "Uradech insisted he would take me to wife, that he had yer blessing, and he was there to force himself on me if I didna take him willingly to my bed."

"Ye understood he had my blessing then?" Aidan asked.

The air stilled in Lachlann's chest. He prayed she would not respond.

"Aye, but *I* didna consent. He chased me, and when he would have ripped my clothing away, he fell back on the stool and it crashed beneath him. 'Twas the leg of the stool that pierced him, killing him."

The chirping of the grasshoppers was the only sound

as the men from her tribe stared at her, mulling over her confession. Aidan did not move a muscle. It seemed as if he was waiting for her to realize what she'd just admitted to.

Lachlann finally broke the silence, his voice low, solemnly quiet, while he hoped against hope that he could somehow save her still. "May I take her with me now?"

Aidan's expression of disbelief said it all, but he did not respond. Instead, Malcolm stepped up to his sister. "Ye have defied the laws of our tribe, Ethne."

No doubt filled with fear at what she'd done, Ethne's mouth went slack and her body began to tremble.

"Please, Aidan." Lachlann's entire body was rigid. "Allow me to take her away."

Aidan turned to him. "Come now, Lachlann. Have ye anything of value to offer for the life of our beloved prince? We are family after all, and we take that bond quite seriously, though others may not feel the same. One of our own has been murdered. The only acceptable payment is the life of the murderer. A life for a life."

"I didna mean to. He fell," she said, her words barely above a whisper and her face stricken with fear.

"Ye knew he had come from me and had been ordered to consummate the marriage, Ethne." Aidan's commanding tone brought the desired result. She took a shaky breath. "Ye defied him. Ye defied me. The result was his death."

Lachlann reached toward his sack, but Thomas grabbed at his arm.

"I have something of value. 'Tis in my bag," Lachlann said, turning back for Aidan's permission.

He nodded his consent. Lachlann burrowed down to the bottom of his satchel and withdrew the silver medallion, the only reminder of who he'd been before Clan MacDonell had taken him in, raised him as their own, and given him a place to belong. The arrow that pierced the hog glistened from the light of the fire, giving the impression it moved right before his eyes.

Lachlann held up the medallion by the chain and turned toward Aidan. "I will pay for the life of Uradech with this."

"Lachlann, no!" Ethne cried.

The fierceness of Aidan's expression could not be denied. When he ripped the item from his hand, Lachlann was taken aback at the barely contained rage. Aidan's scrutiny was intense. He held the medallion close to his face, turning it this way and that, and all the while shooting glances at Lachlann as if he'd suddenly grown a third head. For a moment, he thought Aidan was going to throw it back at him. He just didn't understand why. It held great value. Even greater than all the costly trinkets Domelch covered herself in.

"I will accept this." With a tight scowl, Aidan lowered his hands and lifted his eyes to glare openly at Lachlann. "Take her away. Now! Before I change my mind."

When he would have demanded explanations from Aidan about his strange reaction, Ethne was beside him, grabbing his hand to pull him toward his horse.

"Come," she said. "Let us leave here. Now, as he says."

Lachlann accepted her help, leaning heavily against her. It took several tries before he was able to mount his horse. Aidan's eyes never wavered from them and his men never moved. They never responded in any way except the tenseness in their bodies, the readiness to attack if given the word by their leader. No word came. Instead, they simply watched, probably following them with their eyes until they disappeared down the path that led to the castle.

CHAPTER 26

The travel toward the castle was slow because of Lachlann's injuries. He and Ethne took their time, riding gently rather than galloping. They spoke of Finn. This was the first time she did not have him with her. Her concern touched Lachlann's heart, and he promised to do what he could to see that the child was safe. It was close to nightfall when they arrived at the same glen where Niall, Lachlann, and Aldred had met up with Cull. So long ago now, or so it seemed.

Just clearing the low-hanging branches, Aldred and Niall paced the meadow. They were having a heated argument while their horses grazed nearby. When Niall noticed them approach on horseback, he turned his angry demeanor on Lachlann.

"We've been waiting," Niall stated before Lachlann even had a chance to dismount. His tone, not surprisingly, matched his demeanor perfectly.

"I went a different way." Lachlann's dismount was less than graceful, his side especially aching from the beating he'd received, but he helped Ethne down before facing his friend.

Niall stood there shaking his head, his hands at his waist. "To what purpose do ye disobey my orders?"

Lachlann's face heated. His lips flattened at the sarcastic comment until he gasped at the pain. Gingerly touching the split bottom lip. This was hardly the time to pull rank but Niall seemed intent, his eyes sparkled.

"We worried they'd caught ye!" His gaze finally moved over Lachlann, his blood-encrusted clothes and black eye. "It appears our concerns were well grounded."

Aldred stepped closer and prodded Lachlann's swollen face in several places. Each time, he winced and jerked back. It seemed one wince of pain was not sufficient proof of what had transpired as far as Aldred was concerned.

"Ye are correct." Lachlann raised a hand to halt any further comments. "I should have obeyed and not gone a different way. There's no reason for ye to say more."

Niall seemed appeased with that, relieved even, to have Lachlann with them now.

"Then I will tell ye of our news," Niall said. "We came across Brian and his soldiers heading toward the shore. They received word from their mormaer to be on alert for Olaf and his men. They were ready for a fight, so we joined up with them to search out the islanders. With our greater number of warriors, Olaf was easily convinced to surrender."

Niall held up the sack of coins, waggling his brows and smiling. "And we've recovered the silver for the priory."

Lachlann fisted his hip but grimaced and relaxed his stance when pain shot through his entire body. "Did the mormaer not demand to be given the silver?"

Shrugging, Niall explained, "He was impressed by the earlier tokens given in his absence, the tokens *my uncle* had offered. The mormaer required nothing more." Niall finally turned to Ethne. "We ask forgiveness for not telling ye we'd come from the priory to retrieve their silver. We meant no harm in keeping the truth from ye."

Her jaw tightened but she said nothing.

"Will we be seeing ye to the church for protection now that ye can no longer return to yer clan?"

Her eyes rounded, and she pulled back as if she'd been struck, but just as quickly stiffened her back and turned to Lachlann. "'Twould be best."

"Nay!" Lachlann winced again before responding with less emotion. "Nay, ye're coming with us." Lachlann glared at Niall. The man was dumb as a sack of rocks sometimes. "She will not need to be left at some church."

Aldred's face contorted with disgust. "We canna have a lass join us. 'Tis dangerous and uncomfortable and she'll complain the entire way."

"And we need to get to the priory and return to our clan before the first snow," Niall said to her matter-of-factly. "We've taken longer here than we intended."

"I will not leave her behind." Lachlann hoped his tone was emphatic enough for them this time. Then he turned to her, contradicting their idiocy. "This way *I'll* know ye're safe."

"And she'll ride with ye? On yer horse? The entire way?" Niall glanced heavenward with a sigh. "Ye'll be dragging out an uncomfortable journey, Lachlann."

"I dinna want to be any trouble." Ethne nodded in agreement with Niall and turned that nod toward Lachlann.

"Ye're no trouble." Lachlann offered her a reassuring smile, but was fuming and turned on Niall. "Would ye have me just up and leave my wife? Abandon her on the steps of a church?"

Niall and Aldred exchanged glances. It was Niall who spoke first. "Yer wife? And when did this take place exactly?"

"Well...it...has not happened *yet*." Lachlann hated how sheepish he sounded.

He turned to Ethne, holding her close and blocking

out Niall and Aldred. "A formality only. A visit to the chapel here seems like a fine idea. Surely, someone there can witness our agreement and vows." Under his breath, he added, "I want ye as my wife, and I'll not wait another moment."

Aldred stepped closer, his face contorted with his confusion. "Ye've promised ye'd marry her?"

"I *promised* nothing," Lachlann bellowed, regretting it only because of the pain that shot down his side. More quietly, he added, "'Tis what I want."

Ethne shifted uncomfortably. Damn! She was getting the wrong idea.

He set his jaw tight before taking a breath and responding, nearly matching the man in his angry response. "I *asked* her if I could take her to wife, ye knave."

"And she told *ye* aye?" Aldred matched his outraged tone.

"And why would she not?" Lachlann's defensive words and fierce scowl received no answer, but he still added, "She has agreed."

"Actually, I dinna agree." Her quiet voice had all eyes on her.

"What are ye saying?" He didn't like the way her eyes were downcast, and he tipped up her head. "Ye know I love ye. Dinna make me live without ye. Not now. Not after I've found ye."

She glanced at Aldred. "Yer friends have sage advice."

"They're no better than horse dung." Lachlann ignored the boisterous objections to the label and continued. "They know nothing. And they certainly dinna know me as a man in love."

"They seem to think I need only protection, and 'tis true, I can receive that from the church." Her eyes rounded. "That was all I had planned to do when I decided to leave. I decided to come here, Lachlann. I even lied to Domelch, so she would send me here. That was when ye got hurt."

Taking her delicate hand in his, he asked, "So, I got in the way of your escape?"

One slim shoulder tucked up. She dropped her gaze, withdrawing her hand from his to clasp them tightly together.

"Then I owe ye." He offered his most charming of smiles, but got no response. "Ye'd prefer to follow through with those plans? Even now?"

Her eyes remained downcast. "Yer friends are righ—"

"They're no longer my friends."

She made a sound that could have been a giggle. "Regardless…they are correct. 'Tis just protection I need. Surely, the church will provide that for me."

"But ye deserve better." He tugged one hand free to kiss her open palm. "My love, ye need look no further than me."

"Ye are a good man, Lachlann." When she finally looked up at him, her eyes were filled with tears. "Ye would be honor bound for what we have shared, but I will not have it. I would not have ye give up not only the treasured link to yer past, but yer life for me."

And there it was. The guilt she was feeling over the loss of his father's medallion. He would not deny the loss was heavy on his heart. Nor would he deny the price he paid for her life was well worth it.

"I would be honored to give up my life for ye. And if that is all ye want from me?" He shrugged, unsuccessfully ignoring the sudden tightness in his chest that had nothing to do with his beating. "I will accept it, but I will not go on with my life as if I'd not found the lass I want to spend that life with."

Her face tight. "Lachlann, do not—"

"Ach, but I *will*."

He wrapped her in an embrace and held her close

before taking her lips in a most persuasive kiss. A gentle kiss meant to stir her heart and set afire her passionate core. To hell with anyone else watching. To hell with anyone else deciding what should be done. To hell with never being able to make love to her again. All these things he put into the gentlest of kisses and prayed it would be enough.

When he broke the kiss, he waited for her passion-drunk vision to clear before he spoke again, still holding her close. "My past matters little now. *Ye* are my present and *ye* are my future."

Ethne blinked. He held her gaze steady, reading every emotion she wrestled with until he was certain she knew that he meant every word.

Aldred coughed behind them. "Well, we could see if they have room for us in the castle. 'Tis getting quite late."

"We can find Cull. Mayhap he can help find us a place to sleep." Niall's voice held that same uncertain tone, but Lachlann refused to look away from Ethne.

"Are ye two coming?" Niall asked.

"Are ye ready?" Lachlann asked. "Or would ye prefer to stay under the stars again tonight?"

Ethne said, "The castle will be a fine change from the loud caves."

Niall and Aldred got on their horses, but when he began to put all of his weight on one foot to mount, Lachlann moaned.

Ethne pulled back on his hand. "Mayhap we can follow on foot?"

He turned to the other two. "We will be close behind."

They must have had some reaction, but he only had eyes for her.

"Will yer friends ever forgive me?" she asked. "For taking ye from them?"

He grinned, understanding her concerns, but not certain if she referred to tonight or the rest of his life.

He shrugged. "It matters not how they feel about it. Only that I dinna choose to be without ye."

With his courser trailing behind, its long reins dragging along the ground, and their joined hands swaying between them, they continued to the castle.

Ethne knew walking would lessen the pain in Lachlann's body so she forced him to take it slowly. They arrived at the castle just as the gates were closing. He stopped several times to share greetings with people he'd met earlier and to be welcomed back. The meal in the Great Hall was about to begin, but she felt compelled to follow her heart and seek out the priest.

When she came with Malcolm and Domelch, she'd always been afraid to approach the priest. With Finn at her side, it would have been difficult to keep the visit from them, and she wasn't sure what they might do to her had they learned of it.

Lachlann strode past the Great Hall, leading the way to the chapel with a tight grip of her hand as if afraid he might lose her. That warmed her heart as much as the way he blocked the masses from smashing into her. Those people were hurrying by, paying little heed to anyone they bumped into in their attempt to make it to the Great Hall.

Ethne paused in the doorway of the small, stone chapel to breathe in the pleasing aroma with closed eyes. The interior was brightly lit with several candles and smelled of incense. "Mmm, it seems a peaceful place." She opened her eyes.

"Mayhap the priest is nearby." Lachlann's eyes were bright with excitement and matched the quickening of her heart.

"Or he is at the meal," she said and hoped he didn't hear the disappointment in her voice.

"There." Lachlann pointed at a small man whose head was barely visible above the altar, his face cast down as he worked. "I believe 'tis him."

The priest spared them the briefest glance. "Ye've missed Mass. Come back tomorrow."

She halted in her steps, but Lachlann pulled her closer and replied, "We've been a long time without a blessing."

The priest ceased his busy preparations of cleaning, wiping, and tidying to study them. "Who would that be? Ye?" He pointed one long finger at Lachlann, then at her. "Or ye?"

The priest held her gaze, and she was overcome by a sense of coming home. "It is I who have been separated, though not of my own choosing."

He nodded as if understanding, but how could he really? "Then let us see to ye."

Guiding them to a bench, the priest sat beside Ethne while Lachlann took the seat on her other side.

"Ye seem familiar, lass. Might I know yer family?"

She ducked her head. Priests must say that to everyone. This man could not know her.

"Ye have a brother Malcolm?" he asked.

Their eyes met and her lips parted. He did seem slightly familiar, but with his simple white tunic and long, dark overcoat, there was little chance she'd recognize one monk from another—

"Are ye Ethne? Little Ethne?"

He recognized her. She closed her eyes and took a slow, steady breath. Opening her eyes, she smiled at him and nodded. "I am."

Covering her hands where they rested on her lap, the priest smiled. "'Tis good to have ye back in the fold. And who is this man with ye?"

"This is my—"

"Protector," Lachlann answered for her.

She turned to correct him. "No. Ye are no mere protector."

"Then what is it he means to ye?" the priest asked with his solemn expression and solid gaze. "Should I be readying some parchment for the contract?"

Her breath caught, and she considered Lachlann for a very long time, or so it seemed.

"I am in love with him." She said the words with great awe before repeating them more emphatically. "I am, Lachlann. I am in love with ye."

Lachlan placed a gentle hand on her back and said, "If ye realize yer love for me, let me take ye to wife."

Her thoughts raced through the short amount of time she'd known him. Finn gripping his leg to hide from her. Lachlann's warm smile had taken her breath away. Her spouting off at Domelch, and that wink! His expression of steadfast support had caused her heart to break out of its chains of complacency.

How could she not love this man?

"Aye, we will be wed." Determined now, she turned to the priest. "Can ye do so now?"

The priest nodded. Confessions were made at Ethne's request. She wanted to come to Lachlann as she would have had her parents lived to meet him. A simple agreement stating all his worldly possessions were hers, and since she had nothing to offer but herself, he accepted her into his tender care with the promise of seeing to her in all ways. And the contract was signed.

"Many thanks, Father. Ye are kind to have helped us with this since the hour is so late," she said.

The priest dipped his head, accepting her thanks, and said, "I am happy to marry a couple so truly in love as ye two. May God shine his face upon ye and be gracious unto ye."

A blessing from the church, and the deed was done. Lachlann was her husband. And she was his wife.

A wife? She had never considered that would be her lot in life. Things were definitely different now.

Standing in the entrance to the Great Hall, she was surrounded by kind faces smiling and enjoying each other's company. There was not one person she recognized and why would she? She was the outsider here and her heart started racing. She resisted Lachlann's tug on her arm.

"What is amiss?" he asked.

"This is wrong. I canna come in here with ye like this." Rejection was something she knew quite well and experienced often from these people. "I am not allowed in here."

"Why would that be?"

His questioning gaze changed to one of understanding right before her eyes.

"If ye prefer, we can eat under the stars."

She located Niall and Aldred. They sat with some castle folk, but the soldiers at the next table, she recognized. They'd been the ones who had run them out of the hall. Taking a slow, deep breath, she fought against the fear worming its way through the pit of her stomach, the one that urged her to make her escape before she was spotted.

"I would be happy to be alone with ye." Lachlann tipped her chin up to look in her eyes. "'Tis *ye* I wish to share my repast with."

"Lachlann." Aldred stood at the table where he sat beside a young man with dark, curly hair and waved them closer.

Her gut tightened. "Mayhap I should eat outside and ye can partake with—"

"Never!" Lachlann's words were quiet, but his tone

firm. "Never would I choose another's company over yers."

He must have read her indecision because he tucked her hand into the crook of his arm and walked straight to the table.

"Ladies? Gentlemen? I wish to make known to ye my wife, Ethne." The pride in his voice brought tears to her eyes, but she dared not venture more than a glimpse to see his happiness at the pronouncement.

A young woman about her own age with dark hair bounded forward, excitement lighting her face, and took Ethne in close for a sweet hug. "A wife! Oh, Lachlann, how wonderful." The lass pulled back, lightly taking her hand. "And she's a beauty."

A man Ethne didn't recognize came up alongside the lass. "Aye. Ye've done well, Lachlann." He bowed at the waist. "My name is Cull and this is my wife Rhona."

"Pleased I am to make yer acquaintance." Ethne hoped she didn't appear as awkward as she felt. Lachlann wrapping a possessive arm about her waist was a boon. She smiled up at him. "I believe *I* am the one who has done well."

Ignoring Niall and Aldred, who stood there with jaws dropped, Cull motioned to the table. "Join us. We will celebrate yer good news."

Lachlann sat beside Aldred, so Ethne was placed on the other side, between Lachlann and Rhona. Cull remained standing and lifted a glass.

"My friends. We have our pilgrims back with us this night."

A large red bearded man at the next table huzzaed.

"With exciting news." Cull smiled at Ethne. "Lachlann has taken a wife. Let us raise a glass to his good fortune!"

The rest of the assembly huzzaed as well. This was followed by loud banging and carrying on, with all eyes on Lachlann and her. He just smiled at her.

"They're saying we need to kiss."

"What?" Her face heated.

"A simple show of affection. No more." His mischievous grin should have warned her, but as soon as she nodded her consent, her drew her onto his lap and into his tight embrace. His mouth was so warm on hers that she quickly forgot the show they were putting on, getting lost in his passionate kiss. Her heart raced and her breath quickened. When he finally broke the kiss, his solid hand at her back was the only thing that kept her from becoming a puddle on the floor.

The claps and shouts of encouragement were deafening, but he whispered close to her.

"I am not certain I want to wait until we have eaten, my love."

"And how do ye like being in a stone structure compared with the *caves*?" Rhona said the last word as if it was something spooky.

Ethne just laughed. "Much quieter, for certain."

Cull spoke up. "And the pagans? Are they what made it loud? With their human sacrifices?"

"Nay. The wind, it howls constantly," she said. "I dinna know anything about human sacrifices."

The lad got excited to be sharing what he knew. "They practiced human sacrifice, the pagans from the past. 'Tis Christians who value life."

She shrugged. "Well, I witnessed killing only in battle. Does that disappoint ye?"

"A little." He grinned at her.

"So, ye'll be staying here with us? When the men go to the priory?" Rhona asked, the musicians just tuning up a short distance away. The tables were being cleared and set aside for the dancing that would soon be taking place.

Long wooden benches were set up along the walls to accommodate the watchers and dancers that needed to rest.

Ethne hesitated, but she'd been over this and didn't need to revisit it. She answered simply, "No, I will be following my husband."

The girl said, "As ye should."

Lachlann looked pleased as well and took her hand to settle on one of the benches. With him beside her, and Aldred and Niall on the other side of him, she wasn't sure how much they had heard.

After they'd eaten and once the music started, Lachlann was quick to stand in front of her, hand extended. "Shall we?"

Immediately concerned, she said, "But yer injuries."

"The pain has subsided." He winked at her. "I feel young and spry."

"Oh, dear!"

"Does that worry ye?" He pulled her to standing and waggled his brows until she smiled.

She slapped at his chest. "Such silliness. One dance only." Her face flooded with heat. She hadn't danced since she was a small child. "I am not sure..."

Taking her hand, he said, "Dinna underestimate yer husband's ability."

And with a tug and a whoosh, they joined the long line of others dancing about the Great Hall. It didn't take long for her to remember the steps, including shifting her weight from one foot to another to keep from stumbling. Lachlann was correct; he was quite good. The big smile never left his face.

When they sat out, he plopped quite hard onto the wood surface, the toll dancing had taken on him more than he would admit.

"'Tis quite late." She stated the obvious.

A wolfish grin on his face, he leaned closer and asked,

"Are ye looking to take advantage of my weakened state, woman?"

"If ye would like me to."

He barked a laugh. "That doesn't sound nearly convincing enough." Dragging her across his lap and turning her face, his passionate kiss quickly stole her breath. "I canna wait any longer to be with ye."

She whispered, "And where shall we go?"

"I've a place just for us."

He led the way to a short hall behind the dais where the mormaer and his lady wife watched the goings-on in the hall. Three deep alcoves lined the outside wall. A heavy tapestry closed off the area with enough room to stand comfortably and a thick cushioned window seat to sleep on.

Ducking into the first alcove, he pulled her against him and kissed her deeply. "Ah, wife," he spoke the words against her lips.

"Husband." She used the same intimate tone. It did sound good to her ears.

"Cull said the wife of the mormaer herself insisted we sleep here." He offered a sheepish grin. "I prefer to sleep alone with my wife."

A hand to her head, he urged her to rest against his chest. It took little urging. She was exhausted.

He suppressed a yawn. "Wife?" A question this time.

"Aye?"

"I am too tired to see to my husbandly duty." Another yawn. "Mayhap if I sleep a bit?"

She led the way to the soft cushion. She lay across it in answer and he settled beside her, holding her in his arms. A gentle kiss on the back of the hand holding hers, she said, "We have the rest of our lives."

CHAPTER 27

True to his word, once Lachlann had rested sufficiently, he woke Ethne with gentle kisses along every part of her body. They made love slowly, touching with gentle hands what they could not see in the darkness. Come morning, they joined the others, but kept to themselves and came back early in the evening to spend the night the same way. The celebration for the return of their leader was ongoing so they were not missed. That suited Lachlann fine. As his injuries healed, he was also getting to better know this woman whom he'd taken to wife.

The third night, he awoke to her sobbing, but when he moved to comfort her, he realized she was still asleep. Gathering her close against him, he asked, "What is upsetting ye so, Ethne?"

"Finn," she cried, her lashes fluttering open, but her sobs continued. "Oh, poor Finn."

"What has happened to the boy?"

She glanced around, a deep furrow between her eyes. "Where has Finn gone?"

Lachlann held her closer and said, "Nothing has happened to the lad. Ye had a bad dream only."

Her sobs finally subsiding, she said, "It seemed so real."

He kissed her firmly on the lips. "'Twas not real. 'Twas only a dream."

She nodded, but her face didn't relax, her look of concern continued. The next morning when they were breaking their fast, she asked him if she'd said anything when she was asleep.

"Ye called out for Finn." Lachlann poured honey over the porridge he'd dished for himself.

"I have this bad feeling still." She pushed aside her bowl. "And I canna even remember my dream."

He took a spoonful of the sweet mix, talking while he chewed. "That is probably why ye sense something is wrong. If ye could remember yer dream, ye'd be less concerned."

"I hope so." She didn't sound convinced.

That night, it was the same, but Lachlann pressed her about the dream while she was just awakening.

"They were in the caves. Verra bad." That was all she'd said before she opened her eyes, only to break down and sob against his chest.

"I think ye miss the boy." He ran an open palm down her back, pressing her to him. "He is like yer son."

She looked hopeful and asked, "Do ye truly believe so?"

"It makes sense, dinna it? He's been left behind, and ye're not sure how he is when he was always yer priority. Mayhap we can see how he fares."

"Are ye saying we could go to the cave and see him?"

It did not go well the last time they saw Aidan, but the price had been paid. Would it be enough?

~

Just the thought of seeing her "family" again brought on more tears. Ethne shook her head. "Think ye they care how I feel about them? No, 'tis better if I leave them in my past, both Finn and Mongfind. Though I cared for them as my own, they are not mine."

Lachlann gathered her close, his scent comforting her as did the way he gently stroked her hair. "If ye change yer mind, come and tell me. We will see what can be done."

"Thank ye." She snuggled against him before righting herself. "I would like to have a good night's sleep and an end to these nightmares."

He grinned. "Mayhap I have not loved ye well enough lately."

"I dinna think *that* is the problem."

She'd heard him discussing their journey to Restenneth Priory with Niall and Aldred, making their plans, but Lachlann had shared none of it with her. There could be only one reason for that. He had changed his mind about her going.

"If ye prefer to leave me here while ye bring the silver to the nuns, I will."

He stilled before answering. "Nay. I said I would not leave ye behind, and I will not. We are merely waiting for the solstice before we leave. The daylight will aid our journey, give us more time to travel before we need to stop for the darkness. Why would ye think I would leave ye now, when I've become so accustomed to ye?"

His words came with a gentle squeeze. Her fears set aside, she closed her eyes, but his words echoed in her mind. The solstice. That had been when she planned to be gone from the caves.

Disorientation washed over her.

The solstice was always an important date for Aidan, the day he planned his most elaborate observances.

She is named for a princess and will be offered at the solstice observance.

"What is amiss?" Lachlann asked, clear concern in his question. "Ye're so pale, Ethne. Sit down."

"Nay!" The memories of past sacred observances carried out on the solstice crowded her mind. This year would include many others. A chance to become powerful again. Performing the rituals exactly correct.

They practiced human sacrifice.

Ethne gasped. "Human sacrifices."

"What about them?"

"Oh, God in heaven!" She stood on shaky legs. "We have to get to the children. We have to save them."

"What? I dinna understand."

"I think they're going to kill the baby, little Mongfind. That's why Domelch was so adamant that Mongfind could not die and then gave her no attention." Ethne started toward the stables at the back of the bailey. "Mayhap even Finn."

Lachlann managed to keep up with her. "Why would they do that?"

She stopped and stared at him with wide eyes. "Because Aidan wants power!"

"Power? How?"

"To appease their gods!"

Lachlann helped her get the blanket on the horse, but urged her back when the young stable boy hurried over to assist. Clearly, they'd awakened him, and he seemed quite insulted she would try to equip the horse on her own. She started rocking uncontrollably while she waited. Thoughts of Finn's laughter, the baby's cooing, and their little faces shot pain across her chest.

"I should have never left them there. Those people show no regard for each other. And Malcolm? He never used to drink as much as he does now. He seems so unhappy." She covered her mouth.

"We will go and see, but ye may not be correct about this."

She took her hand away. "When is the solstice?"

"Tomorrow."

"Tomorrow? Then they'll be at the large cave, Goat's Cave. And others are coming. People they do not know. Aidan contacted Picts from far away. We must hurry."

"Wait, Ethne." When Lachlann took her hands, she finally focused on him. "If that is true, we canna just ride in ourselves. I need to tell Brian. We need to go with others."

She grabbed at him, her fingers jabbing into his chest. "But the baby, Lachlann. We canna let her or Finn die. Please!"

"I will not let that happen, but we need to plan what to do. Tell me what ye remember. Everything."

After she told Lachlann the few details she could remember, he brought her to the Great Hall where she repeated it to the warriors gathered.

Brian asked, "Where is this Goat's cave?"

"Ye walk toward the point, but travel down the goat's path to get to the rocky outcrop along the beach."

"The goat path?" His disbelief caused murmurs among his men. "In the bright of day 'twould be dangerous. Never mind in the dark of night. And ye say there is a cave there?"

"Aye. Ye must climb down the face of the rocks to gain entrance. On any other day, there is little time to get to the cave, perform any rituals, and leave before the water has risen too high to use the path. 'Tis why this sacred ritual was planned for the longest day of the year, when the tide retreats even farther than usual and allows for the time needed for the rituals." She sobbed suddenly, overwhelmed with fear for Finn and Mongfind. "I just didna realize what this ritual would include."

"Ah! A warrior's quest indeed. Glad I am that ye brought it to me, pilgrim." Brian's expression was grave, his eyes scanning the others before he finally spoke. "The path is treacherous in the dark. With the lowest tide midday, 'twill be best to leave before sunrise and arrive when the cave is accessible. If any of ye are not sure-footed or ye're horse is not so, dinna commit yerself."

"Wait!" Ethne's throat tightened. "Ye're not leaving now?"

Brian kept the same solemn tone. "We canna take the chance of losing the path and slipping down the ridge. We need light for that part of the journey."

Her mouth went dry. "We *must* leave now."

Lachlann turned her to him, his eyes imploring. "We will leave anon."

The plans were made and she had no say in them. The tide would be going out at sunrise. but she had a hard time setting that fact aside. She went over and over it again in her head, but she could think of no detail she'd left out.

"Come. Lay down with me. Try to rest a bit." Lachlann stretched out in their cushioned alcove, his arms opened invitingly toward her.

She did as he asked, resting her head on his chest and listening to the rapid beat of his heart slowing. When he started his gentle snoring, she slowly sat up. It was not possible for her to sleep. She had to take action now.

CHAPTER 28

*E*thne knew the sound of Aidan and his people without having to see them. Even the waves crashing ever closer from the incoming tide couldn't drown them out. They were headed toward the point. A seemingly unending, single line, they traveled along the ridge with their bright torches held high to light the way. They mumbled the chants she'd heard as a child. But they became sinister taunts to God Almighty, instead of the songs of praise that she remembered.

Careful to stay hidden in the tall grass, she crouched low to travel alongside them as she moved toward the front of the line. She considered how best to approach them, but could think of no way to rescue the children save revealing herself and begging them to reconsider. Mayhap if she offered herself as a sacrifice?

There were at least ten people in the procession whom she did not recognize. Not such a great number joining them after all. The light from one of the torches revealed Thomas's painted face. She gasped. He looked so menacing. At his side was Finn, being dragged by the tight grip Thomas had of his hand.

She trotted ahead to the bend in the path. A branch broke beneath her feet, and she hunkered down. There was no sound, no sign she'd been heard, but her heart was beating so loudly she was afraid they might yet. She took a slow, deep breath to settle herself. And waited.

Finally, she caught sight of Malcolm. The glow cast on his face showed dark circles under his eyes, making him look sickly. The light of his torch also shined down on Domelch, the babe in her arms. They walked close behind Aidan, who carried a nasty-looking poleaxe and was calling out the words to the ancient song. Not everyone was singing. The people she didn't recognize frowned and glanced about them as if confused.

Something clasped onto her shoulder, and she lost her balance, falling to the ground. She looked up into Thomas's grimace.

He leered at her. "Ah, Ethne, ye've come to join us."

She glanced around for Finn, but the lad was not with him. When she started to shake her head in answer, he only mimicked the action, his mouth opening as if he was ready to dispute anything that came out of her mouth. Nothing did. He glanced toward the procession then back at her. The others continued on, none of them looking their way. When the last of them were around the corner, she got brave enough to speak.

"I...I wanted to come. I was afeared Aidan would punish me."

"Tsk. Tsk. Is that the best ye can do?" The whites of Thomas's eyes were bright even in the darkness. "Dinna lie to me."

Anger darkened his expression, and she spoke more quickly. "Lachlann tossed me aside as soon as we reached the castle."

That incensed Thomas enough that he grabbed her arm, yanking her to her feet. "And ye are a liar now as well as a whore?"

The sound of the ocean and the wind surrounded them. They were completely alone.

"How could ye turn to another and allow him to ...? After all the times I've protected ye from Aidan?" He gritted his teeth, barely controlling his rage. "He would have taken ye right there on the floor in yer cave, Ethne, do ye not remember? Many times, I saw it in his eyes. Aidan wanted ye. And yer brother too drunk to do a thing. *I* convinced Aidan he should take Moira instead of ye."

Guilt flooded Ethne. That poor lass truly could have been her. She'd had no idea Thomas had been so protective of her, and now, she had no idea what to say.

"Do not doubt it." He searched her as if not sure what he wanted to do. "I thought I was in love with ye."

"I wish I had known."

He snorted in irritation. "No, ye didna know." He shoved her toward the path and, when she stumbled to the ground, didn't help her. "Get up. Aidan will be glad to have ye join us."

By the time Thomas had prodded her as far as the beach, the last of the torches were just disappearing inside the cave and the angry ocean churned up the cliffs surrounding the entrance. Either she convinced him now to let her go, or who knew what would happen to her, alone and unprotected.

She dug in her heels and turned to him. "Dinna do this, Thomas. I only wanted to catch a glimpse of Finn."

"Finn?"

He allowed her to stop him. A good sign.

"He is like my own son, and I have missed him." Her voice cracked unexpectedly, surprising her with the depth of emotion she felt toward the boy.

The waves crashed hard nearby.

More quietly, she added, "I am afeared for him."

Thomas put a hand to his hip. "As ye should be."

"Aidan is not right in the head, Thomas. Surely, ye see that as well?"

"I do." He shook his head. "But he is my father."

"What?" Her mind reeled at the outrageous idea. "How can that be so?"

"He knew my mother."

Thomas faced the horizon, the light from the rising sunrise spreading across the surface with its lovely blues and pinks. "I came to him when she died. I had nowhere else to go. I was a young lad. When I realized his anger toward the God that had stolen his first wife was stronger than any love he could ever have for his own child, I thought about leaving. But where would I go? I had no one else." He turned to her, the track of one single tear on his cheek. "I decided I would stay here because it was better than being alone."

"My heart hurts for—"

"Think ye I care what ye feel?"

She fought to control the trembling seizing her. "What…what will Aidan do when he sees me?"

"He will beat ye for yer disobedience." Thomas's voice softened the tiniest bit. "Then he will take ye as his own."

A wave of revulsion washed over her at the thought of that man touching her. She was playing with fire to think she could have saved the children on her own.

"No one will stop him, Ethne. Ye have defied our laws."

She had to convince Thomas of her sincerity. She forced herself to reach out and take his hand. It was cold and damp.

"Lachlann wished to share me with his friends." Her eyes teared. She had to convince him she came back because she'd been rejected, then if she got close enough to the children, she might have a chance to save them.

She held herself still, her face a mask of contrition as Thomas studied her and tried to discern the truth of her words. This was the one time in her life where she must hide every thought. He had to believe her.

He stepped closer, wiping the wetness from her cheek. "And was it their touch that ye feared? Or the man's betrayal of the precious gift ye gave him?"

One by one, she rummaged through every answer that he might believe, but only one rose to the top. "If ye'd ever given me a reason to hope, Thomas, I would not have accepted another."

The man smiled. A sardonic smile. He didn't believe her. She'd failed to convince him and now, she would face the punishment of a traitor and worse. When he turned toward the cave, his hand still holding hers, confusion and panic overtook her.

She forced a calm breath, but compelled her heavy feet to move, walking alongside him to enter the lion's den.

Once inside, Ethne's gaze immediately found Domelch. She sat beside the pool nursing Mongfind. Filled by the ocean's tide, the water sloshed against the stone floor that sloped down toward it. Malcolm squatted beside her, Finn at his side, and watched the touching scene. Ethne's stomach churned.

When Aidan saw her, his eyes flashed. "Ethne!"

Malcolm stood and turned to her, just halting Finn from running toward her.

"Ethne!" the boy cried out, immediately cowed by his father's grip on his shoulder.

"No," Malcolm ordered. "Ye must allow Aidan to approach her, Finn. She no longer belongs with us."

Her brother's voice held no trace of a drunken slur, nor did he waver where he stood. She couldn't help but wonder if the man she'd known her entire life would willingly allow his own children to be slaughtered. The thought chilled her to her very core because she didn't know the answer.

"Ah, Thomas, have ye brought me my Ethne?" Aidan asked.

She held her breath and waited.

"Thomas?" Aidan prompted the man, who clearly struggled.

Thomas tensed right before he responded. "She was coming down the trail, trying to catch up with us. No doubt she meant to join us on this special occasion."

The air *whooshed* out of her in relief, and she fell to her knees before Aidan. "I've come to beg yer forgiveness."

"Forgiveness?" Aidan asked. "What is that?"

She closed her eyes and kept her face downcast. Short of a miracle, there would be no reprieve for her. The sound of horses galloping across the sand sounded like thunder, and she jerked up her head.

When Thomas turned a frightened face toward the sound, he quickly glared back at her. "Ye knew they were coming!"

She shook her head as relief flooded her. "I didna."

The sound of horses echoed in the large cave as Lachlann, Niall, and Aldred entered, flanked on all sides by warriors, both mounted and on foot, with weapons drawn. Aidan was unquestionably outnumbered.

"Well, well, the pilgrims have returned." Aidan moved closer to her. His pleased facade and syrupy sweet voice made her skin crawl. "Savage pilgrims indeed."

"If ye do not wish to be slaughtered, back down and we will show ye mercy," Brian called from where he commanded his men atop a large courser. "But I've no qualms about taking ye down right where ye stand."

Lachlann dismounted, his eyes searching her out.

Aidan never dropped his veil of bravado and countered, "Allow us to leave and return to our homes."

"Never!" Brian's cruel laugh brought smiles to some of the other warriors. "Think ye the church takes kindly to those who blaspheme Our Lord and Savior? Neither do we."

Lachlann stepped closer and reached a hand toward her, but her reaction was too slow.

Aidan yanked her back against him. One hand, shaking with rage, gripped her neck, more than ready to snap it. "Stop right where ye are, or I will kill her."

The old man held her tight, a hand around her waist and his mouth near her lips. Lachlann halted, his face livid.

"I have missed ye." Aidan's breath hot on her skin, she swallowed the bile rising up her throat. "Tell them if they back up, I will release ye."

"Will ye?" she asked.

He chuckled, dropping a disgusting kiss on her lobe. "Ye'll have to wait and see." He tightened the arm he'd wrapped about her neck. "Tell them. Now!"

She grabbed at his arm without thinking. Lachlann's eyes widened with concern that she wished she could wipe away.

"If ye back up, Aidan will release me." Unfortunately, her hoarse voice sounded as frightened as she felt.

CHAPTER 29

*L*achlann swallowed against the tightness in his own throat, incensed at having to witness Ethne being used as a weapon against him yet again. He studied Ethne, then shifted his gaze to Aidan. Seeing nothing that revealed the man's intent, he backed up and spoke in a quiet voice, "I dinna trust him."

"Ye dinna trust me?" Aidan bellowed before squaring his shoulders. "Because I am old and feeble?"

His men chuckled, inching closer to their leader.

He smiled back at them, but turned a nasty grimace on Lachlann. "And I dinna think I like yer insult."

Brian's men shifted as well, but Lachlann signaled them to stop. Aidan's arm across Ethne's delicate neck didn't warrant any sudden moves on anyone's part.

"Release her." Lachlann frantically thought through any scenario that would end well for her. He could only think of one. "I will fight ye. Just ye and I."

Aidan scoffed and his hand slid tighter around Ethne's waist. "Why would I do that? I have the upper hand. A hostage."

Lachlann took a deep breath, struggling to keep his inner turmoil in check. "Because if ye win, we'll back away. We'll allow ye to leave, even return to yer homes."

"Now see her—" Lachlann jerked out his hand to halt Brian's objection.

"Ye'll be allowed time to pack up and leave on yer own." Lachlann nodded slightly, willing Aidan to agree to the damn terms.

Aidan glanced between Lachlann and Brian then tipped his head before narrowing his eyes. "And if *ye* win?"

"Ye'll do as Brian orders, but leave Ethne with me."

With a slow nod, Aidan signaled his consent. "Then let us see this done." He shoved Ethne toward Thomas, who didn't lose a moment securing her tight against him with a blade at her side.

When Aidan puffed out his chest, the sight of the medallion hanging from around his neck as if it belonged there infuriated Lachlann.

It did not.

Colbán had been a good friend to his father and given Lachlann this important link to his past. He would fight Aidan or die trying, but one way or another, he would take back his birthright. *Son of Branan.*

Aidan beamed and took a deep, satisfied breath. He hunched over and yanked at the shoulders of his tunic to pull it over his head. When he straightened once again, Lachlann's jaw dropped. The marks on Aidan's body were a mirror image of those on his own body. He doffed his tunic as well so that the twin designs were seen by all.

Loud gasps issued from those circled around them, followed by questioning murmurs.

"Quiet!" Aidan roared and accepted the sword offered him. "Will ye fight me *now*? Old or not...courage is measured by action not age."

Lachlann's body stiffened, his brain racing to make sense of this. Realization hit hard and his knees buckled before he could catch himself.

"Ah! Do ye recognize me now?" Aidan spoke as if talking to a child.

Lachlann locked his knees tight. His breath catching in his throat made it hard to breathe and harder to speak. "But how—"

Aidan mocked him with a shaking head and a look of disgust.

None of this made any sense. "*Ye* are Branan?"

Aidan spit on the ground. "Wrong twin! I am called Barra."

A flood of memories held Lachlann in their grip. The fire still stung his eyes. Niall's grandfather taking him in, treating him like a favored son. Colbán's voice assuring him his father was Branan, not Barra.

"What did ye do to my father?" Lachlann's voice was tight with an emotion he couldn't name.

Aidan shrugged, his expression relaxed now. "So long ago. Who can remember?"

"Ye lie!" Lachlann said, with as much malice as was in him. "Ye murdered him."

"Life is not always fair." Aidan spouted the platitude as if it explained everything.

"Nay." Lachlann's festering rage bloomed in his chest, but rather than dragging him down, it gave him renewed energy. He'd been a child. But no longer. Revenge for the murder of his father he could see to. His mind cleared. "So be it!"

He lunged ahead with his sword at the ready, but Aidan easily deflected such a blatant assault. He backed away laughing. "Now, now, son, I expect better than that."

"I am not yer son." Anger flooded his mind, and his next thrust was again thwarted.

The others gave them a wide berth as he and Aidan ducked and weaved about the cave. Lachlann kept a keen eye for any opening to end this and take the upper hand, but the man was amazingly agile.

Aidan hunched in his warrior stance. "If ye're trying to be kind to me because I am an old man, ye needn't bother."

Lachlann ignored the jeers instead he focused on the man's steps. Aidan was shorter and stooped in a defensive posture. A weakness. Feigning a step left, Lachlann hammered the pummel of his sword onto the man's back.

Aidan arched up and back. Seeing his opening, Lachlann came in close and swung up and around with his longsword. Too late, pain burned into his side. He dropped to his knees.

"Come no closer." Aidan waved the unseen dagger that had sliced into Lachlann's flesh as he shouted to Brian's men before they could move.

Ethne screamed, but Thomas held her fast. Lachlann rolled onto his back.

Aidan stood over him, his sword hovering above him. Instead of plunging the sharp blade into his heart, the man held Lachlann's gaze. "Do ye doubt I can kill ye now?"

"I doubt nothing about yer cruelty." He worked to block out the burning in his side.

"I am not cruel. I am what the church turned me into."

Lachlann scoffed. "Only a weak man blames his failings on others."

Aidan's lips curled into a vicious smile. "How well ye remember my teachings."

"The memories haunt my waking and my sleeping." Lachlann felt the punch of truth to his gut. He wanted those memories to stop.

"Haunt?" Aidan's brows rose in skepticism. "They made ye the warrior ye've become."

"I became a warrior of integrity despite ye and yer teachings." Lachlann sent a prayer to the saints above for intervention. He had to keep Aidan talking. "Would ye actually believe murdering a child would gain ye the power ye seek?"

"I seek power for all of us. 'Tis not just about me."

"It has always been about ye."

He sensed Aidan's angry snarl in the pit of his stomach. He'd pushed the man too far and sweat broke out across Lachlann's body. He glimpsed Ethne, who sobbed where she stood with the other onlookers. A fair flower indeed. He had let her down in so many ways and now he couldn't even save the children. Turning to the man holding his life in his hand, Lachlann clenched his jaw tight, and nodded. "Aye, I know ye can kill me."

"And will ye ask me for mercy?"

"I dinna believe ye have any. Ye murdered yer own brother." Lachlann was playing with fire, taunting the man when he held Lachlann's life or death in his hands, but he had to ask, "Think ye any man with a soul could do such a thing as that?"

"The church found my wife unfit for their hallowed ground, all because I had sought other means to heal her. I wanted her to live, damn it! And when they condemned me? My pious brother refused to speak for me. Branan would not even try to change their minds. He agreed with their decision."

Aidan doubled his hands on the hilt of the well-honed blade. Lachlann forced himself to watch the man about to end his life, searching deep inside himself to find the smallest speck of forgiveness. There was none. He struggled to control his labored breathing while his heart thudded against his ribs as if desperate to escape this fate. He took a breath deep enough to fill his entire body and blew it out in a long, steady flow. When Aidan lifted the blade for a last, powerful thrust, Lachlann rolled clear of the blade. He scrambled to his feet.

Aidan's face tightened in outrage, but his piercing cry

as he lurched awkwardly at Lachlann sounded more like a wounded animal.

"Ye'd kill yer own nephew?" Thomas's voice boomed as Aidan's shoulders dropped.

When Aidan crumpled face first to the ground, Thomas loomed over him with wide, tear-filled eyes and a dirk covered in blood. "Ye dinna deserve to live."

He dropped to his knees beside his father to again jab the blade into his back. "Ye deserve to die."

And again.

Aidan never moved. No one moved. No one but Thomas. He continued his ranting as the blood sprayed and the cavernous space echoed back the sick sucking and slurping of the blade being shoved into the lifeless body over and over.

Lachlann was the first to edge closer to Thomas until he was able to catch the next downward gesture with a stiffened arm. "Ye've finished him, Thomas."

The stench of the spilled blood surrounded them. Lachlann forced down the bile rising up his throat when his knee squished against something unseen as he knelt beside him. Staring directly in the man's black, vacant eyes, Lachlann willed him to obey.

"Ye can stop now."

Thomas breathed a deep sigh that sounded like relief. "Ye dinna deserve to die. Not ye or yer dah."

"'Tis over now. You can give me yer weapon."

Once Thomas released his grip, Brian and his men came forward. Lachlann stood and handed Brian the bloodied dirk. No one was willing to fight. Their blank expressions reflected his own disbelief of the unexpected and ghastly event.

Coming to Lachlann with faltering steps, Ethne collapsed in his arms. Her warmth against him was a soothing boon that he was in no hurry to let go of.

Finally, she cupped his cheek with a damp palm and searched his face.

"Are ye badly hurt?" Her voice trembled.

"I will be fine." Lachlann's breath finally eased. "Let us see this finished."

"No!" The wild screech caught everyone off guard.

Lachlann placed Ethne behind him with a firm hand, even as he turned toward the source of the awful sound.

The sight of Domelch standing beside the rising waters of the pool with her innocent babe clasped to her bosom set Lachlann's blood to boil.

"I was to be queen!" Her screeching voice was like claws clenching at his heart.

Aidan's men began to murmur, all but Malcolm, who finally allowed Finn to go to Ethne. Running as quickly as his little legs could carry him, Finn's petrified expression tugged at Lachlann's heart.

"Domelch..." Malcolm's voice remained calm as he moved closer to her. "Aidan could not make ye queen no matter what he promised."

She turned on him with an ugly scowl. A mask of fury. "Ye're wrong. We go through the ritual just as it was described, then the gods will make us powerful once again!"

The murmuring increased, as the water rose above her ankles. The tide was coming in and despite searching the area from where he remained riveted, Lachlann could distinguish no possible outlet for the water. The woman was about to be immersed.

"Malcolm, she killed our parents," Ethne called out. The pain in her voice tightened Lachlann's chest.

Malcolm halted. His shoulders rounded. He was a defeated man and his tone said as much. "Is that true? Did ye do that, Domelch?"

"I. Had. To," she screamed. "I needed to come back here. It was Aidan who sent yer uncle to yer family. We needed more men *here*, not to stay behind in yer weak little clan."

"My mother was so kind to ye, Domelch. Have ye no feelings for another?" Malcolm's expression shifted from pity to acceptance. He squared his shoulder and reached his arms out with purpose. "Give me the child."

"I will be queen." Domelch stepped nearer the center of the pool where the water rose above her knees. The baby cried out. "I will not be thwarted."

Horses whinnied behind them, sensing the imminent threat of drowning. Brian yelled, "Retreat! Everyone! Before the path to higher ground is flooded."

The water reached his wife's waist. Malcolm lurched forward.

"Oh, dear Lord in heaven," Ethne turned away so that Finn could not watch his baby sister be murdered.

With water sloshing around their ankles, Lachlann led them toward the entrance. Brian accepted Finn onto his horse, and Lachlann hefted Ethne onto his, then slapped its rump so that the mare lurched forward.

"Lachlann! No!"

But Lachlann headed back into the flooding cave.

CHAPTER 30

Back within the castle walls in the Great Hall, celebrations continued around them. Lachlann sat at a table surrounded by Niall, Aldred, Brian, and Ethne. She was close at his side, as if afraid if she left him, he might end up dead.

"The mormaer has placed a guard on the caves to be certain no one returns," Niall said.

Ethne's silence pushed Lachlann to place an arm around her. In a quiet voice, he asked, "Do ye worry for Finn and Mongfind?"

"I will miss them."

"Is Malcolm not coming by so ye can see them off?"

"He is. The long trip to the clan we were raised with will be a chance for him to heal with them, although Mongfind will have no memory of her mother. That may be a good thing." Ethne turned her loving gaze to him. "Thank ye for aiding him in his escape. I admit I am not sorry Domelch drowned."

Lachlann kissed her gently. "And fear not, we will visit. They are not so verra far away from Niall's clan."

She frowned. "Ye always refer to it as Niall's clan. Why is that? Is it not yer clan as well?"

"He is the son of the true chieftain. I like to remind him of that."

Niall added, "And Lachlann is the most loyal man ye will ever meet, Ethne. I do not exaggerate even the tiniest bit."

Aldred nodded, but remained quiet, preferring to shovel in more of the warmed bread the lovely redhead had just brought to him.

"He leaves it to me to decide where we will belong. Whether it is in my uncle's clan or one I establish on my own."

"And that is what ye will use the money for?" she asked, shaking the leather sack that sat before them in the middle of the table. "Do ye know its worth?"

"Not really," Lachlann said, then signaled to Niall.

Niall emptied the silver coins on the table where they spun and chimed together. A few warriors glanced their way, but they had heard the story of the silver from the caves. They had no interest in money intended for the church.

"Well, see this man?" Niall asked. "A king, I believe someone said."

"That's the Northumbrian king. Alfred, I believe his name is," Brian said.

The coins didn't look to be so very many, but they would do what they could with whatever the nuns offered to them in thanks.

"And the hole is nearly through the top of his head." Aldred squinted at the coin. "Is that how he died then? A hammer to the head?"

Brian laughed. "It could be. 'Twas before my time. And being that I'm not from Northumbria..."

He left the rest unsaid.

Lachlann picked up a coin, also inspecting it. "Are ye certain, Brian, 'tis King Alfred, the Northumbrian?"

"Aye. I've accepted the coins myself in payment when

collecting taxes for the mormaer. Ye need not worry. The silver is of the highest quality. That was why the king had them minted."

Lachlann lay a hand carefully on the trestle table, but said nothing until all eyes were on him.

"What is amiss?" Niall finally asked.

"We need to discuss our plans."

Brian stood, hitched up the leather wrapped around his waist, and said, "Then I'll be off. The mormaer returns today. I've a need to find out how Olaf was received by the islanders. The man is a disgrace to be certain."

Lachlann watched Brian retreat, searched nearby to assure no one was within listening, and moved ever so slightly forward. "These are not the coins that are due to the priory."

Niall and Aldred exchanged doubtful glances before Niall spoke. "How can ye know that, Lachlann? It may not be as much as we expected, but it will make a great difference to the priory's upkeep. Even if we canna accept any payment in kind for what we've done."

"Niall." He waited a moment longer before finally saying, "These coins were minted too late for them to be from Saint Gervadius. Alfred hadn't been born yet when he collected *his* silver, when he worked as a mercenary."

Aldred and Niall searched more closely through the coins.

"They are all the same," Aldred finally said.

Lachlann winked at Ethne, who smiled. "How did ye find these coins?"

"Finn and I collected them from the ground. They would show up in the strangest places."

He glanced at his friends. "The hidden silver is still hidden."

"Then what do we do with this?" Aldred asked, his irritation evident. "Bring it to the nuns or give it back to…" He glanced at Ethne. "Her! She's the one that found it."

She raised her hands in submission. "I have no need of silver coins."

"Am I interrupting ye?" Malcolm's words came just as Finn jumped onto his aunt's lap.

Ethne kissed the boy, squeezing him against her as if it were the last time. "How are ye, my little Finn?"

"I dinna want to be here anymore," he said. "Can ye take me home?"

Malcolm was quickly flustered, the babe in his arms fidgeting against him. "I've told ye, Finn. We go to a new place now." He searched the hall and found the nursing mother who saw to Mongfind. "I'll be but a moment. Ye stay here, Finn."

Finn nodded, slouching forward.

"I have an idea." Niall held one of the coins up to Finn. "Is this yers?"

The boy gasped, taking it into his hand. Just as quickly, he frowned at Ethne. "Am I allowed to say that?"

She chuckled. "Verily, ye are. And anything else ye may wish to tell them. No more secrets. Ever."

"And it looks like ye'll have more than one to wear about yer neck now." Lachlann handed another one to him.

Lachlann glanced at Niall and then Aldred. Both nodded their agreement, so he said, "I believe all of these belong to ye and yer da."

Finn's face lit up with joy. "Is that true, Ethne?"

"If that is what they say."

Niall added, "That means we still have a job to do for the nuns."

"How much time do ye suppose yer uncle is willing to allow us to be gone for?" Aldred asked.

"He has his precious sons to fight his battles," Niall said with a shrug. "I dinna see why we must hurry back."

"Mayhap he'll think ye died." Aldred laughed at his own joke.

Niall did not. "That is one way to deal with it. Something to think about."

Rhona brought fresh creamed butter to the table and placed it down with a thud. Cull and the others were out and about seeing to their duties.

"Where did Sophie go?" Aldred asked, munching on another piece of thick, crusty bread now slathered with butter. A stern gaze remained on him until he noticed and swallowed. "What?"

"Her husband is due back with the mormaer, Aldred."

"What?" His surprise was as sincere as the man could get, but Lachlann had his own suspicions.

"Did she not tell ye?" Rhona's dark expression shifted to concern. "If ye'd accepted one of the willing lasses offered ye, no problems would have ensued, dear Aldred."

He grinned now. "But where's the fun in that?"

Niall and Lachlann exchanged glances.

"Tell us ye didna!" Niall's irritation was shifting to anger. Anger Aldred definitely deserved.

Rhona said, "If the girl didna share her betrothed status, then the law will see no fault on yer part."

Even with all eyes on him, waiting, Aldred refused to respond. His lack of response was as telling as the splash of red rising into his cheeks.

Rhona put a hand to her hip. "Then the devil take ye, man!"

Lachlann rose quickly and helped Finn off Ethne's lap. He led them both to Malcolm. "We need to be leaving, but Niall wanted ye to have this."

Malcolm seemed slightly surprised at a sack being shoved at him, even more so when he looked inside. "I dinna understand."

"With our well wishes." Lachlann hugged Finn tight. "Be a good lad."

"What is amiss?" Ethne asked, but became distracted with her goodbyes, hugging Malcolm and bending down to kiss Finn. "I love ye both."

She palmed Mongfind's little head and dropped her a kiss. Ethne's eyes filled with tears. "Why must we leave so quickly?"

Lachlann watched as Niall and Aldred went out the side door. "This happens on occasion as Aldred is not the wisest man about." He kissed her less than enthusiastic lips. "I promise ye we will see Finn and Mongfind again. Verra soon."

Ethne perked up at that, kissing him a second time with more eagerness. "Thank ye for that."

"But right now, we need to be leaving."

The doors to the front of the bailey swung open wide, and a flood of warriors, laughing and smiling, burst into the room.

"Through the kitchens will work as well." Lachlann redirected them toward the large fireplace in the center of the keep and took the door to the right.

The voices of welcome and celebration were left behind them once they exited to the gardens. He found Niall and Aldred seeing to the three horses in the small bailey where the kitchen herb garden took up most of the space.

"If we'd known about the husband, Aldred, we'd not have come back this way," Niall said.

Aldred shrugged and got on his horse. "It didna seem worth mentioning since they're only betrothed."

"And now what will happen to her?" Niall demanded. "Ye've taken what ye've no right to, and her husband will set her aside on the marriage bed."

"Nay, I gave her several days of more pleasure than she'd have in a lifetime married to some man old enough to be her father."

Lachlann mounted and offered a hand to Ethne,

whose mouth had been gaping open ever since she realized what Aldred had done. She said, "Is that the story she told ye?"

Niall turned his horse about and forced a slow trot through the gates away from the merriment spilling out of the Great Hall.

"Always 'tis the same," Aldred said, "I dinna need to hear specifics each time."

Lachlann rolled his eyes and secured Ethne's arms about his waist. "Someday yer lack of concern for the husband will find ye six feet under."

He tsked his horse into a fast trot to catch up to Niall, who was rounding the bend back toward the sea.

"But not this time," Aldred announced.

The End

AUTHOR'S NOTES

The idea for the three highlanders from *The Gentle Knight* to have their own stories was first suggested to me by one of my readers. Thank you! I had a lot of fun writing Lachlann's story and especially visiting the caves near Lossiemouth and Elgin. The Picts have a glorious past that archeologists are continuing to learn about today.

St. Gervadius was an Irish saint who actually lived as a hermit near Elgin, Scotland, who died in 934. His cave became a place of pilgrimage for many. His back story as a mercenary was from my author's imagination.

Alfred the Great was king of the Anglo-Saxons from 886-899 and is responsible for the conversion of the Viking leader Guthrum to Christianity afterwhich *Danelaw* was established in the north of England.

I ask your indulgence for the timeline discrepancy. This is, afterall, a work of fiction. I hope you enjoyed it.

MORE BOOKS BY ASHLEY YORK

If you enjoy historical romance with a touch of intrigue and
adventure, check out these books by Ashley York

The Warrior Kings Series

Curse of the Healer

Eyes of the Seer

Daughter of the Overking

The Norman Conquest Series

The Saxon Bride

The Gentle Knight

The Irish Warrior

The Seventh Son

The Order of the Scottish Thistle

Lachlann's Legacy

ABOUT THE AUTHOR

Aside from two years spent in the wilds of the Colorado mountains, Ashley York is a proud life-long New Englander and a hardcore romantic. She has an MA in History which brings with it a love for primary documents and the smell of musty old libraries. With her author's imagination, she likes to write about people who could have lived alongside those well-known giants from the past.

Website: www.ashleyyorkauthor.com

www.ingramcontent.com/pod-product-compliance
Lightning Source LLC
Chambersburg PA
CBHW031935110726
47902CB00001B/187